CRITICS PRAISE
SHARON IHLE AND *UNTAMED*!

"Brilliant, funny, and mesmerizing."

—*Affaire de Coeur*

"Gritty realism and down-home humor sparkle in Sharon Ihle's *Untamed*."

—*Romantic Times*

"Award-winning Sharon Ihle writes what may be her best historical to date! Ms. Ihle deserves another award for what should be a bestseller."

—*Painted Rock*

"Spunky, sexy, and heart-warming, *Untamed* is a novel of pure delight from start to finish. When searching for the very best in writing, search no further than Sharon Ihle's name on the cover."

—*Reader to Reader*

"We've come to expect only the best from Sharon Ihle!"

—*Heartland Critiques*

SOMEONE'S BEEN...IN MY BED

"What are you doing?"

Lucy sat bolt upright and scrambled off the bed.

"I, ah, well, see, I thought I heard you knocking, and then you weren't here, but the desk clerk came to the other door, see, and then I went to shut the door, and, and…"

The more she talked, the bigger Sebastian's grin got, but Lucy couldn't seem to stop. "Then I saw your room, see, so big and beautiful, and well, see, your bed was here too, and I wondered if it was the same, and I guess I just got curious, and it *is* like mine. I have to go now."

Laughing softly, Seb caught up with Lucy as she reached the connecting doors. Pinching the throat of her nightgown between his thumb and forefinger, he tugged her toward him, right up close to his face.

"You can crawl around in my bed any time you want to," he whispered darkly. "All you have to do is ask."

DEAR PENELOPE

SHARON IHLE

LEISURE BOOKS NEW YORK CITY

For Stelios, Alexandros, and Ava Caitrin...
our very bright future. And as always, for Larry.

A LEISURE BOOK®

September 2005

Published by

Dorchester Publishing Co., Inc.
200 Madison Avenue
New York, NY 10016

ISBN 0-8439-5599-6

The name "Leisure Books" and the stylized "L" with design are trademarks of Dorchester Publishing Co., Inc.

Printed in the United States of America.

Visit us on the web at www.dorchesterpub.com.

"Women have changed in their relationship to men, but men stand pat just where Adam did when it comes to dealing with women."
—Dorothy Dix, advice columnist, 1896

Chapter One

May 1, 1896

My Dearest Lucille:

The restaurant building (formerly the Pie Shoppe) is everything I'd hoped it would be and more. I finally found out why nobody here in Emancipation bought it, and why it was advertised as far away as Missouri. It seems the previous owner had a habit of poisoning the patrons she didn't like! Needless to say, Charlie's Bakery will not be featuring pies on the menu.

I expect to be open for business in less than two weeks, which brings me to the point of this letter. It pains me more than mere words can express to have to tell you that someone new has come into my life. Despite my deep feelings for you, I have fallen utterly and completely in love with a charming young woman, and we'll soon be married. I realize you expected to join me here in Wyoming for our own wedding, but alas, fate has decided otherwise. The last thing I ever *wanted to do was hurt you, but I'm sure a wonderful, caring person like yourself won't be lacking for male companionship for long!*

Please feel free to return the train ticket I sent you, and understand that you're welcome to keep the refund. I wish you a long and happy life.

With a fondness that lingers, Charlie

Of course, Charlie White had no way of knowing that the train carrying his letter had been set upon by outlaws, or that in their zeal, they had not only planted enough dynamite to blow the door off the mail car but had blown the contents to smithereens. Instead he was blissfully unaware of anything except his own desires. Namely, perfecting his trademark recipe, Hot Cross Buns, gazing upon the comely features of new fiancée, Cherry Barkdoll, and creating a truly unique and dramatic wedding cake for his upcoming nuptials.

Chapter Two

As the conductor passed through the car instructing those who wished to disembark in Emancipation to be getting to it, Lucy was so excited in her haste to exit the train that she almost left her two small bags behind.

As she stepped down onto the wooden platform, she glanced to her right, where a small knot of people stood waiting for family and friends. She didn't spot her fiancé amongst them, so Lucy stepped off the platform and started up the street that led into town. She hadn't gotten but a few feet in that direction before she became aware of a commotion from her left, the thunder of hooves and a man shouting.

Lucy turned to see that the man was on horseback and trying to warn her that the great beast running ahead of him was bearing down on her. Stunned, she froze to the spot for a moment and then backed up a couple of steps. The beast, the biggest bull she'd ever seen, veered along with her. She moved forward and, again, the bull followed her movements. The animal was just seconds from crashing into her when a strong pair of arms suddenly lifted her off her feet and flung her out of harm's way.

The next thing Lucy knew, she was flat on her back in the dirt and the stranger was stretched out on top of her.

"Welcome to Emancipation, ma'am," he said, touching the brim of his hat. "Are you all right?"

She looked up into eyes the color of tempered steel. They were actually twinkling, filled with something akin to mirth despite the dire circumstances. Although the man had propped himself up on his elbows and was barely skimming her body, she could feel his warmth from her breasts to her toes—and realized that she'd stopped breathing.

Lucy eked out, "Can't . . ."

"Are you hurt?"

". . . breathe."

"Oh, sorry."

The stranger leapt to his feet and then pulled Lucy up alongside him. As he spun her around and began dusting her off, uninvited, he said, "You're lucky you weren't gored. Are you sure you're all right?"

Lucy gave herself a moment to consider this. Except for the fact that a full-grown man had pinned her to the ground, she supposed that she was. "I think so."

The man on horseback rode up then, towing the rampaging animal behind him. "Sorry about running you down like that, ma'am, but I guess this ornery bull of mine isn't too interested in taking a ride on the train. Is everyone all right?"

"We're fine," the stranger said.

Lucy was about to agree with him, but then she spotted her new summer bonnet lying a few feet away. "My hat," she said, hurrying over to retrieve the crushed pile of ribbons and straw. "It's ruined."

The cowboy, who'd already begun leading the bull away, said over his shoulder, "Figure up the damages, ma'am, and let Cole know what they are. He'll see you get your money."

"Cole?"

"Sebastian Cole," said the stranger, again touching the brim of his hat. "At your service."

Regarding him, really looking him over this time, again Lucy's breath caught. The man was nothing short of dashing, turned out in a fine three-piece suit of charcoal broadcloth, a white shirt with a high collar, and a thin tie of black silk. Topping the look at an angle as rakish as his piercing gray eyes, he wore a black derby. Cole flashed her a grin then, melting something inside her. Lucy had the distinct impression that he knew she thought him very pleasing to the eye.

Wondering how to respond to such audacity, or if she should even try, she finally made do with a simple, "Thank you."

He tipped his hat. "I assure you, it was my pleasure."

Again with the grin, and again Lucy didn't know what to do or say.

"Is someone meeting you?" Cole asked, saving her the trouble.

"I thought so, but he doesn't seem to be here. Can you tell me where I might find Charlie's Bakery?"

Pointing down the street, he said, "It's a couple of doors past City Hall on the left. You can't miss it. Just follow your nose."

He reached down, collected her bags, and said, "Do you need some help?"

"Oh, no, thank you. I can manage."

"As you wish." After turning her bags over to her, Cole said, "When you figure out what's owed you for the hat, you can find me at the Pearly Gates. It's across the street from the jailhouse."

Then, leaving Lucy to wonder if he was making some kind of joke or if there really was such an establishment, Cole turned on his heel and continued on toward the depot.

She looked after him for a moment, admiring his confident swagger and the way the tails of his jacket hugged his trim hips, and then mentally slapped herself. She was here to wed the man she loved after an absence of several weeks, not to ogle other men.

Thinking only of Charlie again, Lucy plopped her ruined hat on her disheveled hair, renewed her grip on the bags, and headed up Main Street. As Cole suggested, all she had to do was follow her nose. The scent of fresh-baked bread mingled with something sinfully sweet led her along until she was standing in front of Charlie's Bakery. Lucy paused, studying the freshly painted sign and gay curtains framing the windows in checkered squares of blue and white. She was proud of all Charlie had accomplished in so short a time, but somehow disappointed, too. She'd assumed that when she arrived, she'd be the one to apply the finish work, the woman's touch, so to speak, and leave the baking to him. Apparently he'd managed everything all by himself.

Swallowing her disappointment and eager to see her fiancé again, Lucy set her bags down on the boardwalk and opened the door. The tinkle of a little bell greeted her as she stepped inside, and the heads of half a dozen patrons turned toward her. After looking her over and deciding that she was a stranger, they gave off faint but welcoming nods and then went back to their sweet rolls and coffee. Lucy couldn't help but notice that each of the dozen or so tables was decked out in blue and white–checkered tablecloths that matched the napkins and curtains.

"May I help you?" came Charlie's voice just before he stepped up behind the counter.

When he came into view, Lucy's breath caught as it had at the depot. She'd always thought of Charlie as a fine-looking suitor, but he'd somehow changed from a baby-faced boy to a very handsome young man. Oh, his blond hair was still the same, cut short and neatly groomed, and his pale blue eyes were as friendly as ever, but even with the little brush of a mustache he'd grown since she'd last seen him, his face seemed somehow longer, harder. Success had aged him, she noted, and in a very attractive way.

"I certainly hope you can help me," Lucy said, joining him behind the counter. "I'm looking for my fiancé, who was supposed to meet me at the train. Have you seen him?"

Charlie's face got kind of tense and waxy, and his eyes went round. "Lucille."

"You may have forgotten to meet me at the depot," she said coyly, "but at least you haven't forgotten my name."

"No, of course not." He glanced at his patrons, noting that they were all preoccupied with their sweets, and then took her by the elbow. "Let's go where we can talk."

After leading Lucy back to the kitchen, Charlie stepped away from her. He didn't seem interested in apologies or greetings. In fact he almost looked stern as he asked, "Didn't you get my letter?"

"What letter?"

Charlie muttered an oath she'd never heard him use before and pounded his fist against his forehead.

Alarmed, again Lucy asked, "What letter?"

"Ah." Charlie glanced around the kitchen looking at anything but her. "I wrote asking you not to come here."

A trickle of foreboding inched up her spine, but Lucy shrugged it off and forged ahead. "Why shouldn't I have come now? The bakery is open, you seem to be drawing customers, and even though I thought I was going to do the decorating, I see you've managed that as well."

"Yes, but things have changed." He paused to tug on his collar.

Working around his odd behavior, Lucy stepped up close and angled her cheek. "Things can't have changed too much. Aren't you at least going to greet me properly?"

Charlie leaned toward her, looking as if he was going to deliver a quick buss, but then the little bell inside the restaurant rang and he quickly jerked away.

"I've got to tend to business," he said. "Wait right here.

7

When I get back we must have a serious discussion."

Refusing to ponder that or any of the odd things Charlie had said, Lucy took a look around the kitchen as he went on his way. Again impressed with all he'd accomplished alone, she noticed right off how clean and orderly he kept the working area. All of the spices were lined up on the counter, alphabetically, no less. Barrels of flour and sugar were stacked below this counter with nary a trace of their contents dusting the floor, and even the ovens and cooktops sparkled as if they'd never been used. Belying that idea was the heavenly scent of something sweet baking in one of the two huge ovens. Lucy closed her eyes and breathed in, identifying the aroma as Charlie's famous Hot Cross Buns. Her mouth was watering at the thought of sinking her teeth into one of those scrumptious buns when the back door suddenly opened.

Lucy started as a young woman stepped into the room, and then blurted out the first thing that came to mind. "The customer entrance is around front. This is the kitchen."

The woman was a pretty thing with a doll-like face that made her look younger than she probably was, around Lucy's age.

She plopped the packages she was carrying down on the counter and haughtily said, "I know this is the kitchen. I work at the bakery. What are you doing back here?"

Stunned, Lucy couldn't think what to say. She stood there quietly watching as the woman began unloading the bags and storing them in the cupboards above the counter. She was tall for a woman, probably almost as tall as Charlie, and she wore a dated pink dress of dotted Swiss that was adorned with ribbons and bows. Her hair, so blond it would make Charlie's look dirty brown standing beside her, was piled up in a bouquet of ringlets that bounced every time she moved.

Thinking of her dusty olive traveling suit, disheveled hair, and crushed hat, Lucy figured she must look decidedly drab next to this confection in pink. Raising her chin, she asked, "How long have you been working here?"

"Oh," she said with a bob of her ringlet bouquet, "since Charlie opened the place, almost two weeks now."

After pushing the rest of her purchases aside, the girl gave Lucy her undivided attention. "I don't think you ever told me why you're here. Who are you anyways?"

Looking into the woman's big blue eyes, she was proud to say, "I'm Lucille Preston, from Kansas City. I'm Charlie's fiancée."

"You must be thinking about a different Charlie, honey." She slammed her hands to her hips. "The Charlie that owns this bakery happens to be *my* fiancé."

Lucy's hand flew to her throat and she staggered back a step. "That's not possible. The man who owns this bakery is my intended, and has been for almost a year."

Undaunted, the girl advanced, swaggering in the way of a gunfighter. She shook a fist in Lucy's face as she said, "You're making a mighty big mistake, talking like that. Charlie's mine, and if you don't get out of here right now, I'm gonna have to paste you one."

Her face hot, her mind numb, Lucy just stood there listening, not really hearing, following the shape of the girl's rosy lips as she formed the words and wondering which one of them had gone plumb crazy.

"Now then," Lucy heard Charlie say as he came into the room. "As I was trying to explain—oh, Cherry, you're back."

"And none too soon," she said indignantly. "We're going to have to start locking the back door to keep riffraff like this here beggarwoman from getting in."

Lucy thought about objecting to being discussed in such terms, but then remembered her squashed hat and dusty suit. Ignoring the remark, she turned to Charlie, beseeching him. "What is she talking about? Who is she?"

Charlie tugged at his shirt collar. "I, ah, take it you two have met?"

"Not exactly. She did say that she's your fiancée, however. Why would she think that?"

He pressed his lips together, making them flatter than his delicate griddle cakes. "B-because I'm afraid that it's true."

"Afraid?" said the girl, hands still planted on her hips. "That doesn't sound like the man who's been so all-fired crazy to marry up with me."

"You know that's not what I meant, Muffin. What we have here is a little misunderstanding."

Muffin? Misunderstanding? Her head still spinning, anger growing hot in her breast, Lucy glared at Charlie as she said, "Don't you think you should have gotten rid of your first fiancée before taking on another?"

Looking like a man caught between a bear and a mountain lion, Charlie glanced from her to the girl. Settling his gaze back on Lucy, he said, "I thought I'd done that very thing. I explained all this, about Cherry that is, in the letter—"

"Right," Lucy cut in. "The letter that never came."

He shrugged, looking sheepish now instead of successful. "I can't imagine what happened to it. I mailed it almost a month ago."

"Wait a minute," Cherry said, stepping between Charlie and Lucy. "She's telling the truth? She really is your fiancée?"

"*Was* my intended, Muffin. I wrote telling Lucille about us and all, but for some reason she never got my letter."

"Why didn't you tell me about her?" she demanded, practically hovering over Charlie. "Don't you think I have a right to know if some slattern you left behind is going to come chasing after you?"

Sickened by the truth, by the sight of the two of them arguing about her as if she wasn't even there, Lucy raised her chin and sniffed the air.

"Your buns are burning, Charlie," she said dully. "Better tend to them. I'll let myself out."

She never knew how she got her leaden feet to moving,

but somehow Lucy managed to force herself through the back door and slam it shut behind her. She stumbled up the alley and then collapsed against the building before she reached the street. Something was wrong, terribly wrong. She couldn't breathe. Her chest hurt, sharp stabbing pains that jabbed into her soft breast like pins shoved into a cushion. Odder still, the entire world around her had gone curiously silent, the only sound a tiny buzz inside her head. And then she heard something new, a cracking noise, like stepping on the edge of a pond that hadn't quite frozen over. She wondered numbly if the sound was her own heart shattering.

She stood there a while longer, Lucy didn't know for how long, and tried desperately to put the pieces back together again. Gradually she began to hear the sounds of the town; horses plodding along, dragging squeaky wagons behind them; women chatting quietly, whispering secrets into each other's ears as they hurried down the boardwalk; a boy laughing as he skipped alongside the ugliest dog she'd ever seen.

What was she to do? Where would she go? Lucy didn't have the faintest idea. She only knew that she had to leave the area, and now. If she didn't, she'd probably start crying. If that happened, Charlie might open the door to check on her and see her in tears, and then her humiliation would be complete. With nothing but escape in mind, she headed up the boardwalk away from the bakery and the depot.

Taking stock of her situation as she moved along, Lucy figured she had about five dollars left to her name. Hardly enough for a train ticket back home. Even if she had the money, the train was heading west, not east, and probably wouldn't be heading back to Missouri for days. What would she do with herself until then? How would she survive?

Consumed by her mounting problems, Lucy continued up the street. She needed a hotel room for the night and a good meal. Thinking that five dollars wouldn't take her very far in that venture either, she suddenly remembered what the cowboy had said after his bull had nearly killed her. He'd pay for her hat. All she had to do was find this Sebastian Cole again, collect what was due her, and then she'd at least have the night to get some rest and figure out what to do next.

As she strolled through town, Lucy tried to remember the unusual name of the establishment where Cole could be found, but it simply wouldn't come to her. She'd just about given up when she realized that she'd reached the sheriff's office. Remembering Cole's directions, if not the name of his establishment, she glanced across the street and saw an ornate white building with a false steeple perched on the roof. An arch made of rainbow-colored glass framed the single white door, and above the fancy arch were the words THE PEARLY GATES SALOON.

It wasn't enough that her fiancé had jilted her; was she, what most would consider a proper young lady, now expected to disgrace herself by walking into a *saloon?*

Heart hammering in her throat, Lucy swallowed hard, took a deep breath, and headed for this latest in a series of humiliations.

Chapter Three

Sebastian Cole had a taste for Napoleon cognac, chocolate stars, and red-haired women. At the moment he was sitting at his usual table in the saloon and indulging his sweet tooth by stirring three of his favorite chocolate drops into his coffee.

Seb surveyed his kingdom, noting that while all was quiet for now, tonight promised to be the kind of affair to keep the cash register ringing for hours. He'd gone down to the depot when the train arrived and tacked flyers to the walls announcing tonight's big poker tournament. Even now passengers would be heading this way, stopping as they made the trek at establishments like the Lamplighter and the Bucket in the seedier part of town. Eventually the more prosperous of those thirsty travelers would venture into the Pearly Gates, where he would welcome them with open arms.

For now it was just Seb; Pearl, who pretty much ran the bar for him; his gambling manager, Jack Dawkins, known as Black Jack thanks to his penchant for dealing himself aces and face cards on a regular basis; and Little Joe, the kid who mopped the floors each morning.

As he watched Black Jack arranging the tables for tonight's tournament, Seb heard an unusual sound. Turning toward Pearl, who was stacking bottles behind the bar, he asked, "Are you banging something around back there?"

She cocked her head, setting off one of her trademark purple feathers. It bobbed to and fro as she said, "I didn't hear nothing."

Again came the sound, and this time Seb recognized that it came from the opposite direction. The front door. Nobody knocked on the door of a saloon, and yet there it came again, this time a little louder.

Laughing to himself, Seb climbed out of his chair and went to open the door. He immediately recognized the poor gal who'd nearly been run down at the train depot. He'd have remembered her squashed hat, if nothing else.

"You don't have to knock on this door," he said, stepping aside. "Come on in. Everyone is welcome here."

"Oh, I couldn't." Her demure gaze slid to the boardwalk, where it remained. "I came about my ruined hat."

"Ah, yes, but first please come in out of the sun. I assure you, your reputation will suffer no harm. You're in Emancipation, Wyoming, now. Women pretty well run this town, and even the more proper of those women have no problem with visiting the Pearly Gates now and again."

She looked up at him, her brown eyes big and round, not so unlike his favorite chocolate stars. "Really?"

"Yes, really." Taking her by the elbow, Seb gently led her into the saloon and guided her over to his table. After pulling out a chair for her, he took his usual seat and said, "Can I offer you something to drink, some coffee, perhaps?"

"Oh, no, thank you. I just want to settle the bill for my hat." She took the pile of rubble from her head and laid it on the table. A few tendrils of hair escaped her bun, creamy butterscotch locks. Seb thought he'd noticed a few fiery strands in that hair at the depot, but then, he imagined red hair on almost every woman he met.

14

"If I understood your friend correctly," she went on to say, "he promised that you would pay for the damages."

"That's correct." Seb stirred his coffee, the heavenly scent of chocolate wafting up through the steam. "How much do I owe you?"

She cleared her throat. "Ah, fifty dollars?"

Seb had just taken a sip of coffee. He choked on it, nearly strangling as he said, "What? I must have heard you wrong, Miss, er . . ."

"Lucille Preston, from Kansas City, Missouri."

Kansas City. Of course. And fresh off the farm, no doubt. Again Seb glanced at the hat. It was nothing but a pile of broken straw, a mangled pink ribbon, and a few drooping ostrich feathers. Regarding her drab olive traveling suit, still mottled with dusty residue, Seb figured her entire ensemble, hat and all, couldn't be worth more than ten dollars.

"Miss Preston," he said, eyeing her suspiciously, "I'm not a man who spends a lot of time buying ladies' hats, but I can't believe that anyone would give more than, say, five dollars for yours. That is what you meant to say, isn't it?"

Hands clasped together, twisting in her lap, she avoided his gaze. "It's a very special hat, one my mother bought for my trip out West. I don't know what she paid for it, but it's very, very dear to me. Would forty dollars be all right?"

This time Seb had already swallowed his sip of coffee. The urge to choke was no less strong. "No, it would not, but I must say, you've got a lot of guts. Most folks who try to rob me come at it straightforward, waving a gun in my face."

Seb didn't know what kind of reaction to expect after that statement—indignation, at the least—but she surprised him. Miss Preston's eyes rolled to a close and then she took a deep breath. Her hands, still clasped in her lap, were bound together so tightly that her knuckles were white.

"I'm sorry if it seems like I'm trying to rob you," she said breathlessly. "It's just that I'm desperate for money, and I thought . . . well, I don't know what I thought."

Seb didn't know what to think either. Except that she didn't strike him as the criminal sort. "Why don't you start at the beginning," he suggested softly. "Did you find your friend at the bakery?"

"He's not exactly my friend," she said, opening her eyes. They were moist now, all warm and shiny like the melting stars floating around in his coffee.

"If not your friend, then what?" he asked.

"Charlie White and I were to be wed when I got to town," she explained, her voice cracking. "He was surprised I showed up and said that he sent a letter telling me not to come to Emancipation, which I never got of course, and then he introduced me to a girl who looked young enough to be clinging to her mama's apron strings, and she claimed that *she* was Charlie's fiancée, and he didn't state otherwise. Now I'm here."

"I see . . . I think."

"Charlie said her name was Cherry or something silly like that, and then he called her Muffin."

"Ah, yes," Seb commented. "The delectable Cherry Barkdoll." Miss Preston gave him a scowl that would curl paint. Wisely moving ahead, he surmised, "And now you're trying to gather enough money for a ticket back home?"

She nodded miserably.

"It seems to me that Charlie ought to give you train fare back to Kansas City. That's the least he could do." *The blithering idiot.*

"Oh, but I couldn't ask him for money, or even accept it if he offered. You can't imagine how humiliating it was standing there thinking I was Charlie's fiancée, while his new fiancée was laughing at me. I can't face him, not now or ever."

Tears were running down her cheeks, unchecked. Seb had an idea that Miss Preston wasn't even aware she was crying. Looking over his shoulder, he called to Pearl, "A bottle of my personal stock, please, and two snifters."

After Pearl brought the cognac and glasses, Seb poured a measure into a snifter and pushed it in front of Miss Preston. Then he laid his handkerchief beside it. "Here," he said. "Dry your eyes and take a sip of this. It will make you feel better."

Feel better? Until she looked down at the table and saw the linen he'd left for her, Lucy hadn't realized that she'd been crying. She snatched up the handkerchief, dabbed her cheeks and eyes, and then glanced over at the helpful Mr. Cole. As he stared back at her in all her dishevelment, again she was reminded of what Charlie must have seen as he told her about his new love. A miserable, scorned woman wearing a soiled traveling suit and a crushed hat. Something to be pitied and discarded, the unwanted runt of the litter.

Lucy sighed heavily and dropped her face into her hands.

"Please," Cole said, "take a sip of your cognac. It will help."

She peered out from between her fingers. "Oh, thank you, but no. I never touch spirits."

"This is better than spirits. Think of it as medicine."

Since she wasn't up to arguing, and by then she would have swilled the devil's brew if there was a chance it might make her feel better, Lucy lifted the snifter and brought it to her lips. She took a tentative sip, and then a larger swallow. The cognac warmed its way down her throat, heating her to her toes. In moments she could feel the tension draining from her shoulders.

"Thank you, Mr. Cole. I guess I do feel better."

"It's Sebastian, or Seb, if you wish."

"Thank you, Sebastian." She pushed her chair back from the table. "I think I've inconvenienced you enough for one day. If you'll just give me the five dollars, I'll be on my way."

Instead of paying her, Sebastian sat back in his chair and studied her, his index finger curled over his lip. He wasn't wearing his hat now, and Lucy could see that his hair was thick and dark; a little unruly, too, if the length that curled down over his forehead was any indication. Her gaze went to his ear, where more unruly curls fought for position along the side of his neck. It was then she noticed that he had a notch in his ear, a small scoop nicked from the outer edge. She wondered if he'd been born that way or if a bullet had zinged through it, taking a little piece of him as a souvenir. Then he spoke up again, startling her so, Lucy almost knocked over her drink.

"The five dollars is yours, of course," he said. "I'm afraid that won't get you very far, though. Even if you had the fare, the train heading east doesn't stop here until Tuesday. What will you do until then?"

She shrugged. "I honestly don't know."

Keeping a sharp eye on her, Sebastian fell silent. He drummed his fingers against the table, obviously thinking something over, and then shifted in his chair and took a sip of cognac.

Clearing his throat, he surprised Lucy by suggesting, "I don't often do this sort of thing for folks I don't know, but you strike me as an honest woman. I'd be happy to lend you the money for train fare, and even room and board, if necessary. Once you get back home, you can pay me back as you are able."

Stunned by the generous offer, Lucy almost accepted it on the spot. All she'd been able to think about since she left the bakery was running away, as far away as she could get from Charlie White and his childlike piece of confection. Now that her goal seemed within reach, it suddenly gave her pause. The child within was eager to accept, to run back home and into the arms of her family. It would be so easy.

Her family would welcome her back as if she'd never left. They would still love her, too, but she knew what they would be thinking: Poor Lucy, the dreamer who never quite did things right, the girl who couldn't get out of her own way. She'd never truly been able to master the art of cooking; loathed sewing so much it was a challenge to attach buttons to her own gowns; and whenever she was assigned to a household task, she usually got lost in daydreams and invariably wound up making a bigger mess than she'd started with. Now this. She hadn't even managed to hang on to her man long enough to speak her own wedding vows. If she went home, she would still be poor Lucy, the dreamer who'd tried her hand at just about everything expected of a woman but had never mastered anything, not even the art of love. How could she go back to Kansas City a failure again? She couldn't go yet, at least not until she'd done everything in her power to reclaim Charlie as her own.

Settled on that much, Lucy said, "I'm very touched by your generous offer, but I simply cannot accept money from a man I barely know. It wouldn't be seemly."

"I suppose that's understandable." He paused, thinking something over, and then suggested, "Would it be more acceptable if you were to earn the money I'm offering?"

"Earn it?" This was even more startling than his first offer. "How would I do that?"

He glanced around the saloon. "As I believe I already mentioned, the Pearly Gates is a fine establishment, one that our councilwomen visit from time to time. I could use some help, especially during the evening hours, and I think you might be well suited for the job. Interested?"

Horrified was the word that came to Lucy's mind. "You want me to be a hurdy-gurdy girl?"

He laughed. "Absolutely not. I host poker tournaments and other gaming events, and when my customers are busy playing cards, they aren't apt to want to leave their stakes unattended. I just need you to wander around, making sure everyone has a drink and serving those who don't."

Lucy's first impulse was to reject the offer out of hand. Knowing her resources were limited—all right, nonexistent—

she gave herself a moment to look around the saloon. Although she'd never before stepped inside such an establishment, it wasn't nearly as wicked or depraved as she'd assumed of such places. The air was breathable; redolent with the lingering odor of tobacco smoke and whiskey, but tempered with the inviting aroma of fresh-popped corn. Thanks to two large, sparkling chandeliers, the lighting was muted, not murky, and she was able to take more than a cursory look around.

The walls were papered in ruby red velvet and dotted with pictures of President Cleveland, boxing champions, and a few women Lucy didn't recognize. A single billiard table graced the area to the left, and several tables and chairs filled the remaining space. A man arranging decks of cards sat at one of these tables. Behind him, wielding a mop as tall as the top of his head, a young boy washed away the remnants of the night before. In the opposite corner, partitioned from the rest of the business, cigars and newspapers were laid out for sale and inspection. A piano sat quiet to the side of the little enclosure.

Lucy's gaze went to the polished walnut bar that filled the back of the saloon. Against the wall behind this counter were a few shelves displaying sample bottles of wine along with an assortment of spirits, but the thing that caught her eye was the woman behind the bar. Her hair, an unnatural silvery blond, was piled high on her head and adorned with a single purple feather. Her gown, cut indecently low at the bodice, matched the color of the feather and was made of satin and lace. This had to be a hurdy-gurdy girl, or even worse.

Lucy's eyes darted to Sebastian Cole and she blurted out, "If I take this job, am I expected to dress like that woman behind the bar?"

"No," he assured her. "Pearl is one of a kind. You can dress in your own clothing as long as it's something a little less severe than your traveling suit. Maybe Pearl can help you figure out what to wear if you decide to take the job. Well?"

He raised his eyebrows, the question hanging there in his expression, but Lucy wasn't ready with an answer. Would a lady even consider taking such a position? She rather doubted it, and yet at the thought of earning her own keep, her pulse surged with the kind of excitement she hadn't experienced since she'd boarded the train in Kansas City for her first ride on the rails. If she planned on staying in town a while, and Lucy was now determined to do just that, she had little choice.

Again regarding Sebastian Cole, she considered the fact that he owned a gambling establishment and that he was probably as slick as a well-seasoned skillet. She'd never known a man such as this, and yet he had kind eyes. She decided to trust him.

"I think I'd like to give it a try," Lucy declared. "When would you like me to start?"

"How about this afternoon? That way I can show you around and explain what's expected of you before the crowd gets too big. In the meantime, have you given any thought to where you'll be staying?"

"A hotel, I expect. Can you tell me which one is the cheapest?"

"I could," he said with a grin that pulled one corner of his mouth, "but I doubt you'd be pleased with the other guests. Tell you what—why don't you let me go speak to the manager at my hotel? I'm sure I can convince him to offer you a room at a very reasonable price. Where did you put your luggage?"

"Oh, my stars." Lucy slapped her palms against her cheeks. "I forgot all about my bags. I left them in front of the bakery." Tears threatened again. "I can't go back there, not now, not yet."

"You don't have to." Seb waved his arm high overhead. "Little Joe? Would you come here a minute?"

The boy propped his broom against the wall and hurried over to the table. "Yes, Mr. Cole?"

"The lady left two bags sitting in front of the bakery. Would you mind getting them and bringing them to my hotel?" He dropped a couple of coins into the boy's palm. "I'll be waiting for you there."

"Yes, sir, and thanks." With that, the young man took off at a run.

Seb pushed away from the table and got to his feet. Then he said, "Why don't you stay here and enjoy your cognac while I make the arrangements? I shouldn't be long."

It wasn't until some thirty minutes later as Seb was heading back to the saloon that he began to question his sanity. Hadn't he learned his lesson in Denver? He'd always had an eye for the ladies—the more highborn, the better—but the women who really got to him were damsels in distress. He simply couldn't resist lending a helping hand; sometimes two, if the women in question were so inclined. Unfortunately, and more often than not, those efforts usually wound up costing him a goodly share of his money, occasionally a piece of his heart and, in Denver, his self-respect, among other things.

This time he went out of his way to consider the lady's needs, not his own. Thinking of Lucille and her glaring innocence, he foolishly told the hotel manager that he wanted a room close to his so he could keep an eye on his sister. Claiming Miss Preston as kin seemed like a good idea at the time, but it hadn't occurred to Seb that she would be given the small room connecting to his, which was the finest room the hotel had to offer and was actually part of a suite. He'd only meant to make her feel more secure, especially considering the parade of hotel guests she would encounter. At least that's what Seb told himself, even though he had to admit that he found Lucille Preston attractive, if in a homespun sort of way. Besides, she wasn't even a redhead.

Resigned to his fate, whatever that might be, Seb left the

hotel, strolled into the saloon, and found Miss Preston sitting right where he left her. Instead of sobbing into his handkerchief, she had her nose buried in a newspaper. Seb, a silent partner, owned a piece of the *Emancipation Tribune*, a daily newspaper. He noted sourly that the lady was reading *The Weekly Rustler*.

"Catching up on the local gossip?" he asked as he approached.

She looked up from the paper. "Oh, I hope you don't mind. I was careful not to make any extra creases. I don't think anyone can tell it's been read if I put it back on the rack."

Seb dropped into the chair next to hers. "Keep it. My employees are entitled to free newspapers."

"Thank you. May I take one of the other papers, too?"

"Help yourself. I'm sure you'll find it far more informative."

A deeply dimpled smile lit up her features, erasing the image of the sullen-faced girl who'd been so hesitant to come into the saloon. Seb impulsively licked his lips. Shaking off the urge to kiss her, to learn firsthand if she tasted as sweet as she looked, he abruptly turned to the indelicate subject of her lodging situation.

"I got you a very nice room," he said, more gruffly than he'd intended. "It's only two dollars a day, and that includes a small breakfast each morning."

The smile remained, growing ever more radiant. "That sounds wonderful. I should be able to earn that much each day, shouldn't I?"

He nodded. "And with enough left over to save up for that ticket home. The thing is, your room is part of a suite that leads to my room."

She swallowed this information with obvious difficulty.

Seb quickly added, "I assure you that your privacy won't be an issue. There are connecting doors, each with its own lock. I thought you'd feel more comfortable knowing help was just a knock away."

She considered this a moment. "Thank you. I'm sure it will be just fine. I really appreciate all you've done for me."

"Good." Seb pushed out of his chair. "Now I've got to get to work. The hotel is the Palace Arms, across the street and three doors east. Just tell the clerk that you're my sister and he'll give you a key to the room."

"Your sister?"

The confusion in her dark eyes confirmed that Seb had probably made an error in judgment. Too late to back out now, he shrugged and said, "Half-sister, actually, because our names are different. I thought it might help to keep you safe from the unwanted attentions of the other hotel guests."

"In that case, I am again beholden to you." Rising from her chair, the newspaper clutched to her bosom, she asked, "What time do you want me to come back?"

"How about four o'clock? And don't forget to dress differently, as if you're going to a party." He looked her over, adding, "And let down your hair. At least get rid of the bun."

If she was insulted, it didn't show. She gave him another dazzling smile and said, "Anything else?"

"Yes, actually, your name. We can't be calling you Miss Preston, and Lucille sounds a little too stiff for someone who works here. Can we call you Lucy?"

A little gleam flashed in her dark eyes as she said, "That's what my family and friends call me. You've been a very good friend since I arrived, so yes, you may call me Lucy."

"Lucy it is. See you at four."

Seb watched as she waltzed out the door, content in the knowledge that so far he'd been of some help to the gentle young woman. How long that feeling would last was anyone's guess. He just hoped this wouldn't turn out the way things did in Denver—with him packing up and leaving town.

Too excited to rest, buoyed by all the good that had come from her earlier humiliation, Lucy opted to take a walk around town. Instead of heading in the direction of the hotel, she started toward the depot, morbidly drawn to the building that housed Charlie's Bakery. She was doggedly determined to stay on the opposite side of the street but found herself hoping as she passed by that she might catch a glimpse of Charlie looking for her, calling her name, begging her forgiveness.

Of course none of that happened. Head held high, but spirits low, Lucy continued on down the boardwalk until she came to an alley. She'd pretty much decided to turn around and go to the hotel when she noticed an odd sign on the large, barnlike structure directly ahead. It read, B. C. AL-LISON HAY & GRAIN. Directly beneath that a plaque proclaimed HOME OF THE WEEKLY RUSTLER. The idea of housing a newspaper in with a feed store drew Lucy's curiosity, but not nearly as much as the small, hand-lettered sign in the window that read, HELP WANTED. FEMALES ONLY. INQUIRE WITHIN.

The one thing Lucy had always been good at was reading and writing, though not so much arithmetic. She read everything she could get her hands on from books to newspapers, and even such things as labels listing the ingredients for Durkee's Salad Dressing, Scott's Emulsion of Cod Liver Oil, and other seemingly insignificant pieces of printed matter. She didn't delude herself into thinking that she might qualify for the job offered here but felt drawn to the building anyway.

The first thing to hit her when she stepped inside was the scent of freshly milled grain, the bite of new alfalfa, and the loamy odor of all manner of livestock supplies. From the back of the building, Lucy thought she heard the muted sound of chickens scratching and clucking at their fodder. To her left, a woman hunched over a desk behind the counter. She was twirling a loose strand of hair with one hand and making notes with the other. From a counter toward the rear, where the chicken jabbering seemed to be coming from, a male voice called out.

"Kin I help you, miss?"

Lucy turned toward the voice. "I'm here about the newspaper."

He scratched the edge of his bulbous nose and shouted, "Ya got a visitor, Hazel."

The woman's gray head popped up from behind the counter. "You don't have to yell, Buford. I may not hear so good, but I can still see."

She climbed out of her chair and lumbered over to the counter. A big woman, she loomed over Lucy by a good eight inches in any direction. Although she wasn't exactly fat, she was big of bone and as well muscled as a draft horse. Lucy's gaze shot to the thin, balding man at the rear of the store, and her first thought was of Jack Spratt and his wife.

"Well?" the woman said, looking down her nose through a pair of nickel-plated spectacles. "If you've got a complaint about the paper or advice for the editor, write it down and stick it in the box outside the door."

"Oh, neither, ma'am." Lucy inched closer to the counter. "I think your paper is very good."

"Then what? You applying for the job?"

Caught off guard, she could hardly make her tongue work. "Oh, well, I'm not sure, that is, I don't know—"

The woman reached out and grabbed Lucy's hands, jamming the rest of her garble in her throat. Then she squinted through her glasses and said, "You've got the right kind of fingers for the job, nice and small. You ever arranged lead type before?"

"No, ma'am, I sure haven't."

Now she squinted into Lucy's face, a direct gaze that brooked no lies. "How are you at reading and writing?"

"Oh, I love to read and I'm told I'm a fair hand at writing."

"Can you spell?"

"Better than most," she was proud to say. "I always got one hundred percent on my spelling tests."

"Then I guess you're hired."

Lucy pulled her hands out of the woman's grasp. "I am?"

"If you want the job, such as it is. Don't pay much, that's for sure, and I only need you two days a week, Wednesday and Thursday." She glanced around her tiny office. "The way things are going and if circulation doesn't pick up, I may not need you more than next week. Still want the job?"

Lucy had never even allowed herself to dream that she might one day be offered a job at a real, honest-to-gosh newspaper. And this woman wanted to pay her? She'd have taken the job for free.

"I'd love to work here, ma'am. Can I start tomorrow?"

"Hold your horses. First off, what's your name?"

"Lucille Preston from Kansas City, but you can call me Lucy."

The woman nodded sagely. "I expect this is your first time out of Missouri?"

"Yes. How did you know?"

"Lucky guess." The woman stuck out a meaty hand, grabbed hold of Lucy's, and shook it as if she were swinging an ax. "I'm Hazel Allison. You can call me Hazel. The bald fellow in the back is my husband, Buford. You'll be doing yourself a favor if you don't call him at all."

Seeing the twinkle in Hazel's pale green eyes, Lucy took the comment for a joke and chuckled.

Then Hazel added, "I hope you didn't come to Emancipation looking for a husband of your own. Buford is about the best this town has to offer, and it's taken me a good twelve years just to get him house-broke."

Talk of husbands took some of the wind out of Lucy's sails, but she was honestly able to reply, "No, I didn't come here looking for a husband." *I thought I already had one.* "I am curious about the name of this town. Does it have something to do with the suffrage movement?"

"You might say that. We used to be called Percyville after Tom Percy, the mayor. That was fine with everyone until he decided to beat his wife to death. The womenfolk got up in arms over that and picketed City Hall." She laughed at the memory. "The council didn't have much choice but to re-name the place, and to remain in good graces with their wives, the male council went along with Emancipation as the new name. After that, women kind of took over the town."

Lucy couldn't imagine what she meant by "taking over the town," but it did remind her of something that had been bothering her. "Are you saying that women really are allowed in the saloons here?"

Hazel raised one eyebrow. "You a drinker?"

"Oh, goodness, no. It's just something I overheard."

"Well then, yes, I suppose you could say that. Women here are free to do just about anything they want. I will add that the only saloon self-respecting women might gather in is the Pearly Gates down the street."

Exactly as the helpful Mr. Cole had claimed.

"Listen," Hazel went on, "now that we've got that set-tled, I've got to get to work. I'll see you on Wednesday morning, not tomorrow, and be sure to wear something that will look good with inkstains on it." She paused a moment, studying Lucy's dusty traveling suit. "I guess what you're wearing will do."

Too happy to take offense at the remark, Lucy thanked her new employer again and then went on her way. As she headed for the hotel, she didn't even realize that she'd passed Charlie's Bakery until she was well beyond it. All she could think about was the fact that she'd secured not one but two positions in the same day, one of them a dream job with a newspaper.

Her past sorrow temporarily forgotten, Lucy thought she must be the luckiest girl in the world. She could hardly wait to see what the night would bring.

Chapter Four

For the next few hours Lucy's streak of luck held. When she checked into the hotel, she could hardly believe the luxurious accommodations Sebastian had arranged for her. The walls were covered with soft green wallpaper sporting vines of ivy woven through fancy gold trellises, and the floor was carpeted in the same mint green. A puffy white coverlet blanketed her soft feather bed, and she had not one but two large dressers. Best of all, a separate room housed her own private water closet complete with privy and a sparkling enameled tub that spouted both hot and cold running water.

This was a far cry from the outhouse and small wooden tub used for bathing in the kitchen of the Preston farm; more like a palace that made her feel like a princess. Princess Nobody, she thought ruefully, wondering if Charlie had found accommodations as wonderful as hers. Thoughts of her former fiancé pounded the reality of his deception into her, tearing open an aching wound that left her feeling incredibly weary.

Longing for escape from those painful and dreary thoughts, Lucy took a long, relaxing bath and then stretched out on the puffy coverlet for a quick nap. When she awoke hours later, twilight trickled throughout the room. Knowing it must be well past four o'clock, she bolted out of bed, threw on a skirt and blouse, and hastily braided her hair as she hurried toward the saloon.

The Pearly Gates was no longer the sanctuary it had been when Lucy first stepped into the place. The moment she walked through the door, her senses were assailed from every direction. Thanks to the slick-haired man pounding relentlessly on the keyboard, the piano belted out a raucous rendition of *I've Been Working on the Railroad*. All of the tables were filled with gamblers, some of them hooting and hollering, others grumbling or cursing their luck. The bar was hip deep in men, each of them demanding the attention of a very harried-looking Pearl. As she headed that way, Lucy caught sight of Sebastian making his way from the bar to the tables. He carried a large tray filled with beer mugs, whiskey bottles, and shot glasses.

Lucy waved to him, drawing his attention, and that was when her luck ran out. The scowl he shot her in return sent her backing into the corner, where she tried desperately to fade into the newspaper rack.

After Seb delivered the last beer, he headed straight for Lucy, empty tray in hand. "Where have you been?" he snapped. "I told you to be here by four."

"I'm sorry." She dropped her gaze to the floor. "I took a nap, but I didn't realize how tired I was. I just now woke up."

As she spoke, he took note of her appearance. She'd discarded the dusty traveling suit but replaced it with an equally severe getup—a white blouse that buttoned up to her chin and a plain black skirt. She'd gotten rid of the bun all right, but in its place a long braid hung down the middle of her back.

"I thought I told you to dress for a party. You look like a school marm."

She glanced down at herself, color spotting her cheeks. "I

was so late, I put on the first things I grabbed. Do you want me to go back to the hotel and change?"

"No. As you can see, we're very busy here tonight. I should be at the table with the gamblers, not serving drinks." He handed Lucy the tray. "Just work your way around the tables and if you see anyone with an empty glass, ask them what they'd like. Pearl will help you figure out the rest. Can you manage?"

Lucy gulped and said, "I'll do the best I can."

She looked more than innocent now, vulnerable even, and Seb was gripped by the urge to take her into his arms and tell her to forget the whole damn thing. But he had a business to run, and from what he'd seen a moment earlier, a gambler at table four was enjoying an unusual streak of luck.

Instead of consoling Lucy, he said, "You'd better get busy. We've got a mighty thirsty crowd tonight."

Assuming he'd given her instruction enough, Seb turned on his heel and headed for table four. As he approached, a gambler who'd lost his twenty-five-dollar stake vacated his chair and headed for the front door. Seb was happy to take the man's spot, where he could easily observe the stranger across from him. He tossed his money on the table and the volunteer dealer, Charles Wolcott, president of the Commerce Bank, replaced the bills with twenty-five dollars' worth of poker chips.

As he waited for the cards to be dealt, Seb glanced toward the bar to check on Lucy. She was slowly making her way toward table one, both hands clenched on the outer edges of the tray she carried. There were only two mugs of beer on the tray, but she moved as if she carried two sweaty sticks of dynamite, ready to blow at any minute. Intent on her precious cargo, she failed to negotiate the leg of a gambler who was sprawled out in his chair.

Lucy and her tray abruptly disappeared.

Seb pushed back in his chair, thinking of going to her aid, but then she popped up again, empty mugs in one hand, the dripping tray in the other. Seb closed his eyes and rubbed his forehead, wondering what in hell he'd gotten himself into. It would probably be cheaper to send Lucy back to the hotel and take over the hostessing duties himself.

At the bar, Lucy squeezed the excess beer out of her skirt as Pearl refilled the mugs. "Do you think I have to pay for those beers?" she asked when the woman returned.

"Not this time, honey." Pearl positioned the mugs on the tray. "Let me give you a little advice so it doesn't happen again. You're gonna have to learn to carry a lot more than two beers at a time, so listen up and listen good. Don't watch the liquid else you'll have it slopping all over the place. Also, as you might 'a noticed, you can't see where you're going if you're watching the beer."

"But what if it spills while I'm walking?"

"A little slop ain't never hurt anyone, but dumping perfectly good beers on the floor ain't too smart. Just pay attention to where you're going and try not to think about what's on the tray. Now get a move on or you'll never get all those thirsty folks served."

Head down, eyes on the path before her, Lucy slowly made her way to the table. This time she made it. As she carefully unloaded the drinks, the other gamblers at the table began shouting at her.

"Hey, miss, how about a bottle of whiskey and three glasses?"

"And three more beers, sweetheart."

Trying to remember the order, she hurried back to the bar, distracted by the shouts of gamblers at other tables. By the time she'd served all seven tables, her braid had come loose and her hair hung down in all manner of disarray. Some of those strands were damp with beer, as was her skirt and parts of her blouse. Her feet hurt and her legs felt rubbery, but she gamely started in all over again, and heading for table one.

As she approached, Lucy noticed that a new player had joined the game there. Although dressed like a man in Levi's and a checkered shirt, the new gambler couldn't hide her charms and was definitely a woman. Was this what Hazel meant by women taking over the town? Swallowing her surprise, Lucy glimpsed beneath the wide-brimmed hat that covered most of the gambler's fluffy yellow hair and recognized the girlish features. Cherry Barkdoll.

Drawn to the woman the way men are lured to a hanging, Lucy felt herself gravitating toward Cherry, almost against her will. When she was standing beside her, her hand developed a mind of its own. She watched as her fingers took a full beer from the tray, felt her wrist go limp, and then heard the sound of liquid splashing against leather.

As beer rained down on her hat, spilling over the brim and into her lap, Cherry shrieked and jumped to her feet. "What the hell are you doing?" she demanded.

Terrified of the woman's wrath, not at all clear about what had just happened, Lucy set the tray on the table and backed away.

"What have you got to say for yourself?" Cherry said, advancing. "Are you deaf as well as dumb?"

Something boiled up in Lucy, an anger she could taste, like sour pickles dipped in rust. "Leave him alone," she said, her teeth clenched. "He isn't yours to take."

Cherry reared back at this, her exquisite features rumpled in confusion. "What the hell are you talking about? He, who?"

Lucy laughed out loud, a crazy sound. "You know exactly who you, you . . . husband-stealing slattern."

"*Slattern?*" Cherry drew back her fist and took aim at Lucy's chin. Before she could fire, Sebastian Cole stepped between the two women.

"What seems to be the problem, ladies?" he asked Cherry.

She curled her upper lip. "Your hostess here went and dumped a beer on my head."

Sebastian glanced from her to Lucy, one ebony eyebrow raised high.

"It was an accident," she said, not entirely a lie. "The mug just kind of fell out of my hand. Besides," she added, hands on hips, "shouldn't she be down at the bakery icing Charlie's buns instead of gambling with other men?"

Sebastian rubbed his chin, chuckling under his breath. "I think I know what happened here. Lucy, meet Merry Barkdoll, Cherry's twin sister."

Good thing she wasn't holding a tray full of beer. She'd have dropped it. "Twins?"

"We might be born the same day," Merry cut in, "but that's the only resemblance between me and that cotton-headed sister of mine."

Maybe to her way of thinking, but as far as Lucy could see, Merry was identical to her sister, save for the clothing and coarse demeanor. Lucy glanced at Merry's dripping hat and stained Levi's, her heart sinking when she realized what she'd done. She had no right to blame Cherry Barkdoll or her rough-hewn sister for what had happened with Charlie. The blame rested entirely on her own shoulders. Lucy didn't know exactly how or why she'd lost him, but she finally understood that it was her fault, not Cherry's or Charlie's. All her fault.

Maybe she should have written to him more often after he left Missouri, daily perhaps. Or maybe it was something else altogether. Lucy blushed, ashamed to have such thoughts, but had them anyway. Maybe Charlie would still be hers if she'd let him touch her breasts the way he wanted to their last night together. Maybe she should have given herself to him, become his lover in every sense of the word. Maybe, maybe, maybe. She was drowning in maybes.

35

"Are you all right?" she heard Sebastian say.

Lucy blinked and shook herself back into the present. "What? Oh, yes, I'm fine."

She glanced over his shoulder and saw to her surprise that Merry was back in her chair, studying her cards. Head down, Lucy approached her and said, "I'm terribly sorry about the beer. I honestly don't know what happened."

"Forget it," Merry said without looking up.

Again Sebastian intervened. "I'm sure Lucy will be happy to get you another, and of course it's on the house."

Now Merry did look up, but it was only to rest an appreciative and rather dreamy-eyed gaze on Sebastian. "Thanks, Seb. I appreciate it."

Grumbling to herself although she couldn't say why, Lucy delivered the rest of the drinks left on her tray and then went off to refill Merry's mug.

The rest of the night went by in a blur of beer, whiskey, and tobacco smoke. Lucy spilled a few more drinks, accidentally dousing a gambler's cigar once, and mixed up several orders, but as far as she could tell, she'd managed to keep most of the customers happy. She was standing at the bar waiting for her latest order to be filled, seriously wondering if she had the energy left to make it to table five, when Sebastian approached.

"You look tired," he said. "We're down to two tables of winners, so if you want to, I think you can go on back to the hotel now."

If she wanted to? Lucy thought about dropping to her knees and kissing his boots, but she was fairly certain she'd never get up again. "Thank you," she said instead. "I'd love to go to my room now, assuming I'm still able to walk that far."

Sebastian laughed as Pearl came up with a tray full of drinks. Focusing on the bartender, he said, "Would you mind taking those to table five? I'm going to walk Lucy to the hotel."

"Sure, Seb. No problem." That was what Pearl said, but her expression didn't agree. When she took her adoring gaze from him and dropped it on Lucy, it became narrow and intense, like poison-tipped arrows. "Tough night, huh, kid?"

Tough wasn't the half of it. Lucy's feet had gone way beyond merely aching, and she noticed if she stood still for too long—which didn't happen much—her legs would shake uncontrollably.

Using a precious drop of her waning energy reserves, she forced a smile and said, "Very tough. See you tomorrow."

Lucy dragged along rather than walked as Sebastian escorted her back to the hotel. She assumed he'd leave her in the lobby, but he insisted on accompanying her all the way to her room. When they came to her door, he stood there facing her, one hand on the jamb behind her head.

Sebastian was close, not touching any part of her, and yet Lucy could almost feel his body pressing against hers, the sense that his overpowering masculinity might actually seep into her pores. He reached out with his free hand then, and brushed away a beer-soaked strand of hair that had glued itself to her cheek. Lucy shivered, shaking off a spasm that tingled up her spine.

"You must be cold and exhausted," Sebastian said, his voice a velvet fog. "It wasn't fair of me to throw you into a new job on the night of a poker tournament. I'm sorry if I haven't been as much help as you'd figured on."

"Oh, but you have helped," she protested. "Lord knows where I'd be now if you hadn't offered to put me to work."

"I promise that tomorrow will be a lot easier." His gaze bore into hers, occasionally flickering to her mouth, and then he took a deep breath. "Is there anything else I can do before you turn in?"

"Are you offering more help?" she asked, laughing for no particular reason.

"Sure, if there's something else I can help with. I owe you more than your wages for what you went through tonight. You did a fine job for your first try."

Lucy thought of the spilled drinks and general chaos she'd caused at the saloon. She knew darn well that she hadn't performed well but loved the idea that Sebastian was trying to make her feel better.

Following that thought, she said, "Actually, there is something you might be able to help me with."

"Name it."

"Well, you're a man and all . . ."

"That seems to be the consensus."

Acutely aware that she need only lean forward to touch that masculine presence, she ventured, "I was just wondering if you might know the best way to go about getting Charlie back. After tonight with Merry, I'm pretty sure that dumping a beer on his head won't work."

Sebastian's eyes held hers a moment longer but then slid closed like steel doors. He took his hand from the jamb and stepped back. "I'm not sure I can help you there," he said. "I don't know Charlie all that well."

Lucy felt the sudden rift between them, a cold draft. Loathe to let him go this way, she persisted. "Then you can't offer any kind of advice?"

He shrugged. "I wouldn't go chasing after him, begging him to take you back, if that's what you mean by advice."

"But if I ignore him completely, won't he just forget all about me? You know, out of sight, out of mind?"

"Probably," he agreed. "I didn't mean don't see him. It's just that when you do, I think it would be best if you pretend that all is well, that you're getting along better without him."

Lucy considered this, and a myriad of possibilities bloomed in her mind. "I see what you mean. Make him think I don't want him back, right?"

"Something like that, but don't blame me if it doesn't work out."

"Oh, Sebastian, I would never blame you for anything. You've been more than helpful." She impulsively reached out and touched his cheek. "You've been very kind."

He took her hand in his and lightly kissed her fingertips. "I'd better say good night. See you tomorrow, and you don't have to come in until around five or so."

It was almost noon when Lucy finally dragged her aching body out of bed. She smelled of stale beer and tobacco smoke. Indulging herself in a way she never had before, she took a second bath in as many days, and washed the offensive odors from her hair. Dressing more to Sebastian's liking, Lucy chose a scoop-necked blouse with a drawstring bow, a gauzy skirt of silver gray and pink, and set it off with a wide belt of red velvet. She left her hair down, as he'd suggested, but pulled two lengths away from her face and secured them at the back of her head with a satin ribbon that matched her belt.

Ready to face the day and, even more surprising, Charlie, Lucy downed a breakfast of ham, flapjacks, and scrambled eggs and then took to the boardwalk. She headed straight for Charlie's Bakery. This time when the little bell announced her arrival, Lucy saw that Charlie was already standing behind the counter. Taking a deep breath, she headed for him, ignoring the curious glances of the few patrons.

"Good morning, Charlie," she said brightly, even though her heart was in her throat. "Or should I say, good afternoon?"

"Lucille." He dusted his hands on his apron. "You look different somehow."

She thought he did, too, boyish again, the old Charlie. Flipping one of her loose curls, she said, "It's probably the fact that I let my hair down. I usually wear it in a bun, remember?"

Sharon Ihle

She thought she saw some color in his cheeks as he said, "Yes, that's probably it. Where have you been? I've been terribly worried about you."

"Worried? Whatever for?"

He wouldn't look her in the eye as he said, "The way you left here yesterday, you seemed, well, upset. I went looking for you but couldn't find you anywhere."

She forced a laugh. "You must have looked in all the wrong places. I let a lovely room for myself at the Palace Arms Hotel. What did you want?"

"Want?"

"Why were you looking for me?"

Charlie's mustache twitched, and again he avoided her gaze. "I wanted to make sure you were all right, and that you had enough money to tide you over until the next train comes to town."

"Oh, goodness, Charlie. I have my own money."

A thrill ran through her at the truth behind those words. She was actually earning her own money, her keep, for the first time in her life.

Buoyed, she glanced at the display case on the counter. "In fact, that's why I'm here. I just have to have one of your wonderful Hot Cross Buns. I've really missed them."

Lucy hoped he understood that she'd implied she missed his baked goods, not him. Charlie's blank expression told her that he simply took her at her word as he reached into the display, withdrew one of the buns, and then placed it on a piece of parchment.

"How much do I owe you?" Lucy asked, taking the baked good off the counter.

"Nothing," Charlie scolded. "I can't charge you."

"Oh, but I insist." Again feeling a thrill, she dropped a quarter on the counter, undoubtedly enough to pay for several buns. "Thank you, Charlie. Maybe I'll see you around town sometime."

Before he could find his tongue, Lucy turned and swept

out the door. She'd been afraid that seeing him again would be her undoing, and that instead of convincing him that she didn't want him back, she'd do something stupid like throw herself on his mercy. The knowledge that she'd somehow found the strength to do just the opposite made Lucy feel lighter than air, filled with a kind of crazy euphoria. She practically skipped as she walked on down the boardwalk, and was surprised when she looked up to see that she'd arrived at the doors of the Allison Hay & Grain store. Glancing at the bun in her hand, inspiration struck.

Lucy stepped through the door and went right up to the newspaper counter. "Good afternoon, Missus Allison."

She looked up from her desk, correcting, "It's Hazel. What brings you here today? I don't need you until Wednesday."

Lucy put her present down on the counter. "I brought you a Hot Cross Bun from Charlie's Bakery."

A big woman, nonetheless Hazel shot out of her chair. "Oh, I just love those."

It occurred to Lucy that she no longer had a taste for them.

Eyeing the pastry, Hazel asked, "What did I do to deserve this?"

Without waiting for an answer, Hazel bit into the sweet. She had a long face and weary eyes, but the deep creases around her mouth suggested that she was a woman who laughed freely and often.

Testing that theory, Lucy replied, "I bought it in case I'm not as good at spelling as I might have implied."

A mouthful of bun didn't stop Hazel from laughing out loud. "You're smart, I'll give you that," she said, swallowing the last of the treat. "Now, is this little bit of bribery the only reason you stopped by?"

"Actually," Lucy said, thinking back to the previous night, "we could use a few more newspapers down at the Pearly Gates. I think they all sold out last night."

"Is that right?" Hazel puffed up her already impressive bosom, the buttons holding her blouse together suffering from the additional strain. "Am I to assume that you were there participating in the poker tournament?"

"Oh, heavens no. I'm employed there as a hostess."

"You work for Seb?" At Lucy's nod, Hazel's pale eyes went both soft and hard, sparkling like diamonds. "Lucky girl."

Was every woman in town in love with Sebastian Cole? Lucy wondered, wondering too if he loved any of them back.

"I am glad to hear that you have another job," Hazel continued. "I'm not sure how much longer I can keep this paper going. Since the *Emancipation Tribune* came here a few months back, I've barely been breaking even."

Lucy had found the time to read both papers, so this came as no surprise. "It must be difficult to compete with a daily newspaper."

"Darn right it is, especially since they have so much Denver money behind them, and fancy wire services and such. It's all I can do to keep up with the hog and grain prices. I collect most of the big news from the *Tribune* during the week and offer a short version in my paper. I'm going to have to do something different if I want to stay in business."

Lucy wanted to argue with her, to tell her that she thought the *Rustler* was fine just the way it was, but she couldn't lie. Aside from a few local articles and notices, there wasn't much special about Hazel's paper.

"Maybe you could expand the local section," Lucy suggested. "I think most folks would love to read about themselves."

Hazel barked a laugh, and then went to her desk. When she returned, she had a small pile of notes in her hand. "This is a sample of the kind of thing I get from the fine citizens of Emancipation. How much expanding do you think I'll do if I write about this?"

She took one of the notes from the pile and read it out loud. " 'Dear Madam Editor: I think my husband goes to bawdy houses and saloons, and has taken to drink. I heard tell I could cut his arm and set a match to his blood. How big a flame proves he's a tippler?' " She looked up at Lucy. "If I wrote that up in my paper and had the gall to give the woman my honest opinion, I'd be run out of town on a rail."

Although Lucy understood the problem, the letter tickled her funny bone. "Too bad," she said, laughing softly. "This letter is hysterical."

Hazel pondered that a moment. "It is pretty titillating at that. I'd love to put it in the paper, maybe in its own column, but I'd still have to answer to the townsfolk."

"You wouldn't have to if you had other reporters writing for you the way the *Tribune* does. That way you could blame the column on someone else."

Hazel drew her graying brows together, thinking it over, and then said, "An excellent idea, dear, but I'd never find someone fool enough to write about this."

Lucy shrugged. "Well, it was just an idea."

Hazel cocked her head and narrowed her eyes. Tapping her finger against the counter, she said, "Didn't you mention that you were good at spelling *and* writing?"

"Y-yes," Lucy said warily.

Hazel pushed the letter toward her. "Maybe you'd like to try your hand as a reporter."

The thought of writing her own column was so overwhelming that Lucy's breath froze in her lungs. She wanted to hoot and holler, stomp her feet, and twirl in a circle. Then she realized what attempting such an endeavor would involve. She sure didn't want to incur the wrath of anyone, much less people she hadn't even met.

"What about the townsfolk? Won't they be mad at me?"

"There is that. You'd probably become the most unpopular woman in town." Hazel tapped her finger more rapidly. "Unless . . . unless you write the column under another name, something you make up, and we tell our readers that this columnist writes for a fancy wire service somewhere else."

"Like Chicago or New York?"

"Right." Hazel's enthusiasm almost matched Lucy's. "I like the sound of Chicago. By Jove, I think this might actually work."

"You really want me to do it?"

"I think so. Just be warned, if you do write this column, you won't get credit for the work. Most writers can't wait to show off their work and call it their own. Isn't that going to bother you?"

"No," she promised, meaning it. "But are you really, really sure you want me—*me*—to write this?"

"Odds are it won't work out, but there's no harm in you giving it a try." Hazel paused, brought her fist to her mouth, and tapped the knuckles against her lips. At length she said, "We can call it an advice column, but I can't think what we ought to call you. Any ideas?"

Lucy thought of her oldest sister, the one who thought she knew everything. "How about Penelope?"

Tapping her lips a final time, Hazel said, "Penelope. That'll work. If you get busy on this and have a decent answer by Wednesday, something my readers will like, we might even be able to debut the new column with the next edition. Why don't we call it 'Ask Penelope'?"

Chapter Five

It seemed a ridiculously simple task. All Lucy had to do was write down the woman's question, smoothing the words and grammar a little, and then think of an answer. New at the idea of giving anyone advice, she jotted down the first thing that came to mind: follow the man to see where he really went.

When Lucy took her prized column back to Hazel for approval the next day, carrying it as if it were a child, she expected some excitement, maybe even a little praise. What she got for her efforts was a quill through the heart.

"No, no, dear," said Hazel, clucking her tongue. "For one thing, you can't sign Shirley's name to her letter. If her husband reads this, he might shoot her. We're going to have to make these queries anonymous if we want to have any peace in this town."

"That's no problem. I'll just leave it unsigned."

Hazel shook her gray head and tapped her finger against one of her multiple chins. "I don't like that idea any better. What about this? Maybe you can pick something out of her letter, a word or phrase, and sign it that way."

"Oh, I see." Lucy glanced at the letter, considering the possibilities, and then said, "The way this reads, we ought to sign it 'Crazy in Emancipation.'"

Hazel barked a laugh. "Do something like that, but not so blunt."

Thinking the signature was Hazel's only complaint, Lucy said, "I can't wait to see this in print."

"You won't be seeing this column in print, not as is, anyway." Hazel puckered up her lips, dropping her jowls like pouches. "Sorry, dear, but this isn't much of an answer."

Lucy tried not to take it personally but felt her spine stiffen in response. "I thought telling her to follow her husband made a lot more sense than carving him up."

"Of course it does, but it's not very interesting and doesn't get at the heart of the problem. Know what I mean?"

"I'm not sure. What would you do if Buford was the one running off to saloons and bawdy houses? Follow him, right?"

"Nope. I'd sit on him and pluck out his chest hairs, one at a time."

After sharing a laugh, Hazel patted the back of Lucy's hand and said, "Don't get in a fret over this, dear. I know you're new at the newspaper business, so let me tell you about our readers. What you or I would do doesn't matter much. If anyone's going to care about this column, or the paper for that matter, we have to titillate our readers, maybe even make them mad. It's not the mundane that sells papers, you know. Folks like to read about murderers, bank robbers, scandalous trysts, and such."

Her cheeks aflame, still feeling the tip of that quill, Lucy had to admit that Hazel had a point. "I think I understand what you mean. I need to make my answers more inflammatory, maybe adding a dash of humor to keep readers from getting too annoyed."

"Now you're getting it." This time Hazel reached out and pinched Lucy's cheek. Then she suggested, "Read the question again, but as you do, think about what the woman is saying, not about what you think she ought to do."

Lucy picked up her notes and reread the letter.

When she'd finished, Hazel asked, "What does your gut tell you?"

Lucy had never been one to tattle or to malign other folks, so it didn't come easy when she said, "I hope it doesn't sound mean, but I think this woman is seriously deranged and that her plan is idiotic."

"There you go." Hazel gave her a congratulatory slap on the shoulder, nearly knocking Lucy off her feet. "Keep that gut thought in mind and go write your answer again. You can go ahead and tell the woman her plan is idiotic, but make her think it's a compliment. Give our readers something to laugh at, shock them if you want to, but don't bore them. Got it?"

Her mind already buzzing with possibilities, Lucy said, "Yes, Madam Editor, I believe that I do."

Lucy wrote and rewrote the column. As many times as she produced it, Hazel whipped out her editing pencil and went through it like a dose of salts. After they finally agreed that they had produced the perfect column, Lucy could hardly wait to set the type.

First she had to get through Tuesday night at the Pearly Gates. The train heading east had come through town earlier in the day, and Sebastian had arranged to have faro games to help relieve the newcomers of their excess cash. It promised to be an evening that would run her legs off, much the way she'd fared the first night she worked at the saloon. Two hours into the job, Lucy was proved right.

As she stood at the bar waiting for Pearl to fill yet another order, Seb slid up beside her. He moved like a cat, gracefully, full of purpose. Lucy sensed his presence before he leaned over her shoulder and asked, "How are you holding up tonight?"

Warmth flooded her breast as she turned to him and said, "Better than last Friday. I'm up to carrying six beers at a time and hardly spilling a drop." She neglected to mention that when she did have an accident, it was usually a real lollapalooza.

"You keep that up and soon you'll be known as Emancipation's Queen of the Hostesses."

Lucy imagined her father learning that his daughter was thought of as a saloon queen. "If you don't mind," she said, cringing, "I'd just as soon be known as a hard worker."

Pearl shoved a tray of beers toward Lucy then, slopping some of it onto her hands. She doubted that it was an accident, especially since Sebastian was standing so close to her, but chose to ignore the incident. This wasn't the first time Pearl had made her displeasure known when Lucy and Sebastian were deep in conversation, and it probably wouldn't be the last.

Smiling gamely, Lucy picked up the tray and said, "If I'm going to be the queen of the hard workers, I guess I'd better get back on the job."

Sebastian tipped his hat to her, and Lucy headed to table four. After depositing her load, this time without mishap, and taking orders from table five, Lucy and her tray full of empty mugs headed back toward the bar. Before she reached her destination, a familiar voice called out to her.

"Lucille?"

She turned to him, surprised to see Charlie, a teetotaler, gracing the Pearly Gates. It occurred to her that she hadn't seen him since the day she bought Hazel a Hot Cross Bun. Part of it was by design, but how could she have forgotten him so easily?

Charlie's ground-eating gait quickly caught him up to her. "What do you think you're doing?"

Lucy glanced at the tray and then forced a friendly smile. "Hi, Charlie. I'm serving drinks. What are you doing? Thinking about joining a game of faro?"

"Heavens no." He puckered up his mouth. "I came by because some of my customers have been talking about the new hostess here and, I might add, in less than gentlemanly terms. They referred to her as Lucy, the girl with the velvet eyes. I just had to see for myself if it was you."

"Is that right?"

Lucy had endured plenty of stares since she started working at the Pearly Gates, a good many of them from men who gawked at her as if she were a monkey on a leash. None of them, thanks in large to Sebastian and his insistence that his customers behave as gentlemen, had ever been overly friendly or vulgar. To think that some of them thought of her as "the girl with the velvet eyes" touched her deeply.

Meaning it, Lucy said to Charlie, "Thank you for telling me."

"Thank you? Is that all you've got to say for yourself?"

A pair of veins popped out on Charlie's forehead, forming a V. For some reason, this amused Lucy. "I guess there is one more thing I could say: I've got to get back to work. Can I get you a beer?"

In addition to the V, now Charlie's cheeks were mottled with color and puffing in and out like a bellows. "I'd like to speak to you in private."

"I'm working now. I'll try to find time to stop by the bakery tomorrow."

"No. We must talk now," he said, taking her by the elbow.

It suddenly seemed more sensible to get this over with than to make a scene during Sebastian's tournament. "As you wish. Just give me a minute."

When Charlie released her, Lucy burrowed between the men crowded around the bar, shouting to Pearl that she needed six more beers, and that she'd be right back. When she popped back out through the men, Charlie immediately took hold of her hand. After dragging her past the storeroom and out the back door, he led her into the alley.

"How come you weren't on the train home today?" he demanded, throwing her hand from his as if it were a wet rag.

She bristled. "Not that it's any of your business, but I'm still trying to earn enough money for train fare home, as well as room and board. It might be some time before I can afford to leave town, if I decide to leave at all."

"You could have asked me for the train fare. That's the least I can do."

Chin up, Lucy said, "I'm sure your new fiancée would frown on you spending so much as a cent on me. Besides, I'm no longer a concern of yours."

"You came here because of me, even though I tried to prevent it, and that makes you my responsibility. I'll see that you're on that train next week."

"I am my own responsibility, nobody else's, and certainly not yours." She practically growled the words. "I'm not leaving Emancipation next Tuesday. Maybe never."

Charlie's lips flattened with disapproval, the upper one sharp enough to carve out a whipping stick. "How can you degrade yourself this way, dressing like a loose woman, mingling with gamblers and serving up the devil's brew? Your parents must be very proud of what you've become."

That remark struck a bull's eye, dead center of her heart. She'd been thinking the very same thing earlier, but to hear it from Charlie was more than Lucy could bear. Without giving any thought to her actions, she reached out and slapped him across his mottled cheek.

Even though she was appalled by her actions, she said, "You've got no right to talk to me like that."

"Right? You want to talk about rights?"

In a startling move, Charlie jerked her into his arms. Then his lips came down on her mouth, punishing her with a hard, searing kiss. Lucy pummeled his back with her fists and struggled against his hold, but it was no use. He was too strong for her, too angry. Just when Lucy thought she might pass out from Charlie's assault, she heard a voice, low, male, and menacing.

"I'm not one to shoot a man in the back," Sebastian said, "but now seems like a good time to find out how it feels."

Charlie released Lucy and jumped away as if indeed he'd been shot. Looking down at the Colt now pointed directly at his heart, he said, "There's no need for violence. This is a private matter between Lucille and me."

"Lucy is my employee and that makes it my business." Sebastian's gaze flickered to her. "Are you all right?"

Before she could open her mouth, Charlie said, "Of course she is. Lucille and I are, well, better than friends. It's complicated."

"It sure as hell is." Sebastian sheathed his gun. "Does Cherry know just how complicated this is for you?"

"That, sir, is definitely none of your business."

"Maybe not, but you're definitely getting into my business. As I already mentioned, Lucy works for me, and you're keeping her from performing her duties. I think it would be a good idea if you left now."

Charlie threw back his shoulders, dismissing Sebastian, and turned to Lucy. "It does seem like a good time to take my leave, but we need to discuss this further. May I see you tomorrow?"

Still stunned by Charlie's actions, by his bruising kiss and obsessive behavior, all Lucy could think was how much he wanted her, that he still loved her. Sebastian's plan had worked! But now what? Should she see him, or keep him dangling, thinking that she no longer wanted him?

"Lucille?" Charlie said. "Will you come by the bakery tomorrow?"

It suddenly occurred to her that the decision was not in her hands. "Oh, uh, no, I don't think I'll have time. I have to be at work the first thing in the morning."

Charlie shot Sebastian a scathing glance. "You work her both day and night?"

Sebastian smiled. "No. Maybe she just doesn't want to see you."

Charlie looked to Lucy for an explanation. Since she hadn't mentioned the second job to Sebastian, she avoided him as she said, "I took another position, setting type for *The Weekly Rustler*."

"You did?" Sebastian asked. "When did that start?"

"I haven't actually started yet, but it's only Wednesdays and Thursdays for a few hours. I'll be here on time tomorrow night."

Charlie stepped between Lucy and Sebastian. "Perhaps you can find the time for me between jobs tomorrow?"

"I'll try."

"That's all I can ask. I guess I'll be going now." He turned to Sebastian, as if waiting for confirmation.

"Don't let me stop you," he said, fondling the pearl handle of his gun.

Confirmation enough, Charlie left the alley and disappeared from view.

"I'm sorry for leaving my job the way I did," Lucy said. "Charlie seemed so upset, I thought it best to talk to him outside."

"You don't have anything to be sorry for." Sebastian pulled her close and took her chin between his thumb and forefinger. Turning her mouth up toward his, he observed, "Your bottom lip is bruised. The man's a pig."

He lowered his head, skimming the spot with his own lips, and then came fully to her mouth, kissing her softly, gently, like the beat of butterfly wings against her flesh. Her breath caught and her blood surged, and Lucy leaned into him, wanting something more.

Sebastian abruptly set her away from him. "Take another minute if you need to. I'll be right inside the door."

Lucy wasn't sure a minute would be enough to untangle the thoughts and sensations racing through her body, but she gave him a grateful nod and watched as he made his way back into the saloon. She could hardly make sense of all that had happened here. First Charlie, kissing her so passionately, so angrily, in a way he never had before, and then Sebastian, soothing her wounds even as he fired her blood. God help her, the man was irresistible, honey to the females who couldn't help but swarm to his mouthwatering hive.

Lucy didn't delude herself into thinking that she was anything more than Sebastian's pitiful project of the month. She'd seen firsthand that every woman he met fell under his spell. She was pretty sure that better women than she had gotten the key to his heart. Still, she would keep that kiss folded in her own heart like rose petals in a book of poetry, and try not to think about it too much. She had to concentrate on Charlie, the man who was going to be her husband whether he knew it or not.

Lucy still hadn't found the time to stop by the bakery by the following Friday, when *The Weekly Rustler* finally rolled off the press. She was too busy putting her column together and anxiously awaiting its debut. Obsessed with the idea of observing her efforts as they were printed by well-used Campbell County Press, she offered her assistance free of charge. Hazel was more than happy to oblige.

Now, as she spread the front page on the counter, Lucy beamed as she read the *Ask Penelope* column not once, but three times:

─────── *THE WEEKLY RUSTLER* ───────

Emancipation, Wyoming,	Vol. 1
Friday, June 5, 1896	No. 37

ASK PENELOPE! FREE ADVICE

Dear Penelope:
I have reason to suspect that my husband frequents bawdy houses and saloons, and has taken to drink. I'm told I can confirm this matter by removing a small amount of blood from his arm and setting a match to it. How big a flame will prove his guilt?
Signed, a Loving but Lonely Wife

Dear Loving and Lonely:
I must say that I am more concerned about the consequences of your actions than I am about your husband's tendency to visit saloons. Should you test your husband in this manner, the resulting flame or explosion might well injure either of you. Also, and assuming you plan to do this while your husband is sleeping, how will you ever explain the wound you have inflicted when he awakens? This is a very bad idea. I shudder to think of the method you have devised to test his fidelity.

Penelope

Chapter Six

Inside the Pearly Gates, Seb was helping Jack set up the usual Friday night poker tournament when he heard someone banging on the front door. This was no tentative knock, more like someone kicking the door; probably the beer delivery he was expecting.

Looking over his shoulder, he said, "Would you get the door, Little Joe? I think it's a delivery."

Back to arranging decks of cards, Seb recalled Lucy's timid knock when she'd first appeared on his doorstep, bedraggled and heartbroken. She'd come a long way since that day, not so much as a hostess, God help him, but as a young woman quite capable of standing on her own two feet. He laughed to himself as he thought about all the spilled drinks and accidents that seemed to follow in Lucy's wake. He might have fired anyone else, but the customers didn't seem to mind her tendencies toward disaster. Her dazzling smile, sparkling eyes, and kind words went a long way in making amends. Just last night she'd dumped a full ashtray on Morris Field's beaver felt hat. Nobody, but nobody, touched Field's hat at any time for any reason, but

Lucy plucked it off his bald pate, banged it against the back of his chair, and then plopped it back down on his head.

Flashing him that amazing smile, she'd apologized and playfully added, "I guess from now on I'll have to call you old ash head."

Seb, seated directly across from the crotchety old man, could hardly believe his own ears when Field cackled with delight and insisted that Lucy was welcome to use his hat as an ashtray whenever the mood struck. Seb figured that while Lucy and her accidents might cost him a little revenue, she more than made up for it in customer goodwill.

Women like Lucy didn't come along every day, he thought fondly. She was very special indeed. For some reason Seb's thoughts drifted to his mother, a woman who'd put her own needs above all others, including a six-year-old boy. A woman like Lucy would never walk out on her own son, leaving him in the care of a man who could barely care for himself while she ran off to find a better life for herself. A woman like Lucy was loyal to those she cared about, and to a fault, if her determination to win Charlie back was any indication.

Seb immediately thought of the way Charlie had assaulted her in the alley. Although he was a peaceful man, one who could usually defuse a volatile situation with a few well-chosen words, Seb had almost come to violence when he saw Lucy struggling against the man she loved. If she'd been injured, if he'd seen blood, Seb thought he might actually have shot the man without so much as a word or a warning. Oh, not in the heart or gut, but somewhere that would do some good, a spot that would be a constant reminder of the way a man ought to treat a lady.

Seb was lost in those dark thoughts, thinking that maybe he should have just shot the man and been done with it, when Black Jack brought him back to the present.

"Uh, Seb? Is something wrong?"

Black Jack was as tough as they came, a man who was as capable as Seb when it came to keeping the peace in an orderly fashion. Jack's past was a mystery, something he wouldn't talk about, and Seb didn't dare ask, but the bonds of friendship and trust between them were strong. Jack was sharp-featured and sharp-eyed, and Seb had never before seen fear in that intensely dark gaze. He saw it now. And Jack was watching Seb's hands.

He looked down and saw that his gun was on the table, though he didn't remember drawing it. He was also fondling the grip.

"Sorry, Jack," he said, sheathing the weapon. "I was thinking about the cheating drifter that came through here last Tuesday. Turning him over to the sheriff wasn't punishment enough."

"Sure," he drawled in a voice so deep, it sounded as if it rose up from a well. "Whatever you say."

The corner of Jack's mouth twitched, his idea of a smile, and then he went back to sorting cards. That was when Seb heard the sound of Lucy's laughter. He spotted her over by the newspaper rack, up to her pretty little neck in copies of the newest *Rustler,* and Seb realized that Little Joe had escorted her, not a delivery boy, into the saloon. He excused himself to Jack and went to join her at the cigar stand.

"Why are you delivering the papers?" he asked, watching as she and Little Joe finished unloading her burden. "Hazel usually sends Matt Gerdy over with them."

She turned to him, dusting herself off. "I was coming this way, so I told her I'd take them."

Plucking a newspaper from the top of the pile, Lucy handed it to Seb. "What do you think?"

He took the paper but didn't give it so much as a glance. "I've seen it before, and by the way, I'll never sell all of those in a week. You might as well take some of them back to Hazel, starting with this one."

When he tried to hand the paper to her, Lucy backed away. "Look at it first. Isn't it beautiful?"

What he thought was that Lucy was beautiful. She was dressed in her severe traveling suit and most of her hair, save for a few errant strands, was pulled back in a bun at the nape of her neck. Her fingers were stained with ink and looked as if she'd been digging through the remnants of a campfire seeking buried treasure. This wasn't a look he appreciated on her or any woman, and yet Lucy fairly glowed, her smile bright enough to light the room.

Giving in to her the way most of his customers did, Seb gave the paper a quick glance. "Hmmm," he said thoughtfully. "This does look different. Hazel really ought to get someone new to set type for her."

She frowned, but her eyes were still playful. "It's perfect, and you can't tell me that it's not."

Again without looking at the paper, Seb said, "Now that I think of it, I guess it is perfect, but there's still too many of them. I'll have Little Joe take about half of these back to Hazel tomorrow. In the meantime, don't you think you ought to get cleaned up for tonight? The train is due in at any time."

This time when Lucy frowned, the light went out of her eyes. "I was hoping you'd take a minute to actually read the paper. Hazel has done some different things with this issue, including introducing a new column."

Giving in to her yet again, Seb said, "I guess it wouldn't kill me."

Although he was a serious student of the newspaper business, up to and including his financial investment in the *Tribune*, Seb didn't give much credence to papers like the *Rustler*, or rags, as he preferred to think of them. For Lucy, he forced himself to study the headlines and then discovered something called the *Ask Penelope* column. Intrigued, he began reading in earnest.

It was all Lucy could do to keep from hopping up and down as Sebastian examined the newspaper. His expression was one of boredom as he began, but it wasn't long before one ebony eyebrow arched high and then his eyes popped open, showing the whites. He wasn't exactly laughing out loud as he read the front page, but now and then she could hear him chuckling under his breath.

When he finished, Sebastian looked at Lucy and said, "Is this for real?"

"You saw it for yourself," she said, hardly able to contain her excitement. "There it is in black and white."

His expression incredulous, he said, "Did Hazel write this namby-pamby schoolgirl trash?"

All the air went out of Lucy's lungs and she clutched her breast, mainly to keep her heart from dropping into the pit of her stomach. "No, of course not," she managed to eke out.

"Who, then? Surely not you."

Heat flared in Lucy's cheeks and she had to look away as she said, "Penelope wrote it."

"Who the devil is Penelope?"

"I don't know exactly." Lucy hated the lie, hated Sebastian even more for his opinion of her work, and so continued with the fabricated story. "Penelope is one of those fancy wire service writers from back East. Chicago, I think."

Sebastian made a sound, a cross between a grunt and a groan. "She should have stayed back East instead of visiting her silly opinions on Emancipation. I hope this question wasn't sent to her by someone in town."

"I wouldn't know." No longer willing or even able to discuss her work with Sebastian, Lucy snatched the paper out of his hand and placed it on the rack. Then she said, "I'll just run back to the hotel now and get ready for tonight."

As she turned to walk away, Sebastian took hold of her elbow. "Hold on a minute," he said softly. "Don't take my comments about the newspaper so personally."

She raised her chin but didn't quite meet his gaze. "What makes you think I do?"

"Oh, I don't know. Maybe because you look like you'd be happy to take a whiskey bottle to the back of my head."

She managed a little chuckle but still refused to look at him.

"Come on," he wheedled. "I'm not blaming you for Hazel's drivel, or whoever she hired to write it. The type looks really nice. You did a good job."

"Thanks," she said bluntly, peeling his fingers off her arm. "I'll be back in an hour."

Lucy was madder than a rained-on rooster as she marched out of the saloon and over to the hotel, and not a whole lot calmer by the time she reached her room. It wasn't until after she'd scrubbed the ink from her hands—and without benefit of Hazel's turpentine, no less—that she began to seriously consider what Sebastian had to say about her new column. Maybe, she thought grudgingly, he had a point. What did she know about the newspaper business? Only that she enjoyed reading them and that she loved writing her column.

She'd been so enamored of her own work, it hadn't occurred to Lucy that everyone might not feel the same way. What if the townsfolk reacted the way Sebastian did? What if they *hated* her column? She shuddered at the thought, and then consoled herself with the fact that Hazel had insisted the column be written under a fictitious name. At least no one would be pointing a finger at Lucy.

With far less enthusiasm than she'd had when the day first started, Lucy dressed in her usual saloon hostess outfit and left her room and went downstairs. She was surprised to see Charlie sitting in the hotel lobby.

"Lucille," he said, climbing to his feet. He removed his derby and clutched it in his hands. "The desk clerk told me that you were in a hurry when you went to your room, so I thought it best to wait down here rather than send someone for you."

"That was very thoughtful of you." He had a rather forlorn look in his eyes, a pinch of sadness. Thinking of her family back home, Lucy's heart skipped a beat. "Is something wrong?"

"Oh, goodness, no. It's just that you said you'd stop by the bakery and you never did. I was worried about you."

Oh, Lord, she'd forgotten about him again. "I'm truly sorry I didn't make it by, but I've been very, very busy the last few days. I simply haven't had the time."

Charlie approached her, moving in close, looking her over. "You're worn out, Lucille. I don't think you should be hostessing at that saloon. Mr. Cole works you too hard and, well, working there isn't seemly."

She was tired, he had that part right, and grumpy enough to take umbrage at his remarks.

"Don't start on me, Charlie," she warned. "If you keep that up, I swear I might just double up my fist and plant it right between your eyes."

He knew that she would do it, too. Many times Charlie had felt Lucy's knuckles smashing against different parts of his body, and just as many times he'd turn tail and run. Of course, that was when they were younger, before she'd looked at him through a woman's eyes, not a child's.

Obviously remembering her strength, Charlie stepped away from Lucy as he said, "Very well, have it your way. Is there anything else I can do to help you? I'm still willing to give you train fare back home."

"And I'm still not willing to take your money or go back home." She turned and headed for the door. "I can't be late to work today. There's a poker tournament."

Charlie quickly caught up to her. "Do you mind if I escort you? There are some things we need to talk about."

"Suit yourself," she said, keeping her pace at a brisk clip.

"Are you still angry with me?" he said, an idiotic question if ever there was one.

Lucy came to an abrupt halt and turned to look Charlie in the eye. "What do you think?"

"I think . . . angry," he replied, his shoulders drooping. "I never meant for any of this to happen, and I sure never wanted to hurt you, Lucille."

"Well, you did, Charlie. And bad."

He thought to reach out to her, but Lucy flinched and he dropped his hand. "Maybe I didn't do everything right," he admitted quietly. "I'm not sure if what I'm doing now is right either, but I can't let things go on like this."

Part of Lucy wanted to punish him, make him hurt the way she did, but a bigger part—her heart, she supposed—urged her to take a look at things from his point of view. Maybe she shouldn't have let Charlie come here without her in the first place. If she'd married him before he was set up and ready to take a wife, none of this would have happened. She never should have let him out of her sight.

Still, she had some questions. "How could you have forgotten me so quickly and taken up with Cherry?"

Chin down, head low, he muttered, "I don't know how it happened, Lucille. Cherry was there, helping me put the shop together, and I don't know. I was lonely and one thing led to another."

She didn't dare ask what *other* things meant. The concerns of her heart fading rapidly, she asked, "What about the life we had planned, the years we spent planning it?"

"I—I don't know what to say. I'm confused right now, not sure about much of anything anymore."

"Including Cherry?"

He averted his gaze. "I've made a promise to her. I can't just up and—"

"What?" Lucy cut in. "Break her heart the way you broke mine?"

Done with this conversation, if not him, she started across the street. Charlie followed close behind, guiding her between wagons and men on horseback. When they reached the doors of the Pearly Gates, once again he took her by the elbow.

"I didn't get a chance to say everything I wanted to."

"I think I've heard all I want to for one day, and now I really have to get to work."

"All right, but first I'd like to invite you on a picnic tomorrow afternoon. That way we can talk in private and I won't have to worry about you running off somewhere."

Lucy wondered what Cherry would say about those arrangements. With a smile she couldn't hide, she said, "All right, Charlie. Come by the hotel around noon."

As before, poker tournament night at the Pearly Gates was pandemonium. All the tables were filled with gamblers hoping to strike it rich. Those waiting to fill the losers' seats huddled around the bar the way cattle bunch just before a storm.

Lucy was so busy serving drinks, she barely had time to think or to eat more than a bite of the ham sandwich that was supplied for the help. As for Sebastian, she couldn't even look at him without thinking that he considered her work trash. Because she had a hard time hiding her feelings—many times in the past Lucy had been told that she wore her heart on her sleeve—she avoided Sebastian as much as possible.

She was still deep in thought, alternately thinking about the new column she had to write and fretting about Sebastian's opinion of the last, when she arrived at table four with a tray filled with beers. Distracted as she lifted a mug from the tray and lowered it to the gambler to her right, the handle somehow slipped out of her fingers and the mug hit the table.

The gambler, whose cards and money were drowned in beer, leapt out of his chair. "What the *hell* is the matter with you?"

Trying to balance the tray and its remaining burden, Lucy flashed her best smile and said, "I'm terribly sorry, sir. I'll just get you another, on the house."

The gambler, a stranger who seemed to be immune to Lucy's charms, reached over and upended the tray, dumping the entire contents on her bosom and skirt.

Black Jack, who was dealing at the table, got to his feet—but that was as far as he got. Before he could take a step toward the stranger, the front door banged open and three men armed with shotguns and pistols stepped inside. They wore their hats down low, and handkerchiefs covered the lower halves of their faces.

"Everyone sit," ordered the middle outlaw. "If you don't have a chair, sit on the floor, and all of you put your hands on your heads. Anyone fool enough to do anything different is gonna git their heads blown off. Do it now."

As he spoke, the other two fanned out on opposite sides of the room. "You," the middle outlaw said, pointing his shotgun at Pearl, who was kind of squatting behind the bar. "Load up the money in that cash register."

The outlaw nearest the bar tossed her a burlap bag.

Then the middle outlaw turned his attention to Lucy. "You," he said, again brandishing his weapon. "Start with these tables here and put all the money in the bag."

As he said it, the other man tossed a sack onto table four.

Lucy just stood there at first, frightened, dripping, and illogically thinking that she really ought to be cleaning up the mess at her feet.

The outlaw advanced on her. "I don't mind shooting a woman. Get a move on or I will."

Mindless now of the broken glass and mugs beneath her feet, Lucy snatched up the bag and began stuffing bills into it.

At the other end of the room, the third outlaw enlisted the aid of a trembling, bespectacled gambler, who began filling a sack from the tables at the back of the room.

Her legs trembling more with fear than exhaustion, Lucy

went from table to table, ending with the one where Sebastian sat with his hands on his head. Their eyes met, and he gave her a slight nod.

"Git on over here, woman," the middle outlaw demanded.

By then the outlaw holding the sack Pearl had filled had joined him. Knees knocking, Lucy threaded her way through the tables and met up with them just as the third outlaw arrived.

The middle outlaw passed his shotgun to the third and then he startled Lucy by grabbing her around the neck and hauling her up close to his body.

"Anybody even thinks about following us and this little lady here gets a bullet in her brain." To prove his point, he drove the barrel of his pistol against her temple.

Sebastian shot out of his chair. "Leave the girl here. You can take me instead."

The outlaw laughed, a sound that rang in Lucy's ears.

"I don't need any more problems than I already got. Take your seat or you're gonna be the first to lose his head."

When Sebastian didn't immediately comply, the second outlaw drew a bead on him and cocked his pistol.

"Sit down, Sebastian," Lucy cried. "He's going to shoot you."

Again the outlaw laughed, a cruel sound. "Listen to the lady. She knows what she's talking about."

With obvious reluctance, Sebastian slowly sank back down on his chair.

The outlaw firmed his grip on Lucy, sliding his arm around until her throat was caught in the crook of his elbow.

"Remember," he warned, backing up, "no one follows us or this little gal is as good as dead."

Then, half-strangling her with his fierce grip, the outlaw dragged Lucy out of the saloon and into the night.

Chapter Seven

When the last outlaw had left the saloon and the thunder of galloping hooves met his ears, Seb leapt out of his chair.

"Jack," he shouted. "Run get the sheriff, and then get a posse together."

He turned toward the bar. "Pearl, you handle things here. I'm going after Lucy."

As he started for the door, Merry called after him, "Take my horse. She's faster than anything those outlaws are bound to have."

It wasn't difficult to pick Merry's horse out of the animals tied to the rail. She and Cherry raised and sold Arabian horses, some of the finest examples of horseflesh Seb had ever seen. After he mounted the sleek animal and applied a single heel to her belly, the mare took off at a dead run, quick and smooth.

Inside the jailhouse, Sheriff B. J. Binstock listened raptly as Black Jack explained what had happened at the saloon. Short and squat, B. J. was built like a pickle barrel, knew it, and didn't much give a damn. She wore a man's shirt and trousers, the legs chopped short to accommodate her bowed legs, and a gunbelt wrapped around her considerable girth that contained a Colt .45. Her weapon of choice was a Remington 10-gauge shotgun with double barrels. Getting on in years, B. J.'s eyes weren't what they used to be. She never missed with the shotgun, though she rarely fired it. The citizens of Emancipation thought of her more as the town's mother than anything else, and B. J.'s brand of policing ran more toward a mother scolding a child. Until now.

As Black Jack finished his tale, she banged her fist against her desk. "And you just let Seb ride off after them?"

Black Jack's grim expression held the slightest hint of amusement. "Let him?"

"All right," B. J. conceded. "I guess you couldn't 'a stopped him. I just hope the dang fool doesn't do something 'to get her or hisself killed."

"He won't. What about that posse?"

As she considered all this, B. J. stuck a finger under her wide-brimmed hat and scratched her gray head. For the first time since she'd taken office some three years before, she wasn't sure how to proceed. Never in that time had there been a crime such as this. Emancipation simply wasn't a robbing kind of town.

"Gonna be hard tracking outlaws in the dark," she said. "Maybe we ought to wait until morning."

"If we wait until morning, we'll never catch up to them. We have to go now. Don't forget, Seb and Lucy are out there, too."

"I know, dang it all."

"Then what are we waiting for?"

The decision made, B. J. jerked open her desk drawer and withdrew a tin star. "My deputy's laid up with a broken leg, so I got to stay here. Pin this on and you'll be my official deputy. Round up as many men as you can and get to it."

With a short nod, Jack pinned the badge to his jacket and then went back to the saloon. It took less than a minute to round up more volunteers than there were horses. Many of the gamblers had come to the Pearly Gates halfway expecting to lose their stakes. None of them were happy to have their bankrolls taken without so much as a play on the dollar.

The outlaws had thrown Lucy up behind their leader's saddle, and then the group had taken off at a dead run, heading north. She'd always had a fear of heights, including the relatively short distance from the rump of a horse to the hard ground. Fears aside, she could not bring herself to wrap her arms around the loathsome bandit, and instead clung to the back of the saddle.

Lucy rode like this, bouncing to and fro with knees clamped to the horse's haunches and fingernails digging into leather, until the lights of Emancipation faded into the darkness. She was wondering how long her strength would hold when the horse jumped over something in the road, knocking her sideways. Intent only on saving herself, she threw her arms around the outlaw's head.

He screamed as her fingers dug into his eyes, and instinctively pulled up the reins.

The horse reared and then toppled over sideways, flinging Lucy in one direction and the outlaw in the other.

She landed on her backside with one leg twisted beneath her. She sat there a minute, trying to get her bearings, wondering if she'd been injured, and then suddenly remembered the outlaw. Peering around, she saw his vague outline in the darkness. He was crumpled in a heap at the base of a tree. His horse stood at the side of the road.

Seeing the chance to flee, mindless of the pain in her ankle when she got to her feet, Lucy hobbled over to the outlaw and saw that he was breathing but out cold. Moving quickly and after several awkward attempts to mount the man's horse, she finally managed to throw herself onto the saddle. The outlaw didn't move.

Turning the horse back toward town, Lucy urged the winded animal into a trot that banged against her already bruised bottom. She hadn't gotten but a few feet up the road when she heard the sounds of horses heading in her direction. Remembering the other two outlaws and the fact that they'd been behind their leader, she quickly steered her mount off the road and disappeared into a thick stand of trees and shrubs.

A quarter moon hung low in the sky, dangling there like a silvery scythe. It didn't give much light, making tracking difficult, if not impossible. Seb figured he'd ridden two or three miles straight north of town when he spotted an object in the road ahead. Slowing the sleek Arab, one hand gripping the butt of his pistol, Seb peered into the shadows and the shape gradually came into view. A big clump looking a lot like a sleeping man was butted up against a large oak tree.

Seb quickly dismounted, gun drawn, and headed for the clump.

Approaching cautiously, he made little noise as he crept up on the man. When he reached him, he cocked his gun and kicked the man in the ribs. The outlaw groaned but made no attempt to protect himself. Bending over him, Seb saw that this was the man who had dragged Lucy out of the saloon. Moving quickly, Seb took a coil of rope off his saddle and wrapped it around the man's torso and arms mummy style. Then he propped him against the tree.

"Where's Lucy?" he demanded, slapping the man's face.

The outlaw shook his head and mumbled, "Dunno."

Sheathing his weapon, Seb looked around, listening intently. Where could she have gone? Had the other outlaws taken her with them? Straining his eyes, he looked ahead to the north. As far as he could tell, there were no telltale clouds of dust rising up to the sky. Had they left the road? Turning to the west, concentrating on the slightest sound,

Seb thought he heard a rustling in the shrubs up ahead. Deciding to have a closer look, he led his horse to the side of the road and tied it to a scrub oak. Then, gun drawn again, Seb slipped into the trees.

A mile or so behind Seb, Black Jack and his posse used lanterns to track the outlaws. The going was slow, but it paid off as the group came to a fork in the road that led to the Day ranch.

Jack and two other volunteers with lanterns climbed down off their horses and examined the fresh tracks. Then Jack said, "Looks like they split up three ways, one to the east, one to the west, and the other continuing straight north."

"That's how I read it, too," one of the men said.

Jack turned to him. "Pick four men and follow the tracks to the east."

That done, he turned to the other volunteer. Jack was trying to decide which trail to take for himself, wondering which of them would lead to Lucy and Seb, when he heard the distinct retort of a shotgun blast.

Fairly certain the sound had come from the north, and that Seb was probably in trouble, he said to the volunteer, "Take four men and follow the tracks to the west."

To the others, Jack said, "We're going north. Follow me."

Then he mounted up and took off in that direction, hoping that he wouldn't be too late.

Seb hadn't gotten very far into the trees before a shotgun blast fired pellets over his head, a few of them finding a home along his hairline. He instantly hit the ground and lay there as a few more pellets rained down on him, bouncing harmlessly off his back. Hands shaking, knees curiously liquid, Seb raised his chin and listened. He was rewarded an instant later by the sound of a shell being racked into the shotgun's chamber.

Then another, more surprising sound.

"Don't come any closer," a woman's voice warned. "I know how to use this thing and I will."

"Lucy?" Seb said, daring to raise his head. "Is that you?"

Again her voice drifted out of the darkness, this time softer, more like Lucy. "Sebastian? Is that you?"

"Yes, and for God's sake, don't shoot again. I'm coming for you."

"Sebastian. Oh, praise the Lord."

Following the sound of her voice, it didn't take Seb but a minute to find Lucy leaning against a large oak tree, the outlaw's shotgun propped up beside her. A horse stood off to the side. When Seb came into view, Lucy hobbled toward him.

"You're hurt," he said, taking her into his arms.

"My ankle's sprained and I feel kind of beat up, but that's about it."

Holding her upright, taking as much of her weight as she'd allow, Seb asked, "What happened?"

Lucy looked up at him, her expression sheepish and her eyes rolling. "It was an accident," she explained softly. "I never was much good at riding horses, and when I thought I was going to fall off the outlaw's horse, I grabbed his head. I think I might have gouged his eyes some, but I didn't mean to, and then the horse went down after that, flinging us in two different directions. I landed on my backside with my leg under me. He's up the road, out cold. I thought you were him."

Seb held her away from him, doing his best to examine her in the darkness, and then realized that the front of her blouse was damp. "Are you bleeding?"

Lucy followed his gaze and rolled her eyes again. "No. That's beer. Just before the outlaws came into the saloon, I had a little accident and dumped a beer. I guess you didn't see it happen."

Seb threw back his head and roared, a sound that was as

much laughter as it was a howl. All the tension drained out of him, the fear he'd had for her life, and left him feeling relieved and curiously exhausted.

"Oh, Lucy, Lucy, Lucy," he said, taking her face between his hands. "What am I going to do with you?"

And suddenly Seb knew exactly what he was going to do. Not waiting for an answer or expecting one, he lowered his head and tenderly kissed Lucy's forehead.

It wasn't enough. Filled with the urge to claim her, to wipe the memory of the outlaw and all other men from her mind, Seb boldly took her mouth with his, kissing her greedily and with a pent-up need he'd refused to acknowledge before now.

Startled by Sebastian's kiss and the fierce passion behind it, Lucy hung lifelessly in his arms, a rag doll. When at last he took his mouth away, he remained close, looking into her eyes, seeking something she couldn't fathom. She held that gaze as long as she could, and then her eyes drifted down to Sebastian's lips.

She surprised herself by saying, "Again."

This time when Sebastian's mouth claimed hers, Lucy threw her arms around his shoulders and met him head on. Never had she been kissed like this, so deeply, so fully and passionately, and never had she responded so wantonly. When Sebastian had thrust his tongue into her mouth before, she'd allowed the invasion, fascinated as he probed, tasted, and caressed her. Now Lucy invited him in, and it was she who did the probing, the tasting, she who explored his mouth and felt the flames of desire licking at her belly and below. She never wanted it to end, and yet Sebastian abruptly set her away from him.

Lucy thought to object, to beg him for more if she must, and then she heard the thunder of horses bearing down on them.

Head cocked toward the sound, Sebastian said, "That

should be the posse. You wait here until I know for sure."

Seb crept to the edge of the road, watching as the group of riders came toward him and then slowed at the spot where he'd left Merry's horse. When he recognized Black Jack in the lead, Seb stepped out in the open.

"About time you guys arrived," he said.

Jack rode up to where he stood and asked, "What have you got?"

"Lucy and one of the outlaws." He pointed to the figure trussed up against the tree.

After a glance in that direction, Jack asked, "Is Lucy all right?"

"Banged up a little, but she'll be fine."

Jack gave a short nod. "What happened to you?"

Seb couldn't imagine what he was talking about. Puzzled, he cocked his head.

Jack held the lantern high, illuminating Seb's face. "You're bleeding."

Remembering the shotgun blast, Seb reached up and wiped away the smears of blood on his forehead, wincing as he felt the pellets beneath his skin. "Lucy shot me. Seems she's a lot better handling a shotgun than a tray of beer."

"A beautiful woman with a gun," Jack murmured with an appreciative nod. "Must have been some marvelous sight."

"She'd have looked a hell of a lot better if she hadn't fired the damn thing."

Jack made a small sound in his throat, as close as he ever got to a laugh, and said, "We found tracks heading east and west back a ways, so I guess that's where I'll be heading." Again he looked beyond Seb to the tree. "Going to take him in with you?"

Seb grumbled, but said, "I guess so."

Without another word between them, Jack climbed off his mount and went to help Seb fling the outlaw over the saddle of Merry's horse. Then he mounted again, signaled the others, and they took off.

This time when Seb approached Lucy, he announced himself. "It's me. Don't shoot."

"I won't," she called back.

Seb found her propped against the tree, the outlaw's horse standing beside her. After mounting the animal, Seb tugged Lucy up behind him and headed for the road. Then he took up the reins of Merry's horse and began the long, slow ride back to town.

The minute they got back to Emancipation, Seb pushed the outlaw off the saddle and led him into the jail, leaving B. J. to her business. Then, against her objections, he carried Lucy to her room.

After setting her on her feet and finding that she was still a little wobbly, he asked, "Is there anything I can do to help you?"

She shook her head. "You've been more than enough help. I just want to collapse now."

"If you're sure . . ."

With a short nod, Lucy glanced up at him and smiled. Her serene expression quickly evolved to one of concern. "Your head is bleeding. What happened to you?"

Seb had forgotten about the shotgun blast. Sparing her the details of yet another of her *accidents,* he shrugged and said, "My horse ran me under a tree. It's just a couple of scratches."

She reached up, brushing a lock of his hair out of the way. "I should clean that up for you."

Seb backed away before she had a chance to feel the pellets beneath his skin. "No time for that now. I have to take care of the horses and then get back to the saloon and tend to business. I'll come back later to see how you're doing."

"All right, but before you go, I want you to know that

I'm sorry for all the trouble I've put you through tonight."

Anger flared in him. "Will you stop apologizing all the time? You've done nothing to apologize for, especially tonight."

With that, he stalked out of the room and closed the door behind him.

Lucy didn't spend a lot of time wondering or worrying about what she'd done to cause such a reaction in Sebastian. She was too tired. The first thing she did was draw some water in the tub to wash the beer and dirt out of her clothes, and then she brushed out her hair, cleaned herself up, and donned her plain Mother Hubbard gown. After that, she set about wrapping her injured ankle to keep the swelling down.

Lucy had just pulled back the covers and was preparing to sink into her soft feather bed when she heard someone knocking on her door, the one that adjoined Sebastian's room. She hobbled over to the door, turned the key in the lock, and saw him standing there.

"How are you doing?" he asked. "Are you all right?"

"Yes, much better, thank you. I was just about to turn in."

A small candle flickered on the bedside table behind Lucy, giving off a soft glow and illuminating her vague outline through the thin cotton nightgown. Seb imagined how soft she would feel beneath the gown, already knew that her hair smelled of soap and lavender water, and could still taste the sweetness of her lips. He wanted to taste them again, make her writhe in his arms and more. It was sheer madness, he thought, thinking, too, that he'd taken advantage of her enough for one night.

His voice gruffer than he'd intended, Seb said, "I just want you to know that I'm going to leave my door open tonight. If you should need me for any reason, don't hesitate to give me a holler."

"Thanks, Sebastian. I appreciate your concern."

She looked nervous, plucking at the ribbons on the bodice of her gown, and sounded nervous, too, her voice as tight as a bowstring. She probably thought he was going to kiss her the way he had on the trail, maybe even drag her into his room and have his way with her. The thought wasn't the least bit unpleasant to Seb, but he had an idea that Lucy would see things in a different light.

He sucked in a breath. "I'll just say good night, then."

"Good night."

"Remember to lock your door," he said, not sure he trusted himself. "I'll wait right here to see that you do."

She gave him a shy smile, closed the door, and turned the key in the lock.

"That's good," he whispered, leaning against the door. "Are you off to bed now?"

"Almost."

If the clear sound of her voice was any indication, Lucy was leaning against her side of the door, probably propping up her bad leg. He could almost feel the heat of her on the other side, a beckoning as old as mankind. As Seb spoke, he began to caress the slick painted wood, wishing he were caressing Lucy.

"What does that mean, almost?"

"I never got a chance to thank you for coming after me the way you did. That was very brave of you."

"No," he whispered, his fingers stroking wood. "You're the brave one. I don't know many women who could have saved themselves the way you did."

Lucy couldn't help but laugh. "That wasn't bravery. That was an accident."

She had her face pressed against the door, her ear near the crack. She could almost feel the heat of Sebastian's breath as he whispered to her, warming her cheeks and so much more. She wanted him to kiss her the way he had on the trail, to take her into his arms and render her senseless again. All she had to do was open the door. Just open it and give herself up to him. She stood there waffling, wanting something she couldn't have, wondering how she could be attracted to this man so much when she still loved another. Then she heard, footsteps, followed closely by the closing of another, more distant door. Sebastian was gone.

Late the next morning, after a very restless night, Lucy awakened to the sound of someone knocking on her door. Thinking of Sebastian, as she had all night long, she climbed out of bed and unlocked the door leading to his room. When she opened it, there was no sign of Sebastian. His room appeared to be empty. Again came a rap at her door.

Hurrying over to the source, her outer door, she said, "Who is it?"

"Bellboy, ma'am. A Mr. White is downstairs calling for you."

The picnic. Lord, was it that late already? "Tell him I'll be down in fifteen minutes."

Heading back to the door leading to Sebastian's room, Lucy meant to close and lock it, but something—curiosity, she supposed—beckoned her to take a peek inside.

Calling Sebastian's name as she crept into the room, Lucy saw that it was at least twice as big, if not bigger, than her own accommodations, and just as lavishly appointed. The bed was huge, more than double the size of hers, and she was drawn to the tangle of blankets and sheets there.

Apparently Sebastian hadn't slept any better than she had. Wondering if his was also a feather bed, convincing herself it would be all right to find out, Lucy limped over and sat down on the mattress. It sank deliciously beneath her weight. The next thing she knew, she was reclining against Sebastian's pillow, breathing in his musky scent, an aroma tinged with the tang of spices. What would it have been like if she'd opened her door last night? Would she and Sebastian be lying here now, snuggling and kissing?

Lucy was still there, thinking of Sebastian and wallowing in his bed, when the door opened and he stepped into the room.

"Oh, my stars." She sat bolt upright and then scrambled off the bed. "Oh, my stars."

"What were you doing?" he asked, the corner of his mouth twitching.

"I, ah, well, see, I thought I heard you knocking and then you weren't here, but the bellboy came to the other door, see, and then I went to shut the door, and, and . . ."

The more she talked, the bigger Sebastian's grin got, but Lucy couldn't seem to shut her mouth. "Then I saw your room, see, so big and beautiful, and well, see, your bed was here, too, and I wondered if it was the same, and I guess I just got curious, and it is like mine. I have to go now."

Laughing softly, Seb caught up with Lucy as she reached the connecting doors. Pinching the throat of her nightgown between his thumb and forefinger, he tugged her toward him, right up close to his face.

"You can crawl around in my bed any time you want to," he whispered darkly. "All you have to do is ask."

Lucy's eyes rolled to a close and her cheeks blossomed with pink splotches. Letting her off the hook, Seb released her gown and said, "How's the ankle today?"

"Much better, thank you."

"Do you know that Charlie White is sitting downstairs?"

"Yes. We're going on a picnic and I'm already late."

"A picnic?" He couldn't say why, but Seb didn't much like the idea. "You sure you ought to go off with him that way?"

"Of course, and now I really must get dressed." Still blushing, Lucy ducked into her room and quickly closed and locked her door.

Sebastian had come back to his room because he'd forgotten his hat. As he fit it onto his head, he glanced at his mussed bed, thinking of how tempting Lucy looked lying there, and then shook the thought from his mind and went on downstairs.

Though he hadn't exactly planned on confronting the man, he strode right up to where Charlie sat and said, "I understand you're taking Lucy on a picnic today."

Charlie, who was wearing a cheap seersucker suit and a red bow tie, adjusted his collar. "That's correct."

"Where are you going, and are you taking a chaperone along?"

His forehead creased with irritation, Charlie got out of his chair. "I fail to see what business that is of yours."

"Lucy is my employee, and as such, she is my concern." Seb felt that he might be crossing a line here, but he took the step anyway, adding, "Maybe I ought to go along with you."

"I hardly think so." Charlie puffed out his chest. "Lucy is perfectly safe with me and she knows it."

"Well, I don't," Seb said, enjoying the man's discomfort.

Charlie opened his mouth to reply, but then his gaze went somewhere over Seb's shoulder and his eyes lit up.

Turning in that direction, Seb watched as Lucy stepped into the lobby. For a woman who had spent a harrowing night on the trail, she looked incredibly lovely. She was wearing a light summer dress of printed lawn and yellow organdy, the bodice set off with a panel of white lace. Her hair was a glorious river of milk and honey running down the middle of her back, bound at the nape of her neck with a wide chocolate bow that matched her eyes. Seb's mouth watered even as something clenched in his gut.

As she approached the men, Lucy gave Seb a cursory nod and then greeted Charlie, the lucky dolt.

"Sorry I'm late," she said breezily. "I had a rather long night."

79

Holding out the crook of his arm for her to take, Charlie shot Seb a smug look as he said, "Shall we go, then?"

There was nothing for Seb to do but watch them stroll out of the hotel. After the buggy Charlie had hired rolled out of view, Seb finally headed for the saloon. If he'd owned a dog, he thought darkly, he might have kicked it.

Chapter Eight

Emancipation sat in a lush green bowl surrounded by rolling hills speckled with emerald-hued shrubs and lots of oak and pine trees. Charlie had chosen the banks of Devil's Lake for their picnic, which offered a tranquil view of the Black Hills to the east, along with the purple shadows cast by those dark pines.

As Lucy limped onto the blanket Charlie had spread on the grass, he said, "Is something wrong with your leg?"

"It's just a sprained ankle," she explained, making herself comfortable.

"Humph." Charlie sat down beside her. "I told you that Cole was working you too hard."

Lucy laughed. "It's not from working. The saloon got robbed last night, and one of the outlaws kidnapped me and flung me on his horse. A couple of miles out of town I fell off, and that's when my ankle got hurt."

"Oh, now, that really does it." Charlie's nostrils flared as he took hold of her hands. "I must insist that you quit working at that saloon. It's much too dangerous."

While she appreciated his concern for her safety, Lucy

wasn't interested in his advice. "For the last time," she said, looking him directly in the eye, "I enjoy working at the Pearly Gates and I'm not going to stop. Besides, I owe Sebastian Cole a lot. He's helped me tremendously."

Charlie pressed his lips together and frowned. "Maybe it's not the work you enjoy so much."

Lucy wondered, illogically, if Charlie somehow knew about the kisses she and Sebastian had shared. Feeling defensive, she snapped, "What's that supposed to mean?"

He looked at her with keen eyes as he said, "Just that I think Cole is taking more of an interest in you than is proper. I really don't think it's a good idea for you to be staying at the same hotel where he's let a room either. I ought to write your father and let him know what kind of life you've been leading since you left home."

Lucy almost came up off the blanket. "You wouldn't dare."

Charlie wouldn't look at her and the tips of his ears went red.

Her heart flopped in her chest. "You didn't, did you?"

"I'm concerned about you and I'm sure he will be, too."

Lucy knew she should have written to her family by now, and that they would be wondering how she was getting along. She hadn't been able to bring herself to tell them that she and Charlie weren't married yet, and since she couldn't lie to them, she'd put the idea of a letter out of her mind.

Lucy fired up her temper as she said, "What did you say in your letter?"

He shrugged, still avoiding her gaze. "Just that we had a parting of the ways, and that you refused my offer of train fare back home."

She groaned. "That's it? You didn't mention the Pearly Gates, did you?"

He looked off toward the Black Hills, avoiding the question.

Answer enough for Lucy, who said, "When you wrote

my father, did you happen to mention that you threw me over for a cotton-headed girl named Cherry?"

His face matching his glowing ears, Charlie busied himself by opening up the wicker basket he'd brought along. Then he quietly said, "We came here for a picnic, not to fight. Shall we eat now?"

Eyeing the bounty Charlie had brought, her stomach growling in response, Lucy allowed a truce—for the time being. She would be hearing from her father, and soon, no doubt. If all went according to plan, she would have Charlie back by then, and she could write and tell her family that all was well.

Focusing on the food, Lucy saw that Charlie had prepared a spread of chopped chicken mixed with mayonnaise, minced pickles, and herbs, and slathered it between two thick slices of fresh-baked bread. There were apples and carrot sticks to complement the sandwiches and a bottle of apple cider to wash it all down. Best of all, he'd made four small cakes, each a different flavor.

After she finished her sandwich and sampled the first dessert, prune cake iced with caramel frosting, Lucy moaned. "This is absolutely delicious, and more than enough after that big lunch. Why did you make the other cakes, too?"

"Oh," he said, tasting a bite of sponge cake filled with raspberry jam, "I'm just experimenting, trying to find the perfect cake for my, uh . . ." He hesitated, his voice faltering as he added, "Wedding."

"Right. Your wedding." The words stung her throat, spreading its poison all the way to her heart. Without thinking, she blurted out, "Maybe it would be more appropriate to forget the cake and make some cherry tarts instead."

"Lucille!" He turned to her, astonished. "You didn't used to talk like that."

"I didn't used to be a scorned woman."

Charlie hung his head and sighed heavily.

"Sorry," she said, not meaning it. "It's just that I'd forgotten about your upcoming wedding. Did you?"

"What do you mean?"

"Did you forget about your wedding or, more specifically, your bride? How come she didn't come along today?"

Charlie fiddled with his bow tie. "Cherry and her sister run a very successful horse business. They're out at the ranch today, talking with some big buyers."

"Doesn't your successful fiancée mind your being here with me? Or doesn't she know?"

"Well, uh . . ." He began plucking cake crumbs and bits of bread crust off the blanket. "I'm sure she wouldn't mind."

Seeing an opening, a way to test Charlie's love for his new fiancée, Lucy leaned in close to him and asked, "Do you think Cherry would mind if I kissed you?"

He reared back as if slapped. "Yes, I'm quite sure she would."

"Would you mind?"

Charlie's mouth dropped open, and then he canted his head, looking deeply into her eyes. "We've been friends—more than friends—for a very long time. I'm surprised after everything that's happened that you still want to kiss me."

Suppressing a grin, quite sure that he had no idea what was coming, Lucy wrapped her arms around his neck and pressed her lips against his. It started like any other kiss they'd ever shared, sweet, chaste, a token of affection. Then Lucy eased Charlie's lips apart with her tongue. He immediately stiffened his shoulders and bared his teeth.

Embarrassed by his less-than-eager reaction, Lucy thought to pull away and end it then before she made an even bigger fool of herself. In that moment of hesitation, Charlie opened his mouth and invited her in.

The next thing Lucy knew, he'd rolled her onto her back and then stretched out on top of her, kissing her in earnest. This was the kind of passion she'd hoped to arouse in him, the kind she'd been so careful not to elicit in the past, and yet instead of thrilling her, she became frightened of this Charlie who wasn't gentle.

With a mighty shove, Lucy pushed him away and said, "Charlie! What are you doing?"

He sat up, breathing heavily, and said, "I'm sorry, Lucille. I didn't expect you to be so . . . how did you learn to kiss like that?"

She certainly wasn't going to tell him, nor mention the fact that Sebastian's kisses had made her feel as if she were aflame, not frightened at all.

Lucy shrugged and said, "I don't know. I figured Cherry must be doing something for you that I never did. Is that the way she kisses you?"

"I can't and won't answer a question like that." Charlie looked at her with something akin to regret. "You're not the same girl I left in Kansas City."

"How can I be? The man I loved jilted me for another."

"I'm sorry." He hung his head, reminding Lucy of the boy she'd loved all these years. "I'm so confused. I don't know what to think or what to do."

Lucy's heart went out to him and she had to bite her tongue to keep from telling him how sorry she was to have upset his plans. She'd spent her entire life apologizing for one thing or another. Apologies were as natural to her as brushing her hair. She thought about Sebastian's angry words insisting that she stop apologizing for every little thing, and vowed that this was the end of it, at least where Charlie was concerned.

"I wish I could help you," she finally said, "but this is something you're going to have to figure out for yourself. You can't have both of us."

Later that afternoon, the posse returned with the other two outlaws. Black Jack left the tending of them to B. J. and headed straight for the Pearly Gates.

He found Seb behind the bar taking stock. Dropping two sacks of money on the counter, he said, "We caught up with them napping alongside the road."

Seb eyed the bags. "I'll estimate how much we would have had in the till, then take a head count of how many gamblers say they lost money, and divide the rest up evenly. I don't know how else to handle it."

"Sounds like a good plan."

Jack stretched and yawned.

"Why don't you get some rest?" Seb suggested. "I don't think we'll be doing big business tonight."

"Fine by me."

As Jack headed toward the stairs leading to his room, the door opened, and in came the stranger who had dumped the tray of beer on Lucy just before the outlaws burst through the door.

Marching directly toward him, Jack spoke in a voice so quiet the man had to lean in to hear him. "You're not welcome here. I suggest you find a new place to quench your thirst."

"You ain't got no right to keep me out."

The man never even saw Jack draw his pistol. The first he knew of it was when the barrel found a home between his ribs. "This gives me all the rights I need. You come here again, roughing up our hostess, and you and I won't be having this conversation." He pushed the pistol farther into the man's flesh. "This will do the talking for us."

Grumbling to himself, the stranger turned tail and went on his way.

Seb, who'd overheard part of the exchange, let Jack know he was standing behind him. "What was that all about?"

"A customer we don't need."

"What did he do?"

Jack looked him directly in the eye. "You don't want to know."

Seb and Jack had worked together for so long, what was

unsaid was generally as clear as the few words spoken. He ventured a guess. "Lucy, right?"

His expression as impassive as usual, Jack said, "That man is not a gentleman. It's taken care of."

Then he ambled up the stairs, leaving Seb to wonder if his fondness for Lucy was as obvious to everyone else.

A couple of hours later, Seb was surprised when Lucy stepped into the saloon dressed in her usual hostess getup. He met her near the door and said, "You don't have to work tonight. I'm sure your ankle isn't up to it."

"Actually, it's fine." She flashed a dazzling smile that set off sparkles in her dark eyes. "I want to work."

"Your call," he said, wondering why she was in such a good mood. Then he remembered. "How did the picnic go?"

"Beautifully." She lowered her voice and leaned in close. "You were right about everything, Sebastian. I don't know if Charlie's ready to come back to me yet, but one thing is clear—he still loves me."

With that, she gave him a peck on the cheek and then bounced off toward the bar.

Seb didn't know why he felt so disappointed. He'd hated seeing her brokenhearted, and he had given her the best advice he could on how to get Charlie back. Why was he so surprised and upset that it had worked?

Lucy wasn't a woman to trifle with, and yet, Seb had to admit, trifle with her he had. It was time to back off, to give Lucy room enough to follow her heart. He ought to be grateful that through his interference, Lucy hadn't transferred her affections from the baker to him. So why was it, Seb wondered as he ambled to the back of the room for a game of billiards, that he felt as if he had a boulder lodged somewhere between his throat and his heart?

The following Wednesday morning Lucy went to Charlie's Bakery to purchase a Hot Cross Bun for Hazel. The minute she walked through the door, Charlie ducked back into the kitchen and sent a surly Cherry out to work the counter. Although disappointed, Lucy supposed he was avoiding her because of what they'd shared at the lake. She knew that Charlie still loved her a little, and that he definitely wanted her. It stood to reason that he needed some time to sort through his feelings and, hopefully, figure out a way to get rid of his newest fiancée.

Buoyed by that thought, she flashed a big grin Cherry's way and said, "I'd like a Hot Cross Bun, please."

Scowling as she reached into the display case, Cherry said, "Charlie doesn't like you bothering him this way. Why don't you just leave him alone?"

"Are you sure Charlie doesn't want me around?" she said, flinging a coin on the counter and snatching up the bun. "Or haven't you asked him lately?" With that, Lucy winked and strolled out of the bakery.

As she worked her way to the newspaper office, Lucy considered a more confusing situation than the one with Charlie. Sebastian had been remote the past few days, talking to her in businesslike tones and treating her more like an employee than a friend. She missed his friendly banter, the little innuendos he sneaked in when no one could overhear. Then again, maybe she was expecting too much of him. She was, after all, merely an employee, and one who remained a bit of a liability.

With thoughts of both Charlie and Sebastian spinning around in her head, Lucy reported for work at the *Rustler*, and set the bun on the counter. Hazel, who didn't usually say hello before she gobbled up the treat, was so excited she didn't even notice the baked good was there.

"Can you believe it?" she cried. "We sold out of last week's paper by Sunday, and I'd printed up fifty extra copies of that edition. That's *never* happened before."

"Really? Do you think it has anything to do with Penelope's column?"

"Darn tootin'." She grabbed a pile of papers off her desk. "These are just the complaints."

"Complaints? That doesn't sound very encouraging."

Hazel roared with laughter. "Complaints are good, girl. That means they're reading the paper and it's getting them riled up."

Lucy thought back to Sebastian's opinion of her column. "Is it good if readers think Penelope's column is trash?"

Serious now, Hazel said, "Oh, honey, did someone call your work trash?"

She nodded. "Sebastian Cole."

Hazel laughed again. "Do yourself a favor and remember that this town is run by women. The Penelope column is for women, but believe me, just as many men will read it. In fact, why do you think I give you letters written mostly by men?"

"So they'll read the column?"

"Darn tootin'. They just won't tell anyone they do, and if they do admit it, they'll call it trash like Seb did. It's the nature of the beast. Don't worry about what he says . . . unless, of course, you're worried about him personally."

Lucy blushed, thinking about the way he'd kissed her. "That's not it," she said, a little fib. "He just made me feel like my column was no good."

"It's not good," Hazel said, quickly adding, "it's great. Did Seb say anything else about the paper?"

Lucy thought back to the conversation. "Yes, he also wanted to know if someone in town wrote that question to Penelope."

"What did you say?"

"I was so upset over what he said about the column, I couldn't talk about it anymore. I just told him that I didn't know."

"Good. That's the best way to handle it anyway. Whoever wrote the question will know it's theirs, and it's no concern of anyone else's." She finally noticed the bun. "For me?"

Lucy nodded, and Hazel dove into the sweet. As she stuffed the last of it into her mouth, Lucy, who really valued the woman's opinion, asked, "Does it seem right to you that a man can be engaged to one woman and still want to kiss the one he left behind?"

Licking her fingers, Hazel cocked one eyebrow and said, "Are you asking for yourself or for the column? That's a good question for Penelope."

"It's for me, and I can't use it in the Penelope column until I know the answer myself."

Hazel leaned her elbows on the counter. "You'll have to tell me a little more than that. Who is this fellow?"

Lucy went on to explain about Charlie and Cherry, the mixup with his letter, and the way he'd behaved at the lake. When she finished, Hazel's considerable jowls were sagging like feedbags.

"What a dirty rat," she grumbled. "If he treated you so mean, why do you keep bringing me buns from his bakery?"

"Because Sebastian told me the best way to get Charlie back is to pretend that I don't care about him anymore. I buy buns just so he can't forget me."

"Smart man, that Seb." Hazel rolled dreamy eyes. "He's something, isn't he?"

"He sure is," Lucy couldn't help but agree. Some little devil inside Lucy made her ask, "How come some clever woman hasn't snared Sebastian yet? Does he have a special lady friend?"

Hazel thought about it, but not for long. "Not that I know of. He's only been in town a few months, even though he's owned the Pearly Gates for a couple of years. He pretty much left Pearl in charge of it until he and Jack came here from Denver. That's all I know."

Hazel winked and poked a finger in Lucy's ribs. "He's a bit of a mystery, all right, but he isn't the man you were asking about. Let me think on Charlie some and I'll get back to you. In the meantime, I have a question for you."

"Oh?"

"Yes. What do you know about politics?"

Lucy shrugged. "Pretty much what I read in newspapers. Why?"

"We've got a presidential election coming up in November, and I want you to devote a Penelope column or two to that subject."

"Oh, I don't think I'm qualified to do something like that."

"You will be," Hazel assured her. "Study up on the Populist Party, because the *Rustler* and most suffragists back it. As far as I know, the *Tribune* is backing the Democrats and President Cleveland, so we might even stir up some debates."

Excited by the idea of being involved in the world around her, Lucy said, "How are we going to get political questions?"

"Don't worry, honey," Hazel said with a laugh. She reached beneath the counter and brought out an envelope. "I already have a couple of "Dear Editor" questions that might work better in your column. Why not look them over and see what you can do?"

Lucy stuffed the envelope in the pocket of her traveling suit and then said, "Thank you for trusting me with this, Hazel. I hope I don't let you down."

"I'm not worried. Now, let's have a look at what you've written for this week's column."

––––––––– *THE WEEKLY RUSTLER* –––––––––

Emancipation, Wyoming,   Vol.1
Friday, June 12, 1896   No.38

ASK PENELOPE! FREE ADVICE!

Dear Penelope:
What do you think of this immodest fad some of the ladies in town have taken up? I refer to the impure

desire to go bicycling. Do you not agree that no self-respecting woman would ever dream of climbing astride an indecent bicycle seat and parading herself down the street for the entire town to see? Please tell my wife to stop it.

Signed, A Disgusted Husband

Dear Disgusted:

Unless the women in question, including your wife, ride to excess, both day and night, I do not understand your concerns.

Bicycle riding is an enjoyable way to reap the benefits of exercise, namely a healthy and long life.

I wonder: is it possible that you fear your wife prefers bicycle riding to your company? Perhaps if you were to concern yourself more with pleasing your wife and spend less time worrying about her taking her pleasures elsewhere, your marriage would be more satisfactory for both of you.

Penelope

Chapter Nine

Due in part to last week's robbery, but mostly because Seb liked to mix things up a little, he decided not to have the usual poker tournament that Friday. Instead he hired a band, and then announced that he would be hosting a dance and a raffle. For the men, a dollar ticket would buy a chance at a horse and saddle, compliments of the outlaws, who wouldn't be needing them at the state prison. For the ladies, eight bits bought a chance on a heart-shaped locket of solid gold, complete with hand engraving. Best of all, and a bigger draw for the families in town, was the fact that Seb intended to donate the proceeds from the raffle to the new school building fund.

Preparing for the big night, he and Black Jack covered the billiard tables with planks of wood and crisp white sheets donated by the Palace Arms Hotel, turning them into buffet tables. Later in the evening, those tables would be filled with delicacies donated by restaurants, up to and including a variety of cupcakes offered by Charlie's Bakery.

Seb and Jack were arranging the poker tables along the outer walls, creating a dance floor in the center of the saloon, when Lucy came through the open door. She was carrying a huge stack of newspapers, fresh off the press. He waited until she'd arranged them on the rack before wandering over that way.

Eyeing the stack, Seb said, "That's an awful lot of papers to sell."

She turned her usual bright smile on him. "We sold that many last week. Why would I bring less today?"

"Last week was a fluke," he assured her, hoping he was right. "Folks were just curious about the new column."

"Judging from the mail Hazel got regarding that column, I'd say they're going to be even more curious today."

Again flashing that incredible smile, she flounced on over to the bar to have a word with Pearl.

"Since we're having a dance tonight," Lucy said, watching Sebastian out of the corner of her eye, "should I wear something different or my usual hostess outfit?"

Pearl, who was washing up the last of the glassware, shrugged without looking up from her work. "That's up to you, sugar. I don't know if you're gonna have much time for dancing, though. Seb expects a pretty big crowd. You might be serving folks out in the street before the night's over."

Lucy only half-listened to Pearl's reply since she'd already made up her mind to don the yellow lawn dress she'd worn at the picnic, a more festive gown that could easily be washed in the event of beer stains or other mishaps. Mostly she was concentrating on Sebastian, delighted to see that he'd sidled over to the rack and picked up a copy of the *Rustler*. Watching him as he read her column, Lucy's chest swelled with pride. He was chuckling under his breath and shaking his head, proving that once again Hazel was right. Whether they admitted it or not, men *did* love her column.

Leaving Pearl to her glasses, Lucy casually walked up to Sebastian and said, "Find something you like?"

He laughed. "This 'Ask Penelope' column is really something. Are you sure Hazel isn't making this stuff up?"

"Absolutely sure." As he folded the paper and placed it back on the rack, Lucy added, "Do you still think we won't sell all of these?"

"That remains to be seen."

He turned as if to walk away, but Lucy impulsively blocked his path. "Is something wrong?" she asked bluntly.

His attention finally on her, Sebastian said, "Wrong? How?"

Lucy hadn't meant to get into this conversation now, but it had been building in her over the past few days. It came out in a rush. "I can't help but feel that I've done something to make you mad. I've only spilled a couple of beers this week."

"No, Lucy, I'm not mad about that or anything else."

"Are you sure?" She didn't like the way he was looking at her, looking but not really seeing. "Was it the popcorn I dumped in that banker's lap? Maybe it was the popcorn itself. Pearl usually makes it, but she was so busy the other night I tried to do it myself, and I'm afraid I burned up most of the kernels."

Sebastian sighed heavily. "I'm a little distracted is all. I have a lot on my mind. Why don't you go to the hotel and get ready for tonight? I'd like you to come in a little early."

Then he walked off and left her standing there, more confused than she'd been before, and feeling as if she'd just lost her best friend.

Since this was Seb's first big social gathering since coming to Emancipation, he should have been in fine spirits. Instead he went around preparing for the festivities with a scowl on his face and a grumble in his gut. He'd hated sending Lucy off the way he had, hated the hurt in her eyes, hated even more that he knew how sweet her lips tasted and that he couldn't even look at her without wanting her. Even now, as he considered all this, his loins grew heavy and his mind wandered to things best left unthought.

He'd tried, he'd honest-to-God tried over the past few days to keep a safe distance from her, leaving her to pursue her heart's desire, Charlie White. It was a damn near impossible thing to ask of himself. All she had to do was brighten up his world with that fabulous smile or, God forbid, touch him, and he turned into a quivering puddle of lust. He had no business feeling this way about Lucy. She was looking for a husband, probably lots of babies, and a good solid home in which to raise a family. Seb could give her only one thing—a few moments of pleasure. He was a bastard for even thinking of her in that way.

"Are you trying to scare the customers away?" Black Jack asked as he approached.

His mind elsewhere, Seb didn't get the gist of what he'd said. "What?"

"You look mean enough to wrestle a grizzly with one hand tied behind your back."

"Oh, sorry. I was just thinking about something."

"If you want tonight to be successful, try to think about something besides her."

Seb doubled up his fist and punched Jack in the shoulder. "Who said anything about a her?"

"Not me, boss. Not me." Jack handed him two envelopes. "I picked up your mail while I was down at the depot."

"Thanks." Seb glanced at the letter on top, noting with some interest that it was from the manager of his saloon in Denver, the Fire and Brimstone. Deciding that he had enough on his mind and that Jack was right—if he didn't get in a better mood, he probably would scare the customers away—he stuck the letters in his jacket pocket and headed for the bar.

Although he rarely took a drink on a big night such as this, Seb felt the need for one now. "A cognac, Pearl. Make it a double."

She took out a glass, poured the shots, and then slid it across the bar. "Expecting a bad night again?" she asked, leaning over the counter.

Ignoring Pearl's considerable charms, which wasn't easy, Seb tossed the liqueur down his throat in a single gulp. Shuddering inwardly, he said, "I expect a good night. It's the day that's been a little long."

Pearl nodded toward the door. "It's about to get longer. Here comes the band."

The musicians—a banjo player, a violinist, and a trumpet player—were a sorry excuse for a band, but the best he could round up, given less than a week's notice. Seb welcomed them, set them up in the corner near the piano, and then went to greet his guests as they began to trickle into the saloon.

One of the first was Gerald Moseley, managing editor of the *Emancipation Tribune* and Seb's partner. He was a slight man with thick white hair, a bulbous nose, and small wire-rimmed glasses that made him look as if he were peering out of the wrong end of a telescope.

As he approached Seb, Gerald glanced around to make sure they couldn't be overheard, then whispered, "What's the *Rustler* up to this week?"

"Another column, I'm afraid."

"Is it anything like the last?"

"Pretty much. Why don't you go on over and take a peek at it?"

Gerald glanced around the room as if he were a Pinkerton agent, then edged his way over to the rack. At about the same time, the band started warming up their instruments, struggling, but not succeeding, in bringing them into tune.

"Afternoon, Seb," said Merry Barkdoll from behind him.

He turned to see her holding up a dollar bill. "Where do I buy a raffle ticket?"

Seb pointed out a table at the far corner of the room. "Black Jack is handling the tickets."

"What, or who, are you handling?"

Seb laughed, used to Merry's ribald nature. "Maybe the lucky woman who wins that gold locket. It'll look good on you."

"Oh, for heaven's sake. I'm not buying a ticket for a damn useless locket. I want the horse and saddle."

Seb rapped the side of his own head. "Stupid me. I should have known better."

"Maybe you ought to buy a ticket on that horse. About time you owned one."

He shrugged. "As the saloon owner, I'm not buying any raffle tickets, and besides, I don't have much use for a horse." He grinned, thinking of the sleek mare. "Anytime I need a horse, I'll just borrow one of yours."

Merry moved up close and placed her palm against his chest. "Honey, any time you want to borrow *anything* from me, it's yours."

Seb wondered in that moment if he shouldn't take her more seriously. Even dressed in men's clothing, Merry was certainly attractive enough, with those big blue eyes and that cornsilk hair. Better yet, she was uncomplicated, not the husband-chasing sort, and with a fine head for business. She would probably suit him just fine. Yet in many ways, she reminded him of his mother, a woman who put her own needs first and didn't give a damn about anyone else.

"I might just take you up on that," he said, one eyebrow raised high.

Merry slipped under his arm, then leaned in close to whisper, "You aren't talking about horses, are you?"

Seb threw back his head and laughed and, as he glanced over Merry's shoulder, saw Lucy standing there, eyes wide, features blanched.

He set Merry away from him and said, "I don't know what the hell I'm talking about. Why don't you get on over to Jack's table and buy a ticket before they're all gone?"

She jutted out her bottom lip. "Oh, all right, but I intend to take up this conversation later."

Swaying her hips, Merry slipped away. Seb turned to Lucy, feeling guilty, but not sure why, and said, "There you are at last—the girl with the velvet eyes has arrived."

"Sorry I'm late," she said, sounding tense. "I got locked in my room and couldn't get out."

"How did that happen?"

Her cheeks bloomed, pink roses. "I guess I pulled on the doorknob too hard. The whole thing came off in my hand and I couldn't get it back in the hole right. I hollered and hollered until someone finally heard me. The manager promised to have it fixed up good as new by tonight."

Seb wanted to laugh in the worst way but knew that she already thought of herself as a walking tornado, apt to wreak havoc if the slightest wind blew. Instead he just smiled and said, "You could have gone through my room, you know. I still keep the door unlocked in case of trouble."

"Thanks," she said, lowering her gaze, "but I couldn't go into your room uninvited."

Now Seb did laugh. "You couldn't?"

Lucy's head popped up and her eyes flashed. "Oh, goodness. I'd forgotten about that."

Seb chucked her under the chin. "Me, too. Now, if you're ready to work, it looks like we're getting quite a crowd."

"Yes," she said, looking around. "I guess I'd better."

Lucy stumbled as she started for the bar, apparently tripping over her own feet, and Seb reached out and caught her by the elbow. Rolling her big brown eyes in a way only she could, Lucy murmured her thanks and again headed for the bar.

She somehow managed to get through the crowd without bumping into anyone or knocking a drink off any of the tables. Lucy had days when she felt as if she couldn't get out of her own way, and this was shaping up to be one of them. She took a couple of deep breaths and slipped around to the back of the bar, where Pearl was busy filling beer mugs.

"As you mighta noticed," Pearl said, keeping her eyes on the spout spewing foam and golden liquid, "Seb has the tables all out of order. These four beers belong to that group over by the stove, but from here on out, you're gonna have to figure out who's who by yourself."

Just what she needed: an extra challenge. Her tray loaded, Lucy carefully made her way to the table Pearl had indicated, and found, to her delight and confusion, that it contained Hazel and Buford Allison, along with another man and woman. The women Lucy had known before would never step into a saloon, much less take a drink of alcohol.

"Are these beers for you?" she asked, fairly certain she had the wrong table.

"Yes, sweetie," said Hazel. "Put them right down."

Hiding her surprise and praying that she wouldn't have an accident, Lucy slid the entire tray onto the table instead of trying to unload it first.

"Lucy," Hazel said as she distributed the drinks, "I'd like you to meet our town treasurer, Alice Fremont, and her husband, Abe. He's a cashier over at the Monument Bank."

After Lucy exchanged pleasantries with the couple, Hazel added, "Alice tells me there's going to be a council meeting Monday night. It's open to everyone, and I think you ought to attend."

Lucy had never been to any kind of meeting with the exception of church services. "Me? Why?"

Hazel furrowed her brow. "Because you live in Emancipation now. Women here have worked long and hard for equality, and now that we have it, we're not letting go. Attending these meetings isn't a privilege—it's your duty."

Awash with a sense of freedom and independence she'd never experienced before, Lucy thought for a moment that she might faint. It took everything she had to swallow her excitement as she said, "I wouldn't miss it for the world."

"See you then," Hazel said. "Town Hall, seven o'clock."

Lucy picked up her tray, preparing to roam the room and take drink orders, when Hazel added, "Oh, wait a minute. Here's another council member I'd like you to meet."

About then a short, squat woman dressed like a man

lumbered up to the table. Lucy noticed that she was wearing a badge on her vest.

"Howdy, everyone," she said, dropping into the chair beside Buford.

"Lucy, meet B. J. Binstock," Hazel said. "She's our sheriff, and a mighty fine one at that. Lucy works for me setting type for the *Rustler*."

"Pleasure to make your acquaintance," B. J. said with a nod. "Do we have another one of them Penelope columns in this week's issue?"

Lucy was trying to get over the fact that the town sheriff was a woman, and an older woman at that, but managed to say, "Yes, ma'am."

As B. J. formed her reply, the band started up, most of them on the same key. The sheriff immediately clamped her hands over her ears and said, "Gawd. What the hell is that racket?"

Lucy cocked her head, listening for a moment, and then said, "I believe it's 'Ta-Ra-Ra-Bom-der-e,' but I'm not certain."

"See if you can get them to tone it down, and when you get a chance I'd like a beer and a copy of the *Rustler*."

"Make it two copies of the paper, please," added Alice Fremont.

Her day suddenly brighter, Lucy smiled and said, "I'll get right to it."

The saloon filled up rapidly after that, and before long restaurant owners began drifting in, depositing their wares on the buffet tables. Soon the aromas of carved ham and roast beef, fresh-baked bread and buns fought for dominance over the usual odors of tobacco smoke and stale beer.

Lucy was working her way toward one of those tables, hoping to sneak a quick sandwich before all the food was gone, when Charlie and Cherry came through the door. They each carried a huge tray of cupcakes slathered with thick chocolate frosting.

"Welcome to the party," Lucy said, snatching a cupcake off Charlie's tray. "Are you planning to stay a while?"

Cherry raised her chin a notch. "I doubt it. We're just here to deliver these."

Lucy indicated a spot on one of the buffet tables and nibbled at her cupcake as she led them there. After the two had deposited their loads, Lucy gave Charlie a bright smile and said, "Are you sure I can't get you something? A ginger beer, perhaps?"

He tugged at his collar. "Well . . ."

"We can't stay," Cherry insisted, looping her arm through Charlie's elbow.

"Oh, that's too bad."

As if cued by Lucy words, the band started in with a new song, a rather rambunctious version of "A Hot Time in the Old Town." The dance floor immediately began to fill.

Again speaking to Charlie, Lucy said, "Are you sure you can't stay for at least one dance? You used to love barn dancing. Remember how much fun we had?"

Lucy felt rather than saw the heat of Cherry's glare and took a particular delight in the way Charlie kept tugging at his collar. She wasn't so thrilled when she heard what he had to say.

"What do you think, Muffin?" he said to Cherry. "We've been working very hard, and the bakery's closed for the day. Why not honor me with a dance or two?"

"Oh, all right, honey, if you insist." Cherry turned a smug cheek to Lucy and added, "When we're done dancing, bring us both a ginger beer."

The air came out of Lucy in a long, angry hiss. So much for getting Charlie's attention. Her appetite gone, she tossed what was left of her cupcake into a trash bag and then went back to work. That work did not include taking drinks to Charlie or Cherry. She was pretty sure that if she did try to serve them, she'd have one of her infamous accidents—and that it would be no accident at all.

After what seemed like hours later, Lucy finally grabbed a roast beef sandwich and dragged herself outside the saloon to a quiet corner of the boardwalk. Shutting out the sounds of the band and the noisy crowd, folks who were enjoying themselves a whole lot more than she was, she went to work on her sandwich.

Her meal finished, Lucy continued to sit there, her chin propped up by her fist, and stared out at the lights of the town.

Charlie, she decided, was two different people. When he was with her, Lucy was sure that he loved her, and yet with Cherry by his side, he had eyes only for her. Which was the real Charlie, and whom did he truly love?

Thinking of him reminded Lucy that she hadn't gotten a letter from her father in today's mail. Apparently it hadn't had time to reach her yet, but she knew it was coming and that in it he would demand that she return home. Her only hope for continuing her life of freedom—and that was exactly what it was; pure, delicious freedom—was that the letter had somehow disappeared like the one Charlie had sent her.

Seb stepped out on the boardwalk then, looking for Lucy. He spotted her sitting at the corner with her head bent low, her usual sparkle a distant star on a moonless night. She also struck him as remote, as if she were hundreds of miles away.

Moving up behind her, he eased himself down on the boardwalk beside her. "Is everything all right?" he asked.

She turned to him, startled. "Yes. Sorry I've stayed away so long. I just came outside for some air and a bite to eat."

Lucy moved as if to push herself up, but Seb put his hand on her shoulder, keeping her in place. "Relax," he said. "Everyone is fine inside. I just wondered what happened to you."

She made a sound that almost passed for a laugh.

"What's wrong? Did one of my customers offend you?"

Looking him in the eye, Lucy said, "I guess you could say that, but there's nothing you can do about it."

"I beg to differ," he said, suddenly incensed. "Who was rude?"

"Charlie," she said dully, looking away again. "I did everything I know how to catch his attention tonight, but he's spending all his time dancing with Cherry. It's like he doesn't even see me."

Charlie again, Seb grumbled to himself, wishing the man would make up his mind and quit trifling with Lucy. Better yet, he could pack up his buns and get the hell out of Emancipation.

"I told you, there's nothing you can do," Lucy said quietly.

Seb sighed. Damned if he did, damned if he didn't. "Maybe there's a way."

"There is? I hate to ask you to help me again."

"You didn't ask," he said, making up his mind. "I'm offering."

With that he climbed to his feet and gave Lucy a hand up. "What Charlie needs to help him make up his mind is a healthy dose of old-fashioned jealousy."

As she laughed, a little of the sparkle came back into Lucy's eyes. "And how am I going to do that?"

"We're going to do it." Seb cocked his head toward the opened door. "Do you hear that?"

She listened a moment. "The 'Melba Waltz'?"

"Exactly." Seb held out his elbow. "Miss Preston, would you do me the extreme honor of dancing with me?"

She brightened even more. "Why, I'd be delighted, Mr. Cole."

Seb swept her into the saloon, catching the rhythm of the music even before they reached the dance floor. He held Lucy closer than would be considered proper but told himself he did so simply to make sure they could discuss the plan without being overheard.

Instead of thinking of the plan, Seb's thoughts were

drawn to Lucy. She stumbled a few times and required a viselike grip to keep her on track, and yet she was like a piece of heaven in his arms, an angel on a cloud. What in hell was wrong with Charlie?

"They're behind you," she whispered. "Just move straight back a few feet."

Following her instructions, Seb turned slightly, catching the couple out of the corner of his eye, and then purposely collided with Charlie's shoulder.

"Oh, excuse us," he said with a laugh.

Charlie looked primed for a terse response, but then he saw Lucy. "Lucille—you're dancing."

"Yes," she said brightly, drawing closer to Seb. "And so are you. What a coincidence."

Charlie's mouth dropped open, a gaping maw. "But you shouldn't be dancing with the likes of him."

"It seems to me that thanks to you, I can dance with whomever I please."

Charlie's face reddened and Cherry shot him a vicious glance. He didn't seem to notice and instead kept his incredulous gaze on Lucy. That's when Cherry punched him in the shoulder.

"I think we should move on," Lucy whispered into Seb's ear. He whisked her away, twirling her, dipping her, and generally putting on the dancing performance of his life.

When they were well away from the bickering couple, Seb grinned and said, "Well, how do you like the plan so far?"

Lucy peeked over his shoulder and saw that Cherry was heading for the front door, stomping actually. Charlie was working his way to the bar.

"I think it's working beautifully." She leaned up on tiptoe and kissed his cheek. "Thanks, Sebastian. Now I'd better get back to work."

Feeling a little guilty about causing a spat between Charlie and Cherry, but pleased by the outcome in any case, Lucy hurried over to the bar.

"Can I get you that ginger beer now?" she asked Charlie.

He turned to her. "Oh, no thanks. I already ordered something."

She moved closer to him, almost but not quite touching his arm. "I'm sorry if I upset Cherry. I didn't mean to cause a problem."

He waved her off. "Cherry's a little touchy about some things."

Lucy glanced around the room. "Where is she?"

"Cherry, ah, had to go back to the ranch. She stayed much longer than she'd planned to."

Pearl sashayed up to the bar then and shoved a beer Charlie's way.

"Goodness." Lucy slapped her hand against her cheek. "I've never known you to take a drink before."

He brought the mug to his lips and sipped the brew. Grimacing but nodding thoughtfully, he said, "We all change, I guess. You certainly have. I can't say I was happy to see you cavorting on the dance floor with that, that gambler."

"Why not?" she said, pleased to hear the hint of jealousy in his tone. "You were dancing; everyone was."

"That's different. You're a single young lady who doesn't even belong in a place like this, much less making a spectacle of herself."

"Don't start on that, Charlie," she warned. "Besides, this is Emancipation, and women are different here."

"I'll drink to that." He took another swallow of beer. "Did you get a letter from your father today?"

"No, and I doubt that I will," she lied. "He knows I can take care of myself."

"You shouldn't have to, Lucille." Charlie reached out and touched her cheek. "You belong back in Kansas City with some nice young fellow who will treat you right. Lord knows I haven't."

For a minute there, Lucy thought she saw the spark of tears in his eyes. "Thanks for saying so, Charlie, but I think

I belong here." The truth of it slammed against her chest. "In fact, I know I belong here."

Charlie downed the rest of his beer in one swallow. Then, before he could respond, Pearl approached and said, "You gonna stand here all night or take care of those folks who are hollering for the hostess?"

Lucy grabbed her tray. "Why don't you have another beer?" she suggested to Charlie. "I'll be back before you know it."

By the time Seb locked up the saloon for the night and trudged up the stairs to his hotel room, he was dead tired. He'd walked Lucy to her room around an hour or so earlier, and figured she'd be fast asleep. And probably dreaming about that bastard Charlie. Not that it was any concern of his.

After he let himself into his room, Seb quickly shed his jacket and shirt and then sat down on the edge of the bed. He'd just tugged off both of his boots when he thought he heard a woman cry out. Lucy?

Seb's first thought was that Charlie had followed her to the hotel. The damn fool had spent the last couple of hours at the party drinking beer, dancing with Lucy, and generally pawing her. Had he come to her room and forced his way inside?

Kicking his boots out of the way, Seb hurried to the connecting door and unlocked it. Putting his ear to her door, he listened intently. A moment later Seb heard Lucy cry out again, followed by an exclamation.

"No, no," she cried, "please stop!"

Chapter Ten

Seb didn't waste any time thinking about what he did next.

Forgetting that he was barefooted, oblivious to the coming pain, he reared back and hurled himself at the lock, using his foot as a battering ram. The door flew open and he stepped inside the room.

The dim light from his own room showed that Lucy was thrashing around in her bed, and that she was alone. Seb limped over to her, his foot throbbing where he'd connected with the doorknob, and sat down beside her. Lucy was moaning now, muttering incoherently.

He gathered her in his arms and whispered, "Hush, now. You're having a bad dream. It's all right."

Lucy tried to fight him, obviously not fully awake, and cried, "No, Charlie, stop."

"It's not Charlie," he assured her. "It's Seb. You're safe now. Go back to sleep."

She went limp in his arms, drifting deeper into her slumber, but continued to moan. Seb stretched out beside her and gathered her more fully into his arms.

"It's all right," he whispered throatily. "I'll stay with you until you're resting comfortably."

Lucy responded by snuggling deeper into the crook of his arm, and then her moans faded into faint, occasional whimpers. Seb rested his chin on the top of her head, filling his senses with the smell of her hair, that faint scent of lavender, and idly wove his fingers through those silken locks.

The worst was over. He should go now, he told himself, leave her while he still could. It would be the right thing to do. Something in him—his body, for sure; the stubborn, irrational part of his mind and, if he were honest, a piece of his heart as well—wouldn't let her go.

Ten minutes, he told himself. He would stay with Lucy for ten more minutes to make sure the nightmares had been chased away, and then he would go. Proud of this rational thought, Seb pulled the coverlet around Lucy's shoulders, tucking her in, and then draped the rest of it across his chest.

The next morning Lucy slowly drifted awake, surfacing from her slumber like a diver coming up for a breath of air. She had an overwhelming sense of peace thrumming inside her, a feeling of wholeness and happiness she hadn't experienced in a long, long time. Maybe never before. She stirred, thinking of raising her arms overhead for a good stretch, and realized that she was trapped. And that she wasn't alone.

Fully awake now, eyes wide with disbelief, Lucy saw that Sebastian was lying beside her, one arm draped across her body. His hair was disheveled, that unruly length curled down on his forehead, and the upper part of his bare chest was exposed.

"Oh," she gasped, staring at the mat of dark curls there. "Oh, my stars."

Sebastian stirred, blinking his eyes, and then finally opened them and rested his gaze on her.

" 'Morning," he murmured sluggishly.

"Oh, but this isn't—"

"Right, I know. Sorry, I guess I must have fallen asleep."

"But why are you here? How?"

Sebastian ran his hands over his face and yawned. "You had a nightmare last night. You made so much noise, I was afraid someone had broken into your room. I came to check on you. Don't you remember any of this?"

Lucy thought back to the night, but no matter how hard she tried, she couldn't remember Sebastian coming into her room, her bed. She did, however, recall a part of her nightmare. She'd dreamed that her father had showed up in Emancipation with a fresh-cut switch in his hand, and dragged her kicking and screaming to the train. The worst of it was when he gathered all of her Penelope columns and tore them to shreds, shouting that she was wasting herself on namby-pamby schoolgirl trash. If felt as if her father had torn the heart right out of her chest.

"Lucy?" Sebastian said with concern. "What's wrong?"

Still quaking inside, she admitted, "I'm just remembering parts of the nightmare."

"Do you want to talk about it?"

"No," she was quick to say.

"How about me? Do you remember now that I came into your room?"

She shook her head.

Sebastian laughed. "I suppose that's a good thing. You thought I was Charlie and tried to punch me in the nose."

Lucy's first impulse was to apologize, but she quickly bit her tongue. "I don't know why I'd have thought Charlie was in my room."

Sebastian made a funny noise in his throat, something like a growl. Then he said, "Maybe you thought that because of his behavior last night. I swear, if he grabbed you one more time, I might have punched him in the nose myself."

Lucy laughed softly and then thought back to the night. Charlie had consumed several beers, far more than he should have, and had been overly friendly toward her, almost possessive. He'd gotten himself drunk, or a little google-eyed at the very least. He'd also told her not once but three times that he loved her, something she'd been longing to hear, but not that way. Charlie ended the night by crying when she told him to go home.

Lucy sighed, impulsively pressed her hand against Sebastian's bare chest, and said, "Thank you for taking such good care of me."

Then, even more rashly, she leaned across his chest and gave him a quick kiss that landed slightly off center, at the corner of his mouth. She was thinking that he tasted of chocolate, thinking, too, how much he whetted her appetites—all of them—when Sebastian suddenly pushed up on his elbow and hovered over her. He stared down at her for a long moment, through her, his gray eyes dark, the color of a thundercloud.

At last, in a voice husky with something other than sleep, he whispered, "I should warn you, sweet girl with the velvet eyes—if you're going to kiss a man who's lying in bed with you, you'd better be prepared for the consequences."

The bed was so small, Lucy realized that Sebastian had no choice but to lean up against her. His body was hard everywhere, muscles tense and coiled. She could feel something more than his leg against her thigh, instinctively knew what it was . . . and exactly what he meant by consequences. Part of her was longing to find out what they would be, but she was uneasy, too. This wasn't right, and yet how terrible could those consequences be?

"I'm not sure I know what you mean by consequences," fell off Lucy's lips before she'd even formed the thought.

Before she could take a breath, Sebastian's mouth came down on hers. As his kiss deepened, became more passionate, he threw his leg over hers and eased down on top of her. Giving her a moment to breathe, he drew away from her mouth but never stopped kissing her, his lips caressing her neck beneath her ear and even a sweet spot at her throat. One of his hands was at the nape of her neck, fingers entwined in her hair; the other cupped her breast. As his thumb found her rigid nipple, he moved it in a slow, sensuous circle that made her moan from deep within her throat. Charlie had tried to do something like this at the lake, she thought hazily, and she'd been frightened. Not so now. Now she wanted more of the man in her arms, and Charlie had become a distant memory.

Lucy drove her hand into Sebastian's hair, absently fingering the notch on his ear, and whispered, "These consequences don't seem so bad, Charlie."

Sebastian went rigid and then took hold of her wrist. "What do you think you're doing?"

Caught off guard, embarrassed by her behavior and the fact that she was lying in bed with nothing between herself and Sebastian but a thin cotton gown, she felt her cheeks grow hot as she said, "I don't know exactly. I guess I was wondering what happened to your ear."

"That's something I don't want to talk about."

He abruptly sat up, his back to her, and climbed out of bed. As he crossed Lucy's room and headed toward his own, Sebastian said over his shoulder, "I'm afraid that I broke the door trying to get into your room last night. I'll make sure someone fixes it today." He paused, still looking at her from over his shoulder, and added, "By the way . . . I wasn't Charlie when you were asleep last night and I'm not Charlie now."

Then he stepped over the threshold and closed and locked his own door behind him.

At first Lucy couldn't imagine what he was talking about, why he'd changed so, and then it finally occurred to her. She'd been thinking about the picnic at the lake, comparing Charlie to Sebastian and finding Charlie lacking. Somehow his name must have slipped out. Lucy glanced at Sebastian's door, thinking of going to him, of finding some way to explain without the usual apologies. Before she could make up her mind what to say, she heard his outer door slam hard enough to rattle the jamb on her own door.

That afternoon when Lucy went to the saloon, Sebastian wasn't there. Pearl was busy pouring drinks, and the crowd, while nothing like the hordes of the night before, had filled most of the tables and the elbow room at the bar.

After edging her way between customers and taking up her tray, Lucy caught Pearl's attention. "Where's Sebastian?"

"These go to table five," Pearl said as she deposited six beers on the tray. "Seb's down talking to Hazel about getting some more copies of the *Rustler*. We sold out last night."

"We did?" Although she was still concerned about Sebastian and what he thought of her, Lucy could hardly contain her excitement. "That's great."

With a toss of her purple feather, Pearl said, "Table five. Get a move on."

The rest of the evening went by in a blur. Sebastian returned with another stack of newspapers, and then he promptly took a seat at one of the tables filled with gamblers. He spent the rest of the night dealing poker, never giving Lucy a chance to explain or apologize.

The following day, Lucy pretty much stayed locked in her room working on her newest, more politically inclined Penelope column. By Monday afternoon she felt certain that the column was the best one she'd written, and more than ready for Hazel's review. She hadn't seen Charlie since

Friday night and decided it would be a good idea to stop by the bakery on her way to the hay and grain store. Maybe he would talk to her. Sebastian wouldn't.

As she stepped into the bakery, the little bell above the door heralded her arrival. Charlie hurried out of the kitchen, his apron smeared with flour and streaks of something that might have been butter. He started when he saw her, and then quickly approached the counter.

"You shouldn't be here," he said quietly.

"Why not? I came to get a Hot Cross Bun."

He glanced over his shoulder, fear in his eyes. "Yes, but now isn't a good time."

There were deep smudges under his eyes, making him look as if he hadn't been sleeping well.

"I won't be long," she said, taking pity on him. "All I want is a bun."

Grumbling under his breath, Charlie snatched one out of the display case, wrapped it in parchment, and shoved it across the counter. "I have to go back to work now," he said with another glance over his shoulder. "This one's on me."

Then, before she could even reach for her money, he turned and hurried back into the kitchen.

While disappointed that not even Charlie would talk to her, Lucy wasn't particularly surprised by his behavior. After all, he'd put on quite an embarrassing performance Friday night, one that Cherry had most likely heard about by now. Lucy shrugged and headed toward the door. As she left the bakery, she thought she heard a woman's voice drifting out of the back room, a shrieking sound that didn't bode well for Charlie's already troubled mind.

Leaving thoughts of him and his cotton-headed fiancée behind, Lucy hurried over to Allison's store and went directly to the newspaper counter. Peering over the edge, she saw that Hazel was down under the printing press with a can of turpentine in one hand and an ink-stained rag in the other.

"Cleaning day?" she surmised.

Hazel looked over her shoulder. "I wish you'd showed up an hour ago and saved me all this trouble. These bones aren't as nimble as they used to be."

"Next time let me know when the press needs cleaning. I'd be happy to help."

Hazel lumbered to her feet, made a pass at her hands with the rag, and then joined Lucy at the counter. When she saw the Hot Cross Bun, her eyes lit up.

"Still keeping yourself in Charlie's thoughts, I see." She snatched up the treat and shoved a corner of it into her mouth.

"More than you know," Lucy confided. While Hazel finished off the bun, she told her about Charlie's behavior at the saloon, and finished with, "He told me that he loved me at least three times."

Using the back of her hand to wipe off her mouth, Hazel said, "I'm not sure drunk is the way to get a man's attention. He probably doesn't even know what he said or did."

"Oh," Lucy said, recalling Charlie's demeanor at the bakery. "I think he has a pretty good memory about that night. I also got the impression that Cherry knows something about what happened."

"Then if I were you, I'd watch my back." Done with such talk, Hazel glanced at the papers in Lucy's hands. "Is that what I hope it is?"

Lucy beamed. "It is if you're waiting for my new column."

Snatching the papers out of Lucy's hands the way she'd grabbed the bun, Hazel spread them on the counter and began to read.

For Lucy, the wait was interminable. The few minutes it took the newspaperwoman to read the column seemed like hours, and then suddenly she was finished.

Hazel looked up from the papers, slowly shook her head, and said, "This is incredible."

Lucy gulped. "You mean no one will believe it?"

"No, girl, I mean it's wonderful. I might change a word

or two as I look it over again, but this is exactly what I was looking for. Congratulations. Next thing you know, all the big papers in the East are going to want your column."

If her smile got any bigger, Lucy thought her face might crack. "So you don't want me take it back to my room and make changes?"

"Nary a one."

She wanted to laugh out loud. She wanted to shout. Most of all, she wanted to cry. Somehow Lucy reined in her emotions long enough to say, "Thank you. Your opinion means everything to me."

"Go on now," Hazel replied, patting the back of Lucy's hand, "or you'll have me blubbering all over your column. And don't forget about tonight's council meeting."

Promising that she would be there, even though it occurred to Lucy that she hadn't asked Sebastian if she could leave the saloon during that period, she fairly danced out of the office.

After making a quick trip to her room to change into her hostess getup, Lucy headed straight for the Pearly Gates. As was the norm for a Monday, the crowd was sparse, and once again, Sebastian was nowhere to be seen.

Edging up to the bar, she asked Pearl, "Is Sebastian taking the night off?"

She shook her silvery head, sending the feather on another rampage. "He had some business at the bank. Ain't much going on here, but I expect you could ask the men at the far table if they need anything."

Happy to get to work—anything to keep her mind off the excitement of her new column—Lucy took drink orders from the men and then served them, all without spilling so much as a drop of beer.

She was thinking of checking on the pair of cowboys who were playing billiards when the saloon door banged opened and Merry Barkdoll stomped into the place. As before, she was dressed in men's Levi's, a checkered work shirt, and a floppy-brimmed hat. With blood in her eye, she headed straight for Lucy.

"I need to talk to you for a minute," Merry said tightly.

Lucy glanced around the room. "I guess that would be all right. What do you want to talk about?"

"Outside." Merry pointed to the door that led to the alley.

"Oh, I don't think—"

"Outside would be best." As she said this, Merry fingered the handle of the gun she wore strapped to her hip. "Let's go."

Filled with equal parts curiosity and fear, Lucy put her tray on the bar and led the way out of the bar.

Once they were alone and in the alley, Merry let fly. "This is the first and last warning you're going to get. We don't hold with rustling in these parts, be it cattle, horses, or men. Leave Charlie be or I swear to God, I'll put a bullet right between those big brown eyes of yours."

This shocked her so, Lucy staggered backward a few steps. "But why would you do that? I thought you didn't care what went on with Cherry."

"I *am* Cherry, you dunder-headed idiot."

Taken aback yet again, Lucy looked her over. "Why are you dressed like Merry?"

"This is the way I dress when I'm working out at the ranch, which is where I'd be now if one of the hands hadn't told me what went on between you and Charlie after I left the party Friday night."

With a gasp, Lucy retreated farther.

Cherry advanced, getting right up close to her face. "You think you can just waltz into town and take Charlie back again? Well, you can't, not as long as I'm alive. I've got a big investment in that man and I'm not going to lose it."

"But I—"

"Just know this—no more dancing with Charlie, you

hear? No more talking to him either, and don't even think about looking at him again, you got it?"

"B-but I didn't do anything wrong. It was Charlie who—"

That was as far as Lucy got before Cherry pulled back her fist and then let it fly.

Lucy went down like a sack of wet grain. At first she didn't know what had happened. She was standing one minute and in the next sitting in a puddle of mud. Her nose was throbbing and she could feel something warm and moist trickling out of one nostril. Through her turmoil and confusion, she suddenly heard Cherry's voice as she lit into her again.

"And another thing," she added, shaking a finger in Lucy's face, "don't come into the bakery again, ever. You're not welcome there and if I see you, as a partner I have every right to shoot you."

With that she turned on her heel, stomped to the end of the alley, and disappeared around the corner.

Lucy sat there a long moment, still dazed and confused, and then finally got to her feet and dragged herself back into the saloon. Holding one hand over her nose, she worked her way to the bar.

Her voice sounding nasal to her own ears, she said to Pearl, "Can you give me a clean bar rag, please? I think my nose is bleeding."

Pearl glanced her way, made a face that assured Lucy she was indeed bleeding, and then tossed her a rag. After pressing the length of cloth against her nose, she made her way to the piano bench, out of sight of most of the customers, and sat down. Before she had a chance to assess the damage, Sebastian rushed up to her side.

"You're bleeding. What happened?"

"I'm not exactly sure. I think my nose is broken."

Sebastian sat down beside her.

"Let me have a look," he said, gently easing the rag away from her face. Keeping a corner of the cloth beneath her nostrils, he gently ran his thumb and forefinger up and down the length of her nose. "It's pretty swollen, but I don't think it's broken. What happened?"

"Cherry came in dressed up like Merry. I thought she was Merry, so when she asked to talk to me outside, I didn't think much of it, see, and like an idiot, I went out to the alley with her."

"Slow down a little," Sebastian encouraged. "And keep your head back until the bleeding stops."

Lucy tilted her chin higher and continued. "She told me to stay away from Charlie and a whole lot of other things that didn't make sense, and then she up and hit me. I still can't believe it. I've never met anyone like her before, man or woman. She hit me as hard as any man with a fist like an anvil."

"Cherry and Merry raise, break, and sell horses, so I imagine she's a pretty strong girl. Mean, too."

The trickle in her throat reduced to an occasional drip, Lucy brought her chin down and looked Sebastian in the eye. She saw nothing but concern in his expression, no hint of his earlier anger, and that somehow made her feel as if everything was her fault.

Lowering her chin even more, she whispered, "I don't know. Maybe I deserved a good punch in the nose."

"That's enough of that talk." Sebastian's voice was stern, and yet gentle at the same time. "Why don't you go back to the hotel and lie down a while?"

The idea was tempting, very tempting. "I would, except I have to go to the council meeting tonight and still get some work done here."

"Don't worry about the work. I'm not expecting a big crowd." He paused, thinking something over. "Maybe you ought to come here when you're up to it, though. Cherry might show up at that meeting."

"It doesn't matter. I promised Hazel I'd be there."

Sebastian glanced around the room. "Things are even slower than usual. Jack and Pearl can handle the saloon themselves. Why don't I collect you a little before seven and we can go to the meeting together?"

Lucy was more than touched by the offer, especially since she'd called him Charlie during a rather intimate moment. She wondered again if there might be a way to apologize, or if she ought to just let it drop. Her nose and head throbbing by now, it suddenly seemed best to leave it alone.

When Lucy and Sebastian walked into City Hall, she insisted on taking a seat at the back of the room. After her long nap, she'd glanced into the mirror above her dresser and almost didn't recognize herself. Her nose was swollen, the tip and right side red, looking as if she'd stayed out in the sun too long. What she hadn't expected was the pouch beneath her right eye, the skin there the same color as her nose. Even dabbing the area with a little powder didn't help much, and she didn't want the townsfolk gawking at her and wondering what kind of an accident she'd had this time. Hiding at the back of the room was a far better idea.

City Hall was a large, cavernous building that also doubled as the courthouse. There were seven council members, six of them women, a number that startled Lucy. They sat around a long table situated just in front of the judge's bench, and chairs had been set up throughout the room for anyone interested in attending the meeting. A few of those townsfolk sat in the jury box, Hazel and Buford Allison among them.

The mayor, Mattie Gerdy, was a tiny woman with a head that was too big for the rest of her body. She reminded Lucy of a bedpost, complete with a fancy round knob. When Mattie wasn't running the town, she worked at Gerdy's Mercantile along with her husband, Frank.

Her smile pleasant and her voice kind, Mattie banged the gavel on the table and said, "This meeting is officially underway. I'd like to begin by requesting the treasurer's report."

Alice Fremont, demure in a tasteful black-and-white suit, fiddled with a sheath of papers and then said, "First of all, I'm proud to report that the raffle held at the Pearly Gates netted the new school building fund a total of three hundred and eighty-seven dollars."

After a round of applause, she went on to say, "In addition to that, I'm informed that Sebastian Cole personally persuaded our local carpenters to donate their time when the building actually begins. Mr. Cole, would you please stand so we can all show you our thanks?"

Lucy heard him grumble under his breath, but he gamely got to his feet, took a short bow, and then sat down again in the midst of rousing applause. After that, Alice went on about taxes collected, licensing fees, and other financial matters that failed to stir Lucy's interest.

At length, Mayor Gerdy reclaimed the floor. "Before I turn the meeting over to our other committees, I have something very special on tonight's docket."

She reached into the folder before her and withdrew a single slip of paper. "This," the mayor explained, "is a letter from Mary Lease, asking if the township of Emancipation would welcome a visit from her and other members of the Populist Party in the next month or two."

A great gasp roared up from the audience, and then they began cheering, whistling, and applauding.

The mayor banged her gavel and said, "I thought you might be interested. Before I can write to her accepting the offer, you should know that we'll be expected to organize at least two political rallies, and that means we'll either have to dip into our town improvement funds or schedule some fund-raising activities, and soon."

As the council members discussed ways of soliciting funds, Sebastian leaned over and whispered in Lucy's ear. "It doesn't look like Cherry is going to show up. If you don't mind, I think I'd better get back to the saloon now."

She turned to him, preparing to give Sebastian his leave, but then froze as she saw the expression on his handsome face. His features were set and rigid, made of stone, and his teeth were clenched, a muscle twitching at the right side of his jaw.

"Is something wrong?" she asked.

"No," he said, getting to his feet. "I've just heard about all of this suffrage nonsense that I can stand. Do you mind if I go?"

"No, of course not."

Sebastian left then without another word. Lucy tried to listen to the rest of the meeting, but all she could think about was Sebastian. What had she done wrong this time?

By Friday morning, most of the swelling had gone down in Lucy's nose, but it was still sore. Her right eye was something else entirely. She was, in many folks' opinions, an Irish beauty: in other words, a woman with only one black eye. She had a monumental shiner, a mouse that had grown into a huge fat rat. For the past three days, the color beneath that eye had gone from blue to black to a mottled purple. Today, as she glanced into the mirror, she saw that all three colors had somehow merged into one, and that the resultant combination was set off by streaks of a horrifically green-tinged shade of yellow.

Wondering how much longer she would have to endure her colorful face as well as the endless queries from just about everyone she saw, Lucy headed down to the hay and grain store to collect as many copies of the *Rustler* as she could carry.

First she looked over her column, a procedure that had become a ritual. As she read it, something occurred to her, a feeling she'd never experienced in her entire life. She'd finally found something she was *good* at—a fulfillment beyond her wildest dreams.

THE WEEKLY RUSTLER

Emancipation, Wyoming,   Vol. 1.
Friday, June 19, 1896   No.39

ASK PENELOPE! FREE ADVICE

Dear Penelope:
My otherwise obedient wife is no longer content with voting on local and state matters. She wants to join the American Woman Suffrage Association and participate in their campaigns. How can I convince her that to do so will harm our marriage beyond repair? She is already having trouble maintaining a proper subordination to her spouse.

Signed, A Disturbed Husband

Dear Disturbed:
It is true that many women of our times believe that gaining the vote in the great State of Wyoming was but a small step toward their ultimate goal. I do not doubt that you, sir, are among the good men who believe that with the vote, "women who were once our superiors are now our equals." May I suggest, sir, that the suffrage movement is not your true complaint?

You state that your wife has trouble maintaining the proper subordination—does she prepare your meals in a timely manner and keep your home and clothing in good repair? If the answer is "yes," consider yourself blessed. Sit at her feet and learn.

Penelope

Chapter Eleven

That afternoon, Seb and Black Jack finished setting up the tables for the poker tournament and then settled in with a beer each at the corner table reserved for spectators and so- cializers. In a reversal of their usual roles, Jack was doing all the talking and Seb was a man of few words.

As Jack mixed a deck of cards, something he did almost constantly, he suggested, "How about a couple of hands of blackjack?"

Seb scowled and brought his beer to his lips.

Jack dealt four cards, his the final, face up. "I thought it might take your mind off your troubles. You look like someone stole your underwear."

Seb shot him another dark look but took a peek at his cards. Fifteen. He glanced at Jack's upturned card and saw that it was a king. It figured. Stuck between a rock and a hard place, wondering whether he ought to stand or take a hit, Seb heard Little Joe's broom clatter to the floor.

Glancing at the front door, where the kid had been sweeping dirt, popcorn, and peanut shells over the threshold, Seb saw Lucy come barreling into the saloon with a huge stack of the newest edition of the *Rustler*.

Little Joe, who made no attempt to hide his feelings for her, said, " 'Afternoon, Miss Lucy. Kin I help you with those?"

She thanked him kindly and allowed him to relieve her of part of the load.

Seb made no move to interfere. He simply watched Lucy, studying her the way a coyote considers a rabbit hole as she and the kid made their way to the newspaper rack.

Black Jack blew out an exaggerated sigh and said, "Why don't you get it over with?"

Jerked back to the game, still unable to decide whether to hit or stand, he glanced at his cards again and grumbled, "I'm thinking about it."

"Not that. Why don't you just call her bluff, deal her your ace of spades, and get it over with. I can't stand to be around you anymore."

This was a really big sentence for Black Jack. The surprise of hearing so many words fall from the man's lips softened the impact of his coarse statement, yet the look Seb shot him still managed to promise a long, slow death.

"Sorry," Black Jack said, clutching his chest. "I didn't realize you were holding the ace of hearts."

Was he? Seb wondered, ignoring the remark. Is that why all he could think about morning, noon, and night was Lucy Preston? He cared for her, and deeply, but love? Watching her again, noting her colorful eye, disheveled bun, and ink-stained fingers, all he could see was the most beautiful woman who'd ever crossed his path. Did that spell love? If it did, Seb figured, he was in big trouble. He'd made a lot of mistakes with a lot of women throughout his life, but never before had he been stupid enough to fall in love with a woman who loved another man. There had to be some other explanation.

"You gonna play cards?" asked Black Jack. "Or just sit there staring at Lucy with your tongue hanging out?"

Without giving it another thought, Seb snarled, "Hit me."

The corner of Black Jack's mouth twitched. "You or the cards?"

"The cards, you idiot."

His lips pressed tightly together, Jack flipped a nine onto Seb's cards. "Busted," he said unnecessarily.

"You cheated, you bastard."

Jack flung the deck of cards at the center of the table and pushed back his chair. "You know I don't cheat. Maybe I ought to go on over to the Coyote Gal, where a first-rate gambler is appreciated."

"Don't let the door hit you on your way out."

"Goodness, gracious," came Lucy's sweet voice from out of nowhere. "Are you two fighting?"

After a quick look at Lucy, Seb and Jack exchanged wary glances, and then Seb said, "We're friends who don't fight but rather have the occasional difference of opinion. Right?"

Jack's gaze narrowed to a venomous slit, snake eyes. It took him a minute, but he finally gave a short nod and pulled his chair back up to the table.

Lucy plopped a copy of the *Rustler* on top of Seb's cards. "I thought you might like to see this. Hazel says it's going to have Emancipation buzzing like a hornet's nest before nightfall."

Grateful for the distraction, Seb took the paper between his hands and immediately went to the "Ask Penelope" column. It had taken a while after he moved to Emancipation, but he'd gradually come to accept women in positions of authority; B.J., the town council, all of it, as long as it didn't interfere with his saloon. He wasn't feeling that generous with this upstart, Penelope.

Seb glanced at Lucy and said, " 'Sit at her feet and learn'? How can Hazel print this crap? She's going to have every man in town chasing after her with a noose."

To Seb's surprise, Lucy turned on her best smile. "That's her intent," she said smugly. "Hazel says the worst thing you can do is bore your readers, and that making them mad is one way to get their attention. Guess it worked, huh?"

Seb wasn't about to agree with her, even though he did, or mention that this issue of the *Rustler* would probably sell out before sundown. Instead he asked, "Where did you say this Penelope can be contacted?"

Lucy's expression brightened. "If you have a question for Penelope, all you have to do is write it down and put it in the LETTERS TO THE EDITOR box outside the hay and grain store."

Seb shook his head. "No, how do you contact her personally? How does Hazel send the letters and receive her replies?"

Lucy shrugged and looked away. "You'll have to ask Hazel about that. I only set the type."

Clutching the newspaper in his hands, Seb shoved out of his chair and said to Jack, "I just remembered something I have to take care of. Can you keep an eye on things until I get back? I won't be long."

With a short nod, Jack assured him that all would be well. Then Seb headed straight for the offices of the *Tribune*.

Later in the day, after the train had arrived and gamblers and thirsty travelers began to fill up the saloon, Lucy's mood couldn't have been better. The only dark spot was the letter that most surely had arrived from her father. She probably should have gone down to the depot to collect it but simply couldn't let anything get her down. Nothing was going to spoil her day.

On the plus side, the stack of *Rustler*s had dwindled down to a few copies, the comments she overheard about her column were positively glowing, and she was having an amazing streak of luck. She'd already served countless beers and drinks and so far hadn't spilled so much as a drop. In direct contrast to her good spirits, Sebastian's mood had drifted from somber to sour. Instinct told Lucy that it had something to do with her Penelope column, but what she couldn't imagine.

Too happy to worry about why his attitude had gone from bad to worse, she went about her work with a decided lilt to her voice. She was serving a table, the final beer still on her tray, when a familiar voice crawled over her shoulder.

"Lucy, is that you?"

As she whirled around, praying that her ears had tricked her, that last beer flew off her tray. To no one's surprise, it landed in the lap of a stranger. Lucy didn't even realize it was gone.

"Dusty! What are you doing here?"

"No," he said, anger, disappointment, maybe some hurt, evident in his dark eyes. "The question is, what are you doing here?"

Of her six brothers and sisters, and with the exception of his dark-cinnamon–colored hair, this one more closely resembled Lucy than the others with the same big brown eyes and wide, dazzling smile. Even though he was a year older than Lucy, Dusty had behaved more like her father than her brother since they were youngsters. As he looked her over, still wearing a scowl, it seemed to Lucy that nothing had changed.

"Just look at you," he said angrily. "Dressed like a tart, flaunting yourself in a saloon, and you've even got a black eye. What's got into you?"

Aware that other eyes were upon them, she said under her breath, "Not here, Dusty. I have work to do. I'll talk to you later."

"You don't have any work to do 'cause you're quitting this job this minute." He took hold of her arm. "And we'll talk now."

Nearly a head taller and some sixty pounds heavier than Lucy, Dusty had no trouble dragging her and her tray out of the saloon even though she put up a fight. They'd no more than reached the boardwalk before another male voice drifted over her shoulder, this one filled with malice.

"Take your hands off her now."

Lucy saw a spark of fear in Dusty's eyes, but he said, "This is family business, none of your concern."

"I'm not going to ask you again," came Sebastian's voice, this time punctuated by the click of a gun hammer. "Take your hands off her."

Dusty immediately released Lucy. "I don't want no trouble."

"Neither do I. Just go on your way and we'll forget about this."

Lucy turned to Sebastian. "It's not that simple. Dusty here is my brother. I think my father sent him after me."

"That's right," Dusty agreed, stepping up beside her. "Like I said, this is family business."

Ignoring Dusty, Sebastian sheathed his pistol and asked Lucy, "Do you need to take some time off?"

Lucy thought about it, hating the idea of leaving Sebastian short-handed, knowing if she went back inside, Dusty would just follow and continue to berate her. With a nod, she said, "I'd appreciate it if I could have a few minutes to talk to my brother. His visit is quite a surprise."

"Take all the time you need." He looked past her to where Dusty stood. "Have a nice chat with your sister, but don't put your hands on her like that again. Got it?"

Beside her, Lucy could feel Dusty bristle. "I wouldn't hurt Lucy. She's my sister."

"Remember that."

Then he turned and stomped back into the saloon.

"Who was that?" asked Dusty, spitting out the words like grape seeds.

"Sebastian Cole. He owns the Pearly Gates. I work for him."

"Not anymore you don't."

Unwilling to discuss the situation within earshot of Sebastian's patrons, Lucy led Dusty to the end of the boardwalk and sat down. As he took a seat beside her, she worked on a way of convincing Dusty to let her stay here in Emancipation.

"This is all a big misunderstanding," she began. "I'm doing just fine and I want to stay here."

"You're the one who doesn't understand. When Pa got that letter from Charlie saying that you two decided not to get hitched and that you were a saloon girl, he just about had a heart attack. It was all I could do to convince him to let me come after you instead of him."

Lucy remembered the nightmare she'd had about her father coming to town and dragging her to the depot . . . and worse. With a sigh, she said, "Thank you for that."

"Don't thank me yet. Charlie told me a whole passel of outlaws kidnapped and run off with you. Is that true?"

Lucy grumbled to herself, thinking that she'd like to stuff one of Charlie's buns down his throat. "That's not exactly what happened. Outlaws, just a couple, came into the place and robbed it, but I wasn't exactly kidnapped, see; they just needed me to show them the way out of town. I kind of got off the horse a ways up the road, but I didn't get hurt or nothing. It wasn't my fault, so don't tell Pa."

Dusty gave her a look. "That's some story. True or not, if we're not at the Kansas City depot come Wednesday, Pa will be on the next train west. Count on it."

There was no use arguing the point. She knew for a fact that her father would come for her if Dusty couldn't manage the job. She wouldn't be able to fight the both of them. She had four days, just that short time to figure out a way to convince Dusty, and thereby her father, that she belonged in Emancipation. It seemed an impossible task.

"Make me a promise," she finally said to Dusty. "Leave me be until Tuesday, let me live my life as it is for those few more days, and if you still think it's for the best, I promise to go home with you."

Thinking this over, Dusty rested his elbows against his knees and dangled his arms between his legs. Then he said, "I can't say I'm any too happy to hear that you want to continue working in a saloon."

"It's how I earn my keep." She pointed to the building down the street. "I have a room over there at the Palace Arms, the best hotel in town and where I feel completely safe. Women matter here; they really, really matter, and not just in the kitchen. We've got a woman sheriff, a woman newspaper owner, most of the city council are women—"

"All right, I get it."

"And best of all," she continued, "I'm making enough money to take care of myself, and doing a fine job of it. Besides working here, I also have a job at the newspaper a couple of days a week."

"Huh?" He whipped his head around. "What do you do?"

Lucy longed to tell him exactly what she did at the *Rustler* but remembered her promise to Hazel. Hedging a little, she said, "I set type for the entire paper and help the editor with a little writing here and there. She might even let me be a reporter soon."

"No kidding?"

"No kidding. That newspaper job is the main reason I want to stay here so badly. I wish we could think of a way to convince Pa to let me stay."

"That's not going to happen. The only way Pa would let you stay here is if you married Charlie."

With a groan, Lucy said, "That's not going to happen either. Have you seen Charlie since you got to town?"

"Sure. I stopped at the bakery first to find out where you were. He's putting me up at his apartment above the store."

"How nice," she said acidly. "Did Charlie happen to mention why we didn't get married?"

Dusty considered this. "No, I don't guess he did. What happened?"

"Before I could come to Emancipation, he went and got himself engaged to another woman. I never had a chance."

Lucy could see that this didn't set well with her headstrong brother. Eyes narrow, cheeks blowing in and out like bellows, he said, "Want me to beat him up some?"

While that didn't sound like an entirely bad idea, Lucy shook her head. "No. I've been dealing with him in my own way."

Dusty reached over, took her chin between his fingers, and angled her head his way. Then he asked, "Where did you get the black eye?"

Smiling despite her appearance, Lucy said, "Charlie's new fiancée doesn't much like me dancing with him."

Lucy spent the rest of Friday night working on a plan that would keep her in Emancipation, and that meant that her lucky streak ran out. She was so distracted, she spilled beers, dropped whiskey bottles, and generally caused mayhem at every table she worked. Things finally got so bad, Sebastian sent her to the hotel early and suggested that she get a good night's sleep.

Sleep was hard to come by as she tested one idea after another. No matter how hard she tried, everything always came back to Charlie. By Sunday morning, and seeing no other way out of her dilemma, Lucy gathered all her courage and headed for the bakery. Instead of confronting Charlie in front of his customers, she went straight for the side door and, to her relief, found it unlocked.

To Lucy's dismay, when she stepped into the kitchen, she saw that Cherry was standing at one of the counters frosting chocolate cupcakes. Charlie was stirring a large bowl of batter at another. Determined to ignore the fluffy-haired girl, Lucy marched right over to where Charlie stood.

"You're not welcome here," Cherry reminded her.

Without looking her way, Lucy said, "Be quiet, please. I have business with Charlie."

Looking him directly in the eye, she went on to say, "As I'm sure you're aware, my brother is here to take me back home. It seems the only way I can stay here is if you follow through on your promise and marry me. You have to make up your mind today. Which one of us are you going to marry?"

"Oh, Lucille . . . geez."

Cherry was a little more eloquent. "That's a stupid question. He's going to marry me and that's that."

Without thinking it through, Lucy reached over, grabbed a cupcake off the tray, and shoved it against Cherry's mouth. "I said to be quiet, *Muffin,* and leave us alone."

"Lucille!" Charlie's wide eyes were pinned on Cherry, who was gagging and spitting out bits of cake. "How could you?"

Feeling pleased with herself and unable to hide a tiny smile, Lucy turned back to him and said, "I thought feeding her a cupcake was a bit nicer than the black eye she gave me, but that's neither here nor there. What's it going to be, Charlie?"

She pointed at Cherry, who was still trying to clean the frosting out of her nostrils. "That, or me?"

Charlie buried his face in his hands and slowly shook his head. "I don't know what to do, Lucille. I just don't know."

"What?" said Cherry.

Keeping her eyes and thoughts trained on Charlie, Lucy went on, more determined than ever to settle this once and for all. "You knew what to do at the lake and at the dance. You kissed me and said you still loved me, not once but three times."

"*What?*" Cherry was screeching now.

"I need your answer," Lucy persisted. "And I need it now."

"I can't . . . I don't know; I—"

That was as far as Charlie got before Cherry smashed a

cupcake against his face and said, "You don't know? After all the money I've loaned you, how can you stand there and say you don't know?"

Though Cherry's accusations didn't make much sense to Lucy, Charlie's hesitation was answer enough. "Oh, for heaven's sake, Charlie," she muttered. "I don't know why I ever thought I wanted to marry you."

She turned on her heel and stomped to the door. Before she left the pair of them to their mess and the argument that was firing up, Lucy said to Cherry, "Such as he is, he's all yours."

Then she headed back toward the hotel. As she walked, Lucy was surprised to realize that Charlie's betrayal didn't hurt the way she thought it would. In fact, he was no longer an issue in her life. Her freedom was the only thing that mattered now. She had to think of a new plan, something short of marrying Charlie that would appease her father enough to let her stay in Emancipation. She couldn't leave now, not when she'd finally found some meaning in her life. She could never go back to Kansas City and be the same person again. She loved her family and the farm, but Lucy realized that she no longer belonged there. How ironic, she thought. A few short weeks ago she couldn't allow herself to go back home as a failure. Now she couldn't go back as a success.

As Lucy neared the Pearly Gates, a daring solution popped into her mind. If anyone could help her figure a way out of this mess, it was Sebastian Cole. Even though the saloon was closed on Sundays, he usually came in to take stock of supplies and order whatever was needed. Hoping to find him there, Lucy dashed across the street and knocked on the door.

Inside the saloon, Seb was filling out an order for another two dozen decks of cards. When Lucy had a bad night performing her hostess duties it usually cost him a lot more than a few beers. As he considered her accident rate of late, he scratched out the two and ordered four dozen decks.

When Seb heard a knock on the door, he shouted, "It's open. Come on in."

After he finished writing down his order, he looked up to see Lucy standing next to the table. "I hope I'm not disturbing you," she said. "I need to talk to you if you have the time."

Seb pulled out the chair next to his. "Sure. Sit down."

As she slid onto the seat, Lucy took a quick look around. "Are we alone?"

His curiosity rising, he said, "It's just us. What's the problem?"

She took a deep breath, closed her eyes for a moment, and then said, "I know you've done nothing but help me since I came to town, and that I shouldn't be imposing on you again, but I need a favor, a really huge favor."

Downright intrigued now, and pretty sure he didn't want to know what the favor might be, Seb swallowed his reservations and said, "You know I'll help you in any way I can. What's the trouble?"

"Well, see, you know my father sent my brother instead of a letter, and if we don't show up at the Kansas City depot on Wednesday, my father will come himself. Then I'll have no choice but to go back home with him, and I don't want to leave Emancipation. I'll die if I have to go. See?"

"No. Why would you die?"

"Well, see, because I'm different now. Before I couldn't go home and get laughed at, but now I can't go home because I'm good at something I can't talk about, and I really like feeling this way, see. But it won't happen in Kansas City because I'm not the same there, and neither is Hazel; well, not really Hazel, you know, but something like that. I have to stay."

So confused he couldn't even speak, Seb just stared at Lucy for a long moment. Then he asked, "How can I help? Do you want me to talk to your father?"

Tears sprang into her eyes and Lucy shook her head.

"That wouldn't do any good, especially with you being a gambling man and all."

"Then what do you have in mind?"

Another breath, this one deeper than before, and Seb had a feeling that Lucy was going to launch into another outburst of words that didn't make any sense.

"First off," she began, "I thought if I could get Charlie to marry me by tomorrow, then Dusty could go back home and report that all is well. But when I went to see Charlie, Cherry was there, too, see, and I shoved a cupcake down her throat and asked Charlie to decide right then and there which of us he wanted to marry."

She paused to suck in another breath and Seb stretched out in his chair, making himself comfortable.

"Charlie said he couldn't make up his mind, didn't know, or some such excuse, and then Cherry talked about money and smashed a cupcake in his face. I knew that I had my answer, even though he never really said no, but then I didn't even care so I left and came here. You see, the only thing that could work, didn't, but then I thought of you."

Utterly confused but clear about the fact that Lucy was worried about having to leave town, he surmised, "If I understand you—and believe me, I'm not sure that I do—since Charlie refuses to marry you, your father is going to force you to go back to Kansas City?"

"That's exactly it," she said brightly.

Almost afraid to hear the answer, Seb asked, "Just how do you think I can help you with this problem?"

"There's only one thing I can think of."

Fingers entwined, giving off more than a hint of apprehension, Lucy turned mournful brown eyes on him and said, "Will you marry me?"

Chapter Twelve

Good thing Seb was already sitting down.

The top of his head seemed to float away, his eyes were swimming in a sea of spots, and his legs felt as if they were made out of pudding. Had he been standing, Seb realized with alarm, he might have fainted. He laughed at the thought.

"It's not a joke," Lucy said quietly. "I'm very serious."

"Lucy, I . . . damn."

"I realize this has come as a shock, but it's not as bad as it sounds."

Marriage was marriage, wasn't it? It wasn't as if he thought having Lucy for a wife would be bad—it was the thought of having anyone for a wife that was bad. The very idea lodged in Seb's throat like a shot glass, dredging up memories of Denver. This was the second time a woman had asked him to marry her, and yet Lucy wasn't Kate . . . or was she? They'd both seemed sweet and guileless in the beginning, but in Denver, things had changed rapidly, and for the worst. His life had been ruined.

"Sebastian?" Lucy said tentatively. "Before you say no, can I at least explain what I have in mind?"

He studied her sitting there, thinking that he did not want her to leave Emancipation, guessing that he was probably at least a little in love with her, and knowing that he was in no way ready for a trip to the altar.

Finally Seb sighed and said, "I can listen as long as you take it slow and easy so I can understand what you're saying, but I'm not making any promises beyond that."

"Thank you, Sebastian. All I ask is that you listen." Lucy clasped her hands together, looking as prim and proper as she had the first time he met her. "If I'm married, my father can't force me to go back home. Since Charlie is still besotted with Cherry, I figured that it really doesn't matter who I'm married to as long as I'm legally wed."

Seb laughed, but it was without humor. "Am I to assume that I'm the first man you happened to stumble across?"

Lucy gave him a quizzical look and then said, "Oh, you know what I mean. Just being married is enough to keep me here."

"But if you can't have Charlie, why stay? Why not go home?"

"Because I'm happy here, truly happy in a way that I can't be back home."

Feeling as if he were stepping into a bog, Seb said, "And so your plan is?"

"I figured we could get married tomorrow, but not for real, not living together as husband and wife, see."

Seb just stared at her. Lucy drew a breath and continued.

"I mean, we'd have to be married legally by Justice of the Peace Carroll because Dusty would never take my word that I suddenly had a husband. He's going to want to see the papers."

"And how, may I ask, does that make the marriage not real? Sounds pretty legal to me."

"It would be on paper, but it doesn't have to be for long. I figure two weeks, maybe a month to make sure that my father isn't still planning to come see for himself what I'm up to, will be enough time for us to be married. After that, you can go to Justice Carroll, tell him whatever you have to, and get an annulment or something, right? You can be a bachelor again, and I can stay here and keep working at the *Rustler*."

Actually, it didn't sound like a bad plan, at least from Lucy's point of view. Seb had some concerns, not the least of which was the fact that he would be a married man for at least a month.

"What about later?" he asked. "Births, deaths, marriages, arrests, all are public knowledge and mentioned in both newspapers. Everyone in town is going to know that we got married, and those same folks are also going to know that it didn't last but a month. Gossip is going to run high, especially where you're concerned."

Lucy's bright expression gradually faded as she considered this. Then she shrugged and said, "I'll just have to figure a way to handle the gossip as it comes. Can you?"

"Shouldn't be a problem. Divorces and annulments are a lot harder on women. Have you thought of that?"

She hadn't, actually, especially the part about her being a divorced woman. Lucy cringed, wondering if she could actually face the future under such a dark cloud.

"Doesn't sound like a good idea now, does it?"

Lucy steeled her resolve. "I'll do whatever it takes to stay here. Will you help me?"

Something in Seb balked, a feeling of terror that gave him the strength to turn away from her desperation. "I don't think so," he said with resignation. "There must be some other way for you to continue living in Emancipation."

Although he still wouldn't look at her, Seb could feel Lucy's disappointment. With a sigh, she said, "There is no other way, but I thank you for listening. Maybe I can get Black Jack to marry me."

"No," shot out of Seb's mouth so fast it made him dizzy.

The very idea of Lucy in Jack's arms, even for a moment during a fictitious marriage, was more than Seb could stand. Even so, there were still a million reasons not to follow through with her insane plan. What he ought to do is flat out refuse her and run as far away from her as he could get. Instead, and without examining his motives too closely, Seb pushed out a heavy sigh.

"You win," he said slowly. "I'll marry you, but only for one month."

Lucy leapt out of her chair and threw her arms around his neck. "Oh, thank you, Sebastian, thank you from the bottom of my heart. I'm forever in your debt."

She gave him a quick buss on the cheek and then began to rattle off her plans. "Can you go to see Justice Carroll first thing in the morning? It's imperative that we get this done tomorrow."

His mind reeling and his gut churning, Seb promised. "I'll take care of it."

"Oh, and witnesses. We need someone to stand up for us, don't we?"

Seb didn't consider this long. He knew exactly whom he would choose, and he could already hear him almost laughing. "Black Jack will stand up for me."

"I'm sure that Hazel will do the same for me. Anything else?"

Seb shrugged. "Nothing I can think of unless you want a ring."

A ring sounded wonderful, but Lucy figured she'd asked enough of him. "That won't be necessary, but there is one other thing. We must keep this a secret until after the fact. If my brother gets wind of this before we get married, he might just find a way to stop the wedding."

This suddenly sounded like a very good idea, but again,

Seb bowed to her demands. "Jack won't talk. He hardly ever does."

"I'm not that sure about Hazel. I'd better wait to ask her until just before the service."

Suddenly in need of a drink, Seb pushed out of his chair. "If that's all," he said, heading to the bar, "I've got more work to do."

"Oh, yes, sure, of course. I have some things to do myself." Lucy started for the door and then hesitated. Turning those big brown eyes on him, she softly said, "This is the most wonderful thing anyone has ever done for me. I'll do anything I can for you in return. Anything."

After Lucy had gone, Seb poured himself a good measure of cognac. Anything? As he considered this, he wondered if Lucy would agree to spend their first evening together as man and wife. In his room. In his bed. Would Lucy agree to a phony marriage featuring an authentic consummation? Not bloody likely. Seb raised the glass, a toast to his bride-to-be, and knocked it back.

Lucy spent the rest of the day working on a particularly troubling, and personal, Penelope column. After a restless night's sleep, she'd barely dragged herself out of bed the next morning before Sebastian stopped by to inform her that the wedding was scheduled for noon over at City Hall. He left so fast after that announcement, Lucy didn't even have a chance to thank him.

An assessment of her wardrobe didn't take her long. She decided that she might as well wear the wedding dress her mother and sister had fashioned of silver taffeta. The bodice was trimmed with white chiffon and seed pearl–beaded fringe that could be removed after the wedding, thereby turning the gown into something Lucy could wear for many years on special occasions.

Not wanting to call too much attention to herself, she tossed the white chiffon veil aside and settled for pulling her hair up into a waterfall of sausage curls that spilled down from the back of her head. Satisfied that she looked the part of a bride heading for a very simple wedding, Lucy grabbed her newest Penelope column and headed straight for the hay and grain store.

"'Morning, Hazel," she said as she approached the counter.

"'Morning, Lucy." Hazel glanced up with a smile and returned to the papers on her desk. Then her gaze shot right back to Lucy. "Great snakes, girl. Why are you so dressed up?"

She shrugged. "There's doings at City Hall around noon today."

Pushing away from her desk, Hazel lumbered over to the counter. "Really? I haven't heard anything about a council meeting."

"It's not a meeting. It's a wedding."

Hazel had been looking around for a Hot Cross Bun, frowning when it became apparent that Lucy hadn't brought her one. Now her expression lit up. "A wedding? How come I don't know about this? These things are supposed to be announced in the newspaper before they happen."

"The wedding wasn't arranged until last night."

Too sharp to tease any longer, Hazel narrowed her gaze and took in Lucy's dress again. "So," she surmised. "I guess this means that foolish young baker of yours finally came to his senses."

"Not exactly, but before I tell you the whole story, I was hoping I could convince you to stand up for me. Will you?"

"'Course, I will, girl." Elbows resting on the counter, Hazel leaned up close and whispered, "All right, tell. What's so mysterious about this wedding? Doesn't Charlie know he's getting married?"

Lucy glanced toward the back of the store. Gus was nowhere to be seen. She quickly said, "It's not Charlie, but

I don't want anyone else to know about the wedding until tomorrow. Can you keep it quiet?"

"Sure, but if not Charlie, who?"

Feeling curiously proud, Lucy admitted in a quiet voice, "It's Sebastian Cole."

Hazel clutched her enormous bosom and staggered back a step. "Seb—my Seb?"

"Yes, but it's not what you think." Lucy quickly filled her in on the most basic details, and then said, "So you see, it's more of a favor than anything."

Hazel didn't say anything at first. She just stood there, jaw hanging down, and rolled her eyes. Then she finally said, "Holy smokes. I can't believe you talked Seb into such a fool thing."

Lucy had spent most of the morning thinking the same thing and hoping that Sebastian didn't see it the same way. Abruptly changing the subject, she handed her papers to Hazel and said, "We don't have much time. Here's my Penelope column. It might need some more work because I was kind of distracted when I wrote it. I'm pretty sure I was thinking about Charlie at the time. Is it all right?"

Obligingly, and with no further mention of Sebastian, Hazel studied the column. When she finished, she let out a low whistle.

"It is a little hard to swallow," she commented, thoughtfully tapping her finger against one of her chins. "Then again, it might provide just the right distraction as far as the men are concerned when they read my editorial. Mary Lease has agreed to bring her group here for a political rally in late July. A lot of folks, men in particular, are not going to be too happy about that."

"Oh, but I think it's wonderful." Now more than ever Lucy wanted to be a part of this town. "Is there anything I can do to help get ready for their visit?"

"Just keep on writing your columns for now; speaking of

143

which, I had a little visit from Gerald Moseley over at the *Tribune*. He stopped by Saturday morning and tried to get information on Penelope."

Lucy knew that Moseley was the editor of the rival newspaper. "What kind of information?"

"How to get in touch with her and so on. I told him that Penelope has an exclusive arrangement with us, but that I'd let her know about his interest. Let's hope he lets it go at that."

Lucy could hardly believe her ears. "You mean he wants to buy my column for his newspaper?"

Hazel's grin was broad as she said, "You bet he does. I think the *Rustler* has been cutting into his profits of late."

"That's wonderful news."

"Wonderful, yes, but you can't make a fuss about it and you sure can't sell that column to him."

"I understand that," she said with a pang of regret. "Just knowing that he wants it is good enough for me."

For now, anyway. Not that Lucy would forget what Hazel had done for her or be disloyal in any way, but it did her heart good to know there was a broader interest in her work. Maybe someday she could sell the column to newspapers in other States.

"Now, then," Hazel said, "about this wedding. Whatever shall I wear?"

Back to the task at hand, Lucy studied Hazel's ink-stained apron and sooty shirtsleeves and frowned. "This won't do. How fast can you get into a Sunday-go-to-meeting dress?"

Down the street at City Hall, Seb had just paid for and finished filling out the papers for a marriage license. Jack, who had spent the entire morning trying to talk him out of the insane plan, stood beside him, the corner of his mouth twitching rhythmically.

As he finished his part of the license and laid the pen beside the papers, Seb asked Justice Carroll, "Is that it?"

Fitting a monocle to his right eye, the justice peered at the license and said, "Your part is completed. Miss Preston will have to fill out her information as soon as she gets here, but other that than, we're done until after the services."

Turning to Jack, whose mouth was still twitching, Seb muttered under his breath, "Stop laughing, damn it. This isn't funny."

"I'm not laughing."

"The hell you aren't."

They might have gone on like that for another ten minutes, but the door opened then and in came the bride and her maid of honor.

Seb's breath caught as Lucy came into the room. He didn't know what he expected her to wear at their so-called wedding, but he hadn't figured on her showing up in a silvery gown that made her look like an angel who just stepped off a cloud. A tremor shot through him, a dire warning of what he was about to do, the mistake he might be making. Seb thought about heading straight for the door and never looking back.

"Are we late?" Lucy asked breathlessly, preventing Seb's escape. "Hazel had a time deciding what to wear."

Grateful for the distraction, Seb glanced away from Lucy and saw that Hazel was decked out in a purple satin suit trimmed with wide splashes of yellow and green. She looked like a giant eggplant.

"You're right on time," he finally said to Lucy, and then added under his breath, "and I must say, you look absolutely beautiful."

"Thank you." Leaning in close, she pressed something into his hand and whispered, "Hazel thought it would look more official if I had a ring. She loaned me one for the wedding."

Without looking at it, Seb stuck it in his pocket and said, "You have to fill out some paperwork."

Then he escorted her over to where Justice Carroll sat waiting. When she'd finished providing her personal information, the justice gathered everyone around his podium.

"Now then," Justice Carroll began, "as I'm sure you're all aware, marriage isn't something to be entered into lightly."

As Justice Carroll droned on about the sanctity of their upcoming nuptials, Seb thought he heard Lucy gulp. To his right, Jack made a sound in his throat, something that sounded like a cross between a grumble and a chuckle.

As Seb again considered bolting through the front door, he heard the justice say, "And so if no one has any objections to a union between these two fine folks, we'll just get on with the vows."

He paused for the required moment and then asked, "Do you, Sebastian Cole, take Lucille Mathilda Preston as your lawfully wedded wife?"

Seb cocked his head her way. "Mathilda?" he whispered.

"Family name," she said under her breath.

Seb stood there a moment longer, thinking how little he really knew about this woman.

"Ah, Mr. Cole?" Justice Carroll persisted. "Do you take Miss Preston as your wife?"

Gathering himself up, Seb quietly said, "I guess I do."

Justice Carroll furrowed his brow, then turned to Lucy and said, "And do you, Lucille Mathilda Preston, take Sebastian Cole as your lawfully wedded husband?"

She gulped more loudly than before and said, "I guess so."

Looking even more perplexed, the justice asked, "Are you two sure you want to go ahead with this?"

Lucy let out a whispered "Yes," and Seb gave a short nod.

"I see." But, of course, he didn't. "Will you be exchanging rings?"

"Just the bride," Seb said as he reached into his pocket.

As he slipped the narrow gold ring on Lucy's finger, he saw that three little heart-shaped bangles dangled from the band. A letter was engraved on each small heart: P-E-T.

Seb's eyes cut to Lucy. "It belonged to Hazel's little girl," she whispered.

"Ahem," Justice Carroll said. "If you're ready, I now pronounce you man and wife. You may kiss your bride."

Seb hadn't thought ahead to this moment. Even though it was territory he'd explored before, leaning over and pressing his lips against Lucy's struck him as something new, as if it were the first time they'd ever kissed. He didn't have much chance to figure out what that might have meant, or even wonder if he'd completely lost his mind. In the next minute Hazel was upon him, giving him a congratulatory hug that practically knocked Seb off his feet.

After that, everything went by in a blur of paperwork, handshakes, and an urgency to get back to the relative sanity of the Pearly Gates. Jack, Seb noticed, neither shook his hand nor Lucy's. The corner of his mouth, however, continued to twitch all the way back to the saloon.

It was the strangest thing, Lucy thought the next morning, being married and yet not being married. After the wedding, Sebastian had headed right back to the saloon, and she went to her room to change out of her gown. When she reported for work that afternoon, the two of them were like strangers, as if they'd never met. Oh, they were polite to one another, but they couldn't hold a gaze for more than a second.

As distracted as she was, wondering if she'd made a dreadful mistake by dragging Sebastian into her troubles, Lucy's hostessing duties suffered terribly. Even when she decided to deliver the beers one at a time instead of piled up on her tray, she usually managed to slop liquid all over the table. Once, to her horror, she tripped and dumped a beer down the back of an unsuspecting gambler.

Understandably, Sebastian insisted that since customers were sparse, she ought to retire early. Lucy couldn't get out of the saloon fast enough.

The next morning, as she donned her yellow lawn dress in anticipation of her brother's arrival, Lucy couldn't quit thinking about her strained relationship with Sebastian. She'd gained the husband she needed, but in the process somehow lost a very special friend. Would Sebastian go through with the second part of her plan by meeting with Dusty? Or would he figure that he'd done enough by loaning her his name?

Lucy didn't have to wait long for an answer. The bellboy came to her door to inform her that she had visitors waiting downstairs. With a breath for courage, Lucy unlocked her connecting door and then lightly knocked on Sebastian's door.

"It's open," he called, inviting her in.

As Lucy took a tentative step into his room, she saw that Sebastian was fully dressed, sitting on the edge of his bed and tugging on his boots.

"My brother is downstairs," Lucy said. "Will you join us?"

Sebastian pushed off the mattress, adjusted his tie and jacket, and then said, "That's the plan, isn't it?"

"I wasn't sure you'd still want to be a part of all this."

His lip curled into a grin that looked suspiciously like a smirk as he said, "You must have me confused with Charlie. I'm a man of my word."

With that he escorted Lucy out of his room and down the stairs. When they reached the lobby, Dusty was nowhere to be seen.

Approaching the desk clerk, Lucy said, "The bellboy told me I had a visitor. Do you know what happened to him?"

His nose in the air, pinched as if he'd inhaled a foul odor, the clerk said, "Your visitors are waiting for you in the restaurant." Shifting his gaze to Sebastian, he added, "One of them claims that he is another of Miss Preston's brothers."

Sebastian and Lucy shot each other a quick glance. Then he said, "Oh, that must be Dusty. He's her natural brother and I'm just a family friend who once thought of himself as her brother."

"I see," the clerk muttered, although clearly he didn't.

Taking Lucy's arm, Sebastian extracted her from the uncomfortable conversation and led her into the dining room. She was wondering who her other visitor might be when she spotted Dusty and Charlie White sitting at a corner table. Although she was surprised by his presence, she figured now was as good a time as any for her former fiancé to hear the news about her marriage.

As they reached the table, Dusty looked up at Sebastian and said, "What's he doing here?"

"He's here at my request," Lucy quickly explained. Pointing at Charlie, she asked, "What's he doing here?"

"All in good time," Dusty replied, waving to the two empty chairs across from him and Charlie. "Sit yourselves down."

After she and Sebastian took their seats, Dusty ordered mugs of coffee and biscuits for everyone and then got right to it. "I brought Charlie with me because we found a way to keep you here in Emancipation."

"Really?" She exchanged a quick glance with Sebastian, who was frowning. "I can't imagine it's anything I'm interested in hearing."

"Give him a chance," Dusty said. "I think you'll like what you hear. Charlie?"

After shooting a nasty look at Sebastian, Charlie said, "Dusty and I spent a long time talking last night. I still have to figure out a way to pay Cherry the money I owe her, but I realize that I have no choice but to do my duty and marry you, today if possible."

Swapping another fast glance with Sebastian, Lucy swallowed her surprise. She noticed that his expression fairly screamed "You got me into this, now get me out."

To Lucy's relief, the waiter arrived with their order, giving her a moment in which to think. That was about all it took for her to realize that even if she hadn't married Sebastian yesterday, she wouldn't have jumped at Charlie's magnanimous offer. The idea of being married to Sebastian, even though it was a sham, held much more appeal than the real thing with Charlie White. As she considered all the time she'd wasted on Charlie, Lucy groaned out loud.

Sebastian leaned in close and asked, "Do we need to be excused for a few moments?"

"No," she whispered back. "I still like the plan the way it is."

"Secrets?" said Dusty. "Shouldn't you be whispering them to your intended here?"

"Forgive my rudeness," Lucy said, turning her attention to Charlie. "Thank you for your kind offer, but you're too late. Sebastian and I were married yesterday."

"What?" Dusty said against the rim of his mug, spewing coffee onto the white linen tablecloth. "You can't marry him. He's a gambler."

"I guess you didn't hear me. I already did marry Sebastian." Lucy slipped her arm through his and rested her head on his shoulder. "Last night was our first together as husband and wife."

Charlie went pale and gagged on a bite of biscuit. When he'd recovered, he spat, "This is preposterous."

"No more preposterous than you taking on a new fiancée when you moved here."

Left without a credible retort, Charlie turned to Dusty for advice.

"You might as well go on back to the bakery," Dusty said. "There's no point in your staying here now."

After dabbing his lips with his napkin, Charlie pushed

away from the table and said, "I expected better of you, Lucille. You'll come to regret your rash decision to toss in with the likes of him."

Withholding comment until Charlie had left, Lucy said to her brother, "Thanks for trying to help me, but as you can see, I managed quite well on my own."

Dusty regarded Sebastian, who remained silent, and then asked Lucy, "How do I know you're really married?"

Sebastian reached into his jacket and took out an envelope. As he started to hand it to Dusty, he glanced at it and said, "Oh, hell."

"What's wrong?" asked Lucy.

"This is a letter I got a couple of weeks ago. I stuck it in my jacket and forgot about it." Poking it into his breast pocket, again he reached inside his jacket again and withdrew another envelope. This one he handed to Dusty.

After studying the document a few minutes, Dusty sighed and said, "I don't know much about these things, but this looks pretty legal to me."

"I wouldn't lie to you," Lucy said, reaching over to pat her brother's hand.

"And I can't lie to Pa," he replied. "How do you think he's going to like hearing that you married a gambling man and that you still work in a saloon?"

She shrugged. "Why not tell him a different version of the truth? Say that I married a very nice businessman and that I work at *The Weekly Rustler*. He can't complain about that too much, can he?"

"I guess not." Dusty got out of his chair and walked around to where Lucy sat. "I'll leave you two to your wedding breakfast. Will you come down to the train station later and see me off?"

"Of course I will," she assured him.

Looking to Sebastian, he added, "I wish I could say I'm happy that you married my sister. If you don't take good care of her, you'll find out just how unhappy I can get."

"Point taken," Sebastian replied. "It's been a real pleasure."

After Dusty left the restaurant, Lucy and Sebastian endured several uncomfortable moments of silence. At length he finally said, "Would you mind telling me one thing? Why didn't you go ahead and accept Charlie's proposal? We could get an annulment today."

As she met his gaze, Lucy was struck by a shocking revelation, a sudden thought that exploded in her brain like fireworks: *Because you're the one I want.*

Fumbling around for some other explanation, she muttered, "I, uh, because he still loves Cherry, and besides, I, ah, don't think he'd want his wife getting involved with Mary Lease and her group when they come here in a few weeks for a political rally."

He nodded grimly. "Then I suppose it's just as well you didn't marry Charlie. I'm sure a fellow like him expects a wife who'll be content to care for him and raise his babies. Politics, careers, and babies don't mix."

There was something harsh about the way he said that, something she couldn't understand. Not that this surprised Lucy. How was she supposed to understand this man who was her husband and yet not her husband at all?

The next few days went by in a whirlwind. Hazel had to add four more pages to the *Rustler* to accommodate the new advertising and lengthy Letters to the Editor, which meant that Lucy was setting type almost day and night. She barely made it to work on time Wednesday and Thursday and was so tired, she had to leave early both nights. She supposed it was just as well. Exhaustion kept her from thinking about Sebastian, her feelings for him, and the fact that he continued to treat her as if she were a stranger.

By Friday afternoon, when the last *Rustler* rolled off the press, Lucy was dragging her feet, but elated as well. As usual, and the brightest part of the day was the fact that she was the first to read her column:

──────── *THE WEEKLY RUSTLER* ────────

Emancipation, Wyoming,   Vol. 1.
Friday, June 26, 1896   No. 40

ASK PENELOPE! FREE ADVICE!

Dear Penelope:
My wife has the crazy idea in her head that she is an "advanced" sort, and insists on doing such nonsense as running for public office and general politicking. I am thinking of taking a second wife.

What do you think of that, you [next word deleted at the discretion of the editor]?

Signed, King of His Castle

Dear Mr. King:
If you really must know, what I think is that you should be taken to a sturdy oak and hanged by the neck until you are dead.

In answer to your question, however, I suggest that you refer to your Bible. Adam exchanged a rib for a wife. It therefore stands to reason that you must give up a second rib for a second wife, and so on.

Considering this, perhaps my first suggestion would be a less painful solution to your problem.

Penelope

Chapter Thirteen

Friday afternoon at the Pearly Gates, Seb had just been congratulated on his marriage for something like the tenth time that day. He'd been trying desperately not to think about Lucy or the fact that she was his wife, and yet people kept coming up to him, slapping him on the back, offering well wishes, and reminding him of what he had—and especially of what he didn't have. He was losing the Lucy battle, and badly.

Whenever she was around, Seb watched her closely—as long as she wasn't looking his way—and, with an even keener eye, watched the customers who tried to catch her fancy. He recognized this behavior as possessive even as he understood that the only thing he possessed was a slip of paper.

If all that wasn't bad enough, he was drinking too much cognac, something that had never been a problem for him before. Even now the idea of a shot seemed almost irresistible. He thought he might be losing his mind.

"Seb," came a male voice, interrupting his dark thoughts. "I understand that cute little hostess of yours managed to get a snare around your neck. What hope is there for the rest of us bachelors if someone like you gets caught so easily?"

Seb looked up at Whitey Mills, the albino bartender from the Bucket down the street. "Caught me on my blind side," he simply said, in no mood to converse with the man.

Mills laughed. "Well, congratulations anyway. Some of us over at the Bucket are thinking about putting together a wedding party for you two. I'll let you know when it's settled."

Seb gave him a tight smile and then waited for the man to amble off to more amiable pastures. In a town like Emancipation, he thought darkly, secrets didn't last very long.

As he considered the differences between Denver and Emancipation, liking the slower, small-town life here better with the exception of gossip that spread like wildfire, again Seb pulled the forgotten letter out of his jacket. It was from Billy Renz, his manager at the Fire and Brimstone in Denver. He'd already read it twice but was morbidly drawn to have yet another look at it.

Hello, Seb, it read. *As you've probably noticed by checking your bank account, business is still booming here at the saloon. All is well, but I thought you might like to know that Kate has been poking around the place, asking about you. I don't know what kind, if any, information she has got, but I thought you ought to know. To be sure, she didn't get a thing out of me and never will. Hope all is as good at the Pearly Gates as it is here. Signed, Billy.*

Seb absently rubbed the notch on his ear as he thought back to the past and the fiasco that had been Kate. God, was any of this possible? He'd come to Emancipation ostensibly to look after his business interests, but what he'd really been after was a fresh start. Denver and his life there was a blur. He only knew that all he'd wanted to do in the beginning was to help Kate, to find a way to right the terrible wrong she'd suffered. What he'd gotten for his efforts was a kick in the teeth and a ruined life that had him packing up and leaving town in the dead of night. He wondered if he'd be leaving Emancipation the same way.

Thinking in those terms reminded Seb that in many ways

he'd fallen into the same trap with Lucy. He sighed heavily. The two women were nothing alike and yet, in the beginning, hadn't he been taken in by Kate's sweet disposition and charming ways? And now had she used that side of her nature to convince someone to tell her where he'd gone when he left Denver? Not many people knew his whereabouts, but he supposed it was possible that even now she was on her way to Emancipation. Seb shuddered at the thought, hoping to God those problems were behind him and that they wouldn't follow him here. He had enough trouble in Emancipation without Kate adding to the mix.

In the next moment, trouble of another kind backed into the saloon. Seb immediately recognized Lucy's backside as well as her well-worn traveling suit. She was trying to drag something into the room. Shoving out of his chair, he went to her aid.

"Need some help?" Seb asked, approaching her.

"Yes, thanks."

She straightened, and Seb saw that Lucy had a wheelbarrow filled with the newest edition of the *Rustler*.

"This is a bit much, isn't it?"

"Is it? You keep saying that, and we keep selling out." She plucked a paper out of the pile and handed it to him. "Notice anything different?"

Yeah, he thought: Lucy's eyes and smile were brighter than ever. A few loose hairs were stuck to the side of her neck, damp from her exertions. She'd never looked more desirable. Seb wanted her so badly at that moment, even his teeth ached.

"Well?" she persisted.

Seb glanced at the paper. "Looks the same to me."

"It's bigger," she announced, her smile huge. "Four pages bigger, to be exact. If this keeps up, Hazel is going to have to hire another woman to help set type."

It was bigger, Seb realized, and she'd done something

new to the front page that made the paper look more professional. Moseley wasn't going to like this. Thinking of his partner and another cause for concern, Seb's eye found the "Ask Penelope" column. When he'd finished reading it, he swallowed his admiration and slowly shook his head.

"What's wrong?" Lucy asked.

"It's a good thing this Penelope doesn't live in Emancipation. Where did you say she's from?"

"Um, I don't really know."

"Well, if she lived here, I think she might find *herself* hanging from a sturdy oak."

Lucy laughed. "That's all in how you look at it. I mean, the king of his castle is a bit of a boar, don't you think?"

"What I think doesn't matter." Nudging Lucy aside, Seb took hold of the wheelbarrow and pulled it across the threshold.

As he pushed the load across the saloon toward the newspaper rack, Lucy trailed along behind him. "Are we having the usual poker tournament tonight?" she asked.

"That," he replied as he began to unload the wheelbarrow, "and I'm raffling off a gold watch."

"More funds for the new school?"

Seb didn't answer at first. He finished stacking the newspapers and then finally turned to face her. The jolt he always got when setting eyes on Lucy was as strong as ever, but he finally felt more in control of himself.

"Actually," he explained, pleased by her interest in his work, "the proceeds from the raffle are going toward the political rally the city council is planning for Mary Lease and her band of female militants."

Lucy narrowed her eyes and studied him. "You don't like the suffrage movement, do you?"

"Except for the right to vote, not much."

"How can you feel that way and live in a town like Emancipation?"

Deep inside, Seb thought he knew exactly why, and that it had something to do with his mother. Since he wasn't about to go into that, he shrugged and said, "It's a matter of good business. We all do things we don't want to do in order to further our own causes, don't we?"

She looked away, head down for a moment, and then boldly looked him in the eye. "You've been dying to say something like that to me since Monday, haven't you?" She didn't pause long enough for Seb to get a word in. "You've been treating me like an outcast all week and I'm tired of it. If you're so upset about our arrangement, why don't you march on over to City Hall and get Justice Carroll to make an annulment? I can handle things alone from here on out."

"Lucy, I . . ." But Seb didn't know what to say. She was right—he had treated her badly—but they were his own demons eating him up, not hers. Because he could hardly explain that, even to himself, he simply said, "I'm willing to hold to our deal. I'm a man of his word, remember?"

When Lucy stormed out of the saloon, it was all she could do to keep from going down to City Hall herself and starting annulment proceedings. Instead she went to her room, filled her tub, and took a long, relaxing bath. When she'd calmed down enough to look at things through Sebastian's eyes, she realized that she would probably feel no different in his place. What must he be going through?

When she'd first come up with the idea of their marriage, Lucy'd had no idea that the townsfolk would take such an interest in their affairs. It seemed that was all anyone wanted to talk about these days. If Sebastian was getting even half of the congratulations that she was, and probably a good bit more teasing, she could hardly blame him for his mood.

Armed with a determination to be more understanding of his position, and secretly thrilled by the thought of being the temporary wife of such a man, Lucy donned her usual hostess getup and headed for a long night at the Pearly Gates.

The crowd was larger than usual for a poker night and, thanks to Sebastian's raffle, contained several of the town's leading women. As Lucy was juggling a tray filled with beers, Mayor Mattie Gerdy stopped her.

"I hear congratulations are in order," she said with a wink. "Sebastian Cole is quite a catch."

Struggling under her burden, although the mayor didn't seem to notice, Lucy said the only thing she could. "Thank you. We're, um, very happy."

"I can imagine."

As Lucy turned to head to table four, the mayor added, "Have you seen the new Penelope column yet?"

From over her shoulder, she gave a tentative, "Yes."

"Isn't she fabulous? I'd just love to meet her some time."

The six beers suddenly feeling like a pile of feathers on her tray, Lucy smiled and said, "Hazel will be happy to hear that you're so fond of the column."

Buoyed by the mayor's comments and others like them, the next few hours went by in a happy blur. With the boisterous crowd, Lucy was fortunate to have only spilled one beer, and that mishap occurred at the bar, where it didn't do much damage. Although she occasionally felt Sebastian's eyes on her, he was too busy dealing poker to pay her much mind. All in all, Lucy was having a very good night.

She'd just finished serving a table near the back of the room when she saw Charlie White come into the bar. Lucy noticed with a little flush of satisfaction that he was alone. As she worked her way back to the bar and passed Sebastian's table, he called out to her.

"What can I get you fellows?" she asked brightly.

As she took the orders, Lucy couldn't help but see that Sebastian had a bottle of cognac by his elbow. She knew that he never drank spirits while dealing and wondered if she and their circumstances had anything to do with his change of habits.

Catching his attention, she said, "Do you want anything else, Sebastian? Popcorn, peanuts . . . coffee?"

The eyes he turned on her weren't as cold as they'd been the last few days, but Lucy couldn't exactly think of them as warm. He seemed to be thinking something over, something that definitely had to do with her. Then he suddenly flashed her a tired but genuine smile.

"No, thanks. I'm fine—for now."

Flushed by something so simple as his smile, Lucy weaved her way back to the bar and signaled Pearl that she needed five more beers. As she waited for her order, she realized that Charlie was leaning against the counter about halfway down and shooting her dark looks. He was also drinking a beer.

Remembering the way he'd behaved the last time he'd had a few drinks, Lucy made it a point to stay out of his way. Her luck held until she went to the storeroom to get some more popcorn. When she headed back into the main room, Charlie was waiting for her outside the door.

"Lucille," he said slowly, "how are you?"

"Fine, Charlie, but I'm really busy."

"I need to talk to you."

"Not now. I'm working."

"Please," he begged. "I just need a minute of your time. Will you meet me outside on the boardwalk?"

Even talking to him here was against Lucy's better judgment. "We've said everything that needs to be said. There's no point in any more talk."

Tears sprang into Charlie's eyes. "I haven't said everything I need to. I promise, I won't take more than five minutes. Won't you do that much for me, an old friend?"

Instinct warned her that this was not a good idea, but Charlie looked so miserable, so downright pitiful, she simply couldn't refuse him. "Oh, all right, but just for a minute. You go on ahead and I'll be right behind you."

As soon as he left, Lucy ducked back into the storeroom, grabbed a handful of Sebastian's chocolate stars, and stuffed them into her apron pocket. After hollering to Pearl that she was going outside for a breath of air, Lucy made her way through the crowd of gamblers and headed for the boardwalk.

She found Charlie sitting at the far end, his legs dangling into the alley. Sitting down beside him, she popped a chocolate star in her mouth and said, "What is it?"

"How could you?"

"How could I what?"

"Marry that, that . . ." He made a gesture over his shoulder. "That vile gambler."

She shrugged. "How could you get engaged to a tart while you were engaged to me?"

"It's not the same thing. Cherry is a lovely young woman who was kind enough to loan me the money I needed to finish the bakery. It turned out to be far more expensive than I'd assumed."

"So you had to marry your banker?"

He hung his head. "There was a spark between us, I'll admit that, but after you came to town and I wasn't quite sure of my feelings for her any longer, she threatened to take the bakery from me. How could I leave her?"

Lucy didn't care. "How indeed?"

"Enough about Cherry. I want to talk about you and your dreadful mistake. This Cole fellow is nothing but trash."

Bristling at this, Lucy's voice was harsh as she said, "Don't talk about Sebastian that way. He's my husband and . . ."

She paused, recognizing the truth of what she was about to say. In an admission that shocked even her, she added, "He's also the man I love."

"But you can't love him!" Charlie jumped to his feet. "I can't believe this is happening, that I've lost you forever."

Rising to join him, Lucy said, "You lost me a long time ago, Charlie, about ten minutes after I arrived in Emancipation, to be exact."

"But I love you." Tears were in his eyes again, and this time a few rolled down his cheeks.

"Oh, Charlie, I'm sorry," she said, her heart going out to the boy she'd once loved. "But I'm sure Cherry will make you a fine wife, and you'll forget all about me again."

"Never," he sobbed. "I'll never forget you."

Charlie put his arms around her then, and Lucy allowed this one last embrace, wondering all the while if Sebastian would ever hold her like this again.

Inside the saloon, Seb was having trouble making sense of his cards. He recognized that he was drinking more than he should, and knew that he was spending way too much time thinking about Lucy and his troubles and not nearly enough time watching his cards and the other players. Deciding the best thing for him was a breath of fresh air, he tossed his cards in the center of the table.

"I'm out, boys," he declared, getting out of his chair. "Mack, will you take over the deal? I need a break."

Leaving his drink behind, Seb pushed his way through the crowd and stepped out on the boardwalk. There he stretched his arms high overhead, yawned, and sucked in a deep breath of sultry night air. He popped a chocolate star into his mouth and was thinking of taking a short walk around town when he glanced toward the end of the boardwalk and saw a couple embracing. Light from the saloon window spilled down on the pair, revealing them in profile.

Lucy was just about to push out of Charlie's arms when a chilling sensation washed over her. She actually felt Sebastian's icy gaze before she glanced over and saw him standing a few feet away.

Feeling guilty and not knowing exactly why, she quickly pushed out of Charlie's arms.

By then, Sebastian was bearing down on them, fists clenched, jaw tight.

When he reached them, he didn't say a word; didn't even glance Lucy's way. He simply drew back his fist and buried it in Charlie's face.

Charlie flew off the boardwalk backward and landed on his backside. His voice nasal and high-pitched, he wailed, "You broke my nose."

"I'll break more than that," Sebastian threatened, "if you ever again so much as lay a hand on my wife."

Then he turned to Lucy. She gulped, fearful of the storm clouds building in his gray eyes. She couldn't think of a thing to say.

He snarled, "Don't you think it's time you went back to the hotel?"

It wasn't really a question. Sebastian took Lucy by the hand and pulled her along with him. He so overwhelmed her, she didn't even balk when he dragged her up the stairs, unlocked the door to his own room, and pulled her inside. He didn't bother with lights, not that they were needed. Curtains still opened, the room was bathed in the soft glow of moonlight and flickers of illumination from neighboring saloons.

Without so much as a word, Sebastian swept Lucy into his arms, crossed the room, and dumped her in the middle of his bed.

Mute through all of this, frightened and yet curiously excited, Lucy watched Sebastian as he tore off his jacket and shirt and then kicked off his boots. With the exception of her brothers, and mostly when they were younger, this was the first time she'd ever gazed upon a man who was naked to the waist.

She sucked in a breath, mesmerized by the sight of Sebastian's smooth, muscled body and tapered waist, the way his skin glistened in the semidarkness.

Sebastian was pulling off his belt when Lucy finally found her voice. "W-what are you doing?"

He pinned her with a feral look she'd never seen before; not from anything human, certainly no man.

Then, his voice a husky promise, Sebastian said, "I'm going to get Charlie White out of your mind once and for all."

Chapter Fourteen

Lucy's heart was pounding so hard, she couldn't hear herself think. It occurred to her then that she couldn't think at all. It was always like this when Sebastian got too close, as if her mind was paralyzed.

After stripping off his belt, he climbed onto the bed beside her and slipped one arm beneath her waist. He fumbled there a minute and then deftly pulled off her apron. As he tossed the garment aside, a few chocolate stars rained down on Lucy's head and bounced off the pillow beneath her. Sebastian didn't seem to notice. He was staring into her eyes, his gaze intense and probing, and working on the drawstring that kept her blouse from dipping too low.

His voice deep and a little breathless, he said, "I'm afraid I don't feel like much of a gentleman tonight. Once I touch you, Lucy, I don't think I'll be able to stop. Tell me to leave now, and I'll go."

Apparently her vocal cords were paralyzed, too. Modesty, decency, decorum, everything told her to stop this now, that it was wrong, but Lucy's voice still wouldn't cooperate. Instead of protesting, she just stared back at him, vaguely aware that she was running the tip of her tongue across her upper lip.

Sebastian lowered his head, pulled the drawstring free with his teeth, and pressed a kiss between her breasts. After touching the same spot with his tongue, he traveled up her throat, over her chin, and brought his mouth to rest against her lips. Lucy shivered all over even as heat erupted in her groin.

Sebastian suddenly pulled away from her mouth and said, "God, you taste like chocolate."

"So do you," she murmured back. Vocal paralysis seemed to be a tempermental condition, going and coming at will.

Sebastian kissed her again, his hands busier than before, and the next thing Lucy knew, she was lying there in nothing but her chemise. It was bunched up around her throat. She thought of reaching up and pulling the garment down, but then Sebastian's mouth skimmed the crown of her right breast, paralyzing her entire body.

"You haven't told me to go yet," he whispered against her skin. "This is your last chance."

There were a million reasons to send him away, and at least as many to keep Sebastian right where he was. They were married, weren't they? What difference did it make for how long? An annulment was probably out of the question anyway. No one would believe that they hadn't been intimate after weeks of wedded bliss. She would be a divorced woman whether the marriage was consummated or not.

"Well?" His husky voice washed over her like a warm bath.

Lucy met his gaze. What if she never again had a chance to lie in the arms of the man she loved? She probably would have gone on rationalizing, but her mind deserted her again, completely giving her body up to Sebastian and the fiery sensations evoked by his touch.

"What's it to be?" he whispered darkly, gentle fingertips skimming over her belly, heading south, doing unspeakable things that made her writhe with desire.

Lucy's breath caught in her throat but she managed to say, "Don't go."

Sebastian left her for a moment then, long enough for Lucy to wonder if she'd accidentally told him to go away, and then she realized he was shedding his trousers. When he came back to her, all hard, naked muscle, he rolled onto her body and spread her legs with his knee. She was quivering inside, trembling with anticipation and maybe a little bit of fear as he eased himself into position.

He hesitated there a moment, peering down at her with a tenderness that made her heart ache, and then plunged ahead. Lucy felt the resistance in her body as he sought entrance and instinctly shifted her hips to accommodate him. He pulled back and thrust harder, plunging through the barrier. Unable to stop herself, Lucy cried out as a searing pain shot through her. Sebastian stilled at once.

Breathing heavily, he whispered, "Are you all right?"

She blinked away a single tear. "I'm more than all right."

He laughed softly and nestled his lips in the hollow at her throat. Feeling bold, needing something more than this, Lucy shifted her hips and took him more fully into her body.

Sebastian stiffened all over. "Hold still a minute and relax."

"I'm all right," she insisted, ever so much more than simply all right.

"I'm not. Hold still."

Not understanding, she did as he asked and went limp, as she had that night on the trail when he'd taken her into his arms and ravished her mouth. After a moment Sebastian's lips found the tip of her ear, the soft spot at her temple, and then settled on her mouth, where his kisses became a long, sensuous feast. When he finally began to move again, starting slowly, gently, passion overtook them both, driving them to frenzied peaks that left them drained and exhausted.

He remained entwined with her for several long, pulsating moments, and then Sebastian rolled over onto his back.

"I think my heart exploded," he said, bringing his hands to his chest.

"Something did," she admitted, not able to give her responses a name.

Sebastian abruptly sat up, one of his hands digging at his chest. "What the hell is this?"

Lucy glanced over and saw a dark blob tangled in the hairs there. She had a pretty good idea what it might be. "It could be a chocolate star," she ventured.

Sebastian yanked it out, along with a couple of chest hairs. Then he gave it a sniff. "That's exactly what it is. I wonder how that got there?"

She shrugged.

Leaning on one elbow and looking her over, Sebastian plucked a melted star out of Lucy's hair. "Where did these come from?"

"Umm, my apron?"

"But where did you get them?"

Eyes wide, as innocent as she could make them, Lucy admitted, "Your storeroom?"

"You've been helping yourself to my secret cache of chocolate?"

"Maybe it's not such a secret. I'm not the only one who knows where you keep them."

"Don't try to blame anyone else for this. I caught you red-handed."

"Actually, that would probably be brown-handed."

"You think this is funny?" His eyes told her that it was. "This is a bad thing, stealing from your employer, very bad."

"I'm sorry."

Sebastian hovered over her. "Sorry isn't good enough. I'm going to have to punish you for this."

Lucy watched him with enormous, fascinated eyes as he plucked chocolate stars off the pillow and sheets. He buried a few of them between her breasts and then placed a couple on her tummy and even below.

When he lowered his head and began licking the melting chocolate from her breasts, Sebastian murmured, "I intend to find every last one of these, and then, even if it takes me all night long, I'm going to punish you severely."

Oh, my stars!

When Lucy awoke the next morning, she wondered if any woman alive had ever been punished as thoroughly or deliciously as she had been during the night. As she thought about all the wicked things Sebastian had done, the way he'd used his tongue, she chuckled to herself, something that sounded like a girlish giggle. She stretched her arms high overhead, wriggled her backside against the soft down mattress, and then rolled over to see if Sebastian was feeling the same way.

His side of the bed was empty. Had he left her here alone or simply stepped into the water closet? She was listening intently, hoping he was just those few feet away, when the main door suddenly opened.

Lucy clutched the sheet and drew it up to her chin.

"Oh, you're awake," Sebastian said as he stepped into the room carrying a big silver tray. Kicking the door shut behind him, he crossed the room and deposited the tray on the table next to the bed. Then he sat down on the mattress beside her.

"How are you this morning?" he asked.

Tongue paralysis set in again. She blushed and looked away.

Sebastian brushed an errant strand of hair away from her cheek and said, "I feel that I owe you an apology for taking advantage of you the way I did last night. I'd like to blame cognac for my behavior, but that would be the coward's way out."

Lucy hadn't expected this. More cuddling perhaps, a little more kissing, but not remorse. She held up her chin and said, "I could have told you to go and I didn't. You have nothing to apologize for."

"I don't recall giving you much choice in the matter."

She shrugged, searching for a way to end the uncomfortable conversation. "What happened last night happened. If we hadn't consummated the marriage, anybody, even my father if he came here, could have had it annulled—right?"

He considered this. "I suppose."

"Then it's settled. No more apologizing."

"Fair enough, but I did bring you a peace offering." Gesturing toward the tray, he added, "There's coffee and a sweet cake. If you want something else, I'd be happy to get it for you."

Lucy glanced at the tray. Smiling to herself, she said, "Charlie makes those Hot Cross Buns down at his bakery."

"He does?"

She nodded. "I'm not too fond of them."

Sebastian got up, pinched the sweet roll off the plate as if it were a cockroach, and tossed it out the opened window and into the street below.

"I could get you a biscuit," he suggested.

"I think I'd rather have some more chocolate," she said, her cheeks suddenly on fire. God, how brazen she'd become!

"Chocolate, huh?"

Sebastian tugged the sheet out from beneath her chin and let it drop into her lap. After wetting his fingertip, he dragged it along the underside of her left breast and then brought that finger to his mouth.

"Hmmm, looks like I missed some," he murmured, licking what was left of the star from his skin. "Chocolate for breakfast suddenly sounds like a damn fine idea."

It was noon before Seb left Lucy to her toilette and headed on over to the Pearly Gates. Although he prided himself on hiring only the best, most trusted people he could employ, he had more than just a little remorse about leaving Black Jack in charge of the big poker game and the saloon last night. He hadn't even bothered to tell him that he was leaving, much less that he wouldn't be back.

As he walked, he tried to think of a plausible excuse, something Jack could swallow without guessing the truth. Seb could bluff a gambler out of aces full if he set his mind to it, but he wasn't much of a liar, especially when it came to Jack.

Steeling himself, he walked into the saloon. Pearl was tending to a smattering of patrons at the bar. She glanced over at him, winked, and then went back to her work. Five townsmen sat at one of the tables playing cards; whist, Seb thought. Little Joe was hunkered down by the piano having a meal of peanuts and popcorn. Black Jack sat alone at his usual table, practicing his shuffle.

As Seb approached, Jack looked up from his cards and said, "About time you came back."

Seb dropped into the chair beside him. "Sorry I left you alone like that last night. I had some . . . things to take care of."

"No problem." The corner of Jack's mouth was twitching. "I might have gone looking for you, but then I noticed that Lucy was gone, too."

"Lucy, right. She, ah . . . I sent her to the hotel early. I guess I should have told you so you wouldn't worry about her."

"I wasn't worried." The twitch threatened to break into a full-blown grin.

Not about to be drawn any further into this conversation, Seb asked, "How did business go last night?"

"Safe's full."

He nodded appreciatively. "Anything happen I should know about?"

Jack's eyebrows lifted marginally, his idea of a shrug.

"Not last night, but Moseley came by this morning looking for you."

Seb pushed out of his chair. "Well, I guess I'd better go on down to the newspaper office and see what he wants."

As he turned to leave, Whitey Mills stopped him. In addition to his pale skin, white hair, eyebrows, and scraggly beard, today the man was wearing a white shirt. The only color he could claim was the grim yellow of his teeth, which were few and far between.

"We got it all worked out," Whitey said, excitement gleaming in his pale eyes.

"What's worked out?"

"The wedding party for you and the missus at the Bucket."

Behind him Seb was sure he'd heard the impossible. Laughter. He glanced over his shoulder. The twitch was still there, but Jack's lips were clamped tighter than a spinster's thighs.

"It's going to be next Sunday around noon," Whitey continued. "We're making it an open house so anyone can come."

Wonderful. The entire town would turn out to celebrate a mock wedding, one that was getting way too close to the real thing for Seb's comfort. Then he thought of a way out.

"Did you say the party is next Sunday? You know that saloons aren't allowed to be open on Sundays."

"We got a special permit, just for you."

Left with no choice, Seb muttered, "Thanks. I'm sure Lucy will be pleased, too."

Whitey slapped him on the shoulder. "Hell, it's the least we can do."

As Whitey walked away, Seb heard Jack call to him from behind.

"Seb?"

He looked over his shoulder. "What?"

"You might want to wipe that silly grin off your face before you see Moseley."

Those words rang in Seb's ears as he made his way to the

offices of the Emancipation *Tribune*. The building was plain, made of wooden planks painted white, and nestled between the bank and a millinery shop. The front door opened into the main office, where five workmen were busy at tables and machines. Even though the press wasn't running, a steady clacking assaulted his ears, and the air was thick with the odor of ink and turpentine.

Seb nodded a greeting to the men as he passed them and headed straight for the small office at the back of the shop. Knocking as he opened the door and stepped into the room, he said, "You wanted to see me?"

Moseley looked up from the papers scattered across his desk. "Seb. Thanks for stopping by. Have a seat."

He fell into the lone chair across the desk and cut right to it. "Do we have problems?"

"Nothing too serious, if that's what you mean, but I must say, the *Rustler* is cutting into our business."

This came as no surprise. At the Pearly Gates, the *Rustler* was selling out within hours, while copies of the *Tribune* languished on the rack.

"Any luck tracking this Penelope down?"

Moseley shook his bald head. "None. I've contacted everyone I know in Chicago, and they've never heard of her or her column."

"Maybe Hazel hasn't been entirely honest with us."

"That's why I wanted to talk to you. Since your wife works for the woman, I was thinking maybe you could get her to poke around and find out what she can about Penelope."

Seb considered this and then shook his head. "I've asked her about Penelope before, and she doesn't know who the woman is."

"Quite right, but have you asked her to, you know, dig a little deeper, maybe behind Hazel's back?"

"No." He had an idea it wouldn't do much good if he did ask, but he said, "I'll see what I can do."

"Good. If we can't get that woman to write a column for

us, too, we're going to have to find someone who will. I can't believe the interest this town has in an advice column."

Seb might have agreed but then realized he was just as curious as anyone to see what Penelope had to say each Friday. He laughed under his breath.

"You're looking well," Moseley commented, palms together, fingers tented, eyes twinkling through his glasses. "Marriage must really agree with you."

What was it with his business associates? Seb wondered. And how was it any of their business to pry into his private life? He abruptly got out of his chair.

"If that's all," he said, "I've really got to get back to the saloon."

"Yes, yes, and please make sure to give my greetings to the little woman."

Lucy came waltzing into the saloon shortly after Sebastian left. She'd indulged herself in a lilac-scented bath first, and then dressed in her yellow lawn dress. Feeling completely feminine and as light as a feather, she impulsively made a detour to Gerdy's mercantile and picked out a frilly new bonnet—the first real purchase she'd made using money she'd earned herself.

Feeling ridiculously happy, as if euphoria such as this should be against the law, Lucy practically floated into the saloon.

Spotting Black Jack near the door, she said, "Good afternoon, Jack. How are you this fine day?"

He simply nodded, and the corner of his mouth began to twitch. Lucy wondered if the man had some kind of nervous tick. "Is Sebastian in the storeroom?"

He shook his head. "Had some business to tend to. He'll be back soon."

"In that case, I guess I'd better get to work."

She flounced off to the bar and stashed the hatbox under

the counter. After grabbing a clean apron, she said, "Hello, Pearl. How are you?"

She curled her upper lip. "Not as good as you, I'd say. How'd you do it?"

"What?"

"Trap Seb into marrying you."

The question not only surprised Lucy but also sent a jolt through her. She hadn't looked at it quite like that before, but in many ways she supposed she had trapped Sebastian. Theirs was hardly a normal romance or marriage. In any case, Lucy wasn't going to discuss the hows and whys with this woman.

Ducking the issue entirely, she said, "I think that's a question for Sebastian."

Pearl shrugged. "Then here's a question for you: Are you gonna wear that sappy smile all night long?"

Lucy didn't have to think about that for long. "Probably."

"Then you might as well get to work." She shoved a clean tray across the bar and went back to her duties.

Undaunted by Pearl's attitude—the woman had never warmed to her anyway—Lucy snatched up the tray and went off to check on the smattering of customers. She'd just finished serving a table of cowhands when she saw Merry— or Cherry—come through the door. She was wearing men's clothing and a pair of blond pigtails draped over her shoulders from beneath a floppy-brimmed hat.

Whoever she was, she was making a beeline for Lucy.

Preparing herself for the confrontation, she slid her tray onto an empty table and doubled up her fists.

As the woman approached, she asked, "Is it true that you bamboozled Seb into marrying you?"

Keeping her distance, Lucy said, "First tell me which twin you are and if you ever answer to the name Muffin."

She looked at Lucy as if she'd gone crazy. "What?"

"Just checking . . . Merry?"

"Yes, it's Merry. Now what's all this about you and Seb?"

Lucy relaxed her hands but kept her distance. "There isn't much to tell. We got married."

"But you hardly know each other."

Lucy reached over to pick up her tray, intending to end the conversation. As she prepared to dismiss Merry, Sebastian came into the saloon, and Lucy caught his eye. Their gazes locked and held for several beats.

"Oh, my gawd," Merry muttered. "I think I'm going to be sick." Then she stomped off toward the bar.

By then, Sebastian had reached Lucy. "What was that all about?" he asked.

"I think we'd better talk about this in the storeroom."

He frowned but said, "All right."

Once inside the room, he asked, "What's the problem?"

She meant to tell him what Pearl and Merry had said and then ask his advice on handling such questions. What came out of Lucy's mouth was, "I need a kiss."

Sebastian gave her a hungry look. Lucy was pretty sure he wasn't thinking about fried chicken and mashed potatoes. Chocolate stars were a possibility.

"I think that can be arranged." He pulled her hard against his body and took her mouth with his, giving her lots of tongue. His hands cupped her bottom and held her fast, and all Lucy could think about was what those hands could do to her, how they made her feel. Warmth spread through her abdomen and a sense of heaviness filled her below.

Then Sebastian ended the kiss and set her away from him.

"More," she said, her lashes bobbing against her cheeks.

"Not here."

"But why not?"

"I can't spend the night around my customers looking like this."

She followed his gaze down to the tent he'd made of the front of his pants. "Oh."

"It'll be better for us both if I try to ignore you the rest of the night." He kissed the tip of her nose. "Wasn't there something you wanted to talk to me about?"

"Oh, um, it's about Pearl and Merry and such. They're saying I trapped and bamboozled you, see, and I know that I probably did, but I don't know how much, or even if I should—"

Sebastian cut her off with a finger against her lips, then quickly replaced the finger with a brief kiss. "Tell them our marriage is none of their business."

That sounded good. "All right, I will."

Turning to the shelf behind him, Sebastian lifted the lid on a big tin canister, grabbed a handful of chocolate stars, and dropped them into the pocket of her apron.

"Save those for later," he said with a wink. "You'd better get back to work. I'll be along in a minute."

Blushing, she started for the door.

"And Lucy?" he called after her. "When I get back to the hotel tonight, you'd better be in my bed."

That was pretty much the way things went for Lucy the rest of the week. Townsfolk continued to hurl questions about her marriage, though none so intrusive as Merry and Pearl, and she somehow managed to field them all. Although they'd never discussed their lodging arrangements, and never was it suggested that she move into Sebastian's suite, Lucy kept her room and spent most days there working on the column. Sebastian didn't seem to mind. He was busy working on the festivities for the upcoming Fourth of July celebration. If she wasn't in her room, she was helping Hazel at the *Rustler*. Nights were spent in Sebastian's bed and in his arms. Though Lucy knew the marriage wasn't real and that it would end soon, she couldn't remember a time in her life when she'd been happier.

Now that Friday was upon her, Lucy was again the first to gaze upon her newest, and in many ways most challenging, Penelope column:

THE WEEKLY RUSTLER

Emancipation, Wyoming,	Vol. 1
Friday, July 3, 1896	No.41

ASK PENELOPE! FREE ADVICE!

Dear Penelope:
Some of us in town have been wondering—just who are you, anyway? You've been writing some pretty highfaluting advice for the men and women of Emancipation. What are your credentials and why should we listen to you?

Signed, A Few Concerned Citizens

Dear Concerned Citizens:
In reply to your inquiry, I would very much like to say, who the devil are you? That, of course, would break the code of anonymity this paper has shrewdly initiated, as does your question.

If it will ease your collective minds, you might think of me in this manner: I am every man and woman in this town, the dust in the wind, and the leaves on the trees.

My answers are based, I would hope, on pure common sense and, when necessary, gleaned from the proper authorities.

Perhaps you would feel better if you were to think of me from now on as Penelope, wife of Odysseus, and know that I am your true and faithful servant.

Penelope

Chapter Fifteen

Later that afternoon Seb settled in at a corner table and read the latest "Ask Penelope" column. He read it twice. The first time through he'd been distracted with thoughts of Lucy and the fact that he'd yet to seek her help in identifying the illusive Penelope. The second time he had to shake his head in admiration. The *Tribune* simply had to get this woman on the payroll.

As Lucy fluttered by him with a tray of beers, Seb caught the edge of her skirt. "When you've finished delivering those, would you mind coming back and joining me for a minute?"

She glanced around the room. "Everyone should be all right for a while. I'll be right back."

Seb figured that barring a mishap, this would give him a minute or two to figure out how to broach the subject. As it turned out, one of Lucy's customers decided to get out of his chair at the same moment she arrived. His head collided with the tray and the entire load wound up on the floor. By the time Lucy cleaned up the mess and delivered a fresh order of beers, Seb had a full fifteen minutes to consider the conversation. He still didn't know what to say.

When Lucy arrived at his table, she settled into the chair beside him and said, "Sorry about the mess over there. It wasn't my fault."

He patted the back of her hand. "I know. Don't worry about it."

She eyed the newspaper. "I see you have the new *Rustler*. Have you had a chance to read it yet?"

"That's what I want to talk to you about." Seb tapped his finger against the advice column. "I'd like to know more about this Penelope."

Her smile faded and Lucy raised her chin a notch. "Why? So you can run her out of town on a rail?"

Seb raised an eyebrow. "I thought she lived in Chicago."

"That was, umm, just a figure of speech. I know you hate the Penelope column."

"Actually, I don't hate it at all. Near as I can figure, almost everyone in town can't wait to read her column. I think she's very clever."

"You do?" Lucy's eyes brightened and her smile was like the sun parting the clouds. "But I thought you considered her nothing more than a gasbag."

He shrugged. "She may be a gasbag, but she's a very smart gasbag, and a damn good businesswoman."

Lucy's eyes took on a sheen and her expression softened. For a minute, Seb thought she might even break out in tears.

Then she said, "Thank you. Umm, I'll be sure to pass your praise on to Penelope."

"Then you do know her?"

Lucy hated this conversation, hated even more the lies she would have to tell Sebastian. She looked away from him as she said, "What I meant to say, see, is that Hazel knows her. You know I just set the type. Hazel will pass on your kind words."

"O-k-a-y," he said slowly. "If I understand you, Hazel is the only one who has contact with this Penelope?"

"Yes, that's right."

He nodded thoughtfully. "Then I'd like to ask you to do me a favor. Do you think you could poke around in Hazel's desk and find Penelope's address in Chicago?"

That was the last thing Lucy expected. "Why on earth would you want her address? I already told you to drop a note in the editor's box if you have a question for Penelope."

"I don't have a question for her. Gerald Moseley at the *Tribune* is a good friend of mine. He wants to contact Penelope. I said I'd see what I could do."

So that was it: Moseley wanted the advice column for his own newspaper, thereby possibly putting the *Rustler* out of business. Lucy stiffened her spine. "You can tell Mr. Moseley that Penelope writes exclusively for the *Rustler*, so there's no need to contact her."

Sebastian pressed his lips together, thinking something over. Finally he said, "I didn't want to have to tell you this, but maybe I should. I'm the one who wants the address because I hold a substantial interest in the *Tribune*."

Lucy almost fell out of her chair. "Since when?"

"I was instrumental in bringing the *Tribune* to Emancipation, but I did it as a silent partner. I'd prefer that no one in town knows about my involvement with the paper, so I hope you'll keep this to yourself."

Lucy was stunned, but at least that explained why Sebastian advertised the Pearly Gates in the *Tribune* and not in the *Rustler*. She swallowed hard. "Your secret is safe with me. As for Penelope, I, umm, will see what I can do, but I hope you understand that Hazel is a good friend of mine."

"I understand your loyalty to her, believe me. I just don't see why Penelope can't write for both newspapers, do you?"

"Actually, I do see a problem there. If folks can read her column in the *Tribune,* they'll stop buying the *Rustler* and Hazel will probably have to shut down."

Sebastian shrugged. "Welcome to the business world, Lucy. Sometimes things just work out that way."

Not if she had anything to do with it.

As she went about her hostessing duties that night, Lucy thought long and hard about Sebastian's request, along with her feelings for him and her obligation to Hazel. She even considered taking him into her confidence and confessing that she was Penelope. But then she remembered the vow she'd made to Hazel. She couldn't very well expose her other identity without getting Hazel's permission, and Lucy didn't want to trouble her now that things were finally going so well. In the end, and left with little choice, Lucy decided to leave things as they were, and to tell Sebastian that she couldn't find an address for Penelope. Which was, in fact, the truth. Sort of.

The next day dawned bright and beautiful and a little too hot for Lucy's comfort. As the Fourth of July festivities got underway, the sun gave way to overcast skies and the heat became oppressive. Main Street had been blocked off to all horse traffic, and Emancipation's children had free run of the town. Some were playing organized games like potato races or catching a greased pig, and others were running amok waving sparklers, although the effect was pretty much lost in the daylight. Sebastian's contribution was a watermelon-eating contest, which was just beginning.

Lucy, who absolutely adored watermelon, was the first to sign up. She found herself at a long table in front of the saloon along with a dozen other contestants, none of them over the age of twelve. In addition to the apron around her waist, she tied one around her neck in hopes of keeping her yellow dress reasonably clean.

"Is everyone ready?" Sebastian asked.

Lucy nodded, focusing on the pile of watermelon wedges in front of her.

"On your mark, get set . . . go!"

Lucy dove into the first wedge, barely coming up for air, and then flung the rind to the side. She'd only managed to work her way through three wedges before Sebastian's voice rang out again.

"We have a winner," he announced.

Lucy looked up, startled to see Sebastian holding Little Joe's arm aloft. The kid was as skinny as a bed slat, yet the table in front of him contained a pile of empty rinds.

"How did you do that?" Lucy asked, amazed. "Where did you put it all?"

Little Joe beamed. "I coulda ate more. That weren't nothing."

He snatched the prize out of Sebastian's hand—a certificate for a free supper at the Palace Arms restaurant—and took off running down the street.

Shaking her head in amazement, Lucy said, "Joe's parents must have a time keeping that little boy full."

Sebastian reached over to pick a few watermelon seeds out of her hair. "Little Joe doesn't have any parents. All he had was his father, and he died after a fall from his horse. That's when Joe became the official town orphan."

"Orphan? You mean nobody in this town would take the poor boy in?"

Sebastian laughed. "Oh, plenty tried. We do have laws around here about youngsters on the loose, but every time he got sent somewhere, he just ran away and went back to his father's shack at the edge of town. The council finally gave up and decided to let him live there."

"But who looks after him?"

"We all do. Little Joe can get a free meal just about anywhere in town, and several of us hire him to do odd jobs, like sweeping up the saloon. He makes out all right."

Coming from a large and loving family, Lucy wondered if all right was good enough when it came time to be tucked in at night. With the exception of Fridays, when she brought the *Rustler* to the saloon, Little Joe was usually gone for the day when she came to work. Lucy made a mental note to be extra kind to him from here on out.

"Where are you?" came Sebastian's voice, breaking into her thoughts.

"Huh? Oh, I was just thinking about Little Joe and feeling terrible about him being alone like that."

Sebastian's expression darkened. "Sometimes being alone is better than the alternative."

With that curious statement, he went back into the saloon. Lucy followed after him and resumed her hostessing duties.

The rest of the day went by in a blur of beer mugs and the biggest potluck feast she'd ever seen. Tables set up along Main Street featured pies of every description, several varieties of canned pickles, beets, and other vegetables, and fancy breads and rolls. The heavenly aroma of fried chicken, suckling pig turning slowly over a coal fire, and roasted beef filled the air. In front of Gerdy's Mercantile, Mattie sat churning a big batch of tutti-frutti ice cream. By the time the sun went down, Lucy was not only exhausted from delivering beers all day, she was so full of all the fare she'd sampled that she had to loosen the knot on her apron.

When she walked outside for a breath of air, she saw that Sebastian was in the street helping to set up the fireworks display. He glanced her way, said something to Black Jack, who was down on his knees with a large rocket, and then made his way to the boardwalk.

"You look tired," Sebastian said, brushing the hair out of her eyes. "Are you going to stay awake long enough to watch the fireworks?"

"I wouldn't miss them for anything," she replied with a yawn. "How soon are they going to start?"

Sebastian looked up at the sky. "Soon, or else we're going to get rained out."

Lucy hadn't noticed it until then, but a northern wind was whipping through town and the sky was filled with thunderclouds. In the distance she caught a glimpse of a lightning bolt. An involuntary shiver racked her spine.

"Are you cold?" Sebastian asked, even though the evening was still sultry.

"No. I just don't like thunderstorms very much."

"You must have had your share of them in Kansas City."

"Yes, and that's why I don't like them. It seems like I spent half of every summer hiding in the cellar."

Seb laughed as the first of the rockets blasted into the sky. Walking Lucy over to the edge of the boardwalk and into the alley for a better view, he stood behind her, both hands on her shoulders, taking in the show along with her.

He wasn't sure when his hands slipped down from her shoulders to her waist or how he'd managed to tug her backside up tight against his hips, but it felt right, Lucy cradled in his arms. As he kissed the top of her head, Seb happened to look over and caught Jack watching him intently.

Heading toward them, Jack passed by Seb and muttered, "I'll lock up tonight."

Lucy twisted in his arms to ask, "What did he say?"

"That he's giving us the rest of the night off."

After an explosion of red, white, and blue rockets, someone shouted a countdown, and then twenty or more big rockets went off at the same time. After that impressive display, the sky went quiet.

Sounding disappointed, Lucy said, "Are the fireworks over?"

"No," Seb assured her, taking her by the hand and heading for the hotel. "The fireworks have only begun."

Late the next morning, Seb slipped out of bed, dressed, and went downstairs. When he returned to the room with a tray of coffee, biscuits, and chokecherry jam, he was surprised to see that Lucy wasn't there. After setting the tray on the nighttable, he went to the connecting door. Her side was closed. Hoping to catch a glimpse of Lucy in her bath, he knocked and opened the door at the same time.

Instead of lounging in the tub, she was wearing a dressing gown and sitting at her desk going through some papers. She looked up, wide-eyed, and then quickly shoved the papers into the desk drawer.

"What are you doing?" Seb asked.

"Oh, umm, writing a letter home to my parents. I was sure I'd have heard from them before now, so I'm thinking maybe they're waiting for me to offer some kind of explanation about our marriage."

Seb supposed this was a reasonable explanation, and yet he sensed that Lucy hadn't been entirely forthcoming. He was sure she'd been doing more than simply writing a letter home, but he couldn't grasp what it might be.

As he turned to leave her to whatever she was doing, Lucy called to him. "Could you come in for a minute? I need some advice."

Maybe she would tell him what she'd really been up to. Seb walked into the room.

Lucy moved over to her tiny bed, where she'd laid out a pale blue dress with a gray collar and cuffs. She said, "This is the second-day dress my mother made for the day after my wedding. Should I wear it to the party today, or should I wear the gown we were married in?"

Seb couldn't help but laugh.

Lucy's expression fell. "I wanted to look nice. The wedding gown and the second-day dress are the best things I own."

"Let me explain: The party is at the Bucket, and the Bucket isn't exactly the Pearly Gates."

She cocked her head, still not understanding.

"You'd be too dressed up if you wore your hostess getup to this little shindig."

"Oh, I see." Her wistful gaze fell on the blue dress, and then she said, "I don't want to wear my working clothes to the party. I have a black skirt and a nice white blouse. Will that do?"

"Sounds perfect." Again Seb headed for the door. "I brought you some coffee and biscuits, and then I guess you'd better get dressed. They're expecting us shortly after noon."

The blouse Lucy chose to wear was her favorite, with large leg-of-mutton sleeves and a high collar trimmed in lace. Her bell skirt featured a dust ruffle and made feminine swishing sounds as she walked. Then she topped the look with her new bonnet, a black stiff-brimmed hat trimmed with several loops of pink ribbon that formed a large bow, with clusters of white flowers woven throughout.

When she stepped into the Bucket that afternoon, Lucy immediately wished she'd paid more attention to Sebastian's advice and worn her hostessing getup.

There was no flooring, only dirt, and dust and tobacco smoke hung over the room like a muddy cloud. The walls were covered in chromos advertising brands of whiskey and beer, prints of muscular boxers, and the stuffed heads of a variety of animals, including a deer head with missing clumps of hide. Hanging behind the cherry wood bar was a large print of a semi-nude woman. She was wearing a camisole that barely covered her nipples and a pair of bloomers. One of her legs was drawn up and wrapped around the back of her neck, leaving her foot to stick out from behind her ear like an antler. A battered spittoon sat in front of the bar, but from what Lucy could see, most of the chewers couldn't be bothered to walk over to it. Dark stains spotted the dirt floor, and she was pretty sure they weren't from spilled beer.

"Well?" Sebastian asked. "What do you think?"

"I think I'd like to go back to the hotel now."

"Too late," he said as Whitey spotted them.

"Here they are now," Whitey announced over the noisy crowd. "The happy couple."

Everyone turned to gawk at them, and that was when Lucy realized that the only women in the bar seemed to be of the hurdy-gurdy variety. Hoots, whistles, and catcalls followed Whitey's announcement, and then several of the customers were upon them.

Everyone wanted to meet the bride and offer congratulations. After that was accomplished, someone took Lucy by the hand and led her to a chair that featured ribbons of white satin woven throughout the spindles. After taking a seat as instructed, Lucy and the chair were suddenly airborne, hoisted high above the crowd by a group of men.

As they paraded her around the saloon, cheering and calling to her, Lucy had to duck to avoid banging her head on a chandelier made out of deer antlers. The sudden movement caused a shift to the men who were carrying her, and the next thing Lucy knew, she pitched forward and fell out of the chair.

She landed on two of the men who'd been carrying her.

Sebastian was at her side in an instant. "Are you all right?" he asked, helping her to her feet.

"I think so. Mostly embarrassed."

"Sorry about that," Whitey said as he broke through the crowd of men. "I think some of the fellahs started celebrating your wedding a little early. How about some chow? We got some great eats."

That seemed like a much better idea than being toted around on a chair. Lucy quickly said, "Thank you. That sounds wonderful."

Whitey led them to a table pushed back against the wall where the expected ham, pickles, oysters, and leftover salads from yesterday's festivities awaited. What Lucy didn't expect to see was a beautiful white bride's cake decorated with pale pink sugar roses. Suddenly, her marriage seemed all too real.

"Help yourselves," Whitey suggested. "And why don't you cut the cake, ma'am? I had it made up special over at that new bakery, Charlie's place."

Lucy didn't dare look at Sebastian for fear she'd break out laughing. Instead she took the offered knife, used the tablecloth to wipe butter and ham from the blade, and cut into the cake. It was a fruitcake, filled with nuts, candied cherries, and the overwhelming scent of rum. Lucy hated fruitcake and Charlie darn well knew it.

Smiling to herself, she handed the knife to Whitey and said, "There. I've cut the first slice; and now everyone can help themselves."

"Come and get it," he shouted over his shoulder. Then, again addressing the newlyweds, he said, "We got one more table over here."

Lucy expected more food, but the next table held a dozen or more gifts. She glanced at Sebastian in horror. "We can't accept these gifts. It's too much."

"Nonsense," said Whitey. "I know you're new to town, but Seb's done a lot for folks in these parts. This is the least they can do in return."

"Thank you," Sebastian said graciously. "Maybe you can have someone send them over to the hotel for us."

As the men discussed this, Lucy caught sight of someone waving to her from over near the door. "Excuse me," she said to Sebastian. "Hazel is here. I'm going to go greet her."

When she reached the door, Lucy said, "I didn't expect to see you."

"Oh, I didn't come for the party." Hazel leaned in close, whispering, "The wedding wasn't real, so I didn't think you'd want too big a fuss."

"And you were right. What's on your mind?"

"I know I already gave you a Penelope question for this week, but another one came in last night and it's a beaut. I hope you can get it done by Wednesday. Let me know if you want some help."

Without reading it, Lucy folded the paper and slipped it into her pocket. As it turned out, she didn't need Hazel's help. When Friday rolled around and the new *Rustler* was printed, Lucy was proud enough of her work to pop the buttons on her ink-stained traveling suit.

—————— *THE WEEKLY RUSTLER* ——————

| Emancipation, Wyoming, | Vol. 1. |
| Friday, July 10, 1896 | No.42 |

ASK PENELOPE! FREE ADVICE!

Dear Penelope:
Have you seen what the women of this town have gone and done? They have allowed a man to remain on the city council. This strikes me as one step forward, three steps back. What we should be doing is revoking all the voting privileges for men.

If something isn't done now, it won't be long before our men start grabbing us by the hair and dragging us off to their caves. Show your face, Penelope. Come out and unite the women of this town before it's too late!
Signed, No Longer Inclined
To Polish My Husband's Boots

Dear No Longer Inclined:
My face is of no consequence in this matter. As I see it, the women of this town have not stepped backward but rather achieved parity. In other words, by leaving the right to vote with our fathers, sons, and husbands, the women of this town can finally claim true equality.

Regarding the issue of your husband's boots, I must say that I see this as a personal dilemma. Each woman should decide for herself what she will and will not do in the name of love.

Penelope

Chapter Sixteen

Eagerly expecting at least the same accolades that Sebastian had offered last week, Lucy watched as he read her latest column. When he finished, he surprised her by slamming the newspaper onto the table.

Pinning her with a sharp-eyed gaze, Sebastian said, "Isn't it about time you told me what's really going on with this Penelope?"

Lucy gulped. "What do you mean?"

His eyes cut to the back of the room. "Not here. Go into the storeroom. I'll meet you there in a minute."

Unprepared for Sebastian's anger, and not entirely sure of its basis, Lucy made her way to the storeroom and then paced as she awaited her fate. It wasn't far behind her.

A moment later Sebastian came into the room and firmly shut the door behind him. Again locking on her eyes, he said, "You've been lying to me."

He knew! God help her, he must have found out that she was the one who wrote the Penelope column. With a deep breath and another gulp, Lucy said, "I don't know what to say."

"Why don't you start with the truth?" His gray eyes were stormy, so dark they were almost purple. "I've been trying to find out about this Penelope for weeks, and now I've discovered that you've been lying to me all that time."

Lucy backed up a few steps, giving herself room to breath. Then she tried to find a way to explain. "I, well, see, it isn't that I lied exactly. If you think about it and the things I said, it might be that I didn't quite say everything I could, but I never meant anything different or tried to make a big story, see. Mostly I had an obligation to Hazel, and I couldn't very well ignore that trust, see, so I didn't explain a lot, I know. I don't think I ever lied."

"Damn, Lucy." Sebastian shook his dark head. "Can you ever explain anything in a simple sentence?"

"I, well, I thought I did."

"You did not." He paused a minute and then said, "Moseley has contacts in Chicago, namely the editor of the Chicago *Tribune*. He poked around, checking all of the Chicago newspapers, and guess what?"

Big-eyed, working to look innocent, she said, "What?"

"Nobody in Chicago has ever heard of Penelope or her advice column."

Eyes still round, Lucy shrugged. "Isn't that something?"

"What's something is the fact that you sent me on a wild-goose chase, and I turned up looking like a damn fool."

She was relieved to realize that he didn't know her true identity but felt sick to her stomach knowing that she'd caused him so much trouble. "I'm sorry you got caught up in this, but I simply couldn't tell you where to find Penelope. I promised Hazel that I would keep it a secret."

Sebastian considered this. Then he said, "All right. I can understand your loyalty to Hazel, but maybe you can tell me this much: Is Penelope located east or west of the Mississippi?"

Lucy couldn't see a problem with divulging that information. She smiled and said, "West."

"In the northern part of the States, or the southern?"

She still couldn't see the harm—either that or guilt drove her to say, "Umm, the northern."

Sebastian nodded, looking far less angry. "The state where she writes. First half of the alphabet or the second?"

Thinking fast, Lucy considered the states that fit into those parameters. Again it didn't seem to be a problem. "The second."

"I guess that eliminates Idaho," he said with a sigh. "I don't suppose you'd care to be a little more specific, maybe give me the first letter of the state?"

She resolutely shook her head. "I'm sorry, but I simply can't. Hazel, you know."

"I know." Sebastian advanced on Lucy, leaving her with no escape. Instead of threatening or wheedling, he took her into his arms. "I don't guess I'd like knowing that you'd betray Hazel any more than I like not knowing who this Penelope is. Maybe we can track her down with the little information you did give me."

"Maybe," she said, not believing it for a minute. "Then you're not mad at me?"

"No, Lucy, I'm not mad at you." He brushed his thumb against her cheek and then touched the spot with his lips. "You've got ink on your face. The train will be in soon, so I guess you'd better be getting on back to the hotel for a change of clothing."

She nodded and leaned into him, whispering, "Just so you're not mad."

Sebastian's mouth came down on hers, leaving Lucy in no doubt whatsoever that he definitely was not in the least displeased.

An hour later gamblers and travelers began to trickle into the Pearly Gates and there was still no sign of Lucy. While she wasn't what Seb would call late, he figured she'd be back by now. Since the poker tournament wouldn't get underway for another two hours or so, he kept busy by wandering through the saloon, introducing himself to strangers and telling them about the upcoming tournament.

He'd just stopped by Black Jack's table to see how his warm-up game was going when the door banged open. Seb glanced toward the strangers and then said to Jack, "It looks like we might get a pretty decent crowd tonight. How many dealers do you have lined up?"

"Six plus me and you, if necessary."

Seb was trying to decide whether that would be enough, noting, too, that the strangers were heading his way. Glancing toward them again, he realized that one of the men looked familiar.

"Oh, hell," he muttered to Jack under his breath. "Lucy's brother is back in town."

Jack looked up and took in the pair. The corner of his mouth twitching along with the words, he asked, "Want to wager on who the other fellow might be?"

Seb studied Dusty's companion as they approached. He was an older man, round and squat, wearing denim coveralls, a straw hat, and the expression of a bulldog. He kind of bobbed along more than walked, his shuffling steps slow and measured.

As they reached Seb, Dusty pointed at him and said, "There he is, Pa."

"Good to see you again," Seb greeted Dusty. Although by now he knew exactly who the older man was, he said, "And you might be?"

"I might be a lot a things," the man said gruffly, tilting his head to look up at Seb. "The devil, Satan's little helper, the man who's gonna skin you alive, but mostly I'm Lucy's Pa."

Behind him, Seb thought he heard a chuckle. He stuck out his hand. "Nice to meet you, Mr. Preston. I'm Seb Cole."

"What you are," Preston said without shaking Seb's hand,

"is the son of a buck who stole my little girl away without so much as a 'How'd ya do, can I have your daughter's hand in marriage?' or nothing. And now I'm just supposed to accept it as law? Well, see, we don't do things that a way where we come from, no sir, and I've half a mind to take you out back of this here den of iniquity, see, and beat the tar out of you, and if'n you can still stand up, I'll beat on you some more."

God all Friday, Seb thought as the old man paused to draw a breath. Did the whole damn family talk like that?

"And furthermore," Preston went on, "Lucy's ma isn't any too happy with the way you up and—"

"Pa!"

They all turned to see Lucy standing there. Her expression horrified, she said, "What are *you* doing here?"

"Lucy girl, it's good to see you." Preston, about an inch shorter than his daughter, nonetheless wrapped his burly arms around her and lifted her off her feet. When he set her back down he said, "What's all this about marrying up with a gambling man who didn't even have the decency to ask for your hand?"

Lucy looked over her father's shoulder to where Seb stood and rolled her eyes. "It, umm, wasn't Sebastian's fault. Everything happened kind of fast."

"Fast?" Preston spun around and fixed Seb with slitty blue eyes. "Where I come from a fast wedding means there's a delicate situation I can't discuss in front of my daughter's innocent ears. I swear—"

"Oh, Pa, no. It wasn't like that at all."

Lucy glanced at Seb, beseeching him with her eyes to help her out a little. Damned if he knew what to do or say. He was busy wondering exactly what kind of mess he'd gotten himself into, and how to get out of it. First the wedding party at the Bucket, with congratulations they didn't deserve, not to mention a roomful of gifts they didn't have a right to open, and now this—a full-on attack from the father of the bride.

As he listened to the Prestons discussing him and his intentions, Seb realized that almost everyone in the saloon was listening, too. He tapped the old man on the shoulder and quietly said, "Why don't we take this outside? We don't need to have everyone in the room a party to our business, do we?"

Preston scrunched up his chubby face and grudgingly said, "That might be for the best. Especially if there's any bloodshed."

Seb shook off a little tremor and turned to Jack. "I think I'm going to be busy with these folks for a while. Can you manage without me?"

Jack's entire mouth was atwitter. "I expect I can manage better than you will."

Stifling the urge to bunch up his fist and bury it in his best friend's nose, Seb muttered so only Jack could hear, "Thanks, you bastard. If I'm not back in an hour, have B.J. find and arrest me. I think I'm going to be better off in jail."

Then he turned and followed the Preston family through the front door. When the old man reached the boardwalk, he poked Seb in the shoulder and said, "I have no intention of shaming myself or my daughter by standing out in front of this vile establishment discussing family business. You got a restaurant in this town? I'm starved."

Left with little choice, Seb shot Lucy a narrow look and said, "We have a fine restaurant." Then he escorted his new "family" across the street to the Palace Arms.

Once they were shown to their table in the dining room, Preston made a big fuss about where everyone would sit. Should his little girl sit beside him or across from him, next to her miserable excuse for a husband or her brother? At last he decided that Lucy should sit next to him, with Seb directly across the table.

Good thing she wasn't beside him, Seb supposed. Otherwise he might be tempted to wring her neck. Unfortunately the seating arrangement also meant that Seb would enjoy the pleasure of sitting next to Dusty, who smelled as if he'd rolled in a dead skunk.

As everyone studied the menu, Seb glanced up and saw that Lucy was peeking at him from over the top of hers. Eyes big and guileless, she mouthed the words "I'm sorry," and then went back to choosing her meal.

When the waiter came to take their orders, Preston said, "I'll have the biggest steak you got, baked beans, and some coleslaw. And don't forget the bread."

Lucy ordered a small hamburger steak with a tomato salad, and since Seb had already had his big meal of the day, he ordered the same.

Dusty paused a moment longer and finally said, "I'll have the fried chicken, mashed potatoes and gravy, and corn fritters."

Under his breath, Seb groaned. Fried chicken meant their suppers wouldn't be served for another forty-five minutes. He began to earnestly hope that B. J. would come arrest him.

"So," Preston said, jabbing his fork at Seb, "tell me about this marriage of yours."

Seb pasted on a phony grin, looked directly at Lucy, and said, "I'd love to."

She jumped right in. "Maybe I should explain, Pa. Sebastian has only just met you."

"Actually," Seb corrected, "we've barely been introduced. I don't even know your father's name."

"Jeremiah Preston," the man himself proclaimed. "For the time being, you can call me sir."

Seb could feel the muscles in his jaw tighten. "Sebastian Cole. For the time being, it might be best if you didn't call me anything at all."

Jeremiah gave him a barely discernible nod, then turned

to Lucy and said, "This husband of yours has got some fur on his brisket, maybe a little too much. I guess it might be best if you tell me about this marriage."

With a quick glance at Seb, Lucy began her sordid little tale. "Well, I'm pretty sure Dusty told you that when I got to Emancipation I found out right away that Charlie had a new fiancée, and that he didn't want me anymore. The train was gone and I didn't know what to do, see? Sebastian was kind enough to give me a job as a hostess, and that meant a room and food. Then I fought with Charlie and shoved a cupcake in Cherry's face, and always Sebastian was there helping out, see. He became very dear to me."

As Lucy paused to draw in a breath, her father nodded sagely. "That's understandable."

Understandable? Unbelievable was more like it. Seb knew most of the details of Lucy's life since she'd arrived in town, and even so he could barely make sense of her explanation. He glanced at the waiter across the room, thinking he could use a healthy shot of cognac, and then thought better of it.

"Anyway," Lucy continued, "the more I got to know Sebastian, the better I liked him. And my work, too, especially at the newspaper, where I work three or four days a week now. It all made me happy, see, so when Sebastian asked me to marry him, I knew that I'd be happy forever and that I wanted the same as you and Ma, see, so we got married and it all came true. About me, anyway. I don't want you to worry about me."

"I'll always worry about you." Jeremiah patted Lucy's hand. "You're my baby girl."

Then he turned on Seb. "I'm satisfied with Lucy's story. What's yours?"

Wishing now that he had ordered the cognac, Seb said, "Lucy's a very special young woman. I was happy to marry her."

"You were lucky to marry her, don't you mean?"

"Yes, sir, that's exactly what I meant to say."

"If you're feeling so danged lucky," Jeremiah went on, "how can you force your wife, my daughter, to work in that den of iniquity as a beer slinger? It's a sin, and I won't have it."

Seb raised his arm and signaled the waiter. Directing his remark to Jeremiah, he said, "Working at the Pearly Gates was Lucy's choice, not mine. I don't force her to do anything."

"That's right, Pa," she chimed in. "I really don't mind working there. It's a very nice place."

"It's a saloon and a gambling den, no place for a decent young woman to visit, much less ply a trade."

The waiter, very familiar with Seb's signals, came to the table and delivered two fingers of cognac. Seb glanced from Dusty to Jeremiah and said, "Anyone else care for a cognac or some wine?"

Dusty said, "I'd like a—"

"We are not a family of rum suckers," Jeremiah cut in, waving the waiter away. "I'm sorely disappointed to see that you are, but I can't say I'm surprised."

Seb raised his glass, toasted Lucy, and then knocked the drink back in one gulp. "This has been lots of fun," he said, pushing back his chair, "but I think I'd better get back to work. I'm hosting a big poker tournament tonight."

"Oh, please stay for the meal," Lucy implored. "Pa doesn't mean anything by the things he says. He's just worried about me."

Seb figured the cognac had made him mellow enough to bow to her request, but he had an idea he'd have stayed anyway, drink or not. Pulling back up to the table, he decided a change of subject was in order, one that had a direct bearing on his sanity.

"How long are you and Dusty going to be in town?" he asked Jeremiah.

"Till I'm satisfied that Lucy is going to be all right." He

shrugged, and his expression went from warthog to bulldog again. "We figure on heading back when the train comes on Tuesday."

Four days, Seb thought, considering ordering another cognac. He said, "Where are you going to stay?"

Father and son glanced at each other and shrugged. Then Jeremiah said, "Don't know for sure. I expect we'll get us a room somewheres."

"They probably have a room to let right here," Seb said without thinking.

Jeremiah looked around. "This is too highfalutin for the likes of our bankroll. Besides, why can't we just stay with you and Lucy?"

"Pa," she said, "I guess Dusty didn't tell you that we live here at the hotel."

"Your husband put you up in a hotel?" His eyes cut to Seb. "Why haven't you provided my daughter with a proper home?"

Seb didn't have an immediate reply. Lucy saved him by saying, "We haven't had time to find one yet."

His mouth running ahead of his brain, thinking now that he probably shouldn't have ordered that cognac, Seb changed the subject again. "I'd be happy to get you and Dusty a room here; my treat, of course."

"Is that a fact?" Jeremiah narrowed one eye. "Selling the devil's brew must be a pretty good business."

"I do all right."

"Sebastian," Lucy cut in, "you don't have to do that, *really* you don't."

Her father had other ideas. "Man wants to be generous with his new in-laws, I guess we ought to let him."

Jeremiah propped his elbows on the table, looked Seb square in the eye, and said, "Now about my daughter's lodgings . . . We only have a few days here, but Dusty and I will be glad to help you find something suitable. I can't hardly leave town until I know that Lucy is settled in her very own home."

Things were chaotic that night in the saloon. The place was packed with gamblers eager to throw their money away on the chance they might win a hand or two. Others were clustered around the bar drinking away their sorrows.

Lucy and Sebastian were so busy, they hadn't had a moment alone. She figured that was a good thing. She knew exactly what he was thinking from the looks he gave her. His were accusing eyes; warnings, if not outright threats. He didn't show fury or even anger, but Sebastian was definitely displeased. Lucy felt as if she had a scarlet letter burned into her forehead, a capital i for idiot. Only an idiot would have thought of this foolish plan, or believed that it could actually work. All she'd wanted to do was remain in Emancipation, but in the process she'd turned Sebastian's life upside down. He'd never forgive her, and Lucy wouldn't blame him.

Never in her wildest dreams had she truly imagined that her father would show up in Emancipation, not after he knew she was married. She owed Sebastian much more than a mere apology. As if there wasn't already enough tension between them, Lucy's father and Dusty had followed her back to the Pearly Gates for the express purpose of keeping an eye on her. She showed them to a small table near the newsstand, one that wasn't used for card games, and brought them each a root beer on the house.

Hoping they would stay there until it was time to go to the hotel, Lucy went back to work, starting with the table just a few feet away.

One of the gamblers called out, "Hey, sweetheart, we could use some beers."

"How many?" she asked as she approached.

One of the other men said, "If it ain't the girl with the velvet eyes. You're sure looking pretty tonight, honey."

Sharon Ihle

Before she had a chance to thank him for the compliment, Lucy heard her father's voice slide over her shoulder.

"That ain't no way to talk to a lady, especially since this one is my little girl."

The gambler's gaze shot around the table; then he shrugged and said, "Sorry."

"Don't apologize to me. Apologize to her."

"Uh, sorry, ma'am. We'd like six beers, please."

"Coming right up." Turning to her father, she whispered, "Go sit down. I can take care of myself."

"I'm only trying to help."

"I know, but you're embarrassing me."

"Humph."

Lucy could tell her father didn't like it, but he shuffled back to his table and sat down. Hoping he would stay there, fairly certain he wouldn't, she went back to work. As she went about her duties, Lucy could feel eyes on her—Sebastian's, her father's, and even Dusty's—distractions that turned her into a nervous wreck. She slopped more beer on the players, made more mistakes with orders, and fell over her own feet more often than she had her first night on the job. The harder Lucy tried to do things right, the worse things got.

If all that wasn't enough, apparently her father and Dusty took pity on her. They followed her to the bar, insisted on delivering as many beers as they could carry, and trailed along behind her like eager little puppies, rambunctious and easily distracted. She caught Sebastian's eye as the troupe paraded by his table, and he slowly shook his head.

"That's it," Lucy said to her father. "Why don't you and Dusty go to the hotel now? I can handle the orders from here on out."

"If you're sure."

"I'm positive."

He gave a nod. "We'll just go finish up our root beers and be on our way."

Relieved, Lucy went to the bar, loaded up her tray, and

202

headed for Sebastian's table. As she approached, she realized that he was watching her. His expression was hooded—speculative? Full of censure? Or was he thinking something else altogether? He was dealing cards, his long fingers deftly stroking the pasteboards even as he fired them into neat piles in front of each gambler. Lucy was watching those hands, thinking about the things they could do to her, when she bumped into a customer who was on his way to the bar. The tray and its contents hit the floor.

Avoiding Sebastian's gaze, Lucy dropped down to the floor and began cleaning up the mess. A moment later her father and Dusty came to her aid.

"Get down there and help your sister," said her father. Then he turned on Sebastian. "Can't you see my girl needs help? I'd think you'd want to take better care of her than this."

"Pa," Lucy pleaded, "please leave him alone and go sit down. I dropped the tray and it's up to me to clean up the mess."

Sebastian, who appeared to be in the middle of a high stakes game, abruptly threw in his cards, muttered something to the player next to him, and got out of his chair to march toward them.

Lucy and Dusty had just gotten to their feet, the tray filled with empty mugs, when Sebastian said to their father, "This is a very important tournament I'm hosting tonight, and I'm afraid that I don't have time to be a better host to you. I think it would be best if you were to go to the hotel now."

Her father puffed out his barrel chest. "I understand what you're saying, but Lucy is tired and can't do this all by herself. I think me and Dusty better stay around and help her serve all those beers."

Sebastian rolled his eyes. "I agree with the one thing: Lucy is tired." He pointed a finger her way and added, "You go with them. You're fired."

"Oh, but Sebastian—"

"That's it. I've got to get back to work now. Just let Pearl know that you're leaving and then please, all of you leave."

No point in arguing with him—she and her family had pretty well ruined his business. Lucy said, "If that's what you want."

"It is."

After leaving her tray and apron with Pearl and explaining that she was through for the night, Lucy led Dusty and her father out to the boardwalk.

"Listen, girl," said her father, "I was only trying to help. I didn't mean to cause no trouble."

"I know, Pa. I just hope Sebastian didn't mean it when he fired me."

"Maybe it's for the best if he did. I don't know why you love this job so much. It's messy and degrading."

Suddenly as tired as everyone said she was, Lucy vented some of her frustration. "I work there because I owe Sebastian a lot, more than I can ever repay."

"But you're his wife. How can you owe him anything?"

"I don't want to talk about it now. Let's go on over to the hotel."

"Uh, I'm not ready to turn in yet," Dusty said. "I think I'll take a walk around town."

This was fine with Lucy. Before she could get her father moving, Hazel came barreling up the boardwalk. "Lucy, wait up. I've got news."

After introducing her editor to her father, Lucy asked, "What kind of news?"

"Gus and I were having supper with Mattie and Frank, and she told me that she got a wire late this afternoon saying that Mary Lease and company are coming in from Cheyenne on Tuesday's train, *this* Tuesday."

"I thought she wasn't coming here until the end of the month."

"So did everyone else, but I guess she changed her schedule. Anyway, Gus and I were talking about it on the way home, and it occurred to me that since the town isn't quite ready for those gals, maybe Seb can get a celebration party together quicker than anyone. I just came down to ask him."

Lucy thought of his mood. "Why don't you let me ask him first thing in the morning? He's awfully busy right now."

"Good enough." She turned to Lucy's father. "Nice to meet you, Mr. Preston. Enjoy your visit in Emancipation."

Back at the hotel, Lucy led her father to the desk clerk, made sure he got a key to his room, and then headed for her own room. After a long bath and a lot of thinking, she slipped on a dressing gown and crept into Sebastian's room. He hadn't come in yet, which boded well for her plans.

After lighting a small candle on the bed table, she stepped out of the gown, climbed into his bed, and pulled the sheet up past her breasts, covering her nudity. She brushed out her hair and draped it over her shoulders like a veil. Then she waited.

Lucy was half asleep, sitting up in bed, when she heard the door open. When Sebastian came in, he looked tired.

"Oh," he said. "I didn't expect to see you here."

"Are you disappointed?"

"I don't know yet."

Sebastian glanced around the room, hurried over to the water closet and peeked inside, then crossed the room, where he checked to make sure the connecting door was locked. Then he came over to the bed, got down on one knee, and raised the dust ruffle.

"What are you doing?" Lucy asked.

"Looking for your father."

She laughed a little. "Don't worry. He's in his own room."

Sebastian peeled off his jacket and said, "This wasn't part of our bargain, your father coming to town and riding herd on me."

"I know, and I'm terribly sorry. I didn't expect them to show up like this."

"And I didn't expect them to take over my saloon. Not many of my customers appreciate a bald hostess wearing bib overalls who goes on and on about the evils of drinking."

"I know. Am I really fired?"

As he continued undressing, Sebastian said, "I think as long as your family is in town, yes, you're fired. After that whether you work at the Pearly Gates or not is up to you."

"I guess that's fair enough. I'd like to make it up to you somehow."

"Can we get an early divorce? I believe I've still got something like two weeks left on my contract."

Lucy wouldn't even entertain the idea of an early divorce, not with her father in town. In fact, as she thought about it, she wasn't sure she'd be ready for the divorce in two weeks—or ever.

She let the sheet fall, revealing the fact that she was naked. "I had something else in mind."

"Oh?" Suddenly Sebastian didn't look so tired. "And what might that be?"

"I thought you might like to punish me for all the trouble I've caused."

Reaching under the covers, Lucy grabbed the handful of chocolate stars she'd hidden there. As she let them rain down on her breasts, she added, "Severely."

Chapter Seventeen

Early the next morning, after sleeping less than three hours, Lucy was snuggled in the crook of Sebastian's arm when loud knocking startled her.

She sat bolt upright in bed. "Sebastian?" she whispered. "Did you hear that?"

He grumbled something unintelligible at the same time the knocking resumed, this time accompanied by her father's voice.

"Lucy, you in there? The day's wasting away."

"Just a minute, Pa," she hollered back.

Sebastian lifted his head off the pillow and glanced out the window. "It's still dark outside. What's he doing here?"

"Pa gets up before dawn," she explained as she slipped into her dressing gown.

"Where's my gun?"

"Hush," she said. "Go back to sleep. I'll get rid of him."

Lucy crept to the door and opened it a crack.

" 'Morning, girl. You still in bed?"

"Shush, you'll wake Sebastian." Pointing down the hallway, she said, "Go to the next door. I'll let you in."

Then she closed the door and let herself into her own room. After lighting the lantern, she opened the door and ushered her father into her room.

"What's this?" he asked, looking around. "A married woman with her own bedroom?"

"It's, umm, my sitting room, a private area just for me."

He let out a low whistle. "Nice. Is it like my room? It has its own water closet and a big bathtub with hot and cold running water—can you beat that?"

"I think all of the rooms are like that."

He shook his head in admiration. "Life doesn't get much better than this. No wonder you're dragging your feet getting your own place."

That seemed as good an explanation as any, so Lucy let it rest.

As her father walked around the room looking things over, he paused in front of the pile of gifts. "What's all this?"

"Oh, umm, there was a wedding party for us the other day. We haven't had time to open the presents yet."

"How can you stand the suspense? Now that your family's here, you got to open them."

Lucy and Sebastian had decided not to open the presents, given the fact that they'd have to return them in two weeks. Skirting the issue without actually lying, she said, "Oh, we've been so distracted lately, we haven't given the gifts much thought."

"I hope it don't have anything to do with me." Jeremiah walked over to where Lucy stood, his round face puckered with concern. "I'm sorry if I caused you trouble at the saloon last night. I only meant to help."

"I know, Pa."

"I'm gonna try to do better, at least I want to, but first I need to know one thing—do you love this man?"

Finally, with all the deception around her, Lucy was able to tell the truth. "I love him very much," she declared, her heart soaring.

His blue eyes misty, Jeremiah kissed her cheek and said, "That's good enough for me. I'll start mending fences with that husband of yours first chance I get. In the meantime we're gonna open those wedding gifts."

Before Lucy realized what he was up to, Jeremiah shuffled off to the connecting door. As he opened it, he shouted into the room, "Get on in here, son. We're opening presents."

Lucy thought she heard a muttered oath, and then her father was back, commenting, "We can start without Dusty. I swear, I think that boy was out half the night. I've got him downstairs now trying to scare up some coffee, but he ought to be along shortly."

"Pa," she said, trying to reason with him, "Sebastian got in very late last night, too, and hasn't had much sleep. He usually stays in bed until around noon."

"Balderdash. It's not healthy for a man to stay in bed past dawn. You ought to know that."

Sebastian stumbled into Lucy's room. He was wearing trousers, but his feet were bare and he was buttoning last night's rumpled shirt. She checked to make sure he wasn't also wearing his gun.

"What the hell is going on?" he asked, his eyes barely open.

"You'd best watch your language around my girl," Jeremiah warned. "Us Prestons don't hold with cussing."

As his gaze shot to her, Sebastian's eyes got even smaller. "Lucy?"

"Umm, Pa wants us to open our wedding presents."

She expected him to turn on his heel, go back into his room, and lock the door behind him. Instead, Sebastian dragged himself over to her bed and sat down. "Is this going to take long?" he asked wearily.

Jeremiah bobbed on over to the bed, slapped Sebastian on the back, and said, "Wake up, son. We got wedding presents to open. You can sleep any time."

It was a good thing Lucy couldn't see Sebastian's expression. She had an idea it was darker than the early morning sky. She heard a distant knock then, and quickly went to her door. Peeking down the hall, she saw her brother standing in front of Sebastian's room. He was holding a silver tray.

"We're over here," she said, inviting him in.

"Dang," he complained as he strolled into the room. "I had to go all the way back into the kitchen and practically wake everyone up to get us a pot of coffee. They didn't want to make it at first, but I told them we were Seb's guests and that I was gonna stay right there until I got some coffee. This hotel could use some lessons in keeping customers happy."

Sebastian groaned and threw himself flat out on Lucy's bed.

Fighting the urge to join him there, to pull the coverlet over her head and pretend none of this was happening, Lucy relieved Dusty of his burden. After serving coffee to her family, she cautiously approached Sebastian with a steaming mug.

"Coffee?" she asked quietly.

"Might as well." He forced himself to a sitting position and slowly shook his head. "Am I having a nightmare or is this really happening?"

Lucy glanced over and saw that Jeremiah and Dusty were heading toward the bed, their arms filled with packages. "It's happening," she assured Sebastian. "Try to be nice a little longer. This shouldn't take but a few minutes."

Had she been looking into her father's eyes and remembering her childhood, Lucy would never have made such a claim. With seven children in the Preston family, and even though times were often hard, there were always lots of presents under the tree at Christmas. Depending on their finances, a child's package might contain a small toy or even a shiny new penny. Their mother's gifts ran the gamut from inexpensive brooches to single spools of thread. Always, without fail, and no matter how many gifts nestled under the tree, the biggest kid in the room was Jeremiah Preston. He could hardly wait for one of his little ones to open a package, and often tore into the wrappings himself, even though he knew exactly what he would find.

As her father tossed the presents on the bed, the twinkle in his eye told Lucy that nothing had changed in that regard.

She sat down beside Sebastian as Jeremiah "Santa Claus" made himself at home on Lucy's desk chair. Rubbing his hands together, he said, "Go on, girl, get to it."

First, and in order to keep track of who gave what, she carefully pulled a blank piece of paper and a pencil from her desk drawer. Then she picked out a small package. Determined to save the slender blue ribbon tied around the white wrapping paper, Lucy picked at the knot.

After a couple of minutes of this, Jeremiah's patience ran out. "Oh, for heaven's sake, girl. Give it to me."

Beside her, Sebastian slowly shook his head.

Lucy picked up another package and began to work on it. She hadn't gotten past the ribbon before her father reached over and snatched it out of her hands.

Again Sebastian shook his head, but this time he said, "Give me a couple of those."

Matching Jeremiah with broken ribbons and shredded paper, Sebastian and his new father-in-law ripped through the packages in a matter of minutes. In the midst of the carnage were small treasures such as a crystal sugar bowl, a salt-and-pepper-shaker set shaped and painted to resemble two full beer mugs, cake plates and pie tins, and an assortment of napkin rings. The largest package, a crystal punch bowl, was a gift from the owner of the Bucket.

Patting his round belly, Jeremiah said, "Well, I guess we got that done, and a mighty fine haul it was."

Sebastian pushed off the mattress and yawned. "Great presents. Now if you'll excuse me, I'm going back to bed."

"Aw, you can sleep later." Jeremiah got to his feet. "Why don't you get dressed and we'll go have some breakfast? After that I've got a day planned for you and me."

Sebastian's narrow gaze shot to Lucy. She shrugged.

Catching the exchange, Jeremiah explained, "It's time I got to know the man who stole my little girl. We're gonna take us a little ride."

After choking down a breakfast of pancakes that he didn't want to eat and learning from Lucy that he was supposed to host a party for Mary Lease that he didn't want to organize, Seb climbed into Jeremiah's rented buggy for a ride that he didn't want to take. *Three more days,* he thought to himself as the old man slapped the reins against the roan's back and got the rig to moving. Trying to catch a quick nap, Seb settled back against the cushion and closed his eyes.

"I bet you're wondering why I wanted us to go off alone like this," Jeremiah said.

Seb had long since quit wondering why anyone in the Preston family did anything. He said, "I figured you'd tell me in due time."

Jeremiah slapped his own knee. "See there? Already we're getting to understand each other."

Seb figured it was a one-sided understanding. If Jeremiah knew anything about him at all, he'd know how close Seb was to hog-tying him and locking him in his room until the train arrived on Tuesday. Pushing his hat down low on his forehead, he closed his eyes.

Apparently unaware that his companion was trying to sleep, Jeremiah went on. "There's one other thing I thought we'd do on this little ride. Like I told you before, I can't hardly leave town until I know my little girl is settled. I figured we could find her a place today, or at least a parcel of land where you can build her the house she wants."

Suddenly wide awake, Seb sat up. "What the hell are you talking about?"

"Now, now, son," he said, clucking his tongue. "Watch the language."

Tired of taking orders from the old man, not to mention uncomfortable with the sense of intimacy he was trying to establish, Seb said, "I'm not your son. Why don't you call me Seb?"

Jeremiah cocked his head. "I'd like that. And you can call me Jeremiah."

"Wonderful. Now what's all this about a house?"

"I've been poking around and heard tell there's a nice place for sale on Second Avenue. If you'll just direct me, we can take a look at it."

To shut the man up, if nothing else, Seb reluctantly gave him directions. He shook his head, thinking that he'd come to Emancipation for some normalcy, to escape from the increasingly bizarre circumstances of his life in Denver. Apparently all he'd done was trade one bunch of crazies for another: first Kate and all her problems, and now, Lucy and her nutty family. How could he have let himself fall into another trap?

Part of the answer had something to do with the way he felt about Lucy, the fact that he probably loved her more than just a little. How had that happened? He'd known from the beginning that their relationship was nothing but a fleeting moment in her life, a means to an end. Except for the next two weeks, he didn't figure in her future. So why, Seb wondered with a shake of his head, was he sitting here with her father looking for a newlywed home they would never buy?

"Oh, my stars," Jeremiah said. "This isn't what I had in mind."

Seb glanced at the house. Built in a shotgun style, it was twice as long as it was wide, desperately in need of paint, and more suited as an army barracks than a place to raise a family.

"Oh, I don't know," Seb said, tongue firmly in cheek. "It looks pretty good to me."

Jeremiah rubbed his chin. "It don't look too habable."

"Habable?"

"You know, a place where folks could live. I didn't get much schooling, but I'm proud to say that all my kids did. I pick up some of their fancy words now and again."

Seb had to look away from the man as he said, "I think all this place needs is a good coat of paint."

Jeremiah shot him an incredulous look. "And I think we can do a lot better for Lucy. We'll just have to ride around town some more, unless you know about a nice place for sale."

"I can't say that I do."

As it turned out, Emancipation had only one other house for sale and it was at the edge of town, right next door to a house of ill repute. As far as Seb was concerned, that settled the issue of buying a house for Lucy, but then Jeremiah spotted a trail ahead that led up the side of a hill.

"Where's that go?" he asked.

"To a lake and a nice little picnic area."

"Any houses up there?"

Seb shrugged, worrying about where this would lead. "A couple of ranches, I guess."

"Let's go see," Jeremiah said, urging the horse onward.

Seb settled back in his seat, wondering when or if this day would ever end. When they reached the top of the hill, the first thing the old man spotted was the Carrolls' new cabin.

"Now that's a house," Jeremiah declared.

The cabin was much more than a mere house. It was quite large—two stories with a deep basement—and made of matching pine logs. It sat nestled among tall oak and pine trees and featured a view of both Devil's Lake and the town below.

"Yep," Jeremiah went on, "this is the one. Lucy will love this house. Can you get it for her?"

"I'd love to," Seb lied. "But our justice of the peace and his wife just finished building it and I doubt they want to sell."

"Well, let's go find out."

"I don't want to disturb them. Besides," he added, thinking up excuses as he went along, "even if they're interested in selling, I couldn't afford a place like that."

Jeremiah gave him an odd, jack-o'-lantern kind of smile, and reached into his pocket. "Maybe you can't and maybe you can. Lucy's ma and I don't have much, but we'd be happy to help out any way we can."

With that, he tried to shove a few bills into Seb's hands.

As touched as he was alarmed, Seb said, "Thanks, but no. I can't take your money."

"Too proud, huh?" His grin still in place, the old man shoved the money back into his pocket. "Maybe you can't accept my gift, but I'm sure Lucy will see things my way."

Whether Lucy took money from her father or not was no business of Seb's, but it forced him to realize one thing—he was actually beginning to like the old man. A sudden warmth flooded his chest, a feeling he couldn't remember having for his own father, and Seb searched for a way to satisfy Jeremiah's concerns.

"Tell you what," he said, settled on a plan, "I can check around and see what it would take to buy an acre or two up here, and then I can build Lucy exactly the kind of house she wants. How does that sound?"

"Like a man who loves my daughter."

Surprising Seb, the old man threw one burly arm around his shoulders and squeezed, nearly breaking his collarbone. Then he said, "I guess I ought to get you back to town now. You look like you're about to fall asleep sitting up."

Seb was so grateful, he sank back on the cushion and closed his eyes again. Jeremiah didn't seem to notice. He was wound up like a top, spinning yarns as fast as he could talk.

"When I was a young man of your age," he babbled on, "I could stay up for three days straight. I guess they don't make 'em like they used to, huh?"

Seb laughed and said, "I guess not."

"Come to think of it, my Lucy would have stayed abed half the day if her ma didn't drag her out every morning." He laughed then, more of a bray. "Mighta been a little easier on us all if she'd a just let Lucy stay in bed. I swear, that girl was one awkward child."

Chuckling to himself, Seb said, "That's kind of hard to believe."

"Hah! You wouldn't believe the things she used to do. I swear that girl couldn't get out of her own way. If she wasn't tripping on her own feet, falling out of her own bed, or stepping in pig droppings, then it was a day that she didn't get out of bed."

Jeremiah burst out laughing again. Then he caught his breath and added, "Now don't get me wrong: I love that girl like I love breathing, but there weren't too many things she was good at. I remember asking her to shorten the legs on my new winter overalls not long ago. Know what she done?"

No longer surprised by anything Lucy did, Seb wagered a guess. "Cut the legs right off?"

"Better. She sewed 'em shut on me!" Jeremiah howled at the memory. "There I was in the field on a morning that would freeze your eyeballs shut and I couldn't get my foot past the knee joint in my overalls."

Seb laughed so hard he practically choked.

Jeremiah eyed him and said, "I expect it'd be best if you didn't tell Lucy what I've been saying about her, and I'm not saying that she won't make a good wife. I'm sure she musta growed out of that awkward stage by now."

Seb's eyes rolled so far back in his head, he could almost watch his hair grow.

"Anyways," the old man went on, "when her ma figured

out that she wasn't much good at inside chores, she sent her out to the barn to help with the cows and the chickens."

He interrupted himself to laugh again and then went on regaling Seb with tales of Lucy's clumsy attempts at outside chores until at last the buggy pulled up in front of the hotel. Seb leapt off the rig before Jeremiah had a chance to pull it to a full stop.

"Thanks for the ride," he said jauntily. "You and Lucy have a good time tonight."

"A good time? But isn't she coming to work for you?"

"No. I told her to enjoy herself with you and Dusty until you have to leave. I don't expect much of a crowd tonight or Monday, so it'll be fine."

Seb didn't even give the old man a chance to comment. He took off across the street to check on the saloon. As expected, Jack had opened the place and was busy setting up a few poker tables.

"I didn't think I'd see you so soon," Jack said, glancing up from his work.

"I'm not here for long," Seb explained. "Lucy's father got me up before the crack of dawn so I could go riding around town in a buggy with him."

Jack's mouth twitched. "Was there a reason for that?"

Seb knew what he'd be letting himself in for, but he went ahead anyway. "It seems hotel life isn't what he had in mind for his daughter. He wanted to help me pick out and buy a house for Lucy."

Jack threw back his head and laughed out loud. In all their years together, Seb had never seen the man in a full grin. A few muted chuckles from time to time, but nothing like this.

"Now that I've entertained you," he went on, "I stopped by to let you know that I'm going back to the hotel for a couple hours of sleep."

"That's fine," Jack said, his lips still twitching. "Anything else you want to tell me?"

"Yes, actually. I also came by to let you know that the

town council expects us to host a party for Mary Lease and her group on Tuesday after the train comes to town. If you can think of anything to get things going, be my guest."

Back to his sober self, Jack said, "We're having a party for a bunch of women suffragists—here?"

Seb shrugged. "Apparently that's what they want."

It wasn't, however, what Seb wanted. Mary Lease and her kind represented the type of women he usually avoided at all costs. While he believed in equality, especially in the matter of the national vote, Seb didn't much care for the way some women went about gaining that right. His mother was a prime example.

Left with that dark thought, Seb headed for the door. As he reached it, Jack's voice called out from behind.

"So what kind of house did you buy for Lucy?"

When Tuesday finally rolled around, Lucy took her father and Dusty by the Pearly Gates to say good-bye to Sebastian and then walked them down to the depot. After picking up Seb's mail and as they waited for the train to arrive, she decided that it was finally safe to tell her father the secret that she'd been bursting to share.

Handing him a package she'd bound and wrapped, Lucy said, "This is for you and Ma."

"You got your ma and me a present?" he asked, taking the package from her.

"Sort of." So proud she could burst, Lucy explained, "I wrapped up the last six editions of *The Weekly Rustler*."

Jeremiah examined the package. "You gave us newspapers? Sweetie, we got newspapers in Kansas City."

"Not like this one," she assured him. Reaching into her pocket, she pulled out a copy of her latest column and gave it to her father. "Have you seen this?"

Jeremiah took the column and gave it a fast glance.

"Sure. I've been reading the free papers you bring to the hotel since I got to town."

Unable to contain her grin, Lucy asked, "What do you think of the 'Ask Penelope' column?"

Jeremiah glanced at the paper again and said, "It's pretty entertaining, if you like that sort of thing."

Lucy glanced around to ensure their privacy. Dusty had wandered off into the depot and the train was bearing down on the town, the blare of the whistle drowning out all but the loudest of conversations.

Convinced the other passengers couldn't overhear, she whispered, "You can't say anything after I tell you about this because it's a secret, and it has to stay a secret. I'm Penelope."

Jeremiah laughed. "Your sister's Penelope, silly girl."

"No, I mean I write the 'Ask Penelope' column. It's me."

Again Jeremiah glanced at the paper. "Get out of here."

"It's true, Pa. Hazel used to give me the questions and I wrote the answers, see, but now she gives me all the questions that come in for Penelope and I get to pick the one I want to write about."

"You're a writer?" he said, amazed. "My little girl is a writer?"

"Hush, now," she said quietly. "Like I said, it has to stay a secret for now, so don't even tell Dusty until after you get home. Promise?"

"Course, I do, girl, and I'm so proud of you I could hug the life right outta you." With tears in his eyes, Jeremiah threw his arms around Lucy and squeezed. "I just knew you'd be good at something someday. Wait till your ma hears about this."

Tears threatening behind her own eyelids, Lucy broke out of her father's embrace as the train steamed to a halt. The band, the mayor, the entire city council, and a large cluster of supporters were waiting near the tracks. When the conductor lowered the step and began directing passengers off the train, the band broke out in a noisy rendition of "America, The Beautiful."

"Come on," Lucy said, taking her father by the hand. "Let's go welcome Mary Lease."

Although they could barely see over the crowd, Lucy was impressed to find out that something like a dozen women had accompanied the orator to Emancipation. With the band still playing, the group moved down the street away from the train, and then Mary Lease and two other women climbed onto the boardwalk to address the crowd. She was a sharp-featured woman with a long, narrow face, a high forehead, and dark brown hair pulled back in a severe bun. She wore a plain black dress with a high ruffled collar that touched the tip of her pointed chin.

"Thank you for the warm welcome," Lease said, calming the crowd.

Dusty, who'd joined Lucy and their father, whispered over her shoulder, "That woman's got a real hatchet for a face."

"Looks more like a weasel to me," Jeremiah commented.

"Hush, now," Lucy chided them. "Let's hear what she's got to say."

Lease continued. "I'd like to start by introducing a couple of my companions, invaluable aides who make my life much easier."

She turned to the woman on her left, a plain little mouse dressed in a gray suit who kept her gaze pinned to the boardwalk. "This is Laura Freedman, my secretary and the one who organizes visits such as this."

After a smattering of applause, she turned to the woman on her right. She was taller than the others, probably around five feet eight inches, with a handsome, dignified face and white hair streaked with ribbons of its original auburn color. She wore a beige jacket over a white blouse and full-cut men's style trousers.

"This," Lease went on to say, "is Elizabeth Cole, my

lawyer and one of the finest legal minds this country has ever known."

Jeremiah nudged Lucy's ribs and asked, "What in tarnation is that woman wearing?"

"I think they're called trouserettes."

As her father muttered something about women wanting to be men, Lease finished her brief introductions. "We've had a long journey and will retire to our hotel rooms for now, but I understand we're having a welcome party tonight and I invite you all to come. Be warned, now, that my tongue is loose at both ends and hung on a swivel."

As the crowd laughed and cheered, Lease and her companions started up the street toward the hotel. The band followed close behind, playing, as loudly as possible.

Fascinated by the women and the boisterous crowd, Lucy trailed along behind them, keeping time with the music. After marching for nearly two blocks in this manner, she noticed that her father and Dusty were marching along with her.

Lucy came to an abrupt halt and spun around in the dirt. The train heading east had pulled out of the station and was rapidly becoming a distant plume of smoke.

"Oh, my stars," she said, horrified. "You missed the train."

Dusty and Jeremiah followed her gaze. Her brother slapped his forehead and said, "Danged if we didn't."

Lucy thought about chasing after the train, realized that it was much too late, and said, "What are you going to do?"

Jeremiah scratched his chin. "Dunno."

Remembering something Charlie had suggested to her, Lucy said, "Maybe we can hire someone to take you to Sundance. The train east stops there on Thursdays.

"No need for that," Jeremiah assured her. "We'll just go on back to the depot a little later, exchange our tickets for next Tuesday, and send your ma a telegram saying we'll be a week late."

"But what about the farm?"

Her father shrugged. "Your brothers can pretty well take

care of it, and if they need an extra hand the Daggert boys said they'd come over and help out. I kinda like the idea of staying on another week. I haven't been off that farm for more than a day for my whole life. I thought you'd be happy seeing us a little longer."

"Oh, I am, Pa." And she was, to a point.

"Come on, then. That parade is getting away from us."

As they hurried to catch up with the crowd, which had almost reached the hotel, Jeremiah laughed and said, "Wait till your ma finds out that me and Dusty are staying another week. Boy is she going to be surprised."

At that moment, Lucy caught sight of Sebastian observing the parade from the boardwalk outside the Pearly Gates. Her only thought was: *Ma's not going to be the only one.*

Chapter Eighteen

As the last of the parade marched on by the Pearly Gates, Seb watched Lucy break away from the group and head for the boardwalk where he stood.

"Isn't this exciting?" she said, joining him there.

"About as much fun as watching the grass grow." Seb raised one eyebrow and added, "Then again, maybe I'm not seeing things right. For a minute there, I thought I saw some ghosts in the crowd."

She gave him that big-eyed, innocent look. "Ghosts?"

"Ghosts, or it might have been a couple of fellows who looked a lot like Dusty and Jeremiah walking along beside you." Lucy's eyes got even bigger. "I'm sure my eyes were tricking me because your family is on the train heading east and it left some ten minutes ago."

"Well, uh, see . . ." She took a deep breath and gulped. "Pa and Dusty sort of missed the train. They're at the hotel trying to get their room back."

Seb sighed and rolled his eyes. "I was a lot happier thinking my sight was going bad."

"It wasn't Pa's fault," she insisted. "We got so interested in listening to Mary Lease and her group that we just kind of followed the crowd and didn't even hear the train leave, see?"

"No, as I mentioned before, I'm not seeing so well today."

Lucy twined her fingers, twisting them as she glanced over her shoulder. Then she looked back at Seb and said, "You'd understand if you'd have been with us at the depot. It was really exciting. Mary Lease gave a little speech, and then she introduced her two top aides. Oh, and her lawyer is a woman named Elizabeth Cole. Maybe you're related somehow."

Feeling as if a sudden bolt of lightning had hit him, Seb's entire system lit up and then shut down. He didn't know how he managed the simple sentence, but he somehow forced the words through wooden lips. "Cole is a very common surname."

Then he turned on his heel, forced his uncooperative legs to carry him into the saloon, and fell into the first available chair. Lucy followed and sat down beside him.

"Are you all right?"

Suddenly both hot and cold, frozen at the core, and perspiring freely on the outside, Seb took off his hat and fanned himself. Another excuse magically fell from his lips. "The heat got to me, I guess."

Lucy shook her head. "I don't believe you. You're upset and I think I know why."

How could she know?

"I realize that my father has been giving you a lot of trouble," Lucy continued, oblivious to his pain. "It's not like he missed the train on purpose, you know, but the band was making so much noise we couldn't hear, see. I even offered to hire a rig to take him to Sundance, but now that he did miss the train, he wants to spend some more time with me. See, he hasn't been off the farm for a very long time, maybe never, now that I think about it. It's a vacation."

Her words didn't make much sense, not that they ever did. Seb figured his muddled brain had more to do with his confusion than Lucy's usual rambling. He needed to think yet couldn't make sense of his own mind. It kept telling Seb that he'd deceived himself by investing in a town run by women, a place formerly known as Percyville until the ladies insisted it be renamed Emancipation. He finally realized that his decision had little if anything to do with money. His motives were deeper, buried at the back of his mind for years. Now he was forced to confront them.

Seb could no longer ignore what his gut was telling him. If anything could draw Elizabeth Cole away from her high-powered Washington, D.C., lawyer's office, it would be a town like this, a woman's town. The Pearly Gates and even the *Tribune* hadn't been investments at all, he now realized. They'd been lures.

It sickened and confused Seb to realize that his mother still had so much influence over him, even though it had been over twenty years since he'd last set eyes on her. Yet he was curiously satisfied on the one score. He hadn't gone to her seeking answers or perhaps even some sign that she cared. She'd come to him, even if she didn't know it. Now what?

"Please don't be mad at me or Pa."

Lost in his own dark thoughts, Seb gave Lucy a blank stare.

"I hate it when you're mad."

"I'm not mad, Lucy." He reached out and patted her hand. "Disappointed, I suppose, but not mad."

"I'll do everything I can to keep Pa away from you. I promise."

Too distracted to give the Preston family any more thought, Seb glanced around the saloon. The pool tables had been pushed aside, dressed up as buffet tables once again, and bunting woven in stripes of red, white, and blue draped the bar and the walls. Corn was popping on the stove and a big bowl of lemonade sat on a small table next to the bar. It looked and smelled like the Fourth of July, but Seb didn't feel like celebrating. With or without his enthusiasm, soon the rest of the food would arrive and then the party would begin.

Looking back at Lucy, Seb said, "I don't expect the bar itself to be very busy tonight, but I would appreciate it if you'd come back to work. Jack hates politics and the fact that we're putting on a show for women suffragists, so he took the night off."

She brightened, as if this was a sign of forgiveness. Maybe it was. "I planned to be here all night anyway," Lucy assured him. "I'd be happy to serve drinks or whatever you want me to do."

It occurred to Seb right then that what he wanted was for Lucy to crawl into his arms, to hold him and remain in his embrace forever. That thought, mingled with his random notions of actually coming face-to-face with his mother, was too much to handle. Shaking off the torrent of emotions coming at him from every direction, Seb pushed out of his chair.

"I expect the Lease party in about an hour," he said. "We'd better get to work."

As he ambled away, looking more disturbed than before, Lucy remembered the letter. "Oh, wait," she said, digging it out of her pocket. "I picked up your mail while I was at the depot."

When he took the envelope from her, his expression darkened even more. Then he stuffed the letter into his jacket pocket and headed for the bar.

No matter what excuses Sebastian gave her, Lucy knew that he was still upset, and she knew exactly why. She'd ruined his life. She supposed the honorable thing to do would be to free him from what he referred to as his contract, to divorce him and let him get back to living his life in a way that would make him happy again. To do that, of course, would mean that she'd have to tell her father the marriage wasn't real. Then, if he were still speaking to her, she'd be forced to return home with him next Tuesday.

No longer sure what to do or even wrong from right, Lucy met a few of the townswomen at the door and helped arrange their salads, pies, and fresh-baked breads on the buffet table. She was wearing her yellow dress, something she didn't usually don to work at the saloon. Given the party mood and the fact that she probably wouldn't be toting many trays filled with beers, she decided not to change into her hostessing getup.

As the chef and his crew arrived from the Palace Arms kitchen carrying platters of ham, beef, and turkey, Lucy saw that her father was bobbing along behind them.

"There you are, girl," Jeremiah said, shuffling over to the buffet table. "Boy, did me and Dusty have a time over at that hotel."

Almost afraid to hear, Lucy asked, "What happened?"

"That Mary Lease and her cronies went and took all the rooms at the hotel, including the one me and Dusty had."

Lucy already knew that the other hotels weren't very pleasant, not to mention the fact that she doubted her father had enough money left to take a hotel room for another week.

"I don't know what to do," she said. "Maybe we can find a boardinghouse or something that doesn't charge too much."

Jeremiah beamed, his round face creased like a pumpkin. "Don't get in a fret. I figured it out all by myself. Me and Dusty can stay in that fancy sitting room of yours."

This wasn't a good idea. While she shared Sebastian's bed almost nightly, she'd always left him to his privacy during their waking hours. She glanced at her "husband," watching as he hoisted a small barrel of pickles onto the bar, and noted the deep frown he still wore. He wasn't going to like this at all.

"Pa, listen," she said, determined not to make Sebastian any madder than he already was, "it's an awfully small room and just has the one little bed."

"That's not a problem. I'm taking the bed and Dusty can bunk on the floor. He sleeps on worse when he's camped out with the sheep."

Lucy couldn't think of a way out, not with customers

streaming into the saloon, a few of them already calling their orders to her. Figuring she'd come up with a plan later, for now she said, "I'll talk to the desk clerk when I'm done here tonight."

"No need," Jeremiah assured her. "I already got the key. Dusty is up in that little sitting room as we speak, stowing our gear."

Lucy could see it all now; her phony marriage, her future, the Penelope column, all of it up in smoke. She considered telling Sebastian about this latest turn of events and then decided it would be best for him to discover the new arrangements on his own. Then he would probably throw her and her family into the street.

As her father shuffled over to the buffet table and began picking at the food before the guest of honor showed up, Lucy shrugged off her worries and went to work. It wasn't long before the saloon was crowded and so noisy she couldn't hear herself think. Not such a bad thing.

As she was carting a tray of beers to a table in the back, Lucy noticed that Dusty had arrived. He was sitting at a table with one of the Barkdoll twins—which one was no longer of any consequence—and huddled up close, as if in the midst of an intimate conversation. As Lucy passed them, Merry—she guessed, due to the men's clothing—reached out and whopped Dusty upside the head.

After she delivered her load, Lucy stopped by the table where Dusty and Merry still sat. She noticed that he was practically drooling on her shoulder. "Is everything all right here?" she asked brightly.

"No," Merry said. "Everything here is not all right. Is this hammerhead really your brother?"

Lucy stiffened. "Yes, he most certainly is."

"Didn't your parents teach him any manners?"

Lucy glanced at Dusty. "What have you done?"

"Nothing," he said, his adoring gaze pinned to Merry. "We were just talking, getting to know each other."

"Well, this is all you're going to get to know about me, buster." With that, Merry slapped him again, shoved out of her chair, and stomped off to the bar.

"Oh, Dusty," Lucy said, her free hand on her hip, "what did you say to her?"

"Nothing much. I don't know why a gal expects to be treated like a lady if she's wearing men's Levi's."

"Ladies do that here, so I'd be really careful the next time you try to take up with one of our emancipated gals."

Dusty grumbled, then his eyes suddenly went wide. "Uh-oh. Charlie's here and Pa is going after him."

As if she didn't have enough on her mind. Turning wearily in the direction of the front door, Lucy saw that her father had reached Charlie and was driving his index finger into his shoulder. His face was the color of a ripe tomato and he was shouting, hanging their dirty laundry out for all to see. If that wasn't bad enough, Lucy spotted Mary Lease and her group trying to duck around the quarrel but not having much luck. Banging her tray against her hip as she walked, Lucy marched toward them.

"And another thing," Jeremiah said, again with a jab to Charlie's shoulder. "When I get back home, I'm gonna have me a nice long talk with your pa, see if I can't get back that nice dowry I provided for Lucy."

"What dowry?" Charlie asked as he backed out of Jeremiah's short reach.

"The money it cost me and Lucy's ma to put together her trusso with all them fancy wedding gowns and such."

"Pa, please," Lucy said, worming her way between the men. "Our guest of honor is here and she can't even get into the saloon with you carrying on like this."

With a glance toward the door where the woman with the hatchet face gave them squinty eyes and pursed lips, Jeremiah looked back at Charlie and said, "We can take this up later. I'm not done with you yet."

Then he shuffled aside, allowing the group of women to come into the saloon.

Looking for Sebastian, sure he would be heading her way with fire in his eyes, Lucy took a wild glance around the room. He was nowhere in sight.

Counting herself lucky, she approached Mary Lease and asked, "May I get you ladies something to drink? We have the usual, plus lemonade, root beer, and even a few bottles of Coca-Cola."

Lucy wasn't surprised when Lease puckered her lips and said, "I'll have a lemonade, thank you."

As she took drink orders from the other ladies, Mayor Gerdy and members of the town council swarmed over the Lease group, and Lucy headed to the bar for fresh glasses. As she gathered them, she noticed that Dusty and Merry were leaning against the counter and drinking beer. They were huddled in conversation again, and this time Merry didn't seem to mind so much. Maybe it was the beer.

Despite Sebastian's prediction, plenty of his customers wanted drinks and beers, a real challenge for Lucy, who had to thread her way through elbow-to-elbow townsfolk. The saloon wasn't simply crowded but packed. Even with a pair of giant fans turning overhead, the heat was oppressive. Somehow Lucy managed to struggle through the next few hours.

She was thinking of going outside for a breath of fresh air, at least to get away from the noise for a while, when Mayor Gerdy began to bang on a beer mug with a spoon. As the crowd gradually quieted, she chanted, "Speech, speech, speech."

As members of the council and others joined in, Mary Lease finally allowed herself to be hoisted onto a chair.

With a wave of her arms, Lease quieted the crowd and said, "Thank you so much. I appreciate your support and this lovely party, even though I never imagined it would be held in a saloon. As much as I've enjoyed myself, I think you can rest assured that this is my first and last appearance at such an establishment."

This was met by female chuckles and male catcalls.

Ignoring them, Lease continued. "My purpose here today is not to give a speech. If you'd like to hear my thoughts on the upcoming presidential election, I invite you all to come to the rally at City Hall on Thursday. There I will also explain why this is no longer a government of the people, by the people, and for the people, but a government of Wall Street, by Wall Street, and for Wall Street."

A great roar came up from the crowd, one that was impossible to identity as pro or con, and then Lease was helped down from her makeshift platform.

In the shadows by the storeroom, Seb read the newest letter from Billy in Denver. *Dear Seb: I hate to tell you this, but I believe that Kate has learned your whereabouts. I sure didn't tell her, but there's talk that she's planning a trip out your way. I'll keep you informed as best I can, and if there's any way I can stop her, you know I will. I wish I had better news. Your friend, Billy.*

Seb muttered several oaths under his breath. Kate. Just what he needed in addition to everything else. He considered the possibility that she might actually board a train for Emancipation and then dismissed the idea. Kate was a little nutty, but not completely crazy.

Distracting himself from that possible problem with another, he listened intently and kept his eye on the crowd—on one woman in particular. As often as he'd thought of this moment over the years and as many times as he'd practiced what he wanted to say to his mother should they ever meet again, his mind was blank. Now that the time was finally upon him, all Seb wanted to do was avoid her, shun her the way she'd shunned him for so long.

As the party broke up and folks began to head for the door, Seb breathed a sigh of relief. A knot of men standing a few feet away from him suddenly parted and out popped Lucy.

"I've been looking all over for you," she said breathlessly. Tendrils of damp hair licked the skin at her neck and temples, and her pretty yellow gown was stained with all manner of drink.

Smiling for the first time that day, Seb said, "You've found me. What do you need?"

"It's not what I need. Mary Lease is looking for you to thank you for hosting her party. Isn't she wonderful?"

It galled Seb to think that Lucy was so impressed with this group of women, and distressed him even more to realize that he had to accept their gratitude. He was trying to think of an excuse good enough to ignore the request when Lucy took him by the hand.

"Come on. Mary is waiting for you."

As usual, Lucy didn't give him much choice. Seb allowed himself to be dragged toward the front door. As they reached the group of women, Mayor Gerdy intercepted them.

"There you are, Seb. I'd like to introduce you to Mary Lease."

The woman, her expression as pinched and tight as a new corset, extended a bony hand. "Thank you so much for the lovely welcome party. The fare and the company were grand. It's been a real pleasure to meet you, ah, Seb, was it?"

He was listening to Lease but watching his mother out of the corner of his eye. "It's Sebastian."

The gray eyes so like his own didn't even blink.

"That's it?" Lease persisted. "Sebastian?"

Eyes hard on his mother now, Seb said, "Sebastian Cole."

"What a coincidence," said Lease, turning to her companion. "My lawyer's name is Cole; Elizabeth Cole."

Elizabeth's left eye fluttered, but other than that, she remained impassive. Then, her voice as cool as a mountain stream, she said, "Not so coincidental. Cole is a fairly common name."

Chapter Nineteen

Seb stood there for a couple of beats, waiting for some show of recognition from his mother. The best he got was a curious gleam in her eyes. Maybe it was because she thought him crazy. Could he have been mistaken and there were two female lawyers named Elizabeth Cole? Was this woman a complete stranger? He studied her features, her tall proud carriage, and realized that had he passed her on the street, he never would have recognized her as his mother. Was he kidding himself now?

Seb was shaken out of his confusion as Jeremiah nudged him aside and said, "So you're a lady lawyer, huh? I never heard of such a thing."

Elizabeth barely glanced at him as she said, "I imagine you've never heard of a lot of things."

Jeremiah laughed, looked her up and down, and said, "You're a big one, aren't you?"

Elizabeth looked down her aristocratic nose and said, "And you, sir, are a bloated gnat."

"Oh, goodness, Miss Cole," Lucy said, cutting off the

233

exchange. "Sometimes Pa's mouth gets to running ahead of his brain. Sorry if he offended you."

Finally finding his own voice, Seb felt that some sort of introduction was called for. Addressing Mary Lease, he said, "Lucy works for me and Mr. Preston is her father."

Jeremiah puffed up his chest and said, "Lucy works for you? Is that the best you can do? Seems to me it's about time you got used to introducing Lucy as your wife."

"Newlyweds, doncha know," Jeremiah said, turning to the tall lawyer and offering a wink. "I expect it takes some getting used to."

Elizabeth stared at Lucy for a long moment, taking in the stained dress, disheveled hair, and her basically awestruck expression. Then she looked at Seb, her eyebrows raised high, and said, "*This* is your wife?"

Taking exception again, Jeremiah piped up. "That's right, and she's also my little Lucy, you laced-up, chicken-beaked—"

"Pa, no!" Lucy grabbed his arm and pulled, muttering to Seb as she dragged him away, "I think I'd better take him to the hotel now."

Seb gave a short nod. "That would be a really good idea."

Mary Lease shook her head with a considerable amount of disapproval. "With that bit of nasty business out of the way, I must say that it's been a long day and we're going to retire now. Thank you again for the warm welcome, Mr. Cole. We hope to see you during the rally at City Hall."

As the group of women started filing out the door, Elizabeth said to Lease, "You go on ahead. I want to pick up some newspapers and a cigar. I'll be along shortly."

Lease glanced at her lawyer and clucked her tongue. "One of these days I'm going to break you of that vile cigar habit, Elizabeth. You mark my words."

After the orator had gone, Elizabeth turned her attention

to Seb. She smiled and said, "Do you have any of those little cigarillos?"

Even with his doubts, Seb was almost a hundred percent certain that this was his mother. For the life of him, he couldn't understand her lack of response. That was all she had to say? "Do you have cigarillos?" Where were the "Nice to see you," the "Lord, but it's been a long time since I've seen you, son," speeches?

"Maybe I can get them somewhere else?" she asked.

"I have them. Follow me."

Seb led her to the little alcove and chose a package containing four of the little cigars. As he walked, he straightened his tie and ran his fingers through his hair, plowing the errant lock in with the rest of the thick crop. When he handed the package of cigarillos to Elizabeth, that stubborn hank of hair fell back onto his forehead.

"Thank you," she said, taking the smokes. "Will you sit and have a drink with me?"

At last some kind of recognition, or so he hoped. "That sounds like a good idea. What would you like?"

"Do you have any brandy?"

"Will Napoleon cognac do?

"Oh, yes. That's my favorite."

Amused to think that they shared at least one passion, Seb noticed a few streaks of red in his mother's hair. His mental image of her had faded over the years, but he could have sworn she had brown hair. Thinking of the wide gulf between them, wondering if it was possible to bridge the gap, Seb led Elizabeth to a quiet table and then collected the cognac and two snifters. The saloon was far from empty, but not so crowded they couldn't have a private conversation.

After they were seated Seb poured two measures of cognac and Elizabeth unwrapped one of the little cigars. Then she sat there holding it out like a princess. Seb immediately struck a match on the bottom of his boot and lit the tip.

After taking a long puff of the cigar, Elizabeth slowly let the smoke curl out of her mouth. Then she sighed and said, "I'm proud to be a part of Mary Lease's team, but she's much too straitlaced for my taste. There's nothing like a good smoke and a shot of fine brandy after a tiring day, wouldn't you agree?"

She raised her glass to Seb and then took a long swallow.

"Was that a toast?" he asked, hoisting his own glass.

"I suppose it was," she said coolly. "We might as well toast to stumbling across each other after all these years. It's an uncanny coincidence, don't you think?"

Seb didn't know what to think. How could she be so calm, so unaffected, while sitting across from her grown son after such a long absence? Perhaps it was the shock of coming face-to-face with him. After all, he'd had the entire evening to study her, to know that they were in the same room at long last, and to ponder the many questions he had about their estrangement.

The little boy in him eager for her apologies, even for her approval, the man he'd become tried to keep a tight rein on his emotions as he said, "It was a surprise, all right. I thought maybe you'd come looking for me before now."

Her expression no longer cool, Elizabeth's tight lips and narrow eyes displayed irritation at the least. She took another sip of brandy and said, "Do you have any idea how hard it has been for me, a woman working in this man's world?"

If he could have found his sense of humor, Seb might have laughed. "What does that have to do with us?"

"You seem to be expecting something of me that I'm not sure I have to give." She took another long pull on her cigar. Through another ribbon of smoke, she said, "I've had to learn to be tough, never to show emotion, or for God's sake, cry. The minute a man smells weakness in a woman of my position, he moves in for the kill."

Feeling abandoned all over again, Seb blurted out, "Speaking of kill, are you aware that your husband is dead?"

She closed her eyes for a moment. "Caleb hasn't been my husband for many years. He was murdered?"

"In a manner of speaking. It was a slow death; took him nearly five years to die." His eyes hard on her, knowing he would probably regret the words but unable to stop the spill, he added, "You killed him."

Something skittered across her expression—pain, regret? Or maybe that was what Seb wanted to see. She took another sip of cognac and asked, "How did I do that?"

"When you left, he didn't care about anything, not even me. He let the farm go to ruin, sent me to town to forage for food, money, and all the other things most folks take for granted. His life was reduced to sitting in your chair and drinking himself to death."

Head low, expression thoughtful, Elizabeth said, "I'm sorry to hear that, but I don't see how any of that is my fault. If I had stayed with Caleb, I would have died. Would you have liked that better?"

Seb banged his fist against the table. Aware that heads were turning in their direction, he lowered his voice to a hiss as he said, "My father never raised a hand to you."

"As you've succinctly pointed out, there are other ways to die. I did what I had to do in order to survive. Fault me for that if you must, but it's the truth."

Truth. Seb didn't know the truth of her life or what drove her to leave him and his father, and he wasn't sure now that he wanted to know. She was more lawyer than mother, spinning yarns the way a weaver spins wool, working to convince him that she was utterly blameless. He wondered if she really knew her true self.

Worn out with trying to make himself known to this woman who remained a stranger, Seb finished off his cognac in one gulp and said, "I guess we all do what we must to survive."

Elizabeth glanced around the saloon. "Is this place yours?"

He nodded.

"Nice. You must have been around eleven or so when your father died. Who took you in?"

He almost smiled as he said, "Nobody."

If this distressed Elizabeth in any way, she didn't show it. Again she looked around. "In that case, I'm even more impressed with your success."

Some ugly thing inside Seb wanted to shout that he also owned a saloon in Denver, plus a large chunk of the Emancipation *Tribune,* no thanks to her. Instead he poured himself another two fingers of cognac.

Elizabeth kept at him, interrogating him as if he were on the witness stand. Seb took this as a sign that she cared at least a little. "This wife of yours . . ."

There was no way to explain why he and Lucy were married or even what she meant to him. He said, "I'm sorry, but I'd rather not discuss Lucy with you right now."

A slight nod. And then, "Are there any children?"

"No."

Again the hint of a nod. Then, in a sudden gesture that made Seb's chest feel as if it might implode, she slid her hand across his and gave it a squeeze. "This has been hard for us both. I realize you probably have some rather unpleasant thoughts about me, and I can't say that I blame you."

Seb couldn't deny that, but he wasn't ready to speak of it. "Mostly what I have are questions."

"Of course you do." She finished her cognac, snatched up the pack of cigarillos, and said, "We both have a lot to digest and a lot more to talk about. Would you mind very much if we continue this conversation tomorrow? I'm exhausted and don't feel that I can do you justice tonight."

It felt like another rejection, and yet Seb wasn't entirely ready to delve any deeper into the past just then. He offered a tight smile. "Tomorrow sounds fine."

"Thank you. Now what do I owe you?"

"If you're talking about money, nothing."

"Thank you again." Then she rose, slowly and gracefully, a sunflower stretching and turning its face to the morning sun. Somehow, even in a tailored jacket and trouserettes, his mother managed to look feminine.

"You've grown into quite a handsome man, Sebastian," she said, with the smile he vaguely remembered. "You remind me of my father, God rest his soul."

Seb had only hazy recollections of his grandfather. Neither flattered nor offended, he shrugged.

"I'll just be off to the hotel now." She drifted around the table to where he stood. Touching his elbow, she said, "Until tomorrow then?"

"I'd like that."

"Believe it or not, so would I. Good night, Sebastian."

Seb spent the rest of the night going over the conversation with his mother and trying to understand at least a small part of her, the part in particular that could leave an innocent child behind. In no mood to play cards or even billiards, he kept himself busy doing things usually left to the help. First he went through the storeroom, dusting shelves, organizing supplies, and making notes for future orders. Then he went behind the bar, lining up bottles alphabetically, washing out glasses, and gathering up dirty rags that would be taken to the laundry the next day.

Seb was encroaching on Pearl's territory, not to mention getting in her way, so she finally said, "What in hell are you doing back here? Want to take over my job?"

She stood there with her hands on hips, looking for all the world as if she owned the place. Seb snapped, "I'm just getting things ready for tomorrow."

Her posture unchanged, Pearl said, "Unless you've got another party up your sleeve, not much is happening tomorrow. Little Joe can take care of the rags and such, or are you trying to save the few pennies you pay him?"

He sighed and said, "I'm just trying to keep busy."

"You look like hell." Pearl was nothing if not blunt.

"Why don't you go to your room? Jack will be back soon, and I can look after things until then."

Seb glanced around the saloon. Only a dozen or so customers remained, most of them regulars who had to be tossed out at closing time each night.

"You might have a point."

She puffed up her enormous bosom. "I have two if you'd ever take the time to have a look."

As drained as he was, Seb found some relief in Pearl's bawdy humor. He let his gaze drift down to her cleavage. "And mighty fine points they are. See you tomorrow."

"If you ever get tired of that wife of yours," she called after him as he walked away, "I can give you a point or two that will keep your head spinning for a week—both of them."

Laughing to himself, Seb might have considered the ways Pearl could accomplish such a thing, but she'd also reminded him of Lucy. He'd hardly given her a thought since the Lease group had walked into the saloon. Seb had been so wrapped up in his own misery, he'd forgotten that she had her own family woes to face. Dusty and her crazy father would be in town for another week. He didn't know how troubling that would be to Lucy, but Seb had barely survived the four days they'd already been here. How would he ever manage them for another week?

His thoughts darker than before, frustrated on so many levels he couldn't count them all, Seb let himself into his room and lit the lamp by the door. The first thing he noticed was a worn travel bag sitting on the floor at the foot of the bed. Mounds of female clothing were stacked on his dressers.

"What the hell?" he muttered to himself.

A feminine moan reached Seb's ears, and then he saw Lucy roll over in his bed.

Although he was surprised to see her there, and not entirely unhappy about it either, he gestured toward the clothing and said, "What the hell is all this?"

Lucy sat up and rubbed the sleep from her eyes. She was

wearing a plain muslin nightgown buttoned up to her throat and her hair was loose, spread all over her shoulders and back.

"Sorry," she said, her voice curiously meek. "Mary Lease and her entourage filled up the hotel. They couldn't get their own room back, see, and I couldn't put them in the street or at one of the other hotels. You said they were bad places, remember, and I didn't know what else to do with my things. Pa and Dusty took my room."

"What?"

"I couldn't think what else to do."

Seb stomped over to the connecting door and turned the key in the lock. Then he marched back to the bed and slipped out of his jacket. As he removed his shirt and the rest of his clothing, hanging items on the bedpost along with his jacket, he kept one eye on Lucy.

She was watching his every move, looking a lot like a naughty child caught tossing eggs at a neighbor's barn. Any minute now she would start apologizing all over again, or worse, begin to cry.

"Let's not talk about this anymore tonight," he said wearily.

"But I even used your bathtub. I was such a mess after the party, I just couldn't get into bed without washing up good."

"I don't mind, Lucy." Seb went to the door and doused the light. Then he returned to the bed and crawled in beside her.

In the darkness her voice reached him, chocolate for the ears. "I bet you're sorry you ever met me."

Lucy had given him a lot of pause and more headaches than a man ought to have to endure, but sorry wasn't an emotion he'd ever had when it came to her. After the letter from Billy warning him about Kate, the uncomfortable conversation with his mother, the questions left unanswered and the turmoil stirred up in his mind, Seb was in no condition to delve into his feelings for Lucy.

He rolled over, took her into his arms, and said, "Please, no more talk tonight. I'm tired of talk."

Surprising him, Lucy did as he asked, snuggling closer, her head just beneath his chin. Seb buried his face in her silken hair, inhaling her scent, the hint of lilac, and was struck by a need so strong, it nearly overwhelmed him. He wanted her now, and badly, yet recognized that his need went beyond the physical. Unwilling, perhaps unable to examine himself any further this night, he rolled her over and crushed his lips to hers.

As the kiss deepened, while Seb feasted on Lucy's sweet mouth, he worked at the buttons on her nightgown.

Wedging her hands between their bodies, she gave his chest a mighty shove. "No. We can't."

Seb was already too far gone for thought. "Can't what?"

"You know. Do this."

He would not be denied. "Why not?"

"Pa and Dusty are in the next room, remember?"

His hands back at the buttons, Seb said, "Then we won't tell them what we're doing."

Lucy pushed his hands away. "No, they'll hear us. The bed's too jiggly."

Right then, Seb didn't care if the bed tooted horns and played "A Hot Time in the Old Town."

"I need you, Lucy," he whispered into her hair. "I need you more than ever. Don't turn me away."

"Oh, Sebastian," she murmured. "I wish I could be what you want, but I just can't do this with my pa so close by."

Seb wasn't going to argue about it any longer, nor was he concerned about Lucy's father. He said, "All right, we'll do it your way. Just let me touch you. I have to touch you."

She relaxed then, her head resting on the pillow, and Seb quickly dispatched the buttons on her nightgown and pulled the garment up over her head. Then his hands and mouth went to work, skimming over her body like an ocean breeze, churning up a frothy wake of desire. Lucy moaned and writhed under his touch, and when he finally dipped into the soft flesh beneath the curls at her groin, he found her hot and wet, ready for him.

Taking things further, Seb continued to stroke her there, driving her until she arched her back and muttered, "Oh, my stars, please don't stop."

He abruptly left her then and rolled over onto his back.

All was quiet save for Lucy's panting and the roar in his own ears. Then she quietly said, "Sebastian? Where did you go?"

"I think we were starting to jiggle the bed." It was amazing, Seb thought, how easily a lie could slide off a man's lips when he was hornier than Eros.

Lucy groaned and then slid up beside him. "Maybe if I try," she suggested, "I can keep it from jiggling."

She straddled him then, right where he wanted her, and slowly lowered herself onto his body. "Is that all right?"

Seb couldn't speak. He made a noise in his throat that was supposed to be agreement, but it came out sounding more like a death rattle. Lucy must have understood because she began to pump him, raising her hips high and then plunging back down in wild abandon.

When her release came a few moments later, she cried out and collapsed on his chest, her voice muffled against his skin. Seb didn't know how he'd lasted as long as he had, and when he came, the force of his climax left him shuddering from head to toe.

As he was lying there, spent, exhausted, and exhilarated, Lucy whispered against his chest, "Did the bed jiggle?"

"No," he lied again, this time to protect the innocent. "I didn't hear a thing."

The next morning, right at dawn, there came a loud, incessant knocking at the connecting door. Lucy's eyes popped open and she reached for her dressing gown.

"Son of a bitch," Sebastian growled. "What does a man have to do to get a little sleep around here?"

"I'll take care of it," she said, buttoning the gown as she hurried to the door. "Go back to sleep."

"Yeah, that will happen."

Mindful of Sebastian's mood and the fact that he hated to be awakened so early, Lucy unlocked the door and opened it a crack. There stood her father, his forehead creased with worry.

"Pa, what are you doing? You know Sebastian doesn't like to wake up this early."

"Sorry, Lucy, but I waited as long as I could."

"What's wrong?"

"It's Dusty. He was drinking a lot of beer last night. I'm worried sick about him cause he didn't come back to the hotel. He wouldn't worry me like this. I think something bad happened to him."

Chapter Twenty

Lucy wheeled around and said to Sebastian, "It's my brother. He's missing."

"Lucky him," he grumbled, burying his head in the pillow. "Maybe he's off somewhere getting a good night's sleep."

She came fully into the room. "You don't understand. This is serious. Dusty wouldn't stay out all night without telling Pa. He's worried that something bad has happened to him."

With a start, Lucy realized that her father had followed her into the room. Moving right up to the foot of the bed, he stared down at Sebastian. "My boy was drinking a lot of beer at your saloon last night. Do you think maybe he passed out on the floor and got locked in for the night?"

Sebastian raised his head an inch, gave Lucy one hard, narrow-eyed look, and muttered, "I doubt it. Jack looks for customers sleeping it off before he locks up each night, and then he goes to his room upstairs. Even if he missed your son, Jack leaves the key in the lock. Dusty could have let himself out."

"Then where in tarnation could he be?"

Sebastian's gaze on Lucy again, she could see the crazed

look in his eyes. She gave him a bright smile. He groaned and fell back on the pillow.

Thinking back to the night before, Lucy snapped her fingers and said, "The last time I saw Dusty he was cuddled up with Merry Barkdoll at the bar. Could he possibly be out at her ranch?"

Sebastian laughed into the pillow.

"This isn't funny," Jeremiah declared. "Dusty could be hurt, or maybe something even more awful."

"Sorry," Sebastian said, his head still buried in the pillow. "I just can't imagine Merry putting up with your son."

"Well, he's got to be somewheres, might just as well be with her. How do we find her place?"

" 'We'?"

"He meant me," Lucy said quickly, in fact a little too quickly. "Except I don't know where she lives either."

"I guess you and me are going to have to get us another buggy," Jeremiah said to Sebastian. "Seems you're the only one who can help. Besides, it's the least you can do for your brother-in-law."

Sebastian peered over the edge of his sheet and tried to spear Lucy with another piercing look. She deftly avoided his gaze. Sitting straight up, he said, "You've got to be kidding. I'm not going anywhere but back to sleep."

"Pa's not kidding," Lucy said quietly. "And I also think he's right. I barely know my way around town, and I have no idea where the ranches are out here. I also have to get to work at the paper this morning." Not to mention she hadn't finished her Penelope column. "I can't let Hazel down."

Looking from her to Jeremiah, Sebastian's wide shoulders sagged in defeat. "All right," he said wearily. "Give me a few minutes to get dressed and I'll meet you downstairs. And you'd better have coffee—lots of coffee."

"Thank you, son. I knew you wouldn't refuse to help the family." With that, Jeremiah shuffled out of the room.

"Family?" Sebastian said. "Doesn't he mean *your* family?"

Turning away from him with a shrug, Lucy busied herself with the pile of clothing on his dresser, anything to keep from facing Sebastian's wrath. It wasn't long in coming. She heard him approach, and then he took hold of her elbow and spun her around to face him.

"This is going to cost you," he warned.

She gulped. "You can have everything I've saved from my jobs."

"I'm not talking about money." His gray eyes glittered like fresh-minted coins. "Tonight I intend to jiggle the hell out of that bed, my way. No excuses."

After Sebastian and her father were on their way out of town, Lucy gathered up the first draft of her column and headed for the newspaper office. Hazel was at her desk, pencil flying across her notebook.

"Looks like I'm not the only one who's pushing the deadline," Lucy said, ducking around behind the counter.

"Oh, girl, you don't know the half of it." Hazel shoved away from the desk but stayed in her chair. "I wish Mary Lease would have scheduled her talk for tonight instead of tomorrow. If I don't get something into this edition of the *Rustler* about her speech, the *Tribune* will have all week to run stories about her. By next Friday it will be old news."

"But how can you write about it before she talks?"

"I'm just getting a column set up for it, putting down some personal information and such. We're going to have to write it and set the type after she speaks." She glanced up at Lucy, her eyes hopeful. "Do you think Sebastian will give you the entire night off on Thursday?"

Knowing his mood, Lucy was pretty sure he'd give her the night off for the rest of her life. "I believe that can be arranged."

"Great." Hazel eyed the papers in Lucy's hands. "Is that your new column?"

"Such as it is. I haven't had much time to work on it,

what with Pa and Dusty in town." She sighed and handed over the column. "Did you happen to see them last night?"

As she perused the column, Hazel shook her head. "I thought they went home yesterday."

"They missed the train."

Hazel's chin shot up. "Uh-oh. How did Sebastian take the news?"

"How do you think?"

When Hazel burst out laughing, Lucy was finally able to see a little humor in the situation and joined in with her. Then Hazel's chuckles abruptly died in her throat. Her gaze somewhere over Lucy's shoulder, her small eyes went big and round. Lucy turned to see Mary Lease standing in the doorway. She carried a copy of the *Rustler* in her hands.

"Good morning, ladies," she said, walking up to the counter. "I'd like to speak to the editor of this newspaper."

Visibly nervous, Hazel pushed out of her chair and went to greet her visitor. "That's me, Hazel Allison. Pleasure to meet you, Miss Lease. I didn't get a chance at last night's party."

"The pleasure is all mine, I assure you." She dropped the newspaper on the counter, and that was when Lucy noticed that there were two issues, not one. Jabbing the papers with her index finger, Lease went on. "Most newspapers I read are just politics, politics, politics, but this one is very refreshing. It must be of great interest to the women of this town."

Lucy could almost hear the blush in her voice as Hazel said, "That was my intent when I started the paper."

"In that case, you've done a wonderful job of carrying out those intentions. I just love this little newspaper, and I'm especially fond of your Penelope column. I would very much like to meet her, too."

"Oh, umm, gosh, that's impossible. Penelope isn't from around here."

"Oh? How may I contact her?"

There was a long pause before Hazel said, "You see, due

to the nature of this column, she prefers to remain anonymous. I can pass your kind comments on to her if you like."

"That would be nice, but what I'd really like is to meet her."

Again Hazel paused. Her voice tight, as if she'd swallowed a cotton ball, she finally said, "I wish you could meet her, but Penelope's identity has to stay a secret."

Lease propped her elbows on the counter and leaned in close. Then she said, "My dear Madam Editor, I am an orator, not a politician. I know how to keep a secret."

Hazel glanced over her shoulder, the question looming large in her eyes. Lucy didn't think about it for long. She smiled and gave a tiny shrug. *It's up to you.*

Seb wasn't interested in taking a ride out to the Barkdoll ranch unless he absolutely had no choice. A mug of coffee in hand, he went to the Pearly Gates and took a thorough look around. No Dusty. Figuring he might have moved on to another place, Seb checked a couple of saloons. No Dusty. Thinking he might have gotten so drunk that he got himself tossed in jail, Seb decided to pay a visit to B. J. Binstock. Still no Dusty.

He was coming out of the sheriff's office when Jeremiah pulled up and beckoned him into the rig. As he settled himself, Seb said, "I checked with everyone I can think of and no one has seen Dusty since last night at the Pearly Gates. As strange as it may sound, I can't think of any place he could be but at the Barkdoll ranch."

"Then let's hope that's where he's at." With a cluck of his tongue and a slap of the reins, Jeremiah got the horse to moving.

They hadn't quite left town before the old man turned to Seb, his gaze pinned on the pistol resting on his thigh, and said, "Do you always wear that thing?"

"Just when I need to shoot folks who insist on waking me up before noon." With a sideways glance and the hint of a grin, Seb added, "Actually, in my line of work wearing a gun is pretty much a necessity."

"That's another thing I've been meaning to talk to you about."

Seb stifled a groan, thinking this was going to be another long trip.

"You're a family man now," Jeremiah went on. "Being a gambler and running a drinking establishment isn't a fitting occupation for you."

Seb's eyebrows met the errant hank of hair. "A family man?"

Jeremiah elbowed his ribs. "Didn't take Lucy's ma and me but nine months to produce our first, and I don't expect it will take Lucy any longer than that either. You can't have your little ones running around in a saloon."

Seb felt himself shrinking in the seat. How much more of Lucy's insane plan was he to endure?

"I think we need to find you a new business," Jeremiah continued. "Something worthy of my grandchildren."

Seb's throat was so dry he couldn't even form words. "Huh?"

"Don't worry, I intend to help you out some. What kind of business are you interested in?"

"Saloons and gambling, lots of gambling," he grumbled, hoping that would end the conversation. If that didn't, this would. "I'm even thinking of putting in a house of ill-repute."

Jeremiah shot him a startled look and then laughed. "Now, Seb, I know you're just funning me. What about a barbershop? Know anything about cutting hair and shaving faces?"

Seb groaned under his breath and slid even lower in the seat. Then he looked right through the old man as he said, "The only thing I know about razors is how to slit a man's throat."

Jeremiah studied him, his frown as thick as molasses. "You're not being very cooperative."

"Sorry. I get that way when I don't get enough sleep."

Seb thought that would be the end of it, but Jeremiah picked up where he left off. "Well, what about becoming a farmer? That's what I do, and though the pay isn't much, your family will never go without. You'll grow your own food and have livestock in the barn and such. It's a good life."

"I have absolutely no interest in farming." Seb turned to the old man, showing his teeth. "None. Zero."

"All right, all right, not everyone's cut out to be a farmer." He paused, but not for long. "I know—how are you at butchering hogs? You could open up your own meat market."

And so it went all the way out to the Barkdoll ranch. More than once Seb considered getting out of the rig and walking along behind it, but the fact was, he was too damn tired to sit there with his eyes open, much less move under his own steam. When at last the grove of trees leading to the ranch came into view, Seb breathed a tiny sigh of relief.

Just past the trees and directly in front of the house sat a circular corral. As it came into view, Seb spotted the Barkdoll twins on the outside of the corral. They were dressed alike in men's work clothes and floppy-brimmed hats, and their arms were draped over the top railing. Inside the corral, a dapple-gray horse was bucking wildly as it tried to dislodge the man on its back.

"Oh, my stars," Jeremiah shouted, mouth agape. "Dusty, is that you?"

When he heard his father's voice, the kid, who was clinging to the saddle horn for dear life, straightened up and looked over at the rig. This gave the horse all the advantage it needed. With a mighty lunge, the animal flung Dusty off his back and pitched him through the fence, taking a large chunk of three rails along with him.

"Great Scot!"

With that exclamation, Jeremiah urged the horse over to where his son lay; and then he and Seb hopped out of the rig.

"Son, son, can you hear me?" the old man asked, dropping to his knees and cradling the boy's head on his lap.

Dusty's bloodshot eyes were rolling around in his head, his skin was sallow, and his tongue was hanging out of the corner of his mouth. Seb thought his condition had more to do with too many beers than his journey through the fence.

His eyeballs still jittery, Dusty struggled to focus on his father. "Howdy, Pa," he finally said. "I'm all right. Sorry about last night. I got to drinking beers, and I guess I got drunk."

"You sure as the devil did get drunk." Jeremiah was all disapproving parent, but he continued to cradle his son's head. "What happened?"

"I'm not real sure," Dusty went on, his eyes still red but centered where they belonged. "I think Merry threw me up on the back of her horse and brought me here. All I know for sure is that I woke up in the barn this morning and saw I was sleeping with two goats and a pig."

Jeremiah glanced at the corral, where the horse was snorting and pawing the ground. "Why'd you get on that crazy animal? You don't know nothing about breaking horses."

His expression sheepish, Dusty said, "They told me I had to break the dang thing if I wanted a ride back to town."

"They?"

"Them girls over there."

Seb glanced at the twins, who were heading his way. In addition to being dressed alike, they each sported long blond braids that bounced along with their breasts as they walked.

Watching them as well, Jeremiah said, "Just who are those girls? Am I seeing double?"

"Those are the Barkdoll twins," Seb explained. "Cherry and Merry."

Jeremiah got to his feet and tugged Dusty up along with him. "Cherry?" he said. "That's a silly name, but it sounds kinda familiar."

Seb was happy to inform him that "Cherry is the girl

who swept Charlie off his feet before Lucy got to town."

"Son of a buck." Jeremiah's cheeks were puffed and splotchy. "Which one is she, Dusty?"

He shrugged. "Danged if I know. They keep tricking me."

As the sisters approached, and without any kind of introduction, Jeremiah demanded, "Which of you is the one called Cherry?"

The twins pointed at one another and said in unison, "She is."

Seb laughed out loud, pretty sure by the little wink that she gave him that Merry was the sister to his left.

"You see, Pa?" said Dusty. "That's what they been doing to me all morning. They lie and I can't tell one from the other."

"Now how can you say that?" said Cherry. "We've taken mighty good care of you, considering what we had to work with."

"I know." He hung his head. "They fed me some biscuits and hardtack this morning when I thought I was going to heave my guts out. Fixed me right up."

Jeremiah eyed the girls and then gave a short nod. "I thank you kindly for taking care of my boy. Now, if you don't mind, we'll just be taking him back to town and getting him cleaned up."

"Oh, but we're not done with him yet," said Merry.

Seb didn't like the sound of that. Between the marriage that didn't happen and the marriage that did, both sisters had reason to dislike Lucy and anyone in her family.

"That's right," Cherry added. "Dusty promised to help us out around here for taking such good care of him. We figured he could get cleaned up at the house when he's done, and then we'll bring him back to town later this afternoon."

Jeremiah regarded his son. "Is that what you want to do?"

Dusty dragged the toe of his boot around in the dirt and then said, "Yeah, Pa. I told them I would."

"All right." Jeremiah addressed the twins. "In that case, ladies, I guess we'll just be on our way."

Although Seb still had reservations, there was no good way to put words to them. He speared Merry with a meaningful gaze and said, "You take good care of him, you hear?"

She flashed a toothy smile. " 'Course we will, Seb. He's in good hands."

"And no more breaking horses," Jeremiah tossed over his shoulder as he headed for the rig.

"Wouldn't think of it," one of the twins called back.

Laughing to himself, Seb got into the rig and prepared himself for the long ride back to town.

At the newspaper office, Lucy suffered under Mary Lease's intense gaze for what seemed like hours before the woman said, "So you're the brains behind the sage comments and witty advice?"

Unused to such flattery, Lucy fell all over herself trying to come up with a witty reply. The best she could do was, "Well, uh, see, I just write."

Lease chuckled. Suddenly her features didn't seem as sharp or stern. "Don't be so diffident, dear. Your columns are absolutely delicious. What are your journalistic credits?"

"Credits?"

"College degrees, other newspapers you've worked for, and so on. Surely this column appears in other papers."

Feeling humbled and inadequate, as if her brain had gone far, far away to when she was a schoolgirl struggling through an arithmatic test, Lucy quietly admitted, "I didn't go to college and I don't have any other newspaper credits. I just write for Hazel."

Lease tapped the tip of her pointed chin. "I like that: a young woman of meager learning who has the gumption to make something of herself. I'm a self-educated lawyer, you know, without the fancy papers and degrees that Elizabeth Cole possesses. That doesn't mean I don't I know my way around a law book."

"Thank you, ma'am. That means a lot."

"The name is Mary. You may use it."

"Thank you, Mary."

Looking amused, Lease asked, "Have you thought of selling your column nationally?"

Lucy gulped. "N-no."

"Maybe you should."

Lucy's eyes flashed and cut to Hazel, who wore an almost identical expression. Then Hazel said, "It occurred to me that someday her column might be picked up by other newspapers, but we haven't tried to sell it anywhere else as yet."

"No time like the present," Lease said. "I have some very important contacts with the biggest newspapers in Washington, Chicago, and New York. If you don't mind, I'd like to show your column around. I have a feeling there might be quite a bit of interest."

Lucy clutched her chest. "You'd do that for me?"

"And why wouldn't I, dear? We're all in this together. Who knows?" she added with a wink. "You might be famous someday, and then you can thank me publicly."

"Oh, my stars." Eyes moist, Lucy glanced at Hazel and then back to Mary Lease. "That would be wonderful. Thank you very, very much."

"No, thank you, my dear. I very much appreciate your taking me into your confidence."

Ten minutes into their journey back to town, Seb was wallowing in the luxury of silence, save for the clopping of the horse's hooves. This steady rhythm was far more relaxing than the old man's inane babbling. For some reason Jeremiah was no longer in a talkative mood, which suited Seb perfectly.

He was just seconds away from dozing off when Jeremiah slapped his own forehead, and shouted, "By ginger, I think I've got it."

The old man's voice was like a gun going off in Seb's head. Jolted awake, he nearly toppled out of the rig. "What are you hollering about?"

"I think I've come up with the perfect business for you."

Seb had had just about all of Lucy's family he could stand. According to the terms of their contract, they weren't a family and never would be. Why the hell did he keep putting up with all this?

"I am *not* interested."

"Hear me out, Seb," Jeremiah persisted. "The newspaper business would be perfect for you. You can do whatever editors do, and Lucy can do all the writing."

Pushing his hat down low on his forehead, again Seb slumped in the seat. "Lucy sets type for the *Rustler*. I'd hardly call that writing."

"I'm talking about her column. I can't say I like everything she says, but I'm real proud of her. I just knew that someday she'd be doing something special."

Something cold crawled along the nape of his neck as Seb asked, "What column?"

"Her Penelope column, of course. I know it's supposed to be a secret and all, but surely it's not a secret she's kept from her husband. I figure she could write that column for your own newspaper, and maybe even do more."

Although he was fully awake now, Seb collapsed against the seat. With the clues Lucy had provided, he'd pretty well figured out that Penelope wrote her column in a state where women had the vote, which left Wyoming, Utah, Idaho, and Colorado. He'd also been smart enough to figure that if Lucy hadn't led him astray again, Idaho was out, as were Utah and Colorado, since they could hardly be considered northern States. That left Wyoming. How come he hadn't been smart enough to figure out that the column was being written here in Emancipation and by his own "wife," no less?

"Did Lucy tell you how she came up with the name Penelope?" Jeremiah prattled on, slapping his knee with delight.

"No, she sure as hell didn't."

"She picked it because her older sister is Penelope. Lucy named the column after her because that girl thinks she knows everything about everything. Isn't that about the funniest thing you ever heard?"

Seb just sat there in stunned silence as the old man laughed at his own joke.

"Well?" Jeremiah asked, unaware of the dark cloud sitting beside him. "So what do you think about getting yourself a newspaper business?"

Doing his best to hide his anger, a deep sense of betrayal, and even surprise, Seb looked the old man in the eye. "Trust me, Jeremiah," he said tightly. "You don't want to know what I think."

Something in his expression must have gotten through to the old man, maybe even frightened him, because throughout the rest of the ride, he never said another word.

When they arrived at the hotel, Seb left Jeremiah to return the horse and buggy and inform Lucy that Dusty had been found. With the old man out of the way, Seb hurried upstairs and let himself into his room. Reasonably certain that Lucy was still working at Hazel's, but in no mood to confront her just yet in case he was wrong, he went directly to the connecting door and knocked.

"Anyone there?" he called, making sure.

Silence. As he hoped, the door leading into the room wasn't locked. Once inside, Seb went straight to the desk and pulled open the drawer. Sure enough, there were at least a dozen questions for the "Ask Penelope" column, along with a few attempts at answers.

Seb had been expecting this, and yet it threw him off balance. He dragged the chair away from the desk and fell onto it. Sitting there for a few minutes, he worked at ignoring his personal feelings and instead considered his options.

His mind made up, Seb took a clean sheet of paper from the drawer, took up Lucy's pencil, and wrote: *Dear Penelope*.

Chapter Twenty-one

Usually when Lucy finished her work at the *Rustler* and dashed to her room to change clothing, she was tired and not particularly looking forward to going to work at the saloon. Not so today. In fact, she was so excited by dreams of a successful future in the newspaper business, she doubted if she would sleep for the rest of the week.

After divesting herself of her ink-stained clothing, Lucy scrubbed her hands as best she could, let her hair down and brushed it until it shone like the morning sun, and then donned her hostess getup. When she burst through the door of the Pearly Gates, breathless and longing to shout her joy at the top of her lungs, Sebastian was nowhere to be seen.

Hurrying over to the bar, she asked Pearl, "Where is Sebastian?"

She cocked her head, sending the purple feather on a wild ride. "In the storeroom."

Perfect, Lucy thought as she headed that way. She'd been hoping for a few private moments with him before their work got in the way. Without knocking, she let herself into the room.

Sebastian's back was to her as he searched through the bottles on the shelf.

"It's just me," she said, announcing her presence. "I was hoping we could have a few minutes alone before I get to work."

He turned, spread his arms, and curled his upper lip into an odd grin. Then he said, "I'm all yours, Lucy, your very own personal doormat."

Taken aback by the comment but fairly certain it had something to do with her father, Lucy rushed toward Sebastian and threw herself into his arms.

"I think you're wonderful," she said, hugging him with all her might. "I can't begin to thank you for going with Pa and finding Dusty today. I know you must be getting very tired of having me and my family underfoot."

"More than you know," he said, running his fingers through her hair. "Why must you look and feel so damn good?"

Lucy felt the reluctance in his grip, but nonetheless he set her away from him. There was something in his expression she couldn't fathom, a thing she didn't much like. "Are you upset about something?"

He laughed. "Why should I be upset? I'm always tired because I can't get any sleep with your family around, I spent the entire day in a buggy with your father, who has nothing nice to say about me and is trying to change my life, and I also have a couple of rather unpleasant things on my mind."

Trying not to think about what those unpleasant things might be, she asked, "How is Pa trying to change your life?"

"For starters, he thinks I should be butchering hogs instead of running a saloon. Sets a better example for his grandchildren, you know, the ones he expects you and me to produce."

"Oh, my stars." Lucy clamped her hand over her mouth.

As her fingers fell away from her lips, she shook her head and said, "I'm really sorry about Pa. He worries about me and doesn't always think before he speaks."

"Maybe it runs in the family." Sebastian studied her a moment and then asked, "What did you want to talk to me about?"

Feeling defensive, wondering about that "runs in the family" remark, Lucy put a little space between them. "I, ah, wanted to thank you for going with Pa, and ask if I can have tomorrow night off."

"No problem. Is that all?"

She'd been excited, dying to tell Sebastian about her column and the promise Mary Lease had made, but now it all seemed trivial, unimportant. With a sigh, she said, "I guess so."

"Then maybe you ought to get to work."

"Oh, umm, sure."

Lucy didn't leave the storeroom so much as flee it. She'd never seen Sebastian in such an odd, calculating mood, and didn't know what to make of it. She only knew one thing: It was her fault. She'd pushed him too far with her family demands and probably driven him to the brink of insanity. Any day now Sebastian would hand her divorce papers, and she really couldn't blame him. She never should have asked him to accompany Pa on his search for Dusty. She should have gotten directions and gone herself. Of course, if she'd done that, she would have missed the meeting with Mary Lease. Why did everything have to be so complicated?

No longer dancing on air, Lucy trudged through her duties and made one mistake after the other. She hadn't dropped a whole load of beer yet, praise God, but not much else had gone right.

She was waiting on a table near the door, tenuously balancing six beers on her tray, when Elizabeth Cole breezed into the saloon. She was wearing trouserettes again, black this time, with a matching jacket and a pale pink blouse beneath. As Lucy gingerly distributed her load, she kept one eye on the woman and was surprised to see her walk directly over to where Sebastian sat. Then she leaned over and whispered something in his ear.

After that curious exchange, Sebastian got out of his chair, said something to Jack, then followed Elizabeth to the front door. After the lawyer passed her, Lucy stepped in front of Sebastian, blocking his way.

"What was that all about?" she asked.

"Miss Cole invited me to supper." He still wore that odd expression and his demeanor was cool.

She probably should have let it go at that, but Lucy was far too curious to step out of his way. "But why? I didn't think you even knew her."

Sebastian's smile was tight as he said, "I don't."

"I don't understand."

"You're not supposed to understand," he whispered, tapping the tip of her nose. "It's a secret. We're all entitled to our little secrets, wouldn't you say?" With that, he stepped around her and went on his way.

"Hey, Velvet Eyes," a cowboy shouted from another table. He twirled his index finger and added, "Get us all one."

Drowning in confusion, moving like a sleepwalker, Lucy headed for the bar.

After they were seated at a secluded corner table, Elizabeth said, "The Palace Arms has such a lovely dining room, I thought you'd enjoy coming here."

Seb couldn't help but smile as he said, "I enjoy it a lot. I live here."

"Oh, perhaps you'd like to go somewhere else."

"This is fine."

"You probably come here a lot. It must be hard for your wife to cook for you, living in a hotel room the way you do."

Seb wasn't going to discuss Lucy, especially not now. "Let's leave her out of this."

Elizabeth lowered her gaze, studied the tablecloth, and said, "This is awkward."

"To say the least." Watching her, again Seb noticed the cinnamon streaks among the gray hair at his mother's temples. Trying to make them both more comfortable, he asked, "Where did you get that red in your hair? I remember you as a brunette."

"You do? My hair was auburn, but it lightened a bit before it decided that no color at all was better."

Thinking back to the past, Sebastian figured it might have been easy for a young boy to confuse brown hair with chestnut. Hit by a sudden memory, he could see his mother standing in the sun as she pinned the wash to the clothesline. Sparklers seemed to fly off her head, lighting up the sky like fireworks. He laughed to himself, thinking that he probably hadn't really been so attracted to red-haired women after all. He'd simply been looking for his mother.

"Sebastian," she said quietly, bringing him out of the past. "If you don't mind, I'd like to ask you a couple of questions."

The waiter arrived with their cognacs. After he left, Seb said, "I guess that's a place to start, as long as I'm awarded the same privilege."

"Fair enough." Raising her glass, Elizabeth tapped it against his. After a quick swallow, she asked, "What brought you here to Emancipation?"

Giving away nothing, he said, "Money; what else?"

"Have you lived here long?"

"Less than a year." He took a long pull of his drink.

"And before that?"

"Denver," he said, looking her in the eye. "Right where you left me."

Elizabeth swirled the brandy in her glass and then sighed. "You don't believe that any excuse is good enough for what I did to you, do you?"

"No."

She nodded. "That's one reason I never tried to contact

you all these years. I didn't think you'd understand—I barely understood it myself until recently. Will you at least let me try to explain?"

Seb shrugged and took another sip of cognac.

Answer enough for Elizabeth. "Do you remember when we raised cattle?" At his nod, she continued. "Occasionally we'd have a young heifer who didn't know what to do with her first calf, wouldn't even nurse it. That meant we either had to bottle raise it or find a cow who'd lost her baby and convince her to adopt the heifer's calf. Women aren't so very different from cattle in that respect."

Seb narrowed his eyes, trying to figure out where this was going. "Are you comparing yourself to a cow?"

She laughed and took a sip of brandy. "I'm just trying to say that some women aren't cut out to be mothers. It's not a failing on your part but on mine."

Seb tried to digest this, to see things her way, but he couldn't make sense of it. "If you feel that way, why did you ever get married in the first place?"

"Oh, Sebastian, I never would have married Caleb if not for you."

He cocked his head to the side, eyebrows raised high.

Elizabeth lowered her gaze and elaborated. "It's a rather indelicate matter, I know, but let me just say that Caleb was quite dashing and persuasive when we met. You're a grown man. Figure it out for yourself. Why does a woman who isn't interested in marriage bother to get married?"

As her meaning sank in, Seb could feel the heat snaking up along his neck, slithering toward his cheeks. He quickly raised two fingers, signaling the waiter, then pointed at his chest and his mother.

"That doesn't mean that I didn't love you," Elizabeth went on. "Or that I don't. You needed more from me than I could give, and when I left, I assumed, or at least hoped, that Caleb would marry again, someone who could be the kind of mother you deserved."

Seb almost laughed. "As you know, that didn't work out too well. Turns out my new mother was a man who taught me how to pick pockets and cheat at cards, among other things I'm none too proud to admit."

When the waiter appeared with two more glasses of cognac, he asked, "Would you care to order your suppers now?"

Not even remotely hungry and with no idea what the special was, Seb simply said, "I'll have the special."

"Make that two," Elizabeth added without looking at her menu. After the waiter moved away, she said, "If you can't understand anything else, please know that it's very important for me to get to know the man you've become, if you'll allow that."

Seb wasn't by nature a cruel man—hell, if he was, he'd have tossed Lucy and her crazy family out on the street long ago. Even with the remnants of the bitter past eating away at him, he didn't want to be cruel now.

"I'd say you're allowed. I'd like to get to know you better, too."

His mother's gray eyes went soft and kind of foggy, like mist over a lake. Her voice soft and foggy, too, she said, "I appreciate that, Sebastian. I'd like to let Mary and her group go on to Denver without me. I'll catch the train going east on Tuesday. Mary can get along without me until she speaks to the Social Reform Club in New York next month. If I stay on those few more days, would it be all right with you?"

What could he say to that? "Get your trouseretted backside on the next train out of town?" Or should he welcome her the way any other son might welcome his mother? What *did* he want? It occurred to Seb then that for the first time in his life, his mother had put his needs before hers. She'd also given him a little gift. Whether they parted or remained together, this time it would be his decision, not hers.

Relaxing his shoulders, smiling and meaning it, Seb said, "I think I'd like it if you stayed on a few more days."

"Thank you." She toasted him, adding, "That will also give me a chance to get to know your wife a little better."

After hardly touching their suppers, Seb and his mother parted company at the hotel. Then he headed across the street to the Pearly Gates. He was feeling better than he had in a long time, thinking that although he'd never forget what his mother had done to him, he was confident that he'd eventually get to a place where he could forgive her. He wondered if he'd be able to do the same for Lucy.

Looking at her in this new light, as a successful and revered columnist, Seb wasn't entirely sure that he liked it. He certainly admired her efforts, of that there was no question. His questions were of a more personal nature. What else didn't he know about this woman who'd turned his life upside down? How many other secrets did she have?

Deep in thought, trying to figure out exactly where Lucy fit in his life as well as his future, Seb walked into the saloon—and complete pandemonium.

It took him a few moments to take in the scene and understand what he was seeing. Tables and chairs had been shoved aside and most of his customers were clustered around in a circle, as if he'd staged a prizefight. Except this one hadn't been planned. Everyone was shouting, egging on the combatants.

As he walked toward the crowd, Dusty Preston suddenly flew through a knot of onlookers. He landed heavily on a chair, collapsing the legs, and wound up on the floor in a tangle of splintered wood. A woman screamed, and then a familiar voice shouted with rage.

"You miserable son of a buck." More thumps and groans, and then, "I'm gonna break you in two."

Seb fought his way through the spectators and saw that

Jeremiah and Charlie White were rolling around on the floor, fists flailing as they tried to pummel one another. As Seb looked on, one of the Barkdoll twins—Cherry, he surmised—leapt onto Jeremiah's back and dug her fingers into his eyes.

"No," Lucy cried, heading into the fray.

Merry Barkdoll was right on her heels. She grabbed hold of Lucy's hair and spun her around. Trying to free herself, arms swinging, feet kicking out at Merry's legs, Lucy slipped and tumbled to the floor, dragging Merry along with her.

Jeremiah and Charlie forgotten, the crowd clustered around the women and cheered them on. Both Lucy and Merry were trying to get a foothold while fending off the other, each clinging to a fistful of her opponent's hair.

This was too much. Though he hated the idea of putting a hole in his ceiling, Seb drew his gun, pointed the barrel to the sky, and fired.

"That's it," he shouted over the crowd. "The show's over."

Surprisingly enough, this was all it took to break up both fights. Seb's customers, most of them grumbling about him spoiling the fun, wandered back to their drinks and poker or billiard games.

On his feet again, Dusty staggered over to where his father was struggling to right himself. The kid had two black eyes, a bloody nose, scratches on his face and arms, and a big chunk torn out of the back of his shirt.

After Dusty had tugged Jeremiah up beside him, Seb pointed a finger at them and said, "Out. Now."

"But, Seb . . ." the old man said.

"Out. Don't make me get the sheriff and have you two arrested."

Heads hanging low, the pair slowly shuffled out of the saloon.

Seb glanced at Charlie, who was sitting on the floor. Cherry was hunched over him, tending his wounds. "You, too. And don't come back."

Then he turned to Lucy. She was standing next to the bar, hair flying everywhere, and clinging to the sleeve of her blouse, which had nearly been torn off. "In the storeroom. Now."

To her credit, she didn't balk or even hesitate. Limping a little, Lucy hurried away and disappeared around the bar.

Finally setting his sights on Merry, Seb shook his head and said, "What the hell is the matter with you?"

Adjusting her clothing, which was in all manner of disarray, she gave off a tiny shrug. "Cherry and I brought Dusty back to town and things got a little out of hand."

Seb waited a beat and then said, "I ought to toss you out on your backside, too."

"I'll make it easy for you," she said, walking by him. "I was thinking about going home anyway."

Steeling himself for the upcoming confrontation, Seb headed for the storeroom. Lucy was standing in the corner, still trying to find a way to keep her blouse from falling off. She was flushed and had tried to smooth her hair but hadn't been too successful. She looked exactly the way she did after they made love.

Trying not to think about that, Seb asked, "What happened?" Then he waited for the barrage.

"I'm not sure exactly," she said quietly, head down. "It all happened so fast."

"Try starting at the beginning. You were serving customers the last time I saw you. What happened after that?"

"Well, see, Charlie came in. I don't know why, but he always seems to know when you're not here."

Seb's expression darkened. "Go on."

"I was working, you know, and Charlie sort of followed me around, trying to talk to me. When things got quiet for a while, I went and waited at the bar. He came along saying all kinds of things he shouldn't be saying and, see, putting his arm around my shoulders and such, and anyway, that's when the twins brought my brother to the saloon. Cherry went crazy when she saw Charlie with me, and Pa must have seen them ride up and go into the saloon because he came in and went crazy, too. And that's not all."

She paused to suck in a breath of air. "Something bad happened to Dusty out at the ranch. I don't know what because I never had a chance to ask, but he was all scratched up and with black eyes and such. But that's not why Pa went crazy, see, it was because of Charlie jilting me and then trying to court a married woman. That really set Cherry off, and the next thing I knew, Pa and Charlie and Cherry were on the floor, and then Merry tried to pull out my hair. It wasn't my fault."

Seb turned his back on her and put his hand over his mouth. He wanted to hang on to his anger, but damned if he didn't want to bust out laughing instead.

When he was reasonably certain he could keep a straight face, he turned to Lucy and said, "I think it would be a good idea for you to go back to the hotel now."

She glanced at her torn blouse. "I could change clothes and come back to work."

"No, I think it's better if you don't come back tonight."

Looking forlorn, Lucy wandered over to Seb and placed her hand on his arm. "I'm sorry, really, really sorry."

"Me, too, Lucy." He leaned over and kissed her forehead. "Me, too."

Back at the hotel, Lucy let herself into Sebastian's room, and then knocked on the connecting door. Dusty opened it and stepped aside.

"Are you two all right?" she asked, glancing at her father. He was sitting on the bed holding a towel over his face.

Dusty explained, "Pa's eyes are smarting some, but he's fine."

"Better than fine," Jeremiah bellowed. "I smashed Charlie White's nose, got the better of him, I did. Not that I can say the same thing about my son."

"Charlie threw me across the room," Dusty admitted, a pout in his voice.

"What happened to you before that?" Lucy asked. "You look terrible."

"It was those dang twins." Dusty's eyes rolled to the back of his head. "I can't even tell you half of what they done to me, but some of it involved moving a bull from one pen to another. They didn't tell me the pen the bull was already in was also where they kept the cows." He rubbed his hip. "That bull didn't want to go to that other pen, see."

Lucy shook her head. "Well, as long as you're both all right."

"We're fine," Jeremiah insisted. "Just a little beat up s'all."

Since it was still early and figuring that she might as well get some work done, Lucy wandered over to her desk. She pulled open the drawer expecting to find a pad of fresh paper and found a letter to Penelope instead. A quick glance told her that she hadn't seen it before. In fact, she couldn't remember putting it on top of the pile. Curious, she gathered it along with the papers and headed for Sebastian's room.

As she reached the door, she said, "Good night, you two. Please stay in and don't get into any more trouble."

"Good night, Lucy," said Jeremiah. "And, uh, sorry if we caused your husband a bit of trouble tonight."

"Yeah, me, too," said Dusty. "But it wasn't our fault."

Chuckling to herself, Lucy closed and locked the door and then made her way to Sebastian's desk. Settling herself in the chair, she perused the letter. Unwilling to believe what her eyes told her the first time, she read it again, one astonishing word at a time.

Sharon Ihle

Dear Penelope:

I'm told you are the smartest woman alive. If that's true, maybe you can help me figure out my wife, because I sure as hell can't. The problem? My otherwise adorable wife lies to me.

I have helped her in many unusual ways and done far more for her and her crazy family than would be expected of any man. And how does she repay that kindness? She deceives me and keeps her little secrets pressed between the pages of her black heart.

What do you think I should do, oh smartest woman of them all? Divorce her? Too easy.

Have her drawn and quartered? Too messy.

Or maybe, just maybe, I should take out an advertisement in your newspaper and expose her for who and what she really is.

I await your wise counsel.

Signed,
Deceived, Disheartened, and Slightly Deranged

Chapter Twenty-two

Unwilling to face Sebastian when he came to his room that night, Lucy kept her eyes closed and feigned sleep. When he rolled onto the mattress beside her, she suddenly remembered that he'd promised to jiggle the hell out of the bed. She halfway expected him to wake her up, but he didn't. He simply buried his head in his pillow and went to sleep. Both relieved and troubled, it was a long time before Lucy actually dozed off.

Late the next morning and still determined to evade him for as long as she could, Lucy decided to slip out of bed without waking Sebastian. With any luck, she might even be able to dress and creep out of the room unnoticed. As she raised the sheet, he caught her wrist and pulled her back down beside him.

Sebastian didn't seem the least bit sleepy. In fact, he looked as if he'd been waiting for her to wake up. With a gulp she said, "Ah, good morning."

"Is it?"

Knowing the time of reckoning was upon her, Lucy sank back down on the pillow. There was no question in her

271

mind that Sebastian was Deceived, Disgusted, and Slightly Deranged. She didn't know how he'd found out that she was Penelope, but she didn't doubt that he knew.

Bracing herself, she faked an airy innocence as she asked, "Is something on your mind?"

"Yes. Charlie for starters," he said, surprising her. "I've known all along how much Charlie means to you, but what I didn't know is that you're still seeing each other; behind my back, no less."

Stunned, Lucy sat up. "What?"

"This marriage was your idea, not mine." Sebastian sounded hollow, almost devoid of emotion. "If Charlie is what you really want, I'll deliver an immediate divorce to you on a silver platter. I won't be played for a fool any longer."

"But I don't want Charlie." Lucy almost couldn't remember a time when she had. "Why are you saying this?"

"Because I'm tired of secrets."

Lying there, his hair dark against the pillow, Sebastian had deftly avoided her gaze. Now his stormy eyes found hers and they were filled with accusations.

"You've been trying to get Charlie back since you came to Emancipation, and when that didn't work you used me in order to stay here, right?"

"Well, sort of."

"It's clear to me and anyone with a brain that Charlie has regrets about what he did to you, and that he still loves you. I think you feel the same way and only wanted to stay here so you could be close to him."

This couldn't be happening; he couldn't possibly believe this of her. "Sebastian, you couldn't be more wrong. You don't understand."

He laughed, but it was without humor. "I don't understand a lot of things, especially when it comes to women."

"Then maybe you can understand this: Do you honestly

believe that I'm the kind of woman who could love another man and yet willingly share your bed?"

He shrugged. "I thought maybe that was your way of paying off your debt."

No longer defensive but angry, Lucy snapped, "And if I was capable of paying off a debt in such a manner, what kind of woman would that make me?"

This gave Seb more than a little pause. He hadn't considered that. Leaning on one elbow, he brushed an errant length of hair from her face and said, "The kind of woman you're not."

Relief flooded her expression as she said, "Then believe me when I say that Charlie means nothing to me anymore; less than nothing."

Not entirely convinced, Seb asked, "Are you telling me that you don't plan to run after Charlie the minute our contract is finished?"

"No. In fact, not no but . . ." She blushed, considering her words, and said them anyway. "But *hell* no."

Seb had an idea that was the first time that word had crossed her lips. Chuckling, he fell back against his pillow. "Since you put it that way, I believe you. I can't say I believe anything else you have to say, though."

She was so quiet after that, for a minute Seb thought Lucy had fallen asleep. Then, her voice trembling a little, she said, "By that I have to assume that you wrote a letter to Penelope and put it in my drawer."

So she'd found it. Grinning, enjoying himself immensely, Seb slid his hands behind his head and admitted, "Yeah, I sure as hell did."

"How did you find out?"

Seb didn't want to bring her father into the conversation, nor did he want to think about him. "Does it matter?"

"Not really." Head down, Lucy picked at the feathers sneaking out of her pillow.

He hated seeing her so forlorn, but Seb hated all the lies even more. "What does matter," he said softly, "is that I asked you repeatedly to find out who this Penelope was and you repeatedly lied to me."

"Oh, but I wanted to tell you," she said, turning to him with a stricken look in her eyes. "More than anything I wanted to tell you, but I promised Hazel I wouldn't, see. Even if I could have told you, you would have tried to make me write for the *Tribune,* and there's no way that I'd ever betray Hazel like that. I didn't have any choice, see. Do you understand?"

Barely. "I understand and admire your ethics, if that's what you mean. I don't have to like them."

"But why not? Does it bother you to know that I'm good at something besides toting beers?"

Seb raised a single ebony eyebrow and cocked his head her way.

"All right," Lucy conceded, "does it bother you to know that I'm finally good at *something?*"

He paused for a few beats, sorting through a sudden confusion, and realized that he didn't have an answer. "I honestly don't know what bothers me about your column, but something does."

Lucy leaned in close, sliding her warm, honeyed locks across his skin, and Seb's already jumbled brain turned to mush.

Then she said, "If it's any consolation, I was probably going to tell you that I'm Penelope last night."

She filled him in on Mary Lease's visit to the *Rustler* and the surprising offer the woman had made to help her take the Penelope column across the nation.

Fighting off anger and mingled thoughts of his mother, Seb sorted through that unexpected development.

Lucy went on. "I was so excited, I was bursting to tell you, but then you were so—I don't know, cold and in such a bad mood, I didn't."

He remembered the excitement shining in her eyes, and how quickly he'd extinguished that light. Running his hands through his hair, he did what he could by way of apology. "I had a lot of reasons for my mood last night, things that had nothing to do with you."

From out of nowhere, Lucy asked, "Does one of those things have anything to do with that nasty lady lawyer in the men's trousers?"

Seb's plan was to bring Lucy to task over Charlie and her secret Penelope column. The last thing he wanted to discuss with her or anyone else was his newfound and tenuous bond with his mother. And yet, after what he'd just put her through, it hardly seemed ethical to respond with a lie. He'd accused her of having secrets. What about his own? It occurred to Seb then that he probably ought to at least warn her about Kate. And yet what would he tell her? The whole sordid story? Nothing good would come of dredging up a past he didn't want to think about. Besides, the odds were good that Kate would stay right where she was, in Denver.

Taking a deep breath as he made up his mind, Seb let it out slowly and said, "I probably should have told you this before, but it turns out that nasty lady is my mother."

Lucy's breath caught, but she slapped at his chest. "And you accuse me of lying?"

Seb caught her face between his hands and looked directly into her eyes. "I didn't want to talk about this, but you asked, and I felt I owed you the truth. Elizabeth Cole is my mother, if in name only."

She froze and then said, "Oh, my stars."

"Not exactly my first thought when she walked into the saloon the other day, but close."

"Oh, and I just called her a nasty lady."

A bubble of laughter popped out as he said, "Believe me, over the years I've thought of her in much worse terms."

As Seb feared, Lucy's questions fairly flowed. "What do

you mean by 'mother in name only'? Has it been a long time since you've seen her?"

Figuring he might as will give her the basics, if nothing else, Seb explained. "In name only because she hasn't been my mother for twenty-five or -six years, something like that.

"But why? What happened?"

"I really don't want to go into it right now. I'm not even sure I understand it myself."

"Oh, but please," she said, stretching across his chest, her soft breasts warm against his skin. "You can't leave it at that. At least give me some idea what happened."

He wasn't happy about it, but Seb came up with a condensed version. "My mother packed up and left me and my father when I was six. All she cared about was a career for herself, which she managed to do on a big scale, and she didn't much care who she hurt in the process." Without thinking, he impulsively added, "I hope that's not something the two of you have in common."

Lucy immediately raised up, fire in her eyes, and Seb held her fast. "Damn, Lucy. I don't know why I said that. It was cruel and it was wrong. Forgive me?"

"I don't know."

She jutted out her bottom lip; pouting, Seb supposed, but to him it was more an invitation. Gripping the back of her head, he guided that pouting mouth to his and kissed her with an intensity that shook him.

When he released her, the anger was gone, and in its place was the warm, gentle woman he'd somehow grown to love. Seb tugged at the hem of Lucy's nightgown, pulling it up until his hands found the silky softness of her bare bottom.

"What do you think you're doing?" she challenged throatily.

Seb buried his face in her hair and nipped the tip of her ear. Soothing the spot with his tongue, he nibbled his way down the side of her neck before finding her mouth again. This time Lucy ended the kiss.

Breathless now, her cheeks glowing, she said, "I asked you what you think you're doing. I haven't forgiven you yet."

"You'll forgive me in a few minutes," he vowed, exploring the valley between her breasts. "As I recall, I made a promise to jiggle the hell out of this bed. If you don't already know it, you'll soon find out that I'm a man of my word."

Late that afternoon, about the time Mary Lease's rally should have been getting underway, Seb was surprised to look up and see his mother walk into the saloon. She was dressed in the same black trousers as yesterday but this time wore a dove gray blouse beneath the matching jacket.

When she reached him, Seb said, "I thought you'd be over at City Hall by now."

"I've already been there half the day, but yes, I am on my way back there for the rally." She glanced around the saloon. "I stopped by to introduce myself properly to your wife and ask her to join me. Is she here?"

"No. She's either at the newspaper office or at the rally. Wild horses couldn't keep her away from Mary Lease's speech."

She smiled warmly and tenderly, the kind of smile he'd longed to see all those years ago. "In that case, I'm sure that she and I will get along just fine. Her name is Lucy?"

Seb nodded, wondering how well Lucy would take to his mother, wondering, too, if Elizabeth remembered she'd also met Lucy's father—and that she'd been less than kind.

"Will you be coming to the rally?" she asked.

"I hadn't planned on it." Considering the fact that she'd probably meet up with Lucy, and possibly Dusty and Jeremiah, too, he added, "I'll probably stop by for a few minutes just to see what's going on."

"What's going on is the speech Mary plans to give in New York. She's testing it out as we travel, honing it to a fine edge."

"I've heard her tongue is already sharp enough to slice leather."

She gave him an indulgent smile. "Some have said that she has a venomous tongue, but rarely do you hear a comment like that coming from a female. Mary has a lot of good, intelligent things to say, and unfortunately, most men don't take her seriously, or women in general for that matter. Do you?"

Seb looked her up and down. "As a rule. But it's kind of hard to take a woman seriously when she's wearing men's pants."

If she took offense, Elizabeth didn't show it. "I've found that they're far more comfortable than trussing myself up in skirts and petticoats. I'm sure if you were faced with the same choices, you'd prefer them, too."

Seb laughed, surprised by his mother's easy candor.

"I really must be getting back to the hall now," she said. "I'll look for you later."

As his mother strolled out of the saloon, it occurred to Seb that stopping by the rally sooner rather than later might be the best option. It wasn't so much that he didn't trust Lucy's reaction to Elizabeth. But there was her crazy family to consider.

Heading for Jack, who was practicing dealing from the bottom of the deck, Seb hollered, "Hey, none of that at the Pearly Gates."

Still dealing, and amazingly smooth, too, Jack said, "I'm not always at the Pearly Gates."

"Fine, but don't let my customers see you doing that."

"Your customers wouldn't notice." His lip twitched. "Takes a thief to know one."

Seb had to let that one slide. They'd known each other

back when that remark was true. "I'm going to take off in a little while. You and Pearl shouldn't have any trouble keeping up. With the rally going on down the street, business will probably be a little slow."

Jack glanced around the room. "In case you haven't noticed, business is already slow. Maybe you ought to put on more prizefights like the one we had last night."

"I like you better when you don't talk so much."

Seb made a gun with his thumb and index finger and shot Jack dead. Then he added, "Speaking of last night, if Charlie White ever comes in here again, throw him out on his ass."

"About time." Jack looked up at Seb with lidded eyes. "He sneaks in here every chance he gets. It's almost like he knows you and Lucy aren't looking at a lifetime marriage."

"I don't care what he does or doesn't know. I don't want him in here again."

"Done. Anyone else you want to ban? What about that harpy in the pants who was just here?"

Seb fired another shot at Jack with his finger gun. "That harpy is my mother."

Jack dropped the cards and his mouth fell open. "I didn't know you had a mother."

"Neither did I."

Later than she'd intended to be, Lucy left Hazel's office and dashed toward City Hall. Right or wrong, and because they were her family, she'd asked her father and Dusty to join her there. She hoped they were already seated and that they'd saved a place for her, preferably in the front row.

As she approached the building, Lucy was amazed to see a smattering of townsmen protesting Mary's speech. Some were throwing tomatoes and other vegetables against the fences and walls, and others were carrying signs denouncing the Populist Party. To Lucy's horror, she spotted her father and Dusty in the middle of the group.

When she reached them, Dusty had just loaded his fist with a tomato and was taking aim on a target.

"Don't you dare," she said, grabbing his shirt and tugging down his arm. "I have to live here after you're gone, and the last thing I need is to have my family thrown in jail."

"Aw, I didn't mean nothing by it. I was just doing what the other fellas did."

Dusty's battered face was a mask of grotesque colors. His eyes looked like a pair of smudge pots, his nose was swollen and red, and the scratches on his cheeks and neck were scabbing over.

"How do you feel today?" she asked, concerned.

"Like somebody put my head in a blacksmith's vise."

Jeremiah edged into the conversation. "That's what you get for filling up your body with the devil's brew. It's paying for your sins is what it is."

Lucy was about to gather her family and head into the hall when she heard someone call her name. Turning, she saw that Elizabeth Cole was practically upon them.

"Hello again," Elizabeth said. "When we last met I was in such a state of shock, I didn't fully realize that you were the woman who captured my son."

Jeremiah tugged up the straps on his overalls and said, "What son are you talking about?"

Elizabeth glanced at him, narrowed her eyes, and said, "We've met before, haven't we?"

"I'm Lucy's pa, and we sure as the dickens have. You called me a gnat."

"Oh, for heaven's sake. I didn't realize who you were at the time. I'm Sebastian's mother."

Jeremiah turned to Lucy and blurted out, "Your mother-in-law wears men's pants?"

"Please, Pa," she pleaded. "We really ought to go inside now."

Undaunted, he turned back to Seb's mother and looked her over. "I guess that makes you one of those suffering teapots."

Chin raised high, she said, "If by that you mean I'm a suffragist, yes, I am."

Dusty laughed and said, "Suffering teapot. That's a good one, Pa."

Since he'd joined the conversation, Lucy felt she had to introduce him. "Mrs. Cole, this is my brother, Dusty."

Turning her gaze on his ruined face, Elizabeth grimaced.

Dusty grinned and said, "A bull throwed me into a bramble bush."

"How very unfortunate." She glanced at the tomato in his hand, looked at the mess splattered against City Hall, and asked, "What were you planning to do with that?"

For a moment, Lucy thought that Dusty might blurt out the truth. Instead he grinned, stuck the tomato in his mouth, and took a bite. The tomato exploded on impact, shooting a stream of juice and seeds all over the front of Elizabeth's silvery blouse.

"Dang," said Dusty.

Pulling a handkerchief from her jacket pocket, Elizabeth dabbed at her blouse as she said to Lucy, "I sincerely hope that you and my son aren't planning to have children."

Then she spun around and marched into the hall.

Lucy had just about decided that things couldn't get any worse when Sebastian strolled by. "How come you're not inside listening to the big speech?" he wanted to know.

"Well, see . . ." Lucy began.

"Let me explain," Dusty cut in, edging up to Sebastian. "See, your ma came by and said she remembered Pa, and he said she called him a gnat. Then he called her a suffering teapot, see, and then Lucy had to introduce me because your ma's eyes kinda bugged out when she saw my face."

As Dusty caught his breath, Jeremiah said, "No call for the woman to think less of the boy 'cause he had an accident."

281

"I had two accidents," Dusty continued. "When me and Pa got here, all these fellas were tossing tomatoes and such against the building and I thought it looked like fun, so I helped out a little s'all, see."

"Understand," Jeremiah said, taking over, "Dusty still had a tomato in his hand when your ma came by, and she wanted to know what he was gonna do with it, see. But my boy wasn't dumb enough to tell her that he was planning to toss it at City Hall."

"That's right," Dusty continued. "I thought it'd be real clever if I looked like I was gonna eat it, but that didn't work out too good because when I bit it, the dang thing blew up on your ma's clothes. Then she said she didn't want you and Lucy to have any kids. It wasn't my fault, see."

Lucy had kept a furtive eye on Sebastian throughout the explanation, and now she braced herself for the coming explosion. Surprisingly, it never came. He just stood there, mouth agape, eyes glazed and far, far away.

Seizing the opportunity, Lucy said brightly, "I guess we'd better get inside if we want decent seats."

They all trailed into City Hall, including Sebastian, whose expression hadn't changed. Lucy found to her dismay that there was standing room only. The best they could manage was the back wall, where they lined up like a row of ducks.

Mary Lease, dressed in a black satin gown trimmed with lace, was already well into her speech. She went on about socialism, old-world tyranny, and British gold, and denounced the wealth of such folks as Rockefeller and Whitney while God's poor were packed in the slums. The hall was very warm. Thanks to Dusty, Elizabeth Cole sat to the side of the orator, her jacket buttoned up to her throat. Lucy could see beads of perspiration dripping from her cheeks and onto her lap, droplets to remind her of the dreadful mistake her son had made.

Lucy stole a glance at Sebastian, who still wore that dazed expression, and noticed that from time to time he slowly shook his head. Pretty sure that like his mother, his thoughts were on her family and not the famous orator, Lucy turned her attention back to the speech.

"What you farmers need to do," Lease expounded, shaking her fist, "is raise less corn and more hell."

The crowd shrieked with approval and then broke into applause. It was only when Lease maligned William McKinley, the Democratic nominee the Populist Party backed for president, that the room got quiet save for a few catcalls and hisses.

The orator finished her speech then, decrying the financiers who were growing into millionaires while the nation sank into bankruptcy. Then she dabbed at her face with a handkerchief and sat down. Again the room exploded in applause.

Taking the opportunity before the crowd overran them, Lucy, her family, and Sebastian slipped through the door and into the relatively cool air.

"Now that's what I call one tart-tongued woman," Jeremiah commented as they proceeded up the street.

Like a man waking up from a dream, Sebastian glanced from Jeremiah to Dusty and then finally to Lucy. "Where's everybody going?"

"Back to the saloon with you?" Lucy ventured.

"After a tongue-lashing like that," Jeremiah said, "I'll bet a lot of those folks will be heading that way. You can probably use all the help you can get."

"I can help, too," Dusty announced.

"Of course you can," Seb muttered, again shaking his head. "That's just what I need. A whole flock of Prestons playing hostess."

Each entertaining their own private thoughts, the group finished the journey to the Pearly Gates in silence. Sebastian immediately went to the bar, leaving Lucy with her father and brother.

"Listen," she said, trying to make things as easy on Sebastian as possible, "maybe it would be best if you two took a table or even better, went to the hotel. I don't think we need any extra help tonight."

Jeremiah thought about this. "I suppose we could take a table. That way we'll be here in case you need us."

Groaning inwardly, Lucy was about to take them to a table where Sebastian wouldn't likely stumble over them. Then Elizabeth Cole breezed into the saloon and waved to them.

"Just the people I want to talk to," she said, joining them. "I feel terrible about some of the things I said and would very much like to make it up to you. May I buy you a cognac, Jeremiah?"

Lucy cringed, waiting for his tart reply, but he surprised her by saying, "That's real neighborly of you, but I'm not a drinking man."

"Oh, come on, Mr. Preston. Cognac isn't spirits. It's more like a balm. I'll be very distressed if you don't join me."

He looked up at Elizabeth, regarding her the way a boy might consider a tree he's thinking of climbing. Again afraid of what might come out of her father's mouth, Lucy flinched. Again, he surprised her.

"Since you put it that way, Mrs. Cole, I'd be happy to take you up on your kind offer. And call me Jeremiah."

Sebastian's mother linked her arm through his, even though she towered over him by several inches, and said as they walked toward the bar, "It's Elizabeth. Please call me Elizabeth."

Struck speechless, Lucy glanced over at Dusty.

"Dang," he said, scratching his head. "What was that all about?"

"I have no idea, and what's more, I don't want to know." She took hold of Dusty's collar and pulled him close. "I'm going to go to work now. I want you to stay out of trouble and out of the beer."

"Don't worry. The way my head feels, I may never drink beer again."

"I'm going to hold you to that."

Relatively certain that things would be all right, Lucy headed for the bar. Sebastian was leaning against the wall where her tray was stored.

As she reached for it, he said, "Is that your father and my mother sitting in the corner sharing a cognac or have I gone crazy?"

"That's them, all right. Your mother came into the saloon," she explained, "apologized to Pa for the things she'd said, and offered to buy him a drink. I should add that I've never known Pa to take a drink of anything stronger than root beer."

Nodding thoughtfully, Sebastian glanced at the corner table again. "If anything goes wrong over there, I don't want to know about it."

She smiled but said, "Me neither."

Meeting her gaze, Sebastian gave her a look that practically melted her toenails. Then, just as quickly, he furrowed his brow. "Where's that brother of yours?"

She glanced around. "I don't know for sure, but he promised he wouldn't drink any beer."

Another short, thoughtful nod. "In that case, I might just make it through the night."

After that, and as her father had predicted, customers poured into the bar, all of them discussing Mary Lease's speech. Lucy was so busy, she actually thought about enlisting her brother's aid. Searching for him, she spotted Dusty at the bar. He leaned in and said something to Pearl. She immediately swatted him as if he were a fly, and then went about her business.

Since Dusty apparently hadn't learned his lesson when it came to women, and there were plenty of females in the saloon, Lucy continued working on her own. The noise was deafening. In addition to heated conversations and the clatter of beer mugs, the piano was getting a real workout, the ivories pounding out one raucous tune after another.

As Lucy was heading back to the bar for another load, Elizabeth Cole and her father twirled by her like a human dust storm, performing their own odd version of a cross between a polka and a waltz. As they passed, Jeremiah laughed and shouted, "Yipee, ki-yi!"

Lucy had seen her mother and father at barn dances on several occasions, but never before had she seen him so animated, so reckless. It was a shocking and unexpected sight. She looked around for Sebastian and saw that he'd also noticed them. He wore that same dazed expression he'd had outside City Hall when Dusty and Pa had tried to explain what happened with his mother.

It seemed like Jeremiah and Elizabeth danced together for the rest of the night, stopping only long enough to refresh their drinks or catch a breath. Lucy didn't know what to make of it. She knew that her mother and father had a deep and abiding love, and that whatever was happening here wasn't the stuff of scandal. Still, it bothered her on some level.

Many times Lucy felt Sebastian's eyes on her throughout the evening. Almost afraid to look his way thanks to her family's antics, she halfway expected to see censure or even anger. Instead each time she caught his gaze it was like a warm caress, sensual and seductive. She could almost feel his hands on her, taste his passionate mouth.

Overwhelmed with emotion for this man, knowing that she would never love another the way she loved him, Lucy dared to dream that when the time came, Sebastian would forget about their contract. With him as her husband for all time, she would be the happiest woman alive.

The next morning Lucy was almost reluctant to get out of bed and go to Hazel's office. She'd given copies of all the Penelope columns to Mary Lease with a promise that the next one would be in her hands before she left town. In order to be certain the *Rustler* was printed in time, she had no choice but to go down to the office early and get to work.

After a very long day and a few misfires, Lucy finally

spread the first copy on the counter and, as usual, perused her column:

————— *THE WEEKLY RUSTLER* —————

Emancipation, Wyoming,	**Vol. 1.**
Friday, July 17, 1896	**No. 43**

ASK PENELOPE! FREE ADVICE

Dear Penelope:
I have never done anything like this before. I ask your advice now because I want to know how a girl who isn't like everyone else—you know, maybe bigger or taller than most folks—can find true love. I really want me a nice tall man, but they always seem to go for short girls. Also, every time a man gets a gander at me, he turns tail and runs. Short of poking out the eyes of a man so he can't see what he's getting, how can I find me a tall fella of my own?
Signed, Looking for Love

Dear Looking for Love:
Please don't think of yourself as unattractive. The measure of a person cannot be found in their height, size, or looks. It is what's in the heart that counts.

May I suggest that perhaps you are looking in the wrong places? Sometimes the thing we want most can be found if we simply look a little harder. Why not consider "lowering" your sights? It's possible the man you seek is already there and you have been blinded by your own high standards. Think of beginning the search for your own true love as if you were building a house. Start from the ground up.

Penelope

Chapter Twenty-three

Late the following Sunday morning, Lucy was cuddled deep in Sebastian's arms, dozing in that delicious chasm between sleep and wakefulness. She couldn't remember a time when she'd been so content, so truly happy. All because of the man beside her.

Sebastian, bless him, never said a word about what went on between his mother and her family outside of City Hall. It was as if the incident had never happened. The only thing he'd expressed about his mother dancing the night away with her father was surprise, along with a certain amusement.

If anything disturbed her on this fine morning, and it was more a curiosity than a concern, it was her father's odd behavior yesterday. He'd hired another rig and left town to do what he called a few errands, as strange as that seemed. When he came back later in the afternoon, he still wouldn't tell Lucy where he'd been or what his mysterious errands were, but his expression was even more secretive than before. She hadn't seen Sebastian's mother either, not during the day or later at the saloon. Hmmm. What could her father have been up to? And did it somehow involve Elizabeth Cole?

As Lucy considered this, there came two sharp raps against the connecting door.

Sebastian slid his hand down her back, pulled her tight against his body, and grumbled, "Tell your father we're not home."

"I'll get rid of him," she promised, pulling on her dressing gown. When she opened the door, sure enough, there stood Jeremiah.

"Good morning, my beautiful daughter," he boomed. "I see you're awake at last."

"Not exactly, Pa. We were still kind of dozing."

"You've done enough of that," he said, a mysterious grin lighting up his eyes. "We've got big doings going on today, so get up and get dressed. Elizabeth and I expect to see the two of you downstairs in ten minutes."

With that he closed the door in her face.

Confused, Lucy turned to Sebastian. By then he was sitting up in bed. He asked, "Did I hear your father mention something about my mother?"

"Yes," she said as she crossed the room to her temporary dresser. "He said that they have something big planned and that we're supposed to be downstairs in ten minutes. Did your mother mention anything about this yesterday?"

Sebastian shook his tousled head. "I didn't even see her yesterday, which strikes me as strange, considering she stayed over a few more days just to get to know me better."

Discussing the possibilities as they dressed and coming up with nothing, when Lucy and Sebastian got downstairs and walked outside they were surprised to see a platform spring wagon with seating for four. Jeremiah and Elizabeth occupied the seat in front and Dusty dangled off the platform at the rear.

"Come on, you two," Jeremiah said, waving them over. "Time's a' wasting."

"But where are we going?" Lucy asked.

"On a picnic," Elizabeth replied. "We planned it right down to the toothpicks. Now come on, get in."

With an uneasy glance at one another, Lucy and Sebastian climbed into the rig and settled back for the ride.

They hadn't gotten too far out of town before Seb realized where they were headed: up to Devil's Lake. After they'd reached their apparent destination, a grassy area not far from the Carrolls' cabin, Jeremiah surprised Seb by driving past it and around to the other side of the lake.

After parking the rig beneath the shade of a huge oak tree, Jeremiah and Elizabeth made a great show of spreading a large blanket, then setting up the picnic lunch.

As they all settled onto the blanket, Jeremiah spread his arms and said, "Well, what do you think? Isn't it beautiful up here?"

Seb had never been to this side of the lake. In fact, his visit up here with Lucy's father was the first time he'd been to the scenic mountaintop. The majestic Black Mountains loomed in the east, a dark and shadowy lavender upon the horizon that spoke to him of mystery and adventure. The picnic area itself was a rich green meadow dotted with oaks and pines, and tall cottonwoods crept down toward the grassy shoreline of the shimmering emerald lake. Seb couldn't imagine there was a prettier place anywhere in Wyoming.

"Oh, Pa," Lucy said breathlessly. "It's gorgeous. What a great place for a picnic."

The old man exchanged a conspiratorial glance with Seb's mother, and then the two of them shared what could only be described as a giggle.

"What are you to up to?" Seb asked. "Is there something in that picnic basket besides food?"

"How did you know?" his mother asked.

"I didn't really. Maybe it's the juvenile way you two are behaving."

"Go on," Dusty urged, moving in tight with the group. "Just tell them so we can get to the chow."

Jeremiah gestured for Elizabeth to do the honors. She opened the basket, removed a mound of sandwiches, a container of potato salad, a bag of what might have been rolls, and five bottles of Coca-Cola, no doubt pilfered from the saloon. After setting out tin plates and forks, she finally pulled out a slip of paper from the bottom of the basket.

With a shy glance the old man's way, Elizabeth said, "This is for Mr. and Mrs. Sebastian Cole. It's our wedding present."

"It's from me, too," Dusty said. "I chipped in along with them."

Seb suddenly didn't want to know what was written on the paper, and from the horrified look on Lucy's face, she didn't either.

"Well, aren't you gonna look at it?" Jeremiah demanded.

Elizabeth said, "I doubt the document will make much sense to them, so maybe we ought to explain. Go ahead."

"Thank you, my dear." Beaming, Jeremiah said, "It's a deed to these here two acres you're sitting on."

Stunned, Seb blurted, "You bought us land?"

Still beaming, the old man nodded. "For you to build that house you and Lucy been wanting."

"It's a perfect spot," Elizabeth added. "Just right for a family."

"But we don't want a house." Panic gripping him, Seb glanced at Lucy, seeking confirmation. She was in another world, dreamy-eyed and misty. No help there.

"I'm surprised by your reaction, Sebastian," said his mother. "It almost sounds as if you don't appreciate our gift."

"Oh, I doubt that's it, Elizabeth," Jeremiah said. "Your Seb is a proud one, wants to do things his own way. I'm sure he likes our gift just fine, don'tcha, son?"

Trapped, he had nowhere to go but where they led. "Of course, I—we do. It's just that it's too much. I don't see how we can accept it."

He nudged Lucy with his elbow. "Right, Lucy?"

"Huh?" She blinked, and then said, "Oh, right. We can't accept such an expensive gift."

"Nonsense," said Elizabeth. "Jeremiah and I ran all over town yesterday trying to find out who owned the land, if it was for sale, and then trying to get someone to sign over the deed. It's a gift from our hearts more than our pocketbooks, and we don't want to hear another thing about it."

"Except maybe a thank you," Jeremiah added.

Seb and Lucy exchanged glances, flickers of guilt filling the space between them. Seb was the first to say, "Thank you. It's beautiful."

"Oh, yes," Lucy said. "I just can't believe it's ours."

Jeremiah rubbed his hands together. "Maybe the fella that built the log cabin on the other side of the lake can help you two some when it comes time to build the house."

By now Seb was desperate to end the conversation. "That's something to think about, all right. What did you bring to eat? I'm starving."

With that the group gobbled up the sandwiches and potato salad, and then Elizabeth tore open the mysterious bag. "Look what I found—the most delicious Hot Cross Buns ever. I got them from Charlie's Bakery, which I'm told is the best in town."

Lucy had just taken a swallow of her Coca-Cola. She choked, fizz shot up her nose, and the rest of the drink ran down the front of her yellow lawn dress.

Dusty burst out laughing. "I don't think Lucy is gonna be having any of those buns."

Elizabeth glanced around at the group; Seb, who was patting Lucy on the back, Dusty, who was still laughing, and Jeremiah, who was grumbling.

"Did I miss something?" she asked.

"Nothing of any consequence," Seb replied.

Dusty burped, a long baritone sound. "Oops," he said. "Guess I'd better go take a walk."

He pushed off the blanket and headed toward the back of the property.

Lucy, who'd regained her composure, said, "That sounds like a good idea. A nice walk."

"Sure, you two, go on ahead." Jeremiah handed the deed to Seb. "Take a look at the whole property. There's a little map in here that shows you where it starts and ends."

When he and Lucy were far enough away from the picnic site, Seb said, "I never expected anything like this. What do we do now?"

"I don't know." There was a catch in Lucy's voice, almost a sob. "It's the most wonderful thing, your mother and my pa working so hard on this surprise, and yet we don't deserve it."

"Exactly. So what do we do about it?"

Lucy knew that he felt trapped, not only in the marriage, but also by the lies he was forced to tell his mother. And it was all because of selfishness, Lucy admitted to herself, that single-minded determination to stand on her own personal mountaintop as a free woman, able to make her own choices and live her own life. That dream had somehow turned into an avalanche, destroying everything she loved and cared about as it tumbled into an abyss of deceit.

Her heart heavy, Lucy suggested, "Maybe we ought to tell them the truth, Sebastian. I can't hold you to your promise any longer. It's not fair; none of this is fair to anyone."

"One thing is for damn sure—your plan has gotten a hell of a lot more complicated than I thought it would be."

"I know, and I'm truly sorry."

"Please, no more apologizing."

Sorry almost slipped out of Lucy's mouth again. She bit it back and said, "So, do we tell them the truth?"

Sebastian didn't answer at once. They continued to walk, passing through mottled shadows tossed by oak leaves and soaking up sunshine. And then he said, "Here's what we'll do: We'll thank them for being so thoughtful, then sell the land a few weeks down the road—sending them the money, of course. If not that, we'll figure out something else."

Stunned, Lucy came to an abrupt halt. "You'd do that after all you've been through because of me?"

Sebastian turned to her and pulled her gently into his arms. "You bet I will. When you get that divorce, I don't want everyone in town to think you got rid of me because I was a rotten husband."

Longing to kiss him, to hug him until her arms ached, Lucy was also aware that two pairs of eyes had been following them since they left the picnic blanket. Instead she settled for a quick kiss on the cheek and a whispered, "I intend to repay you for this. Bring lots of chocolate."

Sebastian held her at arm's length, his expression suggesting an equally ribald reply. Before he could speak, Dusty's voice filled the air.

"Hey, you two. Get on over here. You can see Merry's ranch from up here."

Dusty was just a few feet ahead, standing at the edge of a slope near the end of the property. Joining him there, they glanced down to where he was pointing into the valley below.

"See," he said. "I think that's Merry out in the corral."

He took off his hat and waved it as he shouted, "Hey, Merry. It's me, Dusty."

She looked up from her work, took off her own hat, and waved him down.

"She wants to see me." Dusty's eyes were bright with hope. "If I'm not back when you're ready to leave, ask Pa to come by the ranch and pick me up."

He took off down the hill, running part of the way. After tripping over something, probably his own feet, he rolled head over heels all the way to the bottom.

Lucy gasped and waited until he got to his feet and appeared to be all right. Then they headed back to the picnic site.

As they walked, Sebastian said, "You will make sure that Dusty and your father are on that train Tuesday, right?"

She laughed. "If I have to get on it myself."

He gave her a look then, something suggesting that he might not like that very much, but then they were back by the lake, within earshot of another conversation.

"And by the way, Elizabeth," Jeremiah was saying, "you lied to me about that cognac. It wasn't no balm, it was spirits, plain and simple. When I woke up yesterday morning my head felt like a gourd."

She laughed, reached into the picnic basket, and pulled out a bottle of cognac. "I'm told the best cure for that is a shot of what ailed you."

Elizabeth was holding out the bottle toward Lucy's father when she stepped onto the blanket. "Pa? Do you really think that's such a good idea?"

"No, my sweet girl, I do not. I was just having a look at the label."

Despite his reassurance, once Sebastian and Lucy joined them, it was decided a toast to the new property was in order. Everyone took a sip as Elizabeth passed the bottle around, and then the group fell into conversation as if they'd been friends for years.

When they finally decided to head back to town and were packing up the basket and folding the blanket, a silvery horse came galloping up the slope at the rear of the property. One of the twins was urging the horse on and Dusty, behind her, was clinging to her waist for dear life.

As the horse slid to a stop near the rig, Dusty tumbled off sideways and landed in a heap.

"You all right, son?" Jeremiah said.

"Sure, Pa." Dusty got to his feet and dusted his bottom. "I was just practicing the quick dismount."

The twin laughed as she climbed down off the horse. "Sure you were, Dusty. You're such a liar."

"Merry?" Lucy asked, never certain which twin was which.

"That's Merry, all right," Dusty affirmed. "I can tell them apart now, and besides, ever since Pa beat Charlie up at the saloon, Cherry kinda likes him again."

Merry shot Dusty a sideways glance. "She never liked you, you dolt."

Never one to let his children be criticized, Jeremiah said, "Dusty isn't no dolt, but we do thank you for bringing him back to us."

"She isn't bringing me back, Pa. We were just letting you know that I'm gonna stay at the ranch a while and help out a little. Cherry is off to town to help at the bakery, and Merry said she could use the company."

Jeremiah narrowed his gaze at Merry.

Before he could speak, she said, "Calling Dusty a dolt was all in fun. I like him, and when he isn't falling all over himself, he makes a pretty fair ranch hand. I'd like to keep him until tonight, or maybe even tomorrow sometime."

"I'm not sleeping with no pig," Dusty declared.

"You won't have to," Merry assured him. "Ma will let you use the couch."

Jeremiah turned to his son. "Is that what you want to do?"

"Sure, Pa. I'll be back before tomorrow night."

"You'd best be. We got a train to catch the next day."

The train. Lucy didn't need Sebastian's elbow in her ribs to remind her of what she already knew was imperative. She wagged a finger toward her brother as she said, "You'd best be back by tomorrow *afternoon,* Dusty, or I'll come out here and get you myself."

That settled, Merry and Dusty rode off. Then the Coles

and Prestons headed back to town. Later that night the four of them dined at the Palace Arms dining room, one big, happy family. .

As promised, Merry returned Dusty late Monday afternoon, giving him plenty of time to gather his things and prepare for the trip back home. When Tuesday afternoon arrived, Seb was in a fine mood. He'd already said his farewells to Jeremiah and Dusty, and soon they would be on the train heading out of town and out of his life. Now all he had to do was collect his mother from the hotel and escort her to the train station.

He and Jack had just finished setting up the last table for tonight's poker tournament when the door opened, and to Seb's surprise, there stood his mother.

Joining her at the door, he said, "I was just on my way to get you. Are you ready to go?"

As he leaned over to pick up her traveling bag, Elizabeth blocked his hand. "No, I'd rather you didn't."

"How will it look if I let my mother carry her own bag?"

"Just fine, because I don't want you to go to the depot with me."

Some of the old, ugly feelings crept into his voice as he said, "Why not? Are you embarrassed to be seen with me?"

"Oh, Sebastian, of course not." For a minute there, Seb thought she was going to slap him. "It's just that getting on a train and leaving you behind will bring up too many sad memories I'd like to forget. As it is I won't be able to look out the window and watch Emancipation fade away, and I can't bear the thought of you standing out there watching me go. Can you understand that?"

Seb considered this, imagining the way he might feel as he stood there watching her disappear from his life again, and gave an appreciative nod. "I understand," he said. "And I approve. Saying good-bye here seems less final somehow."

Elizabeth slid her hand up to his shoulder, patting him as if he was still a boy. "Thank you, Sebastian. I'm really happy to know that you feel that way."

He thought he'd prepared himself for this moment, but now that it was upon him, Seb didn't know what to do or say.

Apparently sensing this, Elizabeth removed her hand and flashed a bright smile. "I also want to be clear on something else: The wedding gift Jeremiah and I gave you is simply that, a gift. I know it can't make up for the past, and it's not meant to. I only hope that from now on we can look forward to a future of mutual understanding and respect."

"What?" he said with a grin. "You expect me to write?"

"Yes, actually, I'd like that very much. I'd like it even better if you'd come visit me whenever you can—if you want to, of course."

This was much more than he'd expected from his mother. In some ways Seb had halfway believed that he'd never hear from her again. Something swelled in his throat, making it difficult to swallow as he asked, "Does all that work both ways?"

"Absolutely," she assured him. "I have no intention of ever interfering with your life, Sebastian, but I would very much like to be a part of it again, if you'll have me."

His throat growing tighter, Seb looked into her sincere gray eyes, then impulsively pulled her into his arms. Squeezing her as hard as he dared, he whispered, "I wouldn't have it any other way."

When he released her, Seb was surprised to spot a tear rolling down his mother's cheek.

She turned her head away, brushing at her face, and said, "I'd better be going. Good-bye for now, son. We'll be in touch soon."

"Soon," he promised.

She took a deep breath. "Now go inside and play some cards. I don't want you standing out here watching me walk away either."

* * *

At the train station, Lucy had just urged her father to duck into the depot and buy their tickets while he still could.

Dusty stepped between them and said, "Uh, wait a minute, Pa. I gotta talk to you."

"The train's almost on us, boy. Can't you hear it? Just let me get the tickets and then you can talk all you want."

"That's right," Lucy said. "You simply can't miss the train today."

"But that's what I gotta talk about." He sucked in a breath and squared his shoulders. "I'm not going home."

"What do you mean?" Jeremiah bellowed. "Dang tootin' you're going home." He started for the depot.

"You can buy that ticket if you want to," Dusty called after him, "but I'm not going to use it. Least ways, not today."

Jeremiah stopped in his tracks.

Lucy grabbed hold of her brother's shirt. "Dusty, have you lost your mind?"

"Nope. I want to stay right here in Emancipation, maybe see what happens between me and Merry."

His movements deliberate, his voice thunderous, Jeremiah stalked up to his son and said, "Them twins tried to kill you, or did you forget that? Maybe you have gone crazy."

Dusty laughed. "Oh, Pa, they were just funning with me. Cherry don't care about me anymore since she likes Charlie again, but I think Merry might be kinda sweet on me."

By now the train had arrived and was already disgorging its passengers.

"The tickets, Pa," Lucy reminded him. "You'd better hurry."

With a scowl, he stormed into the depot.

Lucy took the opportunity to bring her brother to task. "What in the world is wrong with you? Now you've gone and gotten Pa all in a dither over this foolish notion of yours."

"Foolish, is it?"

Lucy couldn't remember a time when he'd been so fired up.

"How come it's not foolish when you want to stay here," he continued, "and foolish when I want to?"

"That's different."

"I don't see how. You came here to get married and you did. Maybe I'll just get myself hitched, too."

For some reason Lucy thought it highly unlikely, at least where Merry Barkdoll was concerned. She sure couldn't tell him that, which left her with few arguments.

Jeremiah came down the steps then, a pair of tickets in hand, and held one out to his son.

Dusty's mouth was set in a firm, defiant line. As he snatched the ticket from his father, he said, "I'll take it, but I'm not gonna get on that train."

"That's enough nonsense out of you," Jeremiah said, equally defiant.

Noticing that passengers were beginning to board the train, Lucy quickly explained Dusty's situation. "He wants to stay here because he thinks that Merry Barkdoll would like to make him her husband."

Jeremiah laughed and shook his head. "Then he really has gone crazy."

"No, I haven't, Pa. I'm staying here until she either marries me or tosses me out on my backside."

"But what are you gonna do?" Jeremiah asked. "How will you live?"

Dusty shrugged. "Merry said she'd hire me on as a ranch hand. I might be good at it."

Lucy and her father exchanged a horrified glance. And then, with equal horror, she noticed that the platform was nearly empty.

"It's time to go, Pa."

Jeremiah eyed the train. "I don't like going off this way and leaving Dusty behind."

Lucy figured it was bad enough that she couldn't get her brother out of town as promised. If her father stayed behind, too, Sebastian would never forgive her.

"Oh, don't worry about Dusty," she said, taking her father by the arm and walking him toward the nearest car. "I'll keep an eye on him for you, and if you want the truth, I expect he'll be home a lot sooner than you think."

Jeremiah grumbled a bit but then gave up the battle. Glancing to where Dusty still stood, feet spread, arms crossed over his chest, he said, "Good-bye, son. I sure hope you know what you're doing."

Back to the old Dusty again, big grin, loose joints and all, he waved to his father. "I'll write home as soon as I have news. Give Ma a big kiss from me."

"Give her the same from me," Lucy said, throwing her arms around her father's neck. "And tell her that I love her."

Jeremiah mashed her in his burly arms and planted a kiss on her forehead. "You take good care of yourself, and see if you can't get that husband of yours to find another kind of business."

"I'll try, Pa," was the best she could do. "And I promise to write home once a week. Now you'd better get on board."

As they reached the wooden steps set out on the platform for easy boarding and disembarking, a stout woman appeared at the top step, dragging her baggage behind her. Then she began an awkward descent.

When she saw Lucy and Jeremiah standing at the bottom, she said, "Oh, pardon me. I dozed off during the trip and almost missed my stop."

Jeremiah stepped to the side, then reached out to give the lady a hand. As she neared, Lucy noticed that the woman appeared to be a few years older than she was, and handsome, if not attractive. But her hair was the thing that stopped Lucy in her tracks. Never had she seen such a star-tling and unnatural shade of red, although it couldn't truly be called red. Her head resembled an orange that had been struck by lightning.

As the woman stepped down onto the platform, Jeremiah hefted her bag and started for the depot.

"Pa," Lucy called, following after him. "You have to get on the train now. I can do that."

Determined to do this much, he toted the bag over to the bench sitting in front of the depot and dropped it there. Then he said to the woman, "Your husband's the one ought to be helping you with this heavy stuff."

Behind them the conductor called, "All aboard."

"Oh," the woman replied with a little chuckle. "I had to stay behind in Denver for a while, but he's already here in Emancipation."

"Then why didn't he meet you and help you out?"

"Pa . . ." Lucy pleaded.

"It's a surprise visit," the woman explained. "In fact, I'm not quite sure where to find him."

"Get on the train, Pa," Lucy said. "I can help this lady. I've gotten to know most folks in town. What's your hus-band's name?"

"Cole," she said, her eyes dreamy. "Sebastian Cole."

Chapter Twenty-four

The world spinning wildly around her, Lucy's vision went gray and fuzzy. And then everything went black.

Later—it could have been hours or days for all she knew—Lucy came around enough to realize that she was lying in the dirt. Blinking, dumbstruck, at first she couldn't fathom what had happened.

"Sweetie, sweet girl, are you all right?"

Pa's voice, his hat fanning her.

Lucy opened her eyes and smiled at her father. Then she saw the woman with the orange hair standing beside him. "Oh, no. It can't be true, it just can't be."

"Hush, now," Jeremiah said. "We'll talk about this later. Can you stand up?"

All Lucy could think was that Sebastian had a wife, and it wasn't her. How could this be? How could he have married her while married to another?

"Come on, Lucy girl," Jeremiah encouraged, reaching under her arms and lifting her to her feet. "It's gonna be all right."

"My goodness, is she hurt?" asked the woman with the orange head.

Sounding protective, Jeremiah quickly said, "It's the heat, just the heat. Poor girl can't stand the heat."

"Pa—"

"I know, I know." Turning to Dusty, Jeremiah said, "Go inside the depot and see if you can't get a cup of water while I settle Lucy down."

He dragged his limp daughter over to the bench and sat her down beside the woman's bag. When Dusty returned with the water, Jeremiah held it to her lips. "Come on, drink."

Obedient, but numb all over, Lucy downed the entire cup of water.

"Are you better now?" Jeremiah asked, offering her his handkerchief. "You're not gonna faint again, are you?"

"No, Pa," she said, tears rolling down her cheeks like rain. Lucy could see the heartache in her father's eyes, knew that he couldn't stand to see her this way, but was helpless to cure herself. She was melting from the inside out, and no amount of handkerchiefs or kind words could stem the tide.

"You listen to me, girl," Jeremiah went on. "I want you to stay right where you are. Don't move from this spot until I come back for you."

"But Pa—"

"I'm taking care of this," he said in a tone that brooked no argument. "And I want you to promise me."

Choking on a sob, she managed to say, "Okay, Pa."

He patted the top of her head and kissed her wet cheek. "I'll be right back. Don't you move."

Then he turned to Dusty, who stood there looking as dazed as Lucy, and said, "Come on over here, boy."

When he reached the bench, Jeremiah said, "Grab hold of the lady's bag and then walk her slowly, *very slowly*, down to the Pearly Gates."

"Slow, Pa?"

"Slow. I got some business down there first and need a little time to get it done."

"All right, Pa."

"And one more thing: Don't say nothing to that woman about Lucy and Seb. That's a conversation he can have all to hisself."

Then he took off toward the saloon, moving faster than Lucy had ever seen him move in her entire life.

At the Pearly Gates, Seb was sitting with Jack playing a few quick hands of five-card stud. He heard the train blow three short whistles, a signal that meant "Clear the tracks, we're rolling on our way." He couldn't think about his mother being on that train, or wonder when he might see her again, so he entertained himself in another way.

Breathing a big sigh of relief, he said to Jack, "You hear those whistles?"

Jack didn't look up from his cards. "Music to the ears."

"Yep, but not because we'll soon be full of gamblers eager to lose their hard-earned money. That sound means that Jeremiah and Dusty are finally on their way home. It's about time we had a little peace around here."

Seb reached into his pocket, pulled out a small box, and popped it open. There, nestled in a bed of dark velvet, was a wide gold band engraved with roses. He pushed the box toward Jack and said, "This is going to make it for real. What do you think?"

Jack glanced at the wedding ring and shrugged. "Thanks, but I think you know I'm not the marrying kind."

"Idiot. It's for Lucy." Seb closed the box and put it back in his pocket. "Maybe you ought to give marriage a try, Jack. You don't know what you're missing. I feel like the luckiest man alive."

The door banged open then, and Jeremiah Preston stormed into the room.

Under his breath, Jack said, "Looks like your luck just ran out."

"You miserable son of a buck," Jeremiah shouted as he headed for their table.

Seb jumped out of his chair. "You're not on the train."

"Dang tootin' I'm not on the train, you, you . . . *biggist*."

"Biggist?"

By then the old man was on him, and Seb never saw it coming. Jeremiah drove his fist under his chin.

Seb hit the floor like a sack of potatoes, down, but not out.

Jack hopped out of his chair and advanced. Seb held out his hand, waving him off.

Hovering over him, Jeremiah said, "My sweet girl, my sweet baby Lucy passed out in the dirt because of you."

Still stunned, trying to figure out what the man was talking about, he couldn't think fast enough to suit Jeremiah. The old man took Seb's momentary confusion as an opportunity to kick him in the ribs.

"Damn," whooshed out of Seb along with his breath. He rolled to the side, away from Jeremiah's boot, and then staggered to his feet. "What the hell is going on?"

The old man strutted right up to Seb, acting for all the world as if he were ten feet tall. His fists were bunched, ready for action, as he said, "That's a foul-mouthed question I ought to be asking you, you biggist."

Seb was trying to figure out what the hell a biggist might be when Jeremiah took another swing at him. This time Seb was ready. He caught the old man's fist in his hand and held him there at arm's length.

"I don't want to fight you, and I won't," Seb promised, "but you've got to tell me what's happened. I can't defend myself against invisible charges."

Struggling against Seb's grip but not having much luck, he said, "They were sure visible enough to Lucy. That poor girl's sitting down at the depot now crying her eyes out, and you know what? Them tears are red. You sucked the life's blood out of my little girl, and I mean to see you pay for it."

Suddenly picturing Lucy crying at the depot and, if he'd heard correctly, lying in the dirt as well, Seb released the old man's fist. A mistake.

This time when Jeremiah fired away, he caught Seb's jaw, a glancing blow that sent him sideways and halfway onto a poker table.

Seb righted himself and spun around in time to duck another of Jeremiah's wild swings. Then he reached out and flattened his hand across the old man's bald head, gripping his skull as best he could.

Holding him at bay, Seb demanded, "What happened to Lucy? Why is she crying and in the dirt?"

With his short reach, Jeremiah couldn't possibly touch Seb, but he kept swinging anyway as he said, "I told you, you went and broke her heart, you biggist."

"And what the hell is a biggist?"

"You ought to know." Jeremiah kicked out with a stubby leg, again unable to reach Seb. "You're the one with too many wives."

As Seb thought about that curious statement, Dusty suddenly appeared in the doorway. "Are we here too fast, Pa?"

"No, bring her on in. I'm about done here."

Dusty stood there a moment longer, watching his father swing away at nothing but air. Then he stepped aside, and a woman entered the saloon.

Seb's first reaction was to cringe when he saw the orange hair. And then he took a look at her face.

His mouth fell open and his hand slid off Jeremiah's head. *"Kate?"*

"That's what I been trying to tell you about, you biggist." The old man added as he advanced, "You got one wife too many."

Then, and with his full weight behind it, Jeremiah drove a vicious uppercut into Seb's chin.

This time when he hit the floor, he didn't even feel it.

Lucy was still sitting at the depot when her father and Dusty returned, and not because of any promise she'd made. She couldn't have moved if she wanted to. Her entire system had shut down, everything, that is, except an endless supply of tears along with her mind. It kept telling her that Sebastian had another wife, and she kept on denying it, as if this would somehow make it all go away. So far it wasn't working.

When her father came up and sat down beside her, he gently asked, "Are you doing better now, Lucy?"

Without looking at him—she simply couldn't—she asked, "Is it true, really true?"

"I'm afraid so, darling. When the miserable biggist set eyes on her, he called her by name. Kate is what he said."

Hands over her face, Lucy collapsed into her own lap.

"There, there," her father soothed, patting her on the back. "It'll take some time, but you'll get over all this."

"Never," she sobbed against her palms. "I'll never get over Sebastian. I love him so."

"Well, you'll just have to get over him, and in due time you will. For now, we got things to do, and we'd best get right to them."

Lucy didn't care what needed to be done. All she cared about was Sebastian and her broken heart.

"Dusty and me talked about it some on the way back here," her father went on, apparently oblivious to her pain. "And here's what we're gonna do."

When Lucy didn't respond, her father tugged at her shoulder.

"Come on, girl," he urged. "This is important. Sit up and take notice."

Ever the obedient daughter, Lucy forced herself to push back and straighten her spine.

"That's better." Again he patted her back. "We got to get a place for the three of us to stay, but we're dang short of

308

funds. There isn't but one place we could think of for us to go, so we're headed there now. Think you can walk?"

Anywhere was all right with Lucy, anywhere that wasn't in sight of Sebastian. "Of course I can walk," she said, dabbing at her nose.

After she got to her feet and found her legs a little wobbly, Jeremiah took one arm and Dusty took the other. Propping her up between them, the trio headed up the street.

As they walked, Jeremiah explained, "Once we get you settled, Dusty and I are gonna go back to that hotel and gather up all your clothes and such. That way you don't have to worry about bumping into that biggist and his other wife."

Lucy's tears had finally ebbed some, enough to be manageable. With that statement they came back with a vengeance, flooding the very dirt that she walked upon. She wasn't crying so hard, however, that she didn't recognize the building her father had chosen as her refuge.

There on a neatly painted sign above the door were the words CHARLIE'S BAKERY.

As Seb slowly came around, he became aware of a deep ache radiating from his chin and jaw and felt something cold and clammy covering a large part of his face and neck. When he was able to keep his eyeballs from spinning, he slowly lifted his lids.

Two Jacks were hunkered down next to him, pressing wet bar towels against his skin. "Welcome back," they said.

Seb blinked a couple of times, and the twin Jacks merged into one. "What happened?"

"You probably don't want to know."

As the pieces of his mind gradually came together again, he had a sudden vision. "Jeremiah."

"Yep. He and Dusty are still in town. Kate's here, too."

Seb groaned, remembering it all, and then heard a voice from the not-too-distant past.

"Oh, my darling. Are you all right?"

Turning his head to the left, Seb didn't see Kate so much as the nightmare he thought he'd left behind. Thinking back through the past and how hard he'd tried to escape this woman, Seb's stomach did a slow roll.

Back in Denver he'd actually been forced to move three times, once to a boardinghouse, then to an apartment, and finally to a seedy little shack outside of town. Each time Kate somehow managed to find him. At the last place he'd actually come home after closing the Fire and Brimstone and found her cooking a late-night supper for him. That was when he decided the only way to escape Kate's relentless stalking was to leave town and come to Emancipation. He should have paid more attention to Billy's warning.

Frustrated and angry, Seb sat up and shook his head to clear it. Then he gingerly climbed to his feet.

"I can't believe that old man hit you," Kate said. "He was so helpful at the depot."

"What are you doing here?" he asked, brushing himself off.

"I came to see you, silly."

Seb finally turned to her, again blinded by her bright orange hair. Last time he saw her it had been a dirty blond. She'd also been a lot thinner. Spearing her with what he hoped was a vicious gaze, he asked, "Why would you want to see me again? I told you over and over in Denver that we were through. Why would you follow me all the way out here?"

Showing no hint that his words had hurt her, Kate rested her hands against her belly and said, "I thought you'd want to know about the baby."

Forced to look at her and take in her apparently delicate condition, for a moment Seb thought he might pass out. Beside him Jack made a noise in his throat, nothing close to laughter, and then he excused himself and went back to the poker table.

Dazed, his mind frantically exploring the possibility that this baby could be his, Seb glanced around the room. Customers were beginning to trickle into the saloon, and soon the poker games would start.

Not interested in making a public spectacle of himself, Seb took Kate by the elbow and said, "Come with me."

After leading her to a private table at the back of the room, he seated Kate and then took the chair next to her. Ignoring her claims of impending motherhood for the time being, he tackled the subject that caused him the greatest concern. "You mentioned you met that old man at the depot. What happened down there?"

She gave off a tiny shrug. "The man was kind enough to help me off the train and with my bag, and then the younger one—his son, I suppose—walked me to your saloon."

"What about the old man's daughter?" Seb persisted, sick at heart over Lucy. "Wasn't she there, too?"

Kate pursed her thin lips as if thinking this over, and then breezily said, "Oh, yes, I remember her. She fainted; the heat or something, if I remember correctly."

This didn't sound at all like Lucy. "That's it? You didn't say anything to her?"

Kate smiled, a sickeningly sweet expression that made Seb's stomach roll. Her voice as sugary as her smile, she said, "Since I wasn't exactly sure where you were located, I did ask her to help me find my husband."

Husband. Shelving that issue for later, too, he said rather than asked, "And you told her my name."

"Of course. How would she know where to find you if she didn't know your name?"

Seb propped his elbows on the table and buried his face in his hands. What must Lucy be thinking? Oh, God, he knew this might happen, that Kate might come to town, and he'd even considered warning Lucy about her. Why hadn't he done it? He'd had the opportunity and taken the easy way out. Now it was obvious that she and her family believed Kate's wild tale, especially after the beating Jeremiah had tried to deliver. He had to get to Lucy as quickly as possible, and then somehow try to explain this bizarre situation. But first he had to figure out what do with Kate.

Trying to control his temper, Seb balled his fists and banged them down on the table. "How could you have told Lucy, or anyone, that I'm your husband?"

She patted her belly. "That's a silly question. I told them you're my husband because I can hardly say that I'm unwed."

"I am *not* your husband, I have never been your husband, and I never will be your husband." Seb heard his voice growing louder with each statement, and lowered it considerably as he added, "Why can't you get that through your head?"

Kate recoiled a little, her mouth pinched and tight, and for a minute Seb thought she might burst into tears. She didn't, but her voice quivered as she said, "I don't know why you have so much trouble remembering that we were to wed. If you hadn't come here, we'd have been married in Denver last December."

All Seb could do was shake his head. He looked Kate in the eye, hoping to find a way to reason with her, to make her understand that she was living a fantasy that would never come true. He came away with the feeling that he was looking into the face of madness. How does a man reason with insanity?

As Jeremiah and Dusty burst into the bakery, dragging Lucy along with them, she noticed there was one lone customer. Charlie was nowhere in sight.

Alerted by the little bell above the door, he came around from the kitchen just as Lucy and her family stepped up to the counter.

When he saw them, Charlie's face went as white as the flour he was dusting off his hands. "Oh, my heavens."

"Heaven's got nothing to do with this," Jeremiah declared. "We need to talk to you."

The whites of Charlie's eyes dominated his expression as he said, "Now?"

"Right here and right now."

Charlie glanced at his customer, who had taken an interest in the conversation. "Come back to the kitchen with me."

The minute they all rounded the corner and stepped into the back room, Charlie said, "I don't know what else you people expect of me. I've apologized to Lucy several times. I even offered to marry—"

"We don't need no more apologies from you," Jeremiah said, cutting him off. "We need some help."

Charlie finally took a long look at the family, settling his gaze on Lucy, who did her best to avoid him. "What's wrong? Has something happened?"

"Plenty's happened, but none of it is your business," Jeremiah explained. "We need a place to stay, and Dusty says you got a nice little apartment upstairs."

"Why, yes, but I, ah, live there."

Even though he was shorter than Charlie, Jeremiah got right up in his face. "Guess what? We're gonna live there with you until we figure a way to get out of this miserable town. It's the least you can do after what you put this family through."

Charlie gulped and loosened his collar. "In that case, I suppose you and Dusty could make do with the couch and the floor."

"And what about you?" Jeremiah asked, a twinkle in his eye. "Where are you gonna bunk?"

"In my room, of course, in my own bed."

Jeremiah shook his head and threw his arm around Lucy's shoulders. "My little girl is gonna have your room all to herself. Now where are you gonna sleep?"

Completely ignoring her father, Charlie turned to Lucy in shock. "I can't keep you here. Your husband has made it quite clear that I'm to stay away from you. He'll kill me if he finds you here. Have you all gone mad?"

"Lucy don't have that husband no more," Jeremiah explained. "It seems he isn't what we thought he was. Now again, where are you gonna sleep?"

Still ignoring her father, Charlie said to Lucy, "Is this true? You and Seb are no longer together?"

Lucy couldn't—wouldn't—discuss Sebastian with Charlie or anyone else. She lowered her gaze and refused to answer.

"Leave her be," Jeremiah demanded. "And take us up to the apartment. Lucy needs to lie down for a while."

"But I can't do that. Cherry has agreed to marry me again, and if she finds Lucille here, she'll—"

"I don't give a horse's patoot about any gal except my Lucy. Now take us upstairs."

Staying at Charlie's apartment was the last thing Lucy wanted to do, but in her state of befuddlement she couldn't think of a viable alternative. All she wanted was the total oblivion of sleep, to drift away to a world where there was no pain.

Crestfallen and brokenhearted, she allowed herself to be led out through the back door and then up the stairs and into the relative sanctity of Charlie's bedroom.

Seb glanced around the saloon, noticing that it was filling up rapidly. Getting nowhere with Kate and more than a little concerned about Lucy, he said, "I have to go to work now. Do you have a place to stay?"

She actually had the gall to look surprised as she said, "I had planned on staying with you."

"That's not going to happen."

"Oh, but if we marry today—"

"You will never be my wife." Seb pulled her out of her chair and helped her to her feet. "Let's go find a room for you."

To Seb's surprise, Kate went along quietly, allowing him to lead her out of the saloon and onto the boardwalk. He didn't even look in the direction of the Palace Arms Hotel. There was no way he'd house her under the same roof with him, much less Lucy and her family. As much as he disliked

Kate, he couldn't bring himself to take her to one of the other hotels either, so he settled on something in between. Hoping to God that she had a room available, he headed for Shirley's Boardinghouse.

As they walked, Kate glanced over at him and said, "I see you still have that notch in your ear. Does it bother you much anymore?"

It bothered the hell out of him, but no longer through pain. It was a constant reminder of his guilt. Kate had used that guilt to get to him many times before, and just as many times he'd allowed her to get away with those tactics. Damned if he was going to let it happen again.

When they reached the boardinghouse, Seb's luck held. Shirley had what she called "a lovely room," just right for a lady. After paying for two days' rent in advance and promising Kate that he would return to further discuss their situation at noon the next day, Seb took off for the Palace Arms, moving as quickly as his legs would allow.

Taking the stairs two at a time, he raced up to the second floor and went directly to the little room adjoining his. The door was unlocked, so he let himself in. Except for the furnishings, the room was gutted.

When he opened the connecting door that led to his room, Seb noticed that his door was already open—and that it was splintered near the lock, no doubt by the boot of Jeremiah Preston.

Although he already knew what he would find, Seb searched the entire room, including the water closet and dressers, but not so much as a scrap of Lucy remained. It was almost as if she'd never existed, never spent a night wrapped in his arms. Trembling with both rage and fear, Seb sat down on the bed and buried his head in his hands.

The things Kate had done to him in Denver had been inconvenient, irritating, and frustrating, but not the nightmare he'd thought they were. This was the nightmare, and Seb wasn't sure how to survive it. How could he ever explain all this to Lucy, especially about the baby? He could barely understand it himself.

Seb had only been with Kate the one time, a foolish moment he'd regretted ever since. He'd always been careful with the women he bedded; with the exception of that crazy night when he'd tricked Lucy into climbing on top of him, extremely careful. He was the last man who would ever father a child and abandoned it or its mother. Besides, the timing with Kate didn't feel right. He was sure it must be at least seven months since the one night they'd been together, and yet here she was, looking a little chubby around the middle in a shapeless dress, but not as big as he thought she ought to be. How was this possible?

Flinging himself prone on the bed, Seb picked up Lucy's scent. Reaching for her pillow, he pressed it against his nose and inhaled deeply, trying to drown himself in her essence. He wondered in those few moments of bliss if he'd ever have the chance to hold her again, to tell her how much he loved her.

He had to find her and somehow explain the unexplainable. If he had to tear the town apart or even the entire state of Wyoming, he would do it. Somehow he would find Lucy and make things right between them again.

Chapter Twenty-five

Feeling wounded, damaged in a way he'd never been dam-
~ged before, Seb left the Palace Arms and checked a couple
of other hotels in town. No one had seen or rented rooms to
anyone from the Preston family. In desperation, afraid they
might already be on their way to Sundance to catch the
train heading east, he stopped by Bailey Brothers livery but
got pretty much the same story. The Prestons had not
rented another buggy.

With no clue as to where Lucy might have gone, Seb
headed for the Pearly Gates. The place would be packed
with gamblers by now, and the poker tournament was due
to start at any minute. It wouldn't be right to leave things to
Jack and Pearl, and that thought gave Seb a glimmer of
hope. Above all, Lucy was a trustworthy employee, one
who took loyalty seriously. Even if she hated the sight of
him, she'd probably come to work tonight.

Hoping that when he walked through the door he would
find her balancing a tray of beers—or hell, even spilling
them—Seb stepped into the saloon. Still no Lucy.

* * *

Late the following morning Lucy finally dragged herself out of Charlie's lumpy bed and went through the motions of washing up and brushing out her hair. If not for Hazel, she thought, miserable all over again, she probably would have stayed in bed all day long. Then again, maybe not. She looked around Charlie's tiny room, a space so small the bed nearly took up the entire floor, and sighed. It was a far cry from the Palace Arms, with only a simple washbasin to tend to her most basic needs. Of course, thinking about that made her think of her most basic need of all, Sebastian, and a fresh batch of tears ran down her face.

Drying her eyes as she slipped into her stained traveling suit and stepped out into the living room, she saw that her father and Dusty were sitting on the couch, mapping out their day.

"Lucy," Jeremiah said, "I didn't expect to see you up so soon."

"I have to go to work at the newspaper."

Getting up off the couch, he said, "Are you sure?"

Lucy forced a reassuring smile. "I'm sure. In fact, the newspaper and my column are the only things I'm sure of these days."

"Helps take your mind off things, too, I expect. While you're working, Dusty and me are going to poke around and see what it would cost to rent a rig to take us all to Sundance in time for the train tomorrow."

Lucy hadn't thought about when or if she would leave town, but she knew without question that she wasn't ready to go now.

"I can't leave tomorrow," she said. "Maybe next week, but not now."

Jeremiah hitched up his overalls. "You can't mean you're gonna stay in the same town as that biggist."

"For now I am. I'm not ready to make a decision about whether I go home or stay here. You two go on ahead. Don't worry about me."

Stubborn to the core, her father declared, "I'm not leaving you here alone, not until I know you'll be all right." He turned to Dusty and said, "I guess we'd best go send another wire to your ma telling her we won't be coming home until next week. She isn't gonna like this one bit."

Excusing herself, Lucy hurried down the stairs, ducked into the privy at the back of the bakery, then made her way to the hay and grain store.

Hazel, who was working at her desk, shot Lucy a quick glance and said, "I was wondering if you were going to make it in today. Were you working late at the saloon last night?"

As she rounded the counter and joined Hazel near the printing press, Lucy said, "Not really. Sorry I'm late."

Glancing up from her work again, Hazel's eyes widened as she looked her over. "Gee whillikens, girl. What happened to you?"

Assuming she'd spilled something on her bodice, Lucy glanced down at the front of her suit.

Even though her fingers were stained with ink, Hazel took hold of Lucy's chin and gently raised it. "You've been crying," she said, "and from the look of your eyes, I'd say buckets. What's wrong?"

Lucy had no intention of discussing Sebastian and his wife with anyone, and yet as she looked into Hazel's concerned, almost motherly gaze, the sordid details spilled out, along with a few more tears.

"Oh, Hazel, it's just awful," she said, not knowing where to start. "We went to the train yesterday, but then an orange-haired woman from Denver said Sebastian Cole was her husband, see, and could I find him. The next thing I knew, I fainted, and Pa went to the saloon. I think he got into a fight with Sebastian."

Hazel snatched a handkerchief out of her pocket and dabbed at Lucy's cheeks. "Let me see if I have this straight: Seb already has a wife, and she's here in Emancipation?"

Tears still streaming down, Lucy bit her bottom lip and nodded.

"Well, I'll be dogged. And you're sure it's his wife?"

Nodding miserably, Lucy said, "Pa took her to the saloon and said that Sebastian called her by name."

Lucy hiccupped through a sob and Hazel led her to her own padded chair and sat her down. Speaking more sternly, she asked, "Have you talked to Seb about this?"

She shook her head. "I can't. I didn't even think I could talk to you about it."

"And he hasn't come looking for you?"

Lucy shrugged. "I don't know. I don't think so, but even if he did, I don't think he could find me."

"Where are you staying?"

Sniffing back her tears, Lucy said, "In Charlie White's apartment, but don't tell anyone."

Hands on her plump hips, Hazel said with disapproval, "How could you move in with Charlie?"

Realizing that the older woman probably misunderstood, Lucy explained, "It's not what you think. Pa and Dusty and I kind of took over his apartment. Charlie slept on a bench downstairs in the bakery."

Leaning her bulk against the desk, Hazel slowly shook her head. "Isn't this one hell of a mess?"

Lucy had never heard Hazel cuss before, but in this case, she couldn't disagree. "That's exactly what it is, and I don't know what to do about it."

After a few beats, her voice gentle again, Hazel said, "I can't hardly believe this of Seb, but if it's true, I'm not sure why you feel so betrayed. I hate to be the one to remind you, but your marriage was supposed to be temporary, over in a month. Am I right?"

Until then, Lucy hadn't realized that as of yesterday, the very day his real wife came to town, she and Sebastian had been married for one month. Happy Anniversary.

Even though her father and brother hadn't left town, Sebastian was perfectly entitled to reclaim his freedom and move on with his life, one that apparently included the wife he'd left behind. Lucy had to face the fact that he'd earned the right to be free of her, and she'd selfishly refused him that right.

"It's true," she admitted to Hazel. "I have no right to complain. The contract is up, but—"

"But," Hazel surmised, "you went and fell in love with Seb, and had some very high hopes that he might want to stay married to you."

Cheeks awash again, Lucy squeaked out a barely audible, "Yes."

Hazel rested her hand on Lucy's shoulder and gave her a motherly pat. "What are you going to do now? Leave town?"

"That's what Pa thinks I should do, but I just can't decide what would be best for me."

"It's your decision, of course, but I'd hate it if you left Emancipation, and not just because of the Penelope column."

Thinking about her column gave Lucy the strength she would need to get through this day. She got out of the chair, squared her shoulders, and said, "I'm not going anywhere yet. Why don't we get to work?"

After a miserable excuse for a night's sleep, Seb got out of bed around noon, cranky and out of sorts. His mood was so foul, he couldn't even choke down a cup of coffee. Instead of eating or doing anything he normally did, he resumed his search for Lucy. As he headed for the south end of town, hoping to God that she wasn't holed up in one of the seedier establishments located there, he came to Allison's hay and grain store. Slapping his forehead and wondering why he hadn't thought of it before, Seb was almost certain he would find Lucy there. She might have shrugged off him and her hostessing duties, but she would never let Hazel down.

When he walked into the building, Seb strode right up to the newspaper counter. Lucy was hunched over a long table arranging type and Hazel was down on her knees oiling the press.

"Excuse me," he said. "I'd like to have a private word with Lucy."

She looked up, spotted him, and clutched the edge of the table. For a minute Seb thought Lucy might faint.

She didn't. In fact, she turned back to the table and said, "I'm working. Besides, I don't have anything to say to you."

"Well, I've got plenty to say to you. I can either do it here in earshot of Hazel or anyone who happens by, or you can give me five minutes of your time. That's all I ask."

Hazel, who'd climbed to her feet, said to Lucy, "Why don't you go on back to the tack room and hear him out? It can't hurt."

At first Seb thought she was going to decline the offer; then Lucy grabbed a rag, wiped the ink off her fingers as best she could, and came around to his side of the counter. She didn't look as if she'd slept any better than he had, and her eyes were red and puffy, as if she'd been crying. It was all Seb could do not to take her into his arms and kiss away all the hurt.

"Follow me," Lucy said dully as she led him through a maze of grain sacks and fodder for all manner of livestock. When they reached the back of the store, where saddles and leather goods were on display, she kept her distance and folded her arms across her bosom, looking at him as if to say, "Get it over with."

So he did, and as succinctly as possible. "Kate is not my wife."

Lucy's arms slowly unfolded and fell limp at her sides. "I don't understand."

"Neither do I, actually, but it's the truth."

"Why would she call herself your wife if she isn't?"

Seb jabbed his index finger against his own temple. "I don't think she's right in the head, Lucy. It's the only explanation I can come up with."

She took a couple of tentative steps toward him. "But she knew you, Sebastian, asked for you by name."

"She knows me, all right, and has for the better part of a year," he admitted. "I killed her husband."

Lucy gasped and clutched her throat. "You what?"

"It wasn't intentional, I assure you," he explained. "I own another saloon in Denver, the Fire and Brimstone. Kate's husband—a really nice man and not usually much of a drinker—came in one night and joined my poker game. I didn't realize it at the time, but he was already drunk when he got there and proceeded to get even drunker. He accused me of cheating—I was not—and then pulled out his gun and started shooting."

Seb fingered the notch on his ear and gave her a moment to digest this. "The man damn near blew my head off. I had no choice but to fire back. Kate and her husband were very close, and she was understandably distraught over his untimely death. I felt responsible, even though he left me no choice. I even had a special billiards tournament, using the proceeds to help her out financially."

"Oh, my stars." Lucy moved a little closer, almost close enough to touch. "I understand why you tried to help her, but I still don't know why she says she's your wife."

"She tried to get me to marry her back in Denver. I guess she thought I ought to replace her dead husband." Seb thought back to the past, recognizing the unwitting part he'd played. "In the beginning I did everything I could to help her, but it seems that only made her more dependent on me. When I'd had enough, Kate began to stalk me, and I couldn't get rid of her no matter how hard I tried. That's when I gave up and moved to Emancipation. I still don't know how she found me here."

Lucy could hardly breathe. She knew in her heart that Sebastian was telling the truth, realized, too, that he was still hers, at least for the time being. Without thought or reservation, she threw herself into his arms, buried her head against his shoulder, and sobbed with relief.

"God, how I've missed you," Sebastian whispered against her hair. "I thought you'd left town somehow and that you might never be coming back."

Still too choked up to speak, Lucy continued to cling to him, to wallow in his scent and the marvelous feel of his strong arms surrounding her.

"There's something else you ought to know, Lucy."

Drying her eyes on her sleeve, Lucy backed away from Sebastian. She didn't like his suddenly troubled expression or the fact that he wouldn't look her in the eye.

He finally said, "Kate claims that she's with child."

"Does it, do you . . ." Lucy could hardly make her tongue work. "It isn't yours, is it?"

Sebastian closed his eyes for a moment and then sighed and said, "I don't think so, but I don't really know for sure."

Lucy's heart stopped, but her brain was on fire. "You—you mean, you were with her in that way?"

Head bowed low, still refusing to meet her gaze, Sebastian didn't say a word. He didn't have to.

Lucy doubled up her fist and slugged him in the chest. "You did the jiggly bed with her, the chocolate stars, and punished her, everything we did?"

"Oh, God, no, Lucy, never." As she prepared to launch her fist again, Sebastian caught her wrist. His anger a match for hers, he said, "Don't even think that. It was never like that with her or anyone else. What we have, Lucy, is—"

"Had," she reminded him, spitting the word.

"What we *have* together is something special," he insisted. "Something I've never had with anyone before. Haven't you figured it out yet? I love you, and no matter what happens between us, I'll always love you."

Wrenching her arm free, Lucy clapped her hands over her ears and said as she backed away, "Stop it. Don't say those things to me. It's too late for us."

"It can't be too late." Arms spread, Sebastian came after her. "I've been looking for you my entire life, and I'll be damned if I'll let you go now that I've found you."

Lucy continued backing up the aisle, bumping into grain sacks as she said, "I don't want you to come around anymore, at least not until you figure out just how responsible you are when it comes to Kate. It's no good for us this way, for anyone."

"Lucy, please . . ."

"I mean it," she said, backing into the main aisle. Noticing that Buford had customers at his desk, she lowered her voice and added, "If you really care for me, you'll leave now and not say another word."

His expression grim, Sebastian offered a short nod, gave Lucy a wide berth, and headed on out the door.

After he'd gone, Lucy forced her trembling legs to take her out of the main aisle. Then she sagged against a sack of grain. It was time for her to do the very thing she'd been dreading. Now that she realized how the women in Sebastian's life had used and tricked him, she knew it was way past time. She had to free Sebastian from his obligation to her, release him from what he undoubtedly saw as another of his responsibilities. Maybe then he could see his way clear to do the right thing for himself and everyone else. Maybe then they could all have a little peace. That much settled, Lucy made plans to visit Justice Carroll in the morning.

The minute he left Lucy, and also because he'd promised to visit Kate that afternoon, Seb headed straight for Shirley's Boardinghouse. Kate was sitting on a bench out front, waiting for him.

"I thought you'd never show up," she said, struggling to extract herself from the bench.

"Don't get up," he said. "I'll join you."

Determined that this time, by God, he was going to get some straight answers, Seb settled in beside her. Easing into the conversation, he glanced at Kate's startling head and asked, "What did you do to your hair?"

She patted her brittle pompadour and smiled. "You once told me how much you liked redheads, so I dyed it for you. Do you like it?"

Oh, God, Seb thought, he would never, ever look at another red-haired woman as long as he lived. Butterscotch was his flavor these days, smooth, tasty, and downright satisfying.

Shaking off momentary thoughts of Lucy, Seb steered Kate down a path of his own choosing and bluntly said, "You're going to have to tell me about your baby. Who is the father of the child?"

Blue eyes filled with surprise, she took hold of Seb's hand. "Why, you are, of course. How could you think anything else?"

Uncomfortable with her hand in his, Seb gritted his teeth and let it ride. Maybe if he allowed this small intimacy, she would be more forthright with her answers. "I don't see how it's possible for that baby to be mine. It's been a long time since we were together."

"But I swear to you, Seb, it's true. I've never been with anyone but you; except for my late husband, of course."

The hell of it was that Seb believed her. And yet the timing still felt wrong. "When is the baby supposed to be born?" he asked nonchalantly.

Kate hemmed and hawed, plucking at imaginary lint on her skirt. She finally said, "I really don't know."

"You must have some idea," he persisted.

She rolled her eyes to the heavens, as if the answer was scripted in the clouds. "December?"

"Well, that settles it," he said, greatly relieved. "That baby couldn't possibly be mine."

"Did I say December?" she was quick to respond. "I meant to say September."

Although that put him back in jeopardy, something still

didn't add up. Seb knew next to nothing about women in this condition, and yet it struck him that Kate seemed awfully small for a woman who might become a mother in a month or two. He only knew one thing for sure—he wouldn't find out what was going on with Kate by asking her. He had to take a different route, come up with a foolproof plan that would either point the finger of blame at him or let him off the hook.

Even though it was early the following Friday afternoon, Lucy and Hazel had managed to get the newest edition of the *Rustler* printed in record time. Lucy read through her column, but without her usual exuberance. When she finished here, she would deliver several copies of the *Rustler* to the Pearly Gates and then hand Sebastian his freedom. And she would need some help getting through the ordeal.

THE WEEKLY RUSTLER

Emancipation, Wyoming,	Vol. 1.
Friday, July 24, 1896	No. 44

ASK PENELOPE! FREE ADVICE

Dear Penelope:
I don't know if you keep track of the goings on in our small town, but let me tell you, things here have gotten completely out of hand.

I speak of a recent visit by that profane, venom-tongued orator, Mary Lease. Proper feminine discussions should be about domestics, dustpans and dishware and such.

This woman has convinced my wife that she is entitled to speak of politics, financials, and reform. What's this world coming to?
Signed, A Husband Who Sees a Very Bleak Future
for All Mankind

Dear Bleak Future:

I am very well aware of Mary Lease and her speeches, as well as the good she has done for women across our great nation. If your wife is happy expressing herself on topics that interest her, does she not make you a better spouse?

I assume that you are a farmer, rancher, or perhaps a businessman. Using your logic, you should only be speaking of cows and pigs, corn and wheat, or perhaps the cost of dry goods. The issues of politics affect us all, and therefore should be discussed by all, men and women alike.

Penelope

Chapter Twenty-six

At the Pearly Gates Seb was just getting ready to go collect Kate. His great plan involved taking her for a visit with Doc Smith. If she balked when he tried to convince her to go to the doctor's office, Seb figured he could somehow convince her that he was worried about her health. If a doctor couldn't figure out what was going on with her, then no one could. At the least, he hoped to settle the issue of her unborn child's expected delivery date.

Seb was heading for the door when it opened and in came Jeremiah Preston, pushing a wheelbarrow loaded down with copies of the *Rustler*. Dusty and Lucy were one step behind him. As the trio reached the rack and began filling it with newspapers, Seb warily approached them.

" 'Afternoon," he said, friendly to a fault.

No one answered him.

"Nice day," he added, still hoping to get a response.

Lucy finally turned to him and said, "Hello, Sebastian."

Not so friendly. Seb glanced at Jeremiah and Dusty, behind her. Catching Lucy's gaze again, he mouthed the word *coward.*

Before she could respond to that, if she even intended to, her father and brother took up positions on either side of her and stood there like a pair of fence posts.

Lucy handed Seb a folded slip of paper and said, "This is a bill of divorcement. All you have to do is sign it and return it to Justice Carroll."

Stunned, Seb glanced down at the paper in his hand and said, "Wait a minute."

"Eh, eh." Jeremiah wagged a finger in Seb's face. "Lucy don't want to talk to you now or ever again."

With that, Dusty and Jeremiah each took one of Lucy's arms and escorted her out of the saloon.

Too stunned to move, Seb stood there for a few beats, his mind reeling. This was not happening. How could Lucy walk out of his life so easily, especially after everything he'd told her about the past? Sure, there were a few obstacles to hurdle, but he'd figured on facing them together.

Anger seeping into his bewilderment, Seb tore the bill of divorcement into as many pieces as he could manage and stuffed the bits of paper into his pocket. Then, more than just a little curious about where Lucy was staying, he went on out the door.

To Seb's surprise, he spotted Jeremiah and Dusty climbing into a buggy a few yards down the street and then heading out of town. Lucy crossed the street and made her way south on foot. Staying a block behind her, ducking into shops each time she paused during her journey, Seb darted across the street and followed her until she disappeared into the alley near Charlie's Bakery. Hurrying to the spot, he took a peek around the corner. Lucy was climbing the stairs to the apartment above the bakery.

Seb forced himself to stand there another minute, mostly to keep from ripping out his own hair. In his many frustrations, this was the worst. After all they'd been to each other, after all the promises and nights in each other's arms, he could hardly believe this of Lucy. How much was a man to endure?

Almost able to feel the steam coming out of his nostrils, Seb headed for the stairs.

When Lucy walked into the apartment, she started for the bedroom to collect her papers to work on her next Penelope column. Before she got halfway across the room, Charlie came out of the bedroom. His shirt was open and he was wrestling with one of the buttons.

"Oh, excuse me," she said. "I didn't know you were up here."

He looked up in surprise. "I just wanted to get a clean shirt."

Although he still wasn't her favorite person, Lucy felt terrible about the way her family had moved in on him. "I'm sorry we've caused you so much trouble."

"No need to apologize. The only trouble you caused was with Cherry, but once I told her what happened and she realized that your entire family was staying here, she seemed to understand. We're getting married next month."

Lucy was about to congratulate him when she heard heavy footsteps coming up the stairs. Her father and Dusty were on their way to the Barkdoll Ranch for supper, an invitation Lucy had declined. Figuring that one of them had forgotten something, she didn't give it another thought until the door crashed open and there stood Sebastian.

He stormed across the room to where Lucy stood with Charlie, whose shirt wasn't even half buttoned.

"What the hell is going on here?" Sebastian shouted, his rage settling over Lucy's shoulders like a shroud.

Charlie dropped to his knees. "Oh, God, no."

"What's the meaning of this?" Sebastian demanded, just inches from Lucy's nose.

"Please," Charlie begged, "don't hurt me."

Afraid of the crazed look in Sebastian's eyes, Lucy said, "It's not what you think."

"Please, please," Charlie pleaded, "don't kill me."

As if annoyed by a pesky fly clinging to his pant leg, Seb glanced down at Charlie, knuckled the top of his head a couple of times, and said, "Get out and don't come back."

Half crawling, half stumbling, Charlie scrambled out of the apartment and flew down the stairs.

Sebastian's eyes were dark brimstones as he said, "I thought you were finished with him."

"I am." Lucy hated feeling so defensive, especially while feeling so betrayed. In spite of that, she had to make him understand. "Pa made Charlie take us in because of all the trouble he caused us before, see, and he didn't have much choice or like it too much, but Cherry just hates it. The three of us have been living up here."

As if he'd taken a mental iron to his forehead, the deep furrows there gradually disappeared. "And where, may I ask, does Charlie live?"

She dared a tentative smile. "On a bench downstairs in the bakery."

This settled him down some more, but not enough. Sebastian reached into his pocket, withdrew a fistful of something, and flung it into the air. As small bits of paper rained down on them like confetti, he said, "That's your bill of divorcement. I'm not divorcing you now or ever."

"Oh, but Sebastian—"

"No buts about it. Like it or not, I'm still your husband."

He dragged her into his arms then, and came down on her mouth with a kiss full of both passion and rage. Lucy fought him at first, trying to push out of his arms, but she was no match for Sebastian's strength or determination.

Still kissing her, deeply and thoroughly, he moved across the room, dragging her along with him, kicked the door shut and pinned her against the wall at the back of the apartment. His erection was urgent against her belly, setting fire to her even as she fought the response.

When he finally left her mouth, Lucy said, "No, Sebastian. You don't want to do this."

"Wrong." His hands were busy with the buttons on her jacket. "I want to do this in the worst possible way."

"It's not right. It's—"

He silenced her with another long, searing kiss, and then tugged up the hem of her skirt. Lucy heard the fabric tear, and the next thing she knew her drawers were laying at her feet.

"No, Sebastian, no." Her objections sounded feeble even to her own ears.

Feasting on her mouth again, he reached under her skirt and cupped the mound between her legs. Working his magic with his fingers, he left her mouth long enough to whisper, "Your lips may be saying no, but your body is definitely saying yes. Guess who I'm going to listen to?"

He released her long enough to open his trousers and let them fall into a puddle around his ankles. Then he took Lucy by the waist and lifted her off her feet until just the tips of her toes touched the floor.

She couldn't ever remember wanting Sebastian this badly. She was so heavy with desire, so desperate to have him inside her, she thought she might explode on the spot. He parted her legs with his knees and then guided himself to the place that ached the most. Lucy came before Sebastian had fully entered her, great wracking spasms that took the legs out from beneath her. She'd have fallen if not for his strong arms.

Chuckling throatily, he whispered against her hair, "You missed me."

Gasping for air, Lucy managed to say, "Maybe just a little."

"I missed you a lot." Showing her just how much, Sebastian plunged ahead, filling her completely and, moments later, drove her to another and even more astonishing climax. Right on her heels, he jerked against her, caught up in the throes of his own release, and then called Lucy's name over and over, the sound a balm to her injured heart.

When reason finally returned and she had at least a few of her wits about her, Lucy said, "This doesn't solve anything, you know. Meeting this way can only make things harder for us."

"We're much more than this, Lucy, and I think you know it." As Seb pulled on his trousers and adjusted the rest of his clothing, he tried to remember all the things he wanted to say. "I don't intend to sneak around corners to have you in my life, and I sure as hell don't want that for you. I'm working on a way to straighten things out. Could you trust me for just a little while longer?"

"I want to, honest, I do, but I don't see any way out of this mess."

"That's because you think I'm the father of Kate's child." Catching the stricken look on her face, he pulled Lucy close. "If I'm not, we don't have a problem. If I am, and I kind of doubt it, I'll take responsibility for the child somehow, but know this for certain—I can never marry Kate or live with her."

"But that would make the child a—a—you know."

He nodded wearily. "I don't have all the answers yet. Maybe Kate will let us adopt the baby or something; I don't know. What I do know, and from personal experience, is that there are some things worse than being a bastard."

"How can you say that?"

"Think about it. Would it be better for the child to be raised in a home by a desperately unhappy father who can't stand the sight of its mother?"

It struck Seb then that in many ways his own mother had also chosen the lesser of two evils. For the first time in his life, he could finally see that she'd probably been more interested in his welfare than her own when she left him behind. She couldn't have known how badly his father would react to her desertion, or that Seb would live his life without any kind of mother.

Too stunned and emotional to discuss the issue any further, he said, "Once again, Lucy, I'm asking you to trust me. I'm going to get to the bottom of this baby business one way or another, and I'm late for an appointment that should help me figure it out. Will you be here for me when I get back?"

Lucy bit her swollen bottom lip. "If you want me to be."

Seb took her face between his hands. "I want you, period, for all time and in all things that matter. If you can't understand anything else, understand this: I love you and I always will."

He took her hand then and tugged off the childish ring. Reaching into his pocket, he withdrew the small box, swapped rings, then slipped the shiny new band on her finger.

"Oh, my stars," Lucy said in a breathy whisper.

"With this ring," Seb vowed from deep in his heart, "I thee wed—for now and for always."

With one final kiss, he left her, and headed for his grim business.

As before, Kate was sitting outside the boardinghouse waiting for him. " 'Afternoon, Kate. How are you today?"

She gave him a coy smile. "I couldn't be better now that you're here."

"That remains to be seen." Running short on time, Seb couldn't think of a delicate way to tell Kate his plans. "I've made an appointment for you with Doc Smith."

"Whatever for? I'm in perfect health."

He sighed impatiently. "Look, Kate, we can't settle anything between us until the doc figures out how far gone you are."

She shook her orange head and stared down at the boardwalk. "I already told you when the baby was coming. I'm not going to see a doctor. Why can't you just marry me?"

He thought *biggist* but managed to say, "Because that would make me a bigamist. I'm already married to the woman who fainted at the depot. Her name is Lucy."

This brought her eyes level with Seb's. He flinched a little as he saw a mixture of surprise, anger, even rage shooting barbs at him from their dark blue depths. "You can't be married to someone else. You have to marry me."

"I can't. Marrying you was never my intention in Denver and it's not my intention now, even if it were possible." He took a deep breath. "If I'm responsible for your condition, I will somehow do right by you. Now let's go see the doc."

When he reached for her hand to tug her to her feet, Kate drew away from him and burst into tears. Beyond uncomfortable with the entire situation, Seb sat down beside her and let her cry herself out.

When her sobs eased to an occasional sniffle, he said, "Can we go see the doc now?"

Kate shook her head and refused to meet his gaze. "There's no point."

"What does that mean? Of course there's a point."

She shook her head more violently, tears spilling again. "You don't understand," she sobbed. "I've been told that I can never have children. I'm barren."

Seb felt as if he'd been slapped in the face. Making sure he hadn't heard wrong, he said, "You mean you're not—there's no baby?"

Miserable in her deception, Kate said through her tears, "I just wanted you to marry me. After the way you sneaked out of Denver, I thought this was the only way I could convince you we belonged together."

"My God." She might as well have shot him. "How in the hell could you do this to me, to my family?"

"I—I don't know." Kate buried her face in her hands.

Seb wanted to hang on to his anger—he *was* angry—but

his overriding emotion was pity. Trying not to think of all the heartache she'd caused for him, for Lucy, and for her family, he said, "It's not me you wanted all this time, Kate. I'm just a substitute for Paul."

More tears and then she finally raised her head. "I miss him so."

"I know you do." Seb patted her clenched fist. "I also know that I did everything humanly possible to help you through those first terrible weeks after Paul died. Maybe I was a little too helpful."

"You were wonderful." Kate paused to dab her nose and collect herself. "I just wanted things to be the way they were, I guess, and thought you . . . I thought you could make it happen."

Seb let her think about that for a while and then quietly said, "I think we both know that I'm not the answer to your problems. What will you do now?"

Kate straightened up and blinked her eyes, as if awaking from a dream. "I suppose I'll go back to Denver."

He nodded. "You have friends there, people who care about you."

She turned to look at him with a clarity he'd never seen before. "Your wife . . . I imagine she's not too happy about all of this."

Seb almost laughed. "You might say that."

"Would it help if I had a talk with her? I could try to explain—"

"Thanks, Kate, but you know what? I think I'll just pass on your apologies myself."

Chapter Twenty-seven

The following Tuesday Seb and Lucy walked Jeremiah to the train station. Seb personally exchanged the old man's ticket, from the previous week, and then urged him right up close to an open car door, even though the train was still expelling passengers.

Jeremiah threw his arms around Lucy, gave her a big hug, and then kissed her cheek. When he turned to Seb he said, "I feel like I ought to apologize again for beating the tar out of you."

The only apology Seb wanted was the old man's backside aboard that train. "I've had worse beatings, and besides, in your place I'd have probably done the same thing."

Jeremiah stuck out his hand. "Friends, then?"

Accepting the old man's handshake, squeezing him warmly, Seb admitted, "More than friends. Family."

Jeremiah's face wrinkled up like a basket of laundry, and for a minute Seb thought he might burst into tears. He didn't, but his voice had a ragged edge as he said, "Family. I like that just fine."

Noticing that passengers were beginning to board the

train and warm feelings for the old man aside, Seb restrained himself from tossing Jeremiah into the car as he said, "About time to get on board."

With a nod, Jeremiah gave Lucy one more hug and then started up the steps.

" 'Bye, Pa," she called. "I promise to write home once a week, and I expect the same from you."

"Will do, girl. Will do," he called over his shoulder, apparently too choked up to look back.

After he'd disappeared into the bowels of the train, Lucy said, "I guess we'd better get back to the saloon before it gets crowded."

"No," he said firmly. "I'm not leaving this spot until I'm sure your father and that train are both gone."

Laughing softly, she slipped her hand through Seb's arm and rested her head on his shoulder as the final passengers climbed aboard. When the big engine pulled out of the depot, Seb could hardly believe it. Jeremiah was finally headed home.

As whistles sounded the warning to clear the tracks, he watched in fear, sure that any minute now the conductor would bodily throw the old man off the train. Instead, steaming and puffing, it gathered speed and slowly faded into the distance.

"I miss him already," Lucy said wistfully.

Seb couldn't be that generous, but he did say, "Maybe he can come back for a visit next summer, and even bring your mother along. I'd like to meet her. We should have plenty of room by then."

Lucy cocked her head. "Room? Where?"

Seb winked and said, "The house on the lake ought to be done in a few months."

Lucy's mouth fell open. "Really?"

"Really. I've already talked to a carpenter about it."

Lucy didn't know whether to laugh or cry. This from a man who believed in hotel rooms, restaurants, and no strings attached. And that reminded her of one small obstacle.

"Um, I should probably tell you now that I'm not much of a cook."

He laughed. "Neither am I. How bad are you?"

Lucy sighed. "After more lessons than she could count, my mother finally banned me from the kitchen."

Taking her into his arms, bestowing a quick kiss on the tip of her nose, Seb said, "Then I guess we'll have to learn together."

Several weeks later, as Seb was busy setting up for a Friday night faro tournament, the door opened, distracting him, and Lucy came bouncing into the saloon. Little Joe was right behind her, dragging a *Rustler*-laden wheelbarrow across the threshold.

Joining the pair at the newspaper rack, Seb noticed that Lucy's cheeks were glowing, probably from making the trek to the saloon, and her grin was big enough to light up the entire state of Wyoming. It seemed to him that she got more beautiful with each passing day.

"You're never going to sell all those papers," he said, watching as she and Little Joe unloaded the wheelbarrow.

"You say that every week, and every week you're wrong."

She turned to him then, leaving the rest of the load for Little Joe, and Seb saw that her dark eyes were moist, melted chocolate, and her grin was bigger than ever.

"I've got a couple of surprises for you," she said, brimming with excitement.

"Surprises!" echoed Little Joe, clapping his hands. "Big surprises."

Wary, especially since the kid seemed to know what was going on, Seb said, "What kind of surprises?"

Lucy winked at Little Joe and put a fingertip to her lips. "First off, the Chicago Tribune sent a wire telling me that they want the Penelope column. They also want to make it a daily feature."

"Daily? Can you do that?"

"Sure. In addition to the letters I get at the *Rustler,* the *Tribune* will be sending questions to me from their own readers. I'll have lots of inquiries to choose from, and maybe before long from all over the nation."

By now everyone in Emancipation knew that Lucy was Penelope. Rather than try to run her out of town on a rail, they looked on her as some kind of celebrity. When this got around, they would probably proclaim her the queen of Wyoming.

Seb threw his arms around Lucy and gave her a hug. "That's wonderful news. I'm so proud of you."

Lucy hugged him back, then held him at bay. "And speaking of news, here's the other surprise."

"One more *big* one," claimed Little Joe.

"Hush now," she chided the boy. Lucy picked up a copy of the *Rustler* and handed it to Seb. "This week I did something different," she explained. "I wrote the same column for both the *Tribune* and the *Rustler.*"

That hit Seb as mighty curious. Lucy had struck a compromise with him and the *Tribune,* whereby she would also write a column for them, but never use the same questions that appeared in the *Rustler.*

To Seb's astonishment, when he glanced at this newest column he discovered it was his own damn letter.

————— *THE WEEKLY RUSTLER* —————

Emancipation, Wyoming,	Vol.1.
Friday, September 18, 1896	No.52

ASK PENELOPE! FREE ADVICE

Dear Penelope:
I'm told you are the smartest woman alive. If that's true, maybe you can help me figure out my wife, because I sure can't. The problem? My otherwise adorable wife lies to me.

I have helped her in many unusual ways and done far more for her and her crazy family than could be expected of any man. And how does she repay me? She deceives me and keeps her little secrets pressed between the pages of her black heart.

What do you think I should do, oh smartest woman of them all? Divorce her? Too easy.

Have her drawn and quartered? Too messy.

Or maybe, just maybe, I should take out an advertisement in your newspaper and expose her for who and what she really is. I await your wise counsel.

> *Signed, Deceived, Disheartened,*
> *and Slightly Deranged*

Dear Deranged:

Oh, you poor fool. Can you not tell when a woman is truly in love with you? The only reason a woman ever hides anything from the man she loves is because she's afraid he might find fault with her. We all work to hide the bruises and scrapes we've endured in our lives, do we not? Lord knows you've had your share. May I suggest that you both forget about the past and look forward to a very bright future?

> Penelope

P.S. Speaking of exposing your wife for what she is, I have it on good authority that she may be keeping one other secret from you. It might interest you to know that she is expecting your child in the early spring. And that's no lie.

AUTHOR'S NOTE

Mary Lease is an actual historical figure, an orator and self-educated lawyer who mesmerized mostly male audiences across the Midwest during the 1890s. After earning disfavor with the People's Party leaders by speaking out against their plan to endorse a Democratic candidate for president, she went on to champion women's suffrage, prohibition, and birth control.

The other characters in this book along with the town of Emancipation, Wyoming, are all fictional.